The Mathematician's Journey

by

ANTHONY DALTON

AUGUST WORDS PUBLISHING

unique books by exceptional authors for select readers

Published by **August Words Publishing**

www.AugustWordsPublishing.com

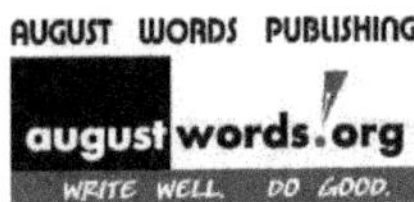

www.augustwords.org

Cover design	Steve Crowhurst, elements courtesy of pixabay.com
Native woman on back cover	© Steve Crowhurst
Additional cover design work	August Words Publishing
Book design	© August Words Publishing
Author photo	© Steve Crowhurst, enhanced by August Words Publishing

ISBN: 978-1-942018-12-4

ADVANCE PRAISE FOR

The Mathematician's Journey

"Anthony Dalton is himself no stranger to the Arctic or sailing. He brings that knowledge to bear in his meticulously researched historical novel to take the reader on a voyage of discovery from the peaceful cloisters of Oxford of King James I's England to the Atlantic wastes and the frigid waters of what will come to be known as Hudson's Bay thence to a native village and finally, after many years, back to upper class London. Peopled with three dimensional characters set against vividly described backgrounds the plot will keep you turning the pages and at book's end hoping the hero's adventures will continue in another work."

Patrick Taylor
New York Times best selling author
of the *Irish Country Doctor* series

"Thomas Woodhouse, a 17th century mathematician by training and a gentleman by birth, longs for adventure. Rejecting his family's wishes and the love of a good woman, he crews on Henry Hudson's ship and begins a peril-filled journey that takes him across the seas, into the far North and a life he could never have imagined. In this rollicking adventure story about the very nature of survival, author Anthony Dalton's gentleman adventurer faces perils from shipwrecks to starvation and from romantic rivalry to redemption in his quest to stay true to the spirit of his secret raven tattoo."

kc dyer
author of *Finding Fraser*
and more

"Whatever happened to Henry Hudson? Told from the viewpoint of one of Henry's crew, this deeply-satisfying, richly-textured adventure story sweeps with confidence from the old world to the new and back again. There are pikestaffs and politics, then mutiny, survival and respect in our hero's adopted tribe, and finally, a man who could not live in England. Once again, Dalton's genius is in the details. Once again, I couldn't stop reading."

Catherine Dook
nautical author of *Offshore*
and more

"I thoroughly enjoyed this book. Such good adventure and an intriguing look into life as it may have been on Discovery during that fateful trip. I liked the characters, but mostly I enjoyed Thomas as sailor and Survivorman à la 17th century. The author's outdoor skills, knowledge and experience make the scenes on the high seas and on land really exciting. The Atlantic crossing, Davis Straits, The Bay of Biscay were filled with, at times, horrific drama. Equally, the characters' adventures and ingenuity when tossed upon unknown shores made history come to life, offering a fine glimpse into the now dormant skills that have kept, and still keep in some areas, our species alive--indeed, indigenous people to this day live, or at least try to live, with the fine skills and sensibilities of the first peoples Thomas came to call family. The castaway scenes, for lack of a better term, felt authentic and were engrossing to read. And I was most relieved that Thomas, after making the arduous trip back to England, realized where his true home lay and returned to his family in the New World. And I loved the Epilogue! It left me smiling."

Shirley Morris, Toronto
historian

ALSO BY ANTHONY DALTON

FICTION

Relentless Pursuit

NON-FICTION

Henry Hudson
Sir John Franklin
Fire Canoes
The Fur-Trade Fleet
Polar Bears
Adventures with Camera and Pen
A Long, Dangerous Coastline
Graveyard of the Pacific
Arctic Naturalist
River Rough, River Smooth
Alone Against the Arctic
Baychimo, Arctic Ghost Ship
J/Boats Sailing to Success
Wayward Sailor

For more about Anthony Dalton and his books visit his website at www.anthonydalton.net

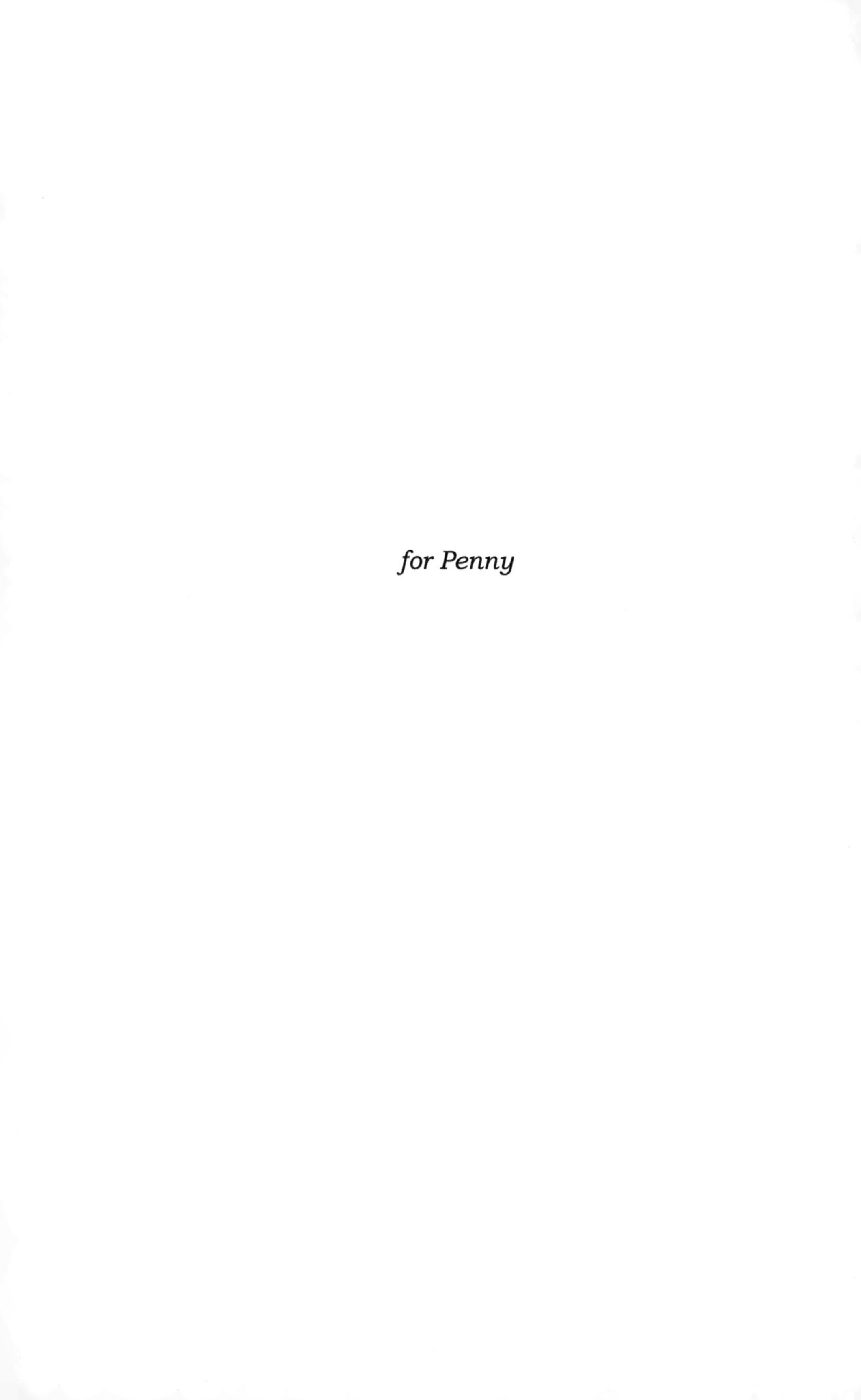

for Penny

"The way is dangerous,

the passage doubtful,

the voyage not thoroughly known."

Richard Willes
The History of Travayle
1577

Contents

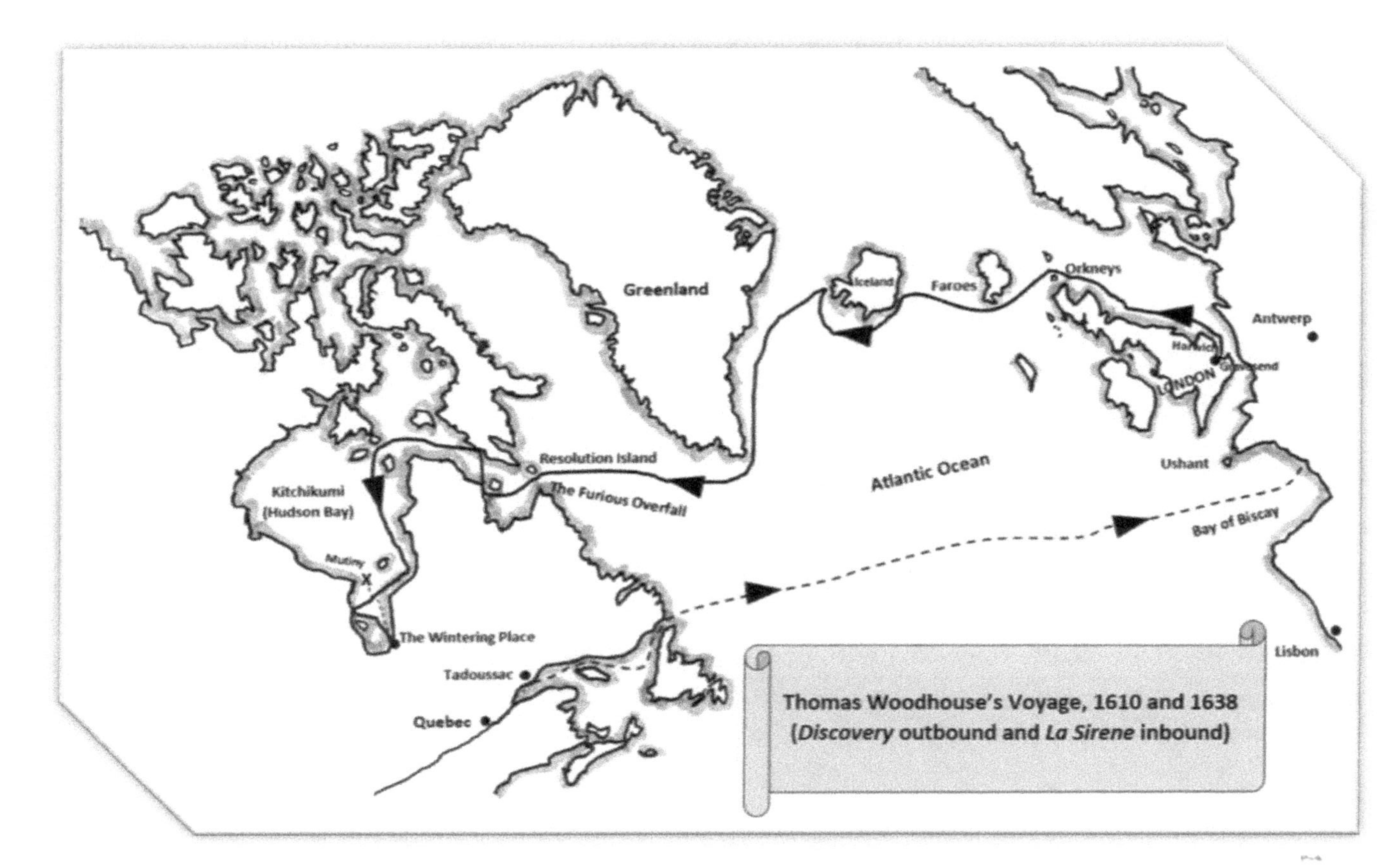
Greenland
Iceland
Faroes
Orkneys
Antwerp
Harwich
LONDON
Ushant
Atlantic Ocean
Bay of Biscay
Lisbon
Resolution Island
The Furious Overfall
Kitchikumi
(Hudson Bay)
Mutiny
X
The Wintering Place
Tadoussac
Quebec
Thomas Woodhouse's Voyage, 1610 and 1638
(*Discovery* outbound and *La Sirene* inbound)

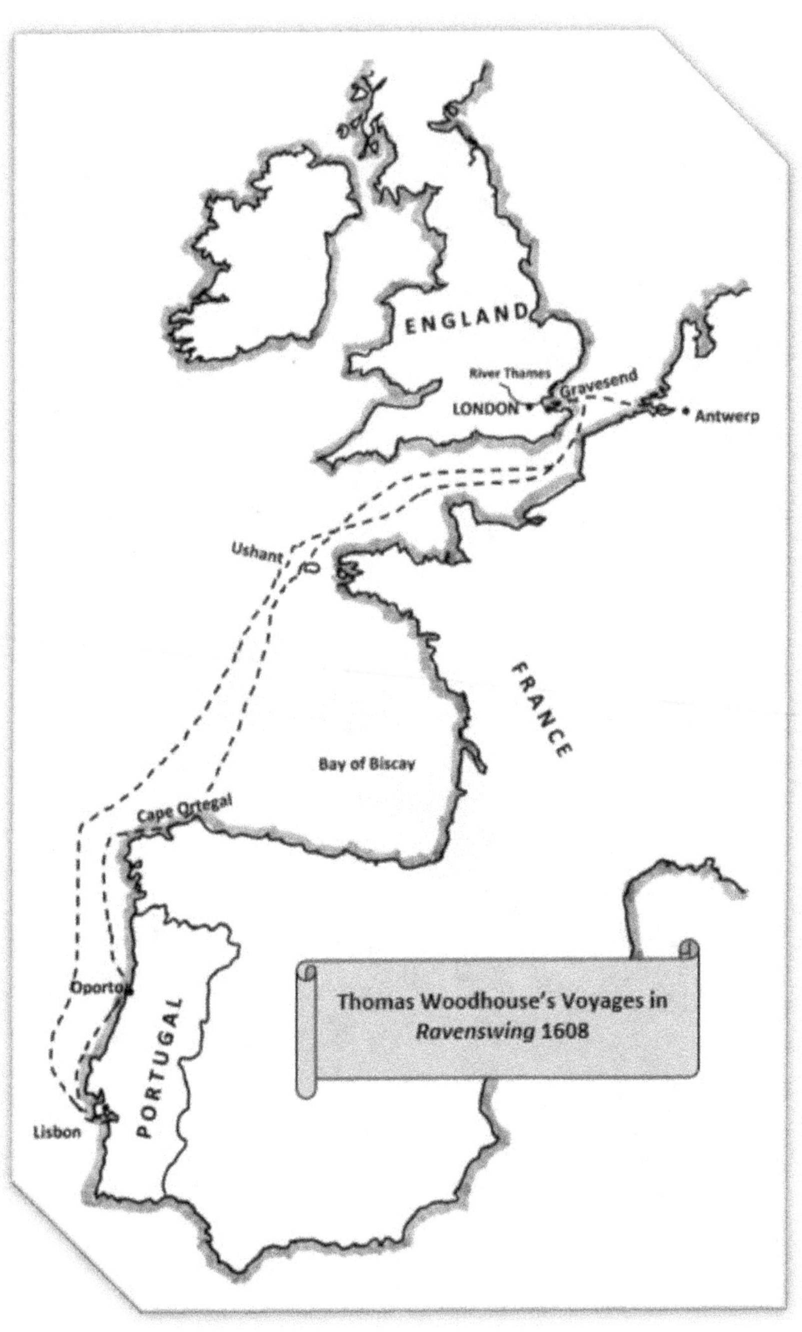
ENGLAND
River Thames
Gravesend
LONDON
Antwerp
Ushant
FRANCE
Bay of Biscay
Cape Ortegal
Oporto
PORTUGAL
Lisbon
Thomas Woodhouse's Voyages in
Ravenswing 1608

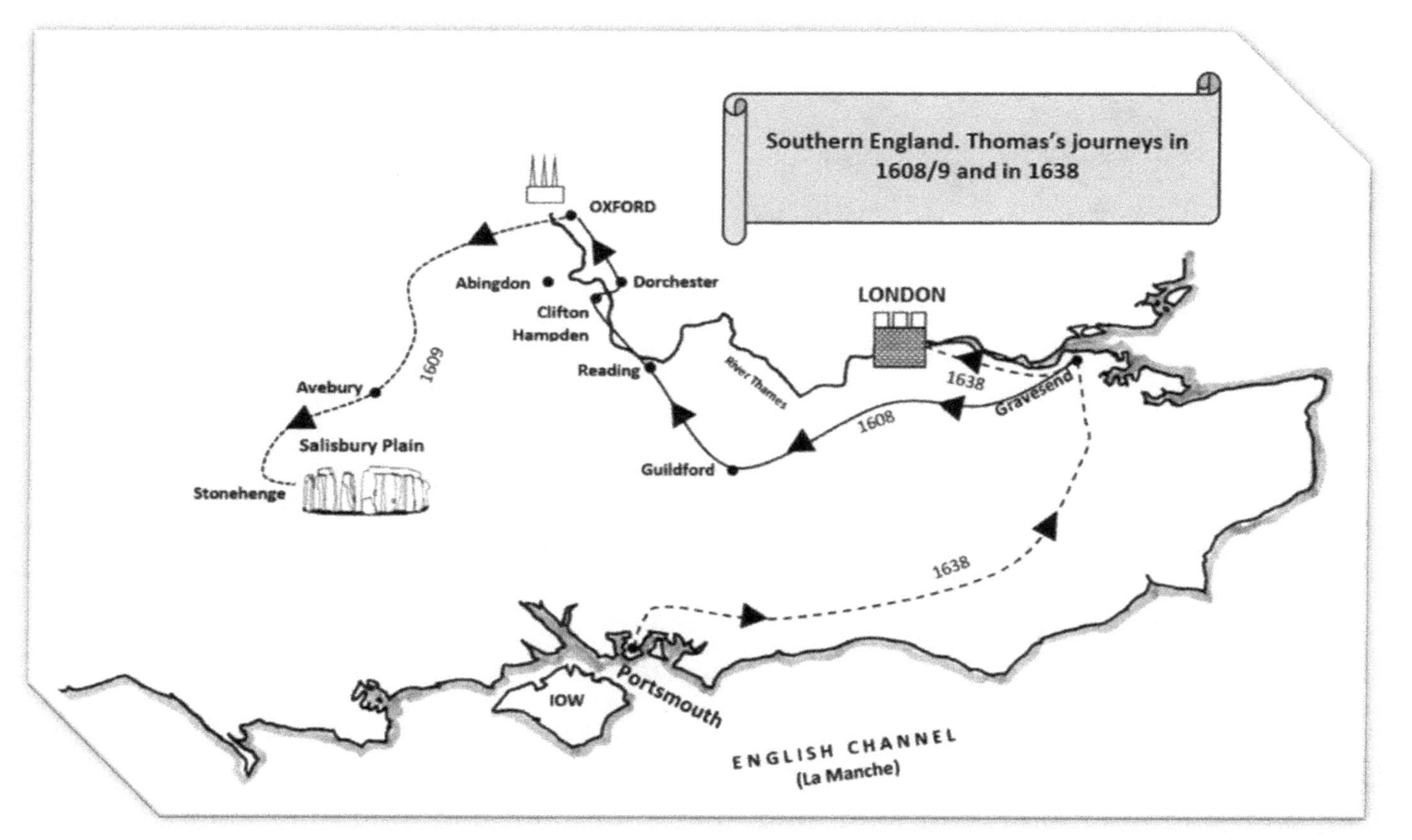
Southern England. Thomas's journeys in 1608/9 and in 1638
OXFORD
Abingdon
Dorchester
Clifton Hampden
Reading
LONDON
River Thames
Gravesend
1638
1608
Guildford
1609
Avebury
Salisbury Plain
Stonehenge
1638
IOW
Portsmouth
ENGLISH CHANNEL
(La Manche)

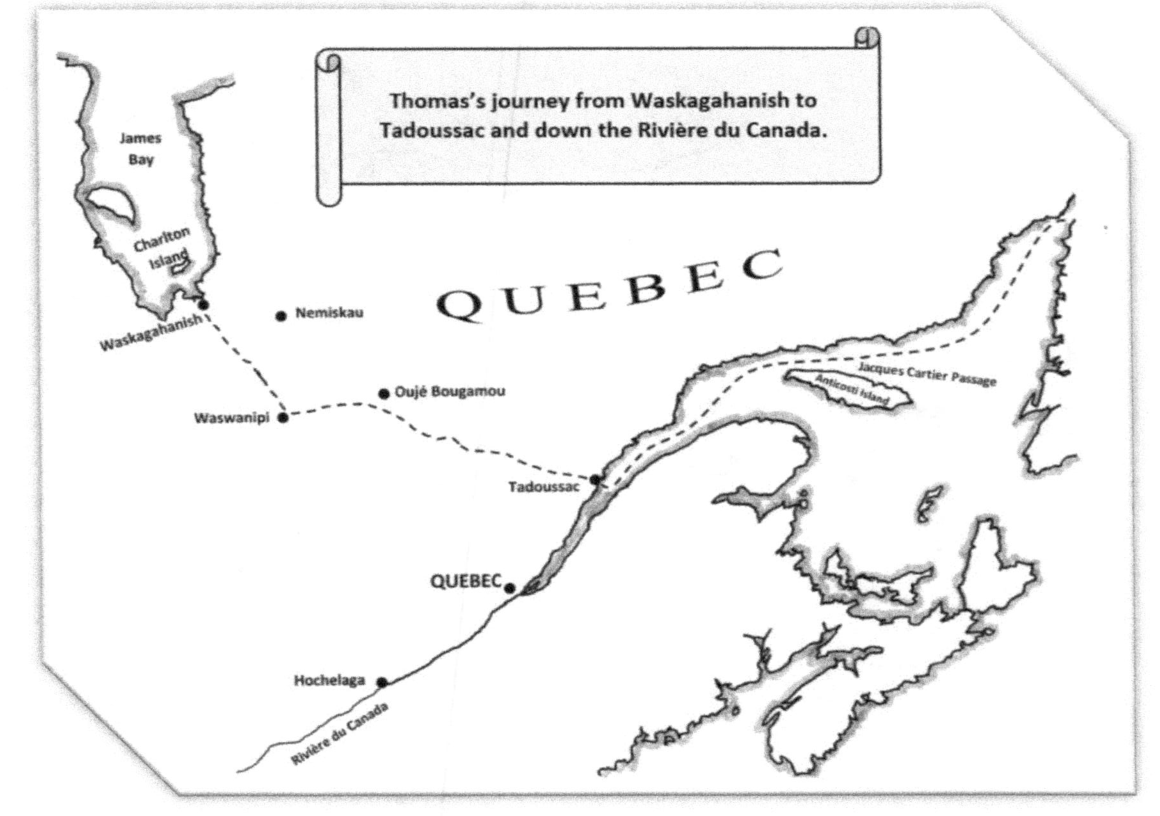
Thomas's journey from Waskagahanish to
Tadoussac and down the Rivière du Canada.
James Bay
Charlton Island
Waskagahanish
Nemiskau
QUEBEC
Oujé Bougamou
Waswanipi
Jacques Cartier Passage
Anticosti Island
Tadoussac
QUEBEC
Hochelaga
Rivière du Canada

BOOK ONE

PRIVILEGE AND POWER

CHAPTER 1

GRAVESEND, ENGLAND, SPRING 1639

The sea breeze whispers across the ancient waterway. Two loaded barques tack up stream separated by no more than a few lengths. They are both working hard, their white sails filled with power. Another stands at anchor, restless, moving with the rhythm of the currents, waiting for cargo. I can see the bare masts, yards and spider-web of rigging on yet another ship towering over the distant pier. Two young men row a loaded wherry past the waterfront in the opposite direction. I lean back against the rough stone wall of the Blockhouse, defender of the old seaport's virtue, the breeze rustling the pages of my book. I feel the sting of tears in my eyes. I imagine I can hear the echo of Captain Hudson's voice warning about ice ahead. But there is no Henry Hudson any more and there is no ice. That was all long ago during the tragic events that played out on the great sub-Arctic bay – the events that helped shape my life.

Last time I sat here to read I was no more than a boy. Reading my journal again so many years after it was taken from me that awful day in June 1611, reminds me of all that I have lost. That was twenty-eight years ago. Now I am back in Gravesend where it all began. I am so much older. Hopefully a lot wiser. Very much alone.

My name is Thomas Woodhouse. It is also Otácimow. I was once a mathematician, and a sailor. Now I am a storyteller. Although this is the land of my birth, I don't really feel at home here. The people are no longer my people. I spent too many years away, living a hard but free outdoor life in the beautiful wilderness of a far-away continent. I miss the fresh air. I miss the thrill of the hunt, the endless cycle of trapping; the flamboyant change of seasons. I miss my friends among the Omushkegowak. Most of all I miss Ahanu, my son, and Alsoomse – my beloved wife.

I was born to a life of privilege, the eldest of four children by Barnaby and Jane Woodhouse. Her Majesty, Queen Elizabeth I, was on the English throne in London when I came into the world no more than seven or so leagues away in the small, but busy, riverside port of Gravesend on an April day in 1590. Good Queen Bess, as her people knew her, had been the English sovereign for over thirty years when I let loose my first lusty yells at the world. I doubt that she heard me from her lofty position. She certainly knew nothing of my birth. Even so, like it or not, I was suddenly one of her subjects and as such expected to be loyal. Pledging allegiance was unnecessary. Loyalty and allegiance to the Crown, to Queen Bess – in other words, was an integral part of the privilege of being born in England, especially in my family. No man dare say a word against the queen in my father's presence. To do so would have provoked a challenge that could only end in a duel by swords.

I remained a loyal subject for the first thirteen years of my life, until Good Queen Bess died at Richmond Palace in March 1603 – at the remarkable age of 70. My loyalty then had to take a new direction, as did the loyalties of most people in England. James VI of Scotland, son of Mary Stuart – the former Queen of Scotland – and Lord Darnley, became King James I of England and was so crowned a few months later. The Elizabethan Era had come to an end. Throughout my short thirteen years of life, I had honoured my queen, as my parents had taught me to do. Now, with her passing, to me it was as though a dark cloud had descended on the land. I found it difficult to accept that I now had to mentally pledge my allegiance to a king – a man I had hardly heard of – and he wasn't even English.

To make the year more difficult and to keep that black cloud hanging over us a new outbreak of plague swept through London, leaving alive in its wake only the strongest and fittest. Twenty thousand or more of the population of our great capital city died in those terrible months. Doctors and other scientists still do not know what causes this pestilence, other than that it breeds in cities and towns where the populations are most dense and conditions are dirty. Perhaps there is a clue in the fact that most outbreaks of the plague take place where there are seaports. We all lived in fear that the dreaded disease that had London in its evil grasp would spread down river to our own port of Gravesend.

William Shakespeare alluded to the plague in his play *King Lear*, which my father gave me to read when I was a young man:

....A disease that's in my flesh,
Which I must needs call mine: thou art a boil,
A plague-sore, an embossed carbuncle,
In my corrupted blood.

Worse news for me was that the king had Sir Walter Raleigh arrested in June on charges of treason. Raleigh was one of my boyhood heroes. It hurt to know he had been confined to the Tower of London awaiting trial, accused of plotting against King James I. My hero was no stranger to the tower. Good Queen Bess had imprisoned him there in 1592 for a few years after he offended her by marrying one of her maids without royal permission. This time, though, the charges were much more serious. Near the end of the year Raleigh was found guilty and sentenced to death. I was devastated when I heard the news. King James later commuted the sentence to life imprisonment. It was not much of an improvement, I thought.

So much of importance happened in the first years of the 17th century to stimulate our young, enquiring minds. There were so many highs and some awful low points. The change of sovereigns and the inevitable political repercussions was a mixture of high and low, some comedy, some serious. The plague was a definite low point – just about as low as could be imagined. William Shakespeare continued to produce wonderful plays that took us to literary heights we could not have imagined. Sir Walter Raleigh's disgrace plunged many of us into depression. And then there was the incredible debacle of the Gunpowder Plot, at the end of 1605. It revolved around the question of religion, a constant topic of conversation, argument and often violence.

Despite the Church of England being the official religion in England since the time of Great Harry – King Henry VIII, there is still much dissension in the land between Protestants and Catholics. Roman Catholics are in the minority and not officially tolerated – or unofficially for that matter. I am no Papist but I have to admit, our dear Bess had certainly not treated them well. The new King James was no different. He had a Catholic mother yet he continued the persecution. Despairing of ever being accepted; denied the right to worship in their own form of Christianity, in late 1605 a group of thirteen young Catholic men decided to complain in a loud way and attract some attention to their cause. Their plan was audacious, outrageous and downright dangerous. They would blow up the Houses of Parliament, with King James and his advisors inside. One of the men went by the name of Guido Fawkes.

In the first week of November 1605, when I was a lad of 15, Fawkes and his companions smuggled some 36 barrels of gunpowder into the parliamentary cellars. Unfortunately for the conspirators, and for their planned extravagant fireworks display, the authorities heard about the gunpowder plot and foiled it. They captured Guido Fawkes red-handed in the cellars and the king sentenced him to death. I discussed the plot with my father one evening because I was confused about the justice involved.

"Why was only one man – this Guido Fawkes – arrested? Where were the other conspirators?"

"Perhaps Fawkes was working alone. There's only his word that there were twelve others involved," answered Papa.

"Well, surely Fawkes did not smuggle thirty-six heavy barrels of gunpowder into the cellars of the Houses of Parliament all by himself. That would have taken hours, perhaps days. Somebody would have seen him, don't you think?"

"Fawkes was found alone in the cellars preparing to light the fuses. I have heard he was an expert with explosives. If there were other men involved, Fawkes will give up their names before the king has him executed. I can assure you of that. Few men can keep secrets from the rack. We'll know more in a few weeks, perhaps by the New Year."

We spent many evenings like that, both enjoying the thrust and parry of intelligent discussion. The gunpowder plot was the big story at the time, a topic of much argument for and against. The audacity of Fawkes and his associates was, in fact, the main talk at all levels of society. In January we learned much more about the plot and its aftermath.

Guido Fawkes, also known as Guy Fawkes, a Yorkshire man who had adopted Catholicism, was just one of a group of young men from good families. His main co-conspirators were Robert Catesby, Thomas Wintour, Francis Tresham and John Wright. The plot was uncovered when Francis Tresham made the mistake of writing a letter to Lord Monteigle, his cousin – a fellow Catholic and Member of Parliament – warning him to stay away from the House on November 5th. That letter somehow found its way into the hands of King James. Found guilty of high treason, all 13 conspirators received the death sentence. That sentence included the instruction that each of the men be drawn, hung, eviscerated and quartered. The executioners received orders that the gruesome act of eviscerating should take place while the guilty men remained alive at the gallows. It was a most barbaric, yet effective way of combating treason.

On January 31, 1606, Guido Fawkes suffered the indignity and fear of being bound with his arms behind him and drawn along the ground behind a horse to the gallows at Smithfield. There, while climbing the steep wooden steps to the scaffold, and before the executioner could mutilate his body while he yet lived, he either fell or threw himself to the ground far below. That precipitous action caused him to break his neck. The king's justice was merciless. Although Fawkes was already dead, his executioners completed the sentence. They eviscerated him. They hung him. They lopped off his head and they quartered his body as a bloodthirsty deterrent to treasonous thoughts and deeds. The other conspirators, Robert and Thomas Wintour, Christopher and John Wright, Francis Tresham, Everard Digby, Ambrose Rookwood, Thomas Bates, Robert Keyes, Hugh Owen and John Grant all suffered similar fates. Robert Catesby and Thomas Percy were shot and killed while trying to escape the law. When I discussed the chilling event with my father, his reply was terse and less than sympathetic.

"Those men deserved their harsh sentences. They plotted against our king and against our country. That is treason. They are not worthy of your concern, besides, they were Papists."

I did not agree. I thought the subject was worthy of everyone's concern. However, I could not argue that point with my father. On certain subjects he had a closed mind. The barbarism of the punishment bothered me very much. The knowledge that the punishment meted out to Fawkes and the others was delivered in public – in front of a jeering and cheering crowd – as if at a sporting event, upset me almost as much. I could think of far more intelligent, much less ghoulish forms of entertainment.

I had heard much of the playwright and actor named William Shakespeare – I mentioned him earlier. My father introduced me to his work and I admired it very much. Shakespeare and his company of actors called themselves the King's Men and regularly performed his plays in London. Early in those years of turmoil I read one of his most popular recent dramas called *Hamlet.* I looked forward to seeing it performed in London at Shakespeare's Globe Theatre one day that summer – if the plague relented.

Unfortunately, the plaque dragged on through July and August, keeping me, and all sensible people, well away from the city.

On days with good weather, one of my favourite places to sit and read was on or sheltered by the thick stone wall of the fort on the waterfront, known as the Gravesend Blockhouse. King Henry VIII ordered its construction long before my birth. He intended it to protect the lower reaches of the river from invasion by enemy forces or pirates. There was a similar strong fort built on the opposite bank of the river at Tilbury. The Gravesend Blockhouse was a substantial military structure dominating the waterfront just east of the town. It consisted of three rectangular buildings fronted by an impressive rounded battlement from which flew the Cross of St. George. The complete fort was surrounded by the wall which was once my reading room.

When I was a boy a boom, made of chain, rope and many tree trunks spanned the river between the two forts. It was there as a strong barrier; another form of defence against enemy warships sailing up the Thames to attack London. The boom could be raised to near surface level by the use of large capstans on either side of the river. In times of peace it was left dormant on the river bed. Once or twice a year the boom would be raised and lowered to make sure the capstans were working properly, and to check that the boom was intact. On those exciting occasions my friends and I would run to the Blockhouse to lend our puny muscles to the task. I do not think the boom ever played a military role while I lived in Gravesend. The presence of the boom did not affect me. Out of sight, out of mind most of the time. The fortification was different. Up against the Blockhouse wall, shielded from the wind, I could read in peace while enjoying the crisp sea air. It was there, in my open-air haven of solitude, that I began to read about the Arctic. It was there by the old Blockhouse wall that I first thought of becoming an explorer. I had no idea where such musings would lead me, only that the feeling of destiny was strong in me.

CHAPTER 2

I was the first child in the Woodhouse family. Emily followed me two years later. James and Mary joined us over the next three years. Papa and Mama doted on their two pretty daughters and showed obvious pride in their pair of sons. Papa was medium height with dark hair and brown eyes. Mama was almost the same height. There any similarity ended. Mama had long golden curls and eyes of bright blue flecked with violet. I had inherited my mother's blue eyes and her golden hair, though mine was much longer than hers and tied back with a black silk ribbon. Emily was mother's double, while James favoured our father and Elizabeth shared the best of both parents, having red hair and dark blue eyes. Mama was one of the happiest people I ever met. She always had a smile on her face. Her laughter rang throughout the house like music. Many years later, in a forest far away, I would hear echoes of her humour in my own son.

My family was rather affluent, by the standards of the time. My father was a gentleman and a merchant. He owned three trading ships in which he imported wines from Spain and Portugal, spices and similar exotic food additives from the Dutch in Antwerp, and exported wool and cloth back to

Antwerp and further afield. My mother came from a gentle family with a religious background, well known and respected in Canterbury. She looked after our spiritual welfare and, because of her own extensive education, tutored us in Latin and French. We all adored her.

We lived in a large, solid four-storey house with twenty rooms in sight of the Thames River in Gravesend, in the county of Kent. Constructed from ragstone carved from the Tovil Quarry near Maidstone, the house had real glass windows, plus six large fireplaces and chimneys. It could be dark, due to the wood panelling in many rooms, but it was always warm and comfortable, even in the worst winters. Most of our furniture had been created from old English oak, though some was more modern, being a thin veneer laid over elm or similar wood. Heavy fabric drapes for the windows and doorways came from Normandy. We had twelve servants to look after us and our home. They included a butler, who effectively ran the house, a cook, maids and serving girls, a groom for our horses and, of course, a valet for my father. A short walk away stood the large warehouse where my father stored his merchandise. He kept half of the space for incoming goods, the other for the wool ready for export. The Thames being a tidal river, the warehouse was accessible to our ships at high tide. With the river full, they came alongside from the anchorages to load and unload.

In those long gone days, I wore fine linen shirts with deep cuffs and full sleeves, and with a broad collar – either lace or linen. I wore a doublet – a tight-buttoned jacket with long sleeves for winter and no sleeves in summer – over my shirt. I often wore a gauffered ruff, in a somewhat narrower style than most people did. I favoured breeches on my lower body and legs, instead of the traditional Venetians and hose. I found them more comfortable, although I still wore Venetians at social events. Fashionable men wore short cloaks or capes, usually hip-length, often with sleeves, usually slung artistically over the left shoulder, even indoors. As a young man of breeding, I felt compelled to adopt this rather flamboyant style. I also had a long, woollen cloak for outside use during inclement weather and a broad-brimmed hat – with a long feather tucked into the band. Of course, I never went anywhere without my sword, a gift from my father when I reached the age of ten. I wore it slung from my waist in a wooden scabbard covered in decorated leather, and a dagger in my belt on the other side. There were too many villains abroad by day and by night for a decent person to go anywhere unarmed.

Dressing as I did; living a life of ease and plenty, I suppose I was the most unlikely looking future explorer. But then, I rationalized, Sir Martin Frobisher had come from a similar background. Sir Walter Raleigh came from the gentry and, I imagined, so did Henry Hudson. What they could do, I could do. Where they had the courage to venture, so would I, but I would go further. The only potential barrier to the fulfillment of my dreams was Papa. He had his own plans for my future.

My father was a dignified man; always dressed in immaculate style. I never saw him with a single hair out of place and his short pointed beard was always perfectly trimmed. To complete the picture of a gentleman, he sported a luxuriant moustache, which curled upwards at both ends. The blond fuzz growing on my face had not reached the stage where I could shape it like his beard. In truth, the fuzz on my chin resembled nothing so much as – well – fuzz.

Our mother and a handful of private tutors schooled us at home. Like it or not, I had to endure up to six hours each day, except Sundays, studying a variety of subjects that my father and mother deemed necessary for my future. The good part of our education was that Mama was an excellent teacher with a wonderful sense of fun. She made all our lessons interesting. As good Christians, we all attended St. George's Church for morning and evening services on Sundays. My parents loved to sing. At church their tuneful voices, one baritone and the other soprano, rang in harmony above the rest of the congregation. As we had all studied music, we raised our voices to sing along with them.

Papa spoke Dutch, Latin and French as well as his native English. Mama was equally fluent in French and Latin. They insisted that their offspring learn Latin, Dutch and French. In our house conversation was often held in a mixture of languages. To any outsider it would have been a veritable Babel of tongues. We were often loud, but our conversations were always intelligent. It was through my tutors, including my mother, that I discovered I had a natural affinity for languages and for mathematics. I especially enjoyed geometry and trigonometry, finding many applications to study in the architecture around Gravesend and London.

The Thames River between the North Sea and London was an important commercial waterway. It carried ships and boats of many sizes, and with assorted cargoes and passengers. Rare indeed was the day when there were not ships in sight on the river opposite the Gravesend waterfront. I loved the smell of tarred rope; of salt-encrusted canvas – it mixed so well with the astringent taste of seaweed on my tongue. I could listen to the voices of the sailors giving and taking orders all day long. One of my greatest joys in those days was to stand on the deck of one of Papa's ships. The sea was in my blood.

Papa wanted me to study. I wanted to go to sea. We were checkmated. I believed the sea held a large place in my future. There I would learn the necessary skills to take me further afield as an explorer: eventually to the Arctic, in fact. We compromised by agreeing that I would learn more about the import export trade and study navigation at the same time – the latter a sensible extension of mathematics for me. To accommodate both of these disciplines, and to allow me the experience I craved, we agreed that I should go to sea for a few months and follow that with university. And so it was that at seventeen I boarded one of my father's ships as a crew member.

The ammoniac smell of seaweed and the tang of salt had been part of the air that I breathed all my life. Ships and boats of all kinds, the necessary transport for my father's cargoes, had been a part of my world since I was born. My father once boasted to a business acquaintance that I took my first faltering steps on the deck of one of his ships at anchor off Gravesend. My excitement was intense as I stepped aboard for my first working voyage. As I said, the sea was in my blood.

At first, the ship – *Ravenswing,* a barque of some 50 tons, sailed back and forth across the North Sea on the short voyage between Gravesend and the Dutch port of Antwerp, always laden with wool on the outbound voyage and carrying spices and wines homeward. All cargo on board belonged to my father or his business associates. Papa's business enterprises handled most of the exports or imports in the Gravesend seaport.

I had made one voyage to Antwerp with Papa when I was eight. On that exciting journey, we enjoyed the relative comfort of the captain's cabin to share for the few days at sea. In deference to the owner and his son, the captain removed himself to a smaller berth.

Life on board ship as a sailor – as opposed to the owner's son – I soon discovered, had none of the comforts of home. At my father's insistence, I signed on as a deckhand. There would be no special treatment for me and none expected. We slept, when we could, in rough bunks or hammocks in crowded quarters. My fellow sailors were dirty, lousy – in fact. I never did get accustomed to the lice. Most of the common sailors were rude and crude. None of them had any but the barest education. None of them could read or write. Few of them could hold a reasonably intelligent conversation. Most people were superstitious to an extent, but sailors took that fragile emotion to an extreme. Without exception, they were all superstitious, reading potential calamity into the most mundane of happenings. In particular, sailors did not approve of women on ships.

"There's no place for a woman on board. Women bring bad luck at sea," I learned that piece of nautical lore from an old salt. Even worse, for some, sailors would not have a priest of any kind on board or anywhere near the ship. Some sailors en route to join their ships would cross the road to avoid a priest. The superstitions made no intellectual sense, yet they were so much part of the lore of sailors everywhere.

Life at sea for me was vastly different from life at home yet, in a strange way, once I adjusted to the coarse speech of most sailors, and some of their less than desirable habits, I enjoyed being with them, despite not having anything in common. I earned a modicum of respect from them because I was never seasick, although I came close to losing the contents of my stomach on more than one occasion. They taught me so much about the sea and they certainly caused me to become tougher and ready for whatever life threw at me. They were good lessons, ones that would stand me in good stead a few years later. On my first day at sea I learned one of the most important lessons for a sailor, and received a reminder of the superstitions at the same time. I was happy, working aloft and whistling to myself when another sailor working on the same yard yelled at me to stop.

"Why?" I asked. "What's wrong with whistling?"

"You'll be whistling up a storm in no time, young 'un. Never whistle on a ship," he warned. I don't think I ever whistled again – at sea or on land.

The short voyage across the North Sea to the estuary of the Scheldt River was calm, with only a rolling swell from the north to set the ship creaking with pleasure. As we entered the wide estuary with a fair wind to carry us east, we passed the Dutch town of Sluis – that told me the waters on which we now sailed had seen at least two mighty naval battles. One between England and France during the Hundred Years War in 1340, and the other only four years past, between the Spanish and Dutch. There were no warships to challenge *Ravenswing* in 1607 as she made her way up the winding river, following the sweeping bends for over 13 leagues through a series of low-lying wetlands to come in sight of the single spire of the magnificent Cathedral of Our Lady.

Antwerp never failed to intrigue me. I always felt a glow as we approached the final bend in the river. I had enjoyed my stay in the city as a little boy. I found so much more to interest me as a young man. Each of the three times we stopped in Antwerp the crew managed to get some free time ashore, due to the complicated and time-consuming customs formalities for the cargoes. Those formalities prevented the ship from being unloaded or loaded until the officials had assessed the duties and received payment. Most of my fellow sailors, all older than I by a decade or more, made straight for the waterfront taverns and the whores waiting inside and close by. I had my own, somewhat more intellectual plans.

Free of the ship for a few hours, I ran up the steep stone steps to the top of the fortifications encircling the city. On board, I was a lowly deckhand. I dressed accordingly – in a long-sleeve shirt, baggy cotton breeches and rope-soled canvas shoes. Ashore in Antwerp, I was again the son of a prosperous gentleman. Dressed in appropriate clothes, which I kept neatly folded in my sea chest in the forepeak, I visited my father's business contacts and often dined with them in the evenings. Making the transition from one to the other, without incurring the derision of my shipmates, was never easy. I was seen leaving the ship in my fine clothes one evening, after I thought the rest of the crew were ashore, and the following day I had to fight to prove I was still one of them. That encounter earned me my first black eye. My second would come years later.

Away from the business aspects of my visits, I had my own favourite place. A few minutes' walk from the wharf where *Ravenswing* was tied up led me along the narrow cobblestone streets leading to the cathedral and the main square. Once a Protestant church, in 1607 when I was there, the unfinished cathedral – the equal of any such edifice in England – was in the hands of the Papists. That religious anomaly did not stop me going in to explore the incredible architecture from the inside. The youthful mathematician in me could not resist calculating the stresses involved in holding up the high, vaulted roof.

Equally, the massive buttresses that supported the exterior walls fascinated my technical mind.

My fourth and final voyage on *Ravenswing* was to Portugal: a long haul on the open sea after the short runs across the North Sea from Gravesend to the mouth of the Scheldt River. For me it was a voyage of discovery and, at last, the real beginning of understanding my own desires. We departed Gravesend with a full cargo of wool for Lisbon. The sky had a slight overcast. The wind was fair. The river busy, as always. We slipped down past Gravesend Reach, out of the estuary and into the North Sea. Rounding North Foreland, we turned south, still holding the wind. Our captain took us well out to sea to avoid the treacherous Goodwin Sands, where many a good ship had foundered. Keeping the distant coast of Kent in sight, we changed course to the west to enter the English Channel. There the wind failed us and we were becalmed for a few hours, with France to port and England to starboard.

The sea fascinated me, then as much as now. It has so many moods; so many unpredictable expressions. The sea and the wind. They work together, as they have always done. Sometimes they favoured our little ship; equally, sometimes they were most assuredly against us. The wind was the driving force in the natural relationship. It could and did tantalize the waves, driving them into a frenzy of spitting white; rolling and crashing like a liquid army on the move. The wind, I soon learned, could do whatever it wished with the sea. It could keep it calm, and it often did. When the black moods were upon it, the wind could lash the surface of the sea until it reared up in fury and attacked any obstacle, natural or manmade, in its path. I had seen many storms raging over the Thames estuary from the comfort of my home, and from the old Blockhouse. I had experienced one while crossing the North Sea to Antwerp. The voyage to and from Portugal introduced me to the true nature of bad weather at sea.

Once the wind again filled our sails, we coursed down the Channel for the open Atlantic Ocean. The winds became contrary, the seas grew into deep, lumpy swells. *Ravenswing* rolled fore and aft and from port to starboard. The motion never ceased. Working high in the rigging, which I was required to do, was a challenge to my determination to live a long life. I felt Death breathing on me every moment aloft and prayed to be spared.

"This be nothing, Thomas," one of the old salts told me with a knowing smile while we were working together far above the deck. His silver curls danced around his face as the wind directed. He pointed a gnarled index finger at me – I noticed the nail was missing – and warned, "You wait 'til we 'its the Bay of Biscay. Then you'll see some fun. The wind and waves there be really fierce."

The Bay of Biscay, between Ushant in French Brittany and Cape Ortegal in north-west Spain, had a reputation for unpleasant behaviour. In a perverse sort of way, I was almost looking forward to a Biscay storm to see how I would measure up. Well, the formidable Biscay proved the old salt wrong and denied me my challenge on the outbound voyage. The winds were fair. The seas no more than rolling swells. The skies remained clear. Day after day, as we made the crossing along an invisible line where the bay meets the Atlantic, the weather treated us to a holiday. We stripped off our shirts and worked with a will, every member of the crew enjoying the voyage.

"Ah, you just wait until we turns for 'ome, Thomas," the old sailor reminded me one hot afternoon as we worked aloft, with the masts and yards swaying in a gentle rhythm. "You'll see. The Biscay will not treat us kindly twice."

In Lisbon, where we unloaded our cargo, I had far too much red wine to drink one night. The result was that I, along with two other sailors, found myself in a tattoo parlour in the docklands beside the Tagus River. When I emerged into the sunlight some hours later, rather more sober than when I went in, I had a black raven, with wings spread wide, tattooed on the front of my right shoulder. That tattoo stretched six inches from wing tip to wing tip. Knowing my mother would not approve of it, I vowed she would never again see me with my shirt off.

The return voyage, with a brief stop at the northern Portuguese town of Oporto in the Douro River to load more casks of wine, was nothing like the outbound journey. Thick black clouds chased us as we rounded Cape Ortegal and set course for Ushant. Within hours of our departure, a typical Bay of Biscay storm overtook us and attacked with full force. *Ravenswing* picked up her skirts and ran for her life to avoid being ravaged. We soon had to take in the square sails, leaving only two small fore and aft sails set for stability. The wind caught us as it ripped the tops off the rising seas and scattered the spray like snow before them. With the wind came the first big wave. Catching *Ravenswing* by the stern, the greyish-black mountain of water lifted her high. It passed under her and left her wallowing in the trough in its wake.

"Here comes another one," a voice screamed above the noise of the storm. "Hold on for your lives."

I wrapped my arms around the mainmast and held on with all my strength. The sea reared up behind *Ravenswing*, a towering ogre of a wave, magnificent in its malevolence; terrifying in its unstoppable power. I closed my eyes and prayed, expecting the ship to be smashed to matchwood. The wave broke over the ship and over me. From far underwater, or so it seemed, I felt my lungs bursting. I could feel *Ravenswing* trembling under me, shaking and skidding sideways, desperate to escape the clutches of the deep. A shrill screaming, accompanied by thunderous roaring, broke the spell over me. Under water one minute, I surfaced – still clinging to the main mast – and took a deep breath, expecting to be submerged again. *Ravenswing* was yet afloat and maintaining an even keel, though suffering. The wind continued to batter us; the seas maintained their punishing attacks, though none as vicious as that first assault. This went on for hours until we were all exhausted. When the storm finally abated, we took stock of our position.

A wave had taken one man from us. Thrown into the scuppers by the water, the next wave washed him overboard. Another had a broken arm. Many of us had cuts and all had suffered bruises. The screaming wind had stripped *Ravenswing* of most of her sails. The remaining shreds flapped in useless protest at the storm. The topmast hung down below the royal yard, held only by some determined rigging. The wind and waves had swept two of the ship's small boats away. The mahogany rail enclosing the poopdeck had suffered damage. There was debris all over the main deck. She was in a mess and wounded, but *Ravenswing* refused to die. In the aftermath of the storm we worked to bring order back to the ship and to our lives. Two weeks later we limped up the familiar waters of the Thames Estuary to Gravesend. I was by then a seasoned sailor. I had learned more about my father's business first hand and I had gained a useful knowledge of basic navigation.

Now I had to fulfill my side of the bargain. I had to make a serious effort to continue my mathematical studies. There was only one way to achieve that goal. I had to take myself as far away from the sea and ships as I could, to remove those powerful distractions from my sight.

CHAPTER 3

The decision to apply to Oxford University to advance my mathematical studies was my own, although with the approval of my parents. My father was particularly pleased when I was accepted. He agreed to cover all expenses for the duration of my stay in the ancient seat of learning, and to make a financial allowance for everyday use. With one week to go before I had to leave Gravesend, I spent as much time with my friends as I could.

On a sunny afternoon, I practiced stick-fighting using quarterstaffs with a friend on the grass field near the Gravesend Blockhouse. We had stripped off our shirts and were soaked in sweat when Emily and her friend, Alice, chanced by. We interrupted our contest and started to put on our shirts to be properly presentable when we greeted them. They reached us before I had covered my shoulders. Emily looked at me in amazement. She pointed to my tattoo.

"Thomas. What is that thing on your shoulder?" she asked, her eyes open wide with horror. Alice stood beside her, one hand covering her mouth; her eyes just as wide.

"It's a tattoo, of a raven," I answered. "Please, Emily, do not mention this at home."

"Where did you get that...that...thing?" she asked with a rare hesitation.

"In Lisbon. Please, do not say anything of this at home."

My sister shook her head in disgust and made a comment about foolish young men. When the girls left us, heads close together under their parasols, they walked towards home without a backward glance. I could only hope Emily would keep her word. Knowing her as well as I did, I doubted she would be able to for long.

Leaving home at the beginning of September 1608, I rode my own horse, Jessie, to Oxford, taking a week for the journey of 30 leagues. The late summer weather was perfect. Avoiding the busy London area and the well-travelled routes, I rode slowly across country by way of small market towns. In Guildford and Reading, both of which were involved in the wool trade, I stayed overnight with merchants who were business associates of my father. Closer to my destination, I delayed for a few hours to rest Jessie at the tiny village of Dorchester while I explored the lovely abbey church of St. Peter and St. Paul.

A church had stood on that site since at least the 7th century, according to the local priest. Originally a Saxon cathedral, the Normans built the abbey in the 12th century. Although it was expanded and improved over the next two hundred years by a succession of architects and priests, it retained an aura of its ancient heritage. A magnificent stained-glass window on the north wall of the chancel depicted the Tree of Jesse. The outer walls of the sturdy square tower appeared to be new, or recently rebuilt. Inside though, the tower is ancient. I climbed the 14th century spiral stone staircase through its heart to the parapet. Polished to a shine by countless feet over the centuries, the individual steps have become well-worn and not for the faint of heart.

The view from the top is almost breathtaking. The abbey is surrounded by lush green meadows, many bordered by aged willow trees bending in tribute to history. In the distance, across the river, are the two rounded hills known locally as Wittenam Clumps; their summits crowned by stands of beech trees.

I made my last stop at Clifton Hampden, a few miles north-west of Dorchester, where I took a room at the delightful 14th century, thatch-roofed *Barley Mow Inn* for one night. That evening, after I had groomed and fed Jessie, I walked along the banks of the Thames, enjoying the peaceful scenery and quiet of the countryside. The fields bordering the river were covered in late summer wildflowers, still smiling with pleasure after a full day in the sun. Bees and butterflies flitted from one bloom to another. Above me, on the opposite side of the Thames, the church of St. Michael and All Angels dominated the rocky cliff hanging over the tiny village and the river. Birds flew low over the river, snapping up mosquitoes, dragonflies and other insects. A tall, slim grey heron stood in the shallows stalking a fish or a frog. It squawked in guttural annoyance at my approach and launched itself into the air, looking more like a carnivorous collection of feathered bones than a harmless bird.

Our final day began early under a cloudy sky. As soon as the dawn broke, Jessie and I forded the river and set off on the last leg of our long journey. The Thames is a meandering river. A few miles south east of Oxford it makes a right turn to flow east through Abingdon. With that accomplished it curves south and then west to find Clifton Hampden. I cut across country to avoid the Abingdon detour, thereby saving myself the best part of a day. Once I picked up the river again, I followed it north by way of Sandford until I could see the spires of Oxford's university buildings. We stopped on a hill for a few minutes to survey the wonderful scene, and to feast on a handful of fresh blackberries I picked from a large bush. Jessie enjoyed the berries as much as I did. Near the blackberries was a large thicket of wild roses, pink and white, still clinging to summer life. As if to welcome me, the afternoon sun peered through the clouds to pick out the highlights on the elegant rooftops. The weather allowed us no more than a brief glimpse of the beauty before the clouds cast their shadows once again over the land. It was enough to spur me on.

Oxford is a walled city with most of the university colleges within its confines, although a few later arrivals have taken up residence outside the walls. When I arrived there for the first time, the university was already ancient, having been in existence for over 500 years. With Jessie nodding her great head in approval, we crossed the stone bridge over the Cherwell River and passed through the wide south-east gate as the rain started. I found University College in minutes on my left where a servant directed me to nearby stables that would look after Jessie.

Oxford is a much finer city than Gravesend. The buildings, especially those owned by the university, are magnificent. Nothing so grand exists anywhere in the region of Gravesend. There is one link between Gravesend and Oxford for me, however: my home-town is on the south bank of a major waterway – the Thames River, Oxford is also on the Thames, and spreads to the banks of feeder streams such as the Cherwell. The Thames at Oxford is considerably narrower and cleaner than in its lower reaches, and much more attractive – though it didn't have any ships.

I spent my first full day at Oxford settling in to my rooms. My leather-covered pine chest of clothes and study materials had arrived by coach a few days earlier. Once I had put everything in its correct place, and after I had introduced myself to the college, I explored the exciting old city on foot for a few days. My studies would commence soon enough and I was looking forward to the work.

Oxford has existed since Saxon times. It is said to have originated in the early years of the 10th century. The university, claiming to be the oldest university in the English-speaking world, followed soon after – dating back to at least 1096. The university buildings, like the defensive wall that surrounds the city, were built with local stone, most likely quarried from the nearby Cotswold Hills. The city had an air of permanence not noticeable in Gravesend or even, perhaps, in London – which was in a constant state of change. Oxford exuded strength, determination and character. As such, it was a perfect setting for a seat of higher learning.

I must admit, I did not spend all my time studying at Oxford. Like many young men at the university, I was fit, healthy and curious. I participated in a variety of sports. I had been a competent swordsman since childhood, thanks to my father's teaching. I was also skilled in the use of the quarterstaff, a stick-fighting sport that I particularly enjoyed. On many chilly mornings the brittle clack-clack of two quarterstaffs in combat echoed across the Oxford meadows. We competed on the banks of the Cherwell without an audience, often with the wraithlike tendrils of early mist snaking around our legs.

At Oxford, under the tutelage of a fellow student, I learned another defensive skill: the art of pugilism. I also took up archery and became quite proficient with bow and arrow. Beyond that, we enjoyed competing with each other kicking large balls across fields. The cowhide balls had an air-filled bladder inside. I also tried another new game for me, called cricket. Played with a wooden bat and a hard, fist-size ball, cricket never did appeal to me. I was happier strengthening my arms and shoulders rowing on the Cherwell or the Thames. Life at Oxford was a rich experience, a mélange of intellectual discussions, concentrated learning, diverse sporting activities and regular forays into the less gentle side of the city.

In the evenings, we – my fellow mathematical students and I – gathered in our habitual pub, *The Bear Inn*, at the corner of Alfred Street and Blue Boar Street. The inn was dark and dingy with low ceilings. It always seemed to be crowded. Often we drank too much ale. We sang bawdy songs until our throats were sore. We flirted with the serving girls and, if sober enough, sometimes one of us would arrange a dalliance for later in the evening. That someone was often me. After my experience with too much wine in Lisbon when I was seventeen, I was rather more careful in my drinking habits than my friends. In effect, they had fun getting drunk. I drank less and had more fun with Brenda – a serving girl about three years my senior. She wasn't beautiful, although her smile could light up a room. The first time she agreed to meet me after the inn closed, Brenda acted coy. She kept asking questions such as, "What's a handsome young gentleman like yourself want with a wench like me, then?"

She knew perfectly well what I wanted and gave every indication of wanting the same from me. First, though, she played hard to get. In between silly questions, she did allow me to stroke her large, smooth breasts and put my hand up her skirt. That was the first time I had ever touched a woman in that way. Brenda's body was soft and felt wonderful, mysterious under my hands. She smelled of smoke and ale, something musky and a certain amount of sweat, as I suppose did I. That mattered not. I was filled with lust and desperate to release the tension in my loins. Brenda took care of that by thrusting her hand down the front of my breeches.

"What have we here?" she asked as she wrapped her fingers around my swollen member. Unable to control myself, I responded by squirting my seed up her arm. With a laugh, she wiped her hand and arm on her petticoat. Taking my face in both hands, she kissed me full on the lips and said, "Next time, young Thomas, I'll teach you to do this properly. I must go now."

She pulled her hood over her dark curls and vanished into the night. I returned to my college room with a smile on my face and a spring in my step. That night I dreamed of what erotic pleasures my next encounter with Brenda would produce.

The Thames River begins its journey somewhere in Gloucestershire to the west of Oxford. It is roughly 72 leagues in length from the source to the mouth of the estuary. I dropped a small stick into the river one morning and watched it drift away to the east. Walking beside it for a while, I calculated the river's flow to be no more than one league in about three hours. That meant, maintaining such an average, the stick would take about nine days to travel from the source, all the way across country, through London and on to Gravesend. I wondered what it would be like to take a small boat the full length of the Thames from the source to the estuary.

My mathematics tutor, Professor Rushworth, had made a study of astronomy. Once he learned of my interest in navigation, he gave me the benefit of additional attention. We often went out on clear nights to study the stars through his special telescope. From him I learned the importance of the celestial bodies and their special relationship to navigation. We discussed and debated the Polish genius – Copernicus, plus Ptolemy and that other erudite Greek – Eratosthenes: all astronomers, all mathematicians of note and all skilled in the science of navigation. To add to my knowledge of great mathematicians, Professor Rushworth introduced me and my fellow students to the works of Euclid, the father of geometry.

I told Rushworth of my interest in the exploration of the Arctic and so we discussed the stars that could guide a navigator through the northern world of ice and snow. Our roles of tutor and student soon merged into a strong friendship. Over a glass of port in his study one evening, he told me of fascinating man-made rings of stone he had seen far to the south and west of Oxford, near Salisbury, and another larger one, north of there, the size of a meadow. He was emphatic in his belief that the stone circles had a connection with astronomy.

"They were certainly designed and built by mathematicians," he said. "I suspect religion had something to do with them too."

"Why do you feel they were possibly built for religious purposes?" I asked.

"Because they are aligned to take advantage of the summer and winter solstices. You should really take the time to see them for yourself, Thomas," Professor

Rushworth suggested. “Why don’t you take a few days off at mid term break to visit the circles? I’m sure you will find them fascinating.”

“We could go together,” I offered. “I have my own horse here.”

Professor Rushworth gave me a rueful smile and scratched his long nose. “No, Thomas. I am no horseman. I would fall off before we had gone half a league.”

We sat talking for hours. The professor told me everything he knew of the two sites and what to look for. I began to get excited about the excursion. The mid-term break was only a week away and I had no other plans. A ride in the countryside seemed like an excellent idea.

The journey was appalling at first. The road, if such it was, contained more mud than the average farmyard and enough stone obstacles to threaten Jessie’s legs at every step. As soon as we could, we left the treacherous road and walked parallel to it on smoother ground for the rest of the way. We followed the valley at the foot of White Horse Hill, taking a detour to climb to the rounded apex and look out over Oxfordshire from the highest point. There is a Bronze-Age replica of an elongated animal etched into the chalk of the hill at Uffington. Locals refer to it as the White Horse, hence the name of the hill. I thought the ‘horse’ resembled a gigantic skinny white cat stretched to extremes. We crossed over the hills to bypass Swindon and followed a pleasant valley to Marlborough, close to the first site I wanted to visit. We arrived on the edge of Salisbury Plain two days after leaving Oxford. There I took a room for a few nights at a coaching inn with stables attached and with reasonable access to both ancient locations.

Avebury is a Neolithic henge site. A henge being the earthworks positioned as a form of defensive barrier to protect the site. Avebury stone circle is enormous, as Professor Rushworth had said. I paced from one side to the other and estimated its diameter to be roughly 1,100 feet. Although the site was not a perfect circle, I calculated the circumference at 3,456 feet and the area as 950,332 square feet. The huge circle of vertical stones, each obviously carved by the hand of man, is incomplete. The stones that remain are gigantic, measuring more than twice my height. Standing on Jessie's saddle with my arms stretched up, I could just reach the top of the tallest one. I have no idea how much more of the stone is buried in the ground, therefore could only estimate the possible weight of the exposed portion at about 25 tons. The overall weight of each stone must be at least twice that. There are two smaller circles inside the main stone circle. The complete complex is ringed by the henge with a ditch on the inside. I wondered what value a ditch would be to a fortification when so placed. That ditch at Avebury could not have slowed a one-legged man.

Stonehenge, through smaller, is much more dramatic. I enjoyed my stay, pacing out the distances between the upright stones, calculating their heights and their probable weights. The professor had told me the builders aligned the stone circle to the sunset of the winter solstice on one side and to the sunrise of the summer solstice on the other. My visit took place almost halfway between these two extremes so I was unable to verify the story. Cloudy skies for the duration of my visit to both sites prevented me from enjoying the circles by moon and starlight, although I did go out in the hope of greater visibility. Intrigued and somewhat mystified by what I had seen, I left these enigmatic ancient structures with far more questions than answers. I thought about their design, construction and their purpose for most of my ride back to Oxford. When I next met Professor Rushworth he could not answer more than a few of the many questions I asked. He had no answer to my question about the strange placement of the ditch, nor could he tell me the purpose of the stone circles, only that astronomy and religion were somehow involved. He did have one comment that gave me hope for an eventual understanding by someone.

"Someday, Thomas, a scholar – perhaps someone such as you – will dedicate his life to studying those stone circles. What a story he will then have to tell the world."

I had not seen Brenda for a few weeks. The night after my return to college, I joined my friends for an evening of libation and song at *The Bear Inn*. When she served us, Brenda leaned towards me, her breast touching my shoulder, and said, "I'll be off at eleven. I've missed you."

Those two brief sentences gave me much to look forward to at the end of the evening. We met, as we had done for a few weeks, in the lane behind the pub. Normally we coupled standing up: an undignified and uncomfortable way to share our bodies. My friends referred to such an exercise as "a knee-trembler." The description was crude but apt. On this night a light rain was falling.

"Come with me," Brenda said, taking my hand and leading me through a maze of alleys to a hay loft. "No one will 'ear us in 'ere."

Brenda was always a noisy partner. She moaned and she cried out, almost screaming at one point. We were fortunate that the hay deadened all the sounds we made. I fell asleep sated and exhausted. Brenda was already snoring softly beside me. I heard nothing more for a few hours until a cockerel announced daybreak, its raucous greeting waking me with a start. I reached for Brenda but she was gone. Daylight told me I must be gone too. I had a tutorial to attend that morning and I was far from prepared.

And so my days and nights at Oxford progressed throughout my first year at university. I had settled in well. During the course of the next few months, at Professor Rushworth's urging, I applied myself more and more to my studies. I spent more time listening to lectures and attending tutorials – and much less time on frivolous activities. Brenda became the first casualty. She accepted the inevitable with a laugh and moved on to a younger student.

About that time, we had an important guest lecturer visit us at University College. Professor Henry Briggs, from Gresham College in London, came to Oxford for a few days at the invitation of his friend Professor Rushworth. Though small in stature, Briggs was an impressive figure to watch. He had large, dark eyes that roved left and right in constant motion. Their intensity contrasted with the silver of his tidy facial hair. He wore a black skull cap and a long robe, also black. His deep voice boomed around the hall when he lectured. Professor Rushworth introduced me to Briggs as a budding mathematical scholar and a dedicated student of exploration. I was delighted when Professor Briggs gave me a copy of his recent publication, *A Table to find the Height of the Pole, the Magnetic Declination being given.* To me it was a treasure beyond value and became one of my favourite possessions.

I enjoyed every aspect of my life at Oxford, the studying as well as the sporting activities, except for one nagging memory. The rivers and the small boats reminded me that I missed the smell of the sea, and I missed seeing real ships every day. That gap in my life became more obvious as the weeks and months went by. I was getting restless and that restlessness began to affect my studies. I knew the only way to solve the problem was to go home for a few weeks, perhaps just for the next Christmas season, or maybe, I thought, to take a few months off and go back to sea once more – maybe, better still, to sign on with an explorer for an expedition.

I went home to Gravesend for Christmas at the end of the Michaelmas term; the first term of my second year at Oxford University, in late 1609. The journey was depressing and bitterly cold. In company with Jessie, I encountered rain, sleet, snow, some ice and high winds. We travelled as far as we were able each day while there was light. At night we bedded down at coaching inns. We were both relieved and happy to reach the sanctity of the family home in Gravesend: Jessie to a bale of fresh, clean straw in her old stall in the stables and me to my warm and comfortable room on the upper floor of the house. I spent the first full day back in Gravesend roaming the waterfront in the rain, visiting the Blockhouse – where I sat by the wall for a while – watching ships and boats, and savoring the familiar exotic tang of the sea air.

CHAPTER 4

Christmas was a wonderful time to be at home. I had spent the previous Christmas with friends near Oxford. Being at home was much better. Although Gravesend was but a small seaport town, it did have a busy social calendar. The festive season offered me any number of dinner invitations, a few musical recitals, two elegant balls, plus the customary church events. I took part in as many functions as I could. At mass on Christmas morning I couldn't help but notice a stunning red head sitting on the opposite side of the aisle and a few pews in front. I am sure every man in the church was aware of her presence.

"Who is that?" I whispered to Emily, inclining my head in the direction of my interest.

"Miss Jane Montrose. Her father is a Scotsman. Landed gentry. Richer than Croesus. Mother is English. They moved here last summer. She's available. She will love your tattoo." Emily's ability to answer a simple question with a series of short, snappy details had always amazed me. On this occasion I was happy to listen.

"Ask Papa to introduce you to her father. They conduct business together. I suspect they know each other quite well by now," she added.

Despite the cold and the threat of snow, members of the congregation milled about outside St. George's after the service, wishing each other the compliments of the season. I was talking to our priest when I saw Emily whispering to Mama while looking at me. Both were smiling. Mama nodded her head. As I walked towards them, Mama took Papa by the arm and steered him towards the Montrose family. Emily grinned up at me in impish delight.

"What have you done, Emily?" I asked, reasonably sure of the answer.

"Oh, I just happened to mention to Mama that you had expressed interest in Miss Montrose, that's all." She put her white-gloved hand to her mouth and giggled. "Come along Mary, and you, James," she ordered. "Let's get in the coach." She turned to me, "You stay here, Thomas. You have people to meet."

Smiling at all around us, she ushered our younger sister and brother to the waiting family coach. Taking a deep breath, I moved to my father's side. He at once introduced me to Mr. Montrose. He in turn introduced me to his wife and his daughter in quick succession. Miss Jane Montrose smiled at me with what appeared to be a mixture of amusement and interest as I kissed her hand.

"Will you be at the New Year's Eve ball next week, Mr. Woodhouse?" she asked.

Until then I had not decided whether to go to the ball or to go carousing with my friends. I made up my mind in a split second. "Yes. Most certainly, Miss Montrose. I hope you will honour me with at least one dance."

"I shall keep that in mind, Mr. Woodhouse. Good day to you."

Jane Montrose walked with her father and mother to their coach. Mama watched her and then said, “She is a lovely young lady, isn’t she?”

Papa narrowed his eyes, looking from Mama to me. He glanced towards the line of coaches where Miss Montrose was just taking her seat.

“Ah, yes. I see,” he said. “Yes, yes. Miss Montrose is certainly a beauty.”

As the Montrose coach pulled away, the two magnificent black horses dancing in concert with each other in their enthusiasm to be moving, a silk-gloved hand waved just once in my direction. I don’t think anyone else noticed, but the simple action put an immediate smile on my face.

That evening, while enjoying a snifter of brandy with my father after dinner, we talked again of my interest in exploration and a life at sea. We were back to the same old argument. I have to say, he was not impressed with my continued dreams and said so, in no uncertain terms.

“Finish your time at Oxford, Thomas,” he barked. “Finish your time there and get your degree.”

I tried to keep my eyes steady on his. It wasn’t easy because, although we were friends, he could still intimidate me at times. I shook my head.

“No, Papa. That is not what I want.”

He glared at me, before softening his face and his tone. “Don’t you see, Thomas, with that mathematics degree behind you, the business world will be yours to explore. You can become my partner. Together we will continue to build this business I have created into a dominant import and export entity with a few more ships: a business, perhaps with other investors, to eventually rival even the East India Company.”

I was not convinced. We argued back and forth in a friendly manner for some time. Eventually, understanding that I would not be side-tracked from the course I desired, he gave in with a deep sigh.

"*Ravenswing* is due to sail for Lisbon again in a week or so. She needs a competent first mate. You have the experience. You could handle that position. Would that suit you for a while?"

I shook my head. "No. Thank you, Papa. That is a really fine offer, but it's not what I want. With your approval, I would be happier searching for a position on a ship bound for real adventure."

Papa sighed and stared at the fire for a few minutes, obviously marshalling his thoughts. He looked up at me again and nodded his head. "Well, Thomas," he said. "if you are so determined, I'll give you a letter of introduction to my friend, Sir Dudley Digges. I'd like you to go and see Digges, anyway. As a governor of the Virginia Colony, he has many powerful contacts, especially with the East India Company. If you are really determined to go to sea again, he might recommend you to one of the captains in the Company's large fleet."

"Where will I find Sir Dudley," I asked.

"He lives at Chilham Castle, here in Kent, between Ashford and Canterbury. He's having that house renovated at the moment so most of the time he'll be at his London residence on Philip Lane. Best to call on him there and present the letter from me."

He stood, as if to leave, and then sat down again. He looked at me with a big smile and his head slightly on one side. "So, my son, the Arctic is your goal for the future, but what about the present? I couldn't help but notice your interest in Miss Montrose – and her interest in you. Does her beauty not make you think less of Arctic adventure and more of family life?"

"Yes, Jane Montrose is gorgeous, isn't she?" I answered, my own smile a mirror to his.

"Well?" he questioned.

"No, Papa. I have to make my mark as an explorer. I believe that is my destiny." I tapped my chest with my right fist. "I feel it in here, Papa. I shall go and see Sir Dudley soon and listen to his advice."

There was no point in going to London until the New Year. Sir Dudley was unlikely to be there and there were too many exciting social events happening in Gravesend to allow me to tear myself away. On New Year's Eve, I escorted Emily to the final ball of the season with my parents. The two younger children stayed at home, despite their protestations of being old enough to attend the evening. I was dancing with Emily to a sedate minuet when I saw Miss Montrose enter with her mother and father. She looked stunning in a full-length silk gown of pale blue fluffed out by innumerable petticoats underneath. I passed Emily over to one of my friends and made my way to the Montrose family.

"Good evening, sir. Good evening, ma'am," I bowed and addressed myself to their daughter. "Good evening, Miss Montrose. May I say how lovely you look?"

"Why, thank you, Mr. Woodhouse. How kind of you to say so."

Jane's fan, which she now used to flutter in front of her face, had the names of her admirers (I assumed that's what they were) written on the leaves. Emily had told me about this custom or ploy being used by some eligible young women. Jane had only been at the ball a few minutes yet her fan was already more than half covered. My dismay must have shown because she looked at her open fan, smiled at me and said, "There are four dances left, Mr. Woodhouse. You may choose whichever one you wish."

One would not be enough. I signed my name in each of the four blank spaces and returned the fan to her. She looked at it and laughed. "Why, Mr. Woodhouse, you have completed the leaves of my fan. That is most demanding of you, sir; interesting, too," she added the last two words in a low voice and with a soft smile.

My smile beamed back at her. I could not have straightened my face if I had tried. I thanked her and went in search of my friends. I would be able to hold Miss Montrose in my arms soon enough. With a glass of rum punch in my hand, I watched as she was whirled around the floor by a succession of suitors. Each time she passed, she acknowledged me with a smile or a subtle movement of her head.

Each time I danced with Miss Montrose that evening I enjoyed myself more and more. She was a delightful partner and an engaging conversationalist. She felt wonderful in my arms, her body moving in a swaying motion in time with the music. I felt we were getting along extremely well. After our final dance, I suggested a walk to find a punch bowl. She took my arm and allowed me to lead her to one of the doors leading away from the ballroom. I opened one door and found a library furnished with large padded leather armchairs.

"Come in here, for a moment," I said leading her through the door.

Inside, Miss Montrose turned to face me, her face straight but her eyes sparkling. "What is it you want of me, Thomas?" she asked in a soft voice.

"To be quite honest, Miss Montrose, Jane, I would like to kiss you."

Miss Montrose took a small step back and studied my face. "You are most forward, Thomas," she said. "Perhaps I should scream for help"

"No, please don't. I mean you no harm, Jane." I hoped I sounded convincing.

"Good. Then if we are to kiss, perhaps we should do it now before anyone else comes in?" She raised her face to mine and offered her lips, her eyes intent on my eyes.

The kiss was brief; no more than a brush of lips against each other, with a subtle promise of something more. She sighed and leaned into me with her rouged lips parted in invitation. I was about to kiss her again with mounting passion when we heard voices coming our way. Miss Montrose pulled away from me saying, "Another time, perhaps, Thomas?"

She opened the door and departed in a rustle of exotic cloth, leaving me alone with a library of silent books and an all too familiar feeling of discomfort in my silk Venetians.

CHAPTER 5

I went to London a few days after the ball to meet Sir Dudley Digges. The nation's capital was not a pleasant place to visit, although it did have undeniable attractions. It was dirty, smelly and it was dangerous in many areas. To offset that, there was an eclectic variety of entertainment. I travelled to London early so that I would have time to attend the Globe Theatre in the hope of seeing one of Shakespeare's plays. I was fortunate in that the King's Men were staging *The Merry Wives of Windsor* that evening. I enjoyed it very much. Shakespeare had a way of using words that thrilled me with their simplicity and their elegance at the same time. The rest of the audience, of course, yelled and catcalled throughout the performance, reducing erudite comedy to the lowest level. The actors often had to shout to make their words audible. Even so, I enjoyed the story and the performance.

Away from the theatre, my feet always seemed to turn to the river. The Thames was the main artery that fed England's heart. Passing through London it pulsated with passenger and commercial traffic all day, every day. Wherries and smaller rowing boats crossed from one side to the other with passengers and freight. Barges hauled cargo from ships at the docks up stream to warehouses. At the docklands, ships stood on cradles in various stages of construction or repair. Operational ships loaded and unloaded cargo. Ships arrived and ships set sail. On any day, even considering the abysmal winter weather, I could have watched the bustling action on the river for hours. Tearing myself away, I went to look at the shops jammed in on both sides of London Bridge. Clustered together and crowding the only pedestrian way of crossing the river, the shops varied from milliners to grocers and from needle-makers to book sellers and publishers. It was the books that attracted me. With an hour to spare, I browsed through three different shops. In the third I found two undeniable treasures. The first was a copy of Euclid's *Elements of Geometry*. That was a prize indeed. I paid far too much for the book but could not leave the shop without it. The second book to enter my possession that morning was a book on Frobisher's three voyages by George Best – one of his crew. Had I the time, I would have sat down somewhere and started studying immediately. Instead, I had an appointment to keep a league or so away on Philip Lane.

Sir Dudley Digges was a well-built man in his mid-forties, I guessed. He was of medium height but appeared taller due to his posture. He stood with head erect and his back straight as a board. His hair was dark brown, with a few streaks of grey. His eyes matched the dominant colour of his hair. His long, thin face had deep creases around the eyes and mouth that spoke of much serious thought. He wore his light brown beard in the same shape as my father. He spoke fast, in an elegant yet staccato style. He obviously did not believe in wasting time.

"Your father tells me you are a mathematician studying at Oxford, Thomas. I too read mathematics there, at University College."

"Yes, sir. I know. I am at University College, also. I have seen your portrait in the gallery of distinguished alumni."

"So, Thomas Woodhouse, why would a mathematician want to go to sea, eh? Not much of a career there for a bright young man, I shouldn't think."

I told Sir Dudley of my interest in the sea as a means to make my mark as an explorer, using much the same arguments as I had employed at home. Digges, like my father, was not impressed. Despite that, I persevered. The discussion swayed back and forth until he came up with an idea.

"My friend and business associate, Sir Thomas Smythe, is the governor of the East India Company. I understand he has vacancies for a few junior officers in his fleet. Are you aware that the largest ship ever built in England is in the final stages of construction at Deptford? She is soon to depart on a voyage to the East Indies."

I knew about *Trades Increase.* She was the talk of the Thames River waterfronts. A behemoth said to weigh more than 1,200 gross tons, she would carry a crew of hundreds – officers and men.

"If you wish, young Woodhouse, I'm sure I could persuade Sir Thomas Smythe to have you signed on as a midshipman. You could learn much from Captain Sir Henry Middleton. What do you think of that idea, heh? She'll be ready to sail in March."

The offer was tempting. I almost accepted, for the experience and the adventure the position would offer. Sir Dudley noticed my hesitation.

"What is it, Thomas?" he asked. "A ship the king has himself blessed is not good enough for you? Is that it, lad?"

"No, sir. Nothing like that. It's just that I have my heart set on a voyage of exploration, rather than trade." I paused for a moment, biting my lip and looking at the floor. Then, "You see, Sir Dudley, much as I appreciate the opportunity you have offered me – and I do not wish to seem ungrateful – I feel my destiny is in a different direction. In the Arctic, to be more precise."

From the way Sir Dudley Digges looked at me, I suspect he thought I was missing a significant part of my brain. He sat there for a long time, staring at the fire in his hearth, darting brief glances at me, yet never meeting my eyes. Finally, he broke the silence with a cough.

"The Arctic, you say," he looked straight me. "The Arctic. Are you sure this is what you want? I doubt that your father will be pleased."

"No, sir. He will not be pleased, but I hope to convince him."

"Well then, I see you have your mind set on this exploration business. Come back tomorrow morning, about eleven o'clock, and I shall have a letter of introduction for you to an acquaintance of mine. He may be able to help."

I was dismissed and so spent an anxious night in a damp room at *The Elephant*, not far away – just across the river in Southwark. That night and the next morning dragged out the longest hours I had suffered through since my last exams at Oxford. The time passed, somehow. I delivered myself to Sir Dudley's house as ordered on the stroke of eleven. A footman handed me an envelope without inviting me in. As the door closed, I looked at the address on the envelope with my mouth wide open. The letter for which I had waited all night with such anxiety was as much a surprise as it was the answer to my dreams. The letter was addressed to Captain Henry Hudson, followed by his address near St. Katherine's Pool. Henry Hudson – commander of three Arctic expeditions – a man I thought of as an exploration hero.

I hastened on foot through the slushy streets towards the river, past the Tower and into the docklands. I arrived at the door of Captain Hudson's house breathless and a little disheveled, with my heart beating a loud tattoo in my chest. There was no way I could allow myself to be seen like that. To calm my nerves, I walked for fifteen minutes or so, straightening my clothes at the same time. When I felt ready to face the man who might hold my destiny in his hands, I returned to the house and knocked loudly. A maid opened the door. She was a comely creature about my own age. She reminded me of Brenda. At any other time...well, I had no time or thought for dalliance that day. I doffed my hat and stated my business.

"I'm here to meet Captain Hudson. I have a letter of introduction from Sir Dudley Digges. Please be good enough to announce me."

"I can't," the maid said, offering a coquettish smile.

"You cannot? Why indeed can you not? This is a matter of some importance to me."

"The Master is in Bristol, sir, visiting Mr. Hakluyt. He won't be home until this day next week."

"Who is there, Betsy?" The voice from inside the house was strong, yet musical.

"A young gentleman to see the captain, ma'am. He says he has a letter of introduction."

"Well, bring him in. We do not keep gentlemen of any age waiting on the doorstep, Betsy. It's not polite."

Katherine Hudson, for the voice did indeed belong to the captain's wife, sat in a comfortable room in an armchair with some papers on her lap. A fire burned in the hearth. I bowed as I entered the room.

"Forgive me for the interruption, Mistress Hudson," I began. "My name is Thomas Woodhouse. I have a letter of introduction to your husband from Sir Dudley Digges. I hope to sail with Captain Hudson on his next expedition."

"Do you, indeed?" There was no smile on her handsome face. "Perhaps you should meet my son, John. He has sailed with his father on three expeditions. Perhaps he can talk you out of such folly."

Unusual for me, I was flustered. Folly? What talk is this from the wife of a famous explorer? I wondered.

"Betsy," Mistress Hudson called. "Ask Master John to join us, if you please. And bring in some refreshments."

John took his time in answering the summons. I was halfway through a glass of wine and desperately trying to maintain a polite conversation with Mrs. Hudson when he walked in. I noticed he fondled the maid's bottom as he passed her. She smiled and raised her eyebrows at him. An invitation if ever I saw one.

"John, this is Mr. Thomas Woodhouse. He hopes to sail with your father to the Arctic on the next expedition. What do you think of that?" Mistress Hudson managed to introduce me and get to the point of our meeting without delay. She stood up and left the room, saying, rather disdainfully, I thought, "I shall leave you two young gentlemen to discuss the North Pole."

John Hudson was two years younger than I with broad shoulders, rough seamen's hands and a firm grip. After we had shaken hands he invited me to be seated again.

"Mother is not happy that we are soon to go back to sea," he explained her parting comment. "We only returned from our last expedition in early November. It's difficult for her, I know: and a great worry, too – she dwells on the dangers so. We have been away from home for much of the last three years, most of that time in the Arctic. And now we hope to leave again in the early spring to search for the North-west Passage to Cathay."

"The maid said your father is in Bristol. Will he be home next week as she said?"

"Yes. Father is visiting Professor Hakluyt. Although he is not an explorer, he probably knows more about the far north than anyone else in England. Hakluyt has a collection of the most valuable maps of exploration, particularly of the Arctic regions. My father is with him to study the most up to date information. When we return from the Arctic, Father will then present Professor Hakluyt with his latest charts."

"I have seen Hakluyt's Arctic map. I have a copy at home, in fact," I told John.

We talked for at least two hours. During that time, I mentioned my mathematical studies, and my brief time at sea as a deck hand and that I was now classed as an able seaman. Mostly I listened to John describing the wonders and dangers of sailing in ice.

John had first gone to sea as a cabin boy on his father's ship at the age of fourteen. On that arduous voyage, his father had attempted – without success – to reach the North Pole. Although the most northerly point on Earth had eluded him, on that expedition Captain Hudson had discovered valuable new whaling grounds in the Arctic. Later, with a different crew, father and son had twice navigated through the North-East Passage across the top of Russia, until they found their course blocked by ice. They had been to Greenland waters together and to the New World, exploring the coast most of the way to the Virginia Colony. John told me of the aggressive savages they had encountered there on a river they followed far inland. He told me of the wondrous sea creatures in the Arctic, of the vicious storms that blow there and of drifting icebergs as big as the Houses of Parliament. It sounded like a wonderful life to me. I gave John my letter of introduction from Sir Dudley for his father and left. I felt we two young men could become firm friends once at sea. In parting, John promised, "Father will send you a message on his return to London." All I could do then was go home and wait for an invitation.

Feeling confident, I walked the short distance to the river. A few small boats mingled just off shore, their owners waiting for passengers. I pointed to one and called, "Sculls."

The boatman pulled hard on his oars and drifted to the steps where I stood. "Where to, Guv?" he asked.

"I need to go to Greenwich, to catch the Long Ferry barge to Gravesend. Will you take me there?"

"You don't need to go that far, young sir. That barge starts from Billingsgate. I'll take you there. It's a lot closer. Much faster for both of us that way. What with the tide and all." The boatman swung the stern of his craft towards the land until I could step in without falling in the river. As soon as I was seated he rowed hard downstream.

A mixture of rain and snow fell for the entire river journey, first on the small rowing boat, later on the much larger and considerably more comfortable barge. Passing Greenwich the winter coated me, two other passengers, both unhappy, and the boatmen in slushy white. I hardly noticed the discomfort. With my heavy woollen cape wrapped around me; the wide brim of my hat tilted over my eyes, I was already fortifying myself for the Arctic. A little snow and sleet on the Thames was nothing compared to the weather I expected to encounter in the far north.

The next few days dragged into a week, and then another with no word from Captain Hudson. I kept busy by helping my father in the warehouse for a few hours each day. For the rest, I roamed the Gravesend waterfront, spent hours on the wall of the Blockhouse watching ships, waiting and hoping. My frustration grew with each passing day. I began to think I had been forgotten.

I visited Miss Jane Montrose and her parents one evening and thoroughly enjoyed the company. Jane was a delight to be with but even she sensed my mind was elsewhere. "You seem preoccupied, Thomas. Is something worrying you?" she asked.

That opening prompted me to tell her of my plans and my hopes for the future. She listened without interruption, a half smile on her face, her hands clasped together in her lap.

"And at the end of these adventures, Thomas...What will you do then?" she looked at me with more than one question in her eyes.

"My father wishes me to join him as his partner. I have promised to consider that opportunity with great care, for my future."

"I think your father is a wise man, Thomas. I hope you follow his lead."

I left the Montrose house with my mind juggling all the possibilities that presented themselves. The idea of a life with the lovely Jane Montrose was extremely appealing. Becoming a successful businessman like my father also had its undeniable appeal. Those two possibilities seemed to fit like hands and gloves. But then there was the other ambition – to become an Arctic explorer. No matter how I weighed the options, and despite the enormous attraction posed by Jane Montrose, the Arctic always tipped the scales. Marriage and business could wait, I decided.

Sixteen days after my conversation with John Hudson, I sat with friends in my customary ale house, the *Eagle and Child,* near the Gravesend waterfront at midday. It was dark and gloomy, as many old taverns are, but the food and drink were good and cheap. I had my usual pint of ale in front of me, along with a plate of bread, cheese and pickled onions. A lad came in, brushing wet snow off a blanket draped over his shoulders. He looked around, asking a serving wench a question. She pointed at me. The boy pushed his way through the crowd until he stood at our small table.

"Master Woodhouse?" he enquired.

"I am Woodhouse."

"Yer pa says to come home right away. There's a message for ya."

"There is? Wonderful." I stood and felt in my pocket for a coin for him. "You can finish my ale and my meal, if you wish."

I placed a coin in his hand and started for the door. The boy downed what was left of my ale in one gulp, belched, grabbed the remaining bread, cheese and two pickled onions with his dirty hands and squirmed through the crowd to reach the door before me.

"Thank you, kind sir," he called as he ran away.

From the *Eagle and Child*, or the *Bird and Baby* as habitual customers usually referred to the ale house, to my home was less than half a mile. Without breaking into an undignified run, I walked as fast as I could to get there in minutes. My father was waiting in his study.

"I have a message for you, Thomas," he said, without preamble. "It is from a Captain Henry Hudson. You are invited to call on him at his home tomorrow, in the forenoon. You had better leave for London at once."

"Thank you, Papa." I shook his hand in my excitement. "I'll be back in a few days with good news, I hope."

That night, once again bedded down at *The Elephant*, I could hardly sleep, despite the tiring journey up river against the current. What would the new day bring for me? Would this prove to be the answer to my dreams? As I was musing on my future, I remembered I had planned to attend a musical recital the following afternoon in Gravesend. Miss Jane Montrose had sent word through one of her father's footmen to Emily that she would be in attendance and requesting the pleasure of her company. Emily, of course, had told me, knowing I would be interested. My plans had changed. Miss Montrose and Emily would have to enjoy the recital without my company.

At the captain's house the next morning, the same maid greeted me with the same inviting smile. "Come in, sir. The captain is waiting for you."

Captain Hudson was a man of about my father's age. He was well dressed in a leather doublet, a linen shirt, leather Venetians and silken hose. His clean white shirt was open at the neck. He had a woollen cape around his shoulders. As he rose to greet me I could see he was about my height, though broader in his shoulders, and appeared extremely fit. A luxurious beard, carefully trimmed, covered the lower half of his face and reached to his upper chest. He had dark eyes and thick black eyebrows to match his long hair.

"Master Woodhouse," he greeted me with a smile and a strong handshake. "Thank you for coming. Sir Dudley Digges tells me you wish to join my ship as a member of the crew. He says you are a mathematician and could prove useful on my next voyage. You have some sea experience – as an able seaman on one of your father's ships, I believe?" He inclined his head sideways as he posed the question.

"Yes, sir. I have made three short voyages to Antwerp and one to Lisbon."

"Aha. Not quite the frozen wastes of the Arctic," he smiled at me. "But, time at sea is useful enough if it helps you find your way around a ship and into the rigging without falling overboard. Why do you want to go to the Arctic?" He shot the question at me so fast it sounded like an accusation.

"I want to learn from you, Captain Hudson. I have studied the voyages of most Arctic explorers, especially the three that Frobisher made, and I believe my destiny lies in the Arctic. I can think of no finer way of learning about the north than to be a part of a serious expedition of discovery, with yourself as commander, of course."

"I accept your compliment, which I hope you meant." He studied my face for a reaction. After a few moments of silence, he nodded – as if deep in thought – and sat down. Leaning back in his armchair, he looked me up and down.

"My ship is the *Discovery,*" he spoke softly. "I plan to leave London in early to mid-March, if we can. If the ship is ready, which seems unlikely at the moment. If not, we must leave before the middle of April. Time is of the essence. We need to be in Arctic waters as soon as possible because of the short navigation season." He raised his voice. "Can you be ready to join my crew by then, Master Woodhouse?"

"Yes, sir." I was so elated I almost saluted. "I'm ready now."

"Calm yourself and have patience, Woodhouse. There is much to be done before we sail."

He told me the arrangements for my pay as an able seaman, and gave me instructions on when and where to join the ship. After that, he fell silent and I realized he had done with me. I thanked him and started for the door.

"Where is our ship now, sir?" I asked as I was leaving.

"Our ship? So, it's our ship now, is it?" The captain was gracious enough to laugh at my presumption of part ownership. "She's at Woolwich, getting her hull strengthened and re-caulked before the rest of the fitting out. You'll see *Discovery* soon enough, Master Woodhouse."

As he showed me to the door, I could see the shadow of another young man, not John, standing at the foot of the stairs.

"Wait for me in the parlor, Henry," Captain Hudson called to him. "I'll be there in a minute."

I left Captain Hudson's home with a smile on my face and a light heart. I was on the captain's crew list, and I knew that our ship would be the stalwart *Discovery* – already a veteran of the Arctic having been Sir George Weymouth's ship a few years before. My mathematical knowledge, therefore my education, and my previous experience at sea, had helped convince Captain Hudson that I could be a useful addition to his crew. Of course, my introduction from Sir Dudley Digges, one of his patrons, had not gone amiss. The pay was a little better than expected too, though nowhere near what I could have earned working with my father. Most important of all, I was about to live my dream. It is needless to say, I am sure, I never did return to my studies at Oxford. However, I could not know on that exciting day that my dream would turn into a nightmare.

While in London I took the opportunity of visiting Gresham College and was rewarded by a brief meeting with

Professor Henry Briggs. When I reminded him we had met the previous year at Oxford he remembered me.

"Ah, yes," he smiled. "Rushworth's protégé, the future Arctic explorer."

"Indeed, I am, Professor," I burst out. "I am to join Captain Henry Hudson on the good ship *Discovery* for an expedition to find the North-west Passage to Cathay. We leave London in a few weeks."

Professor Briggs nodded. "Yes," he said. "I know about the expedition. I have met Captain Hudson through my friend Professor Hakluyt. Hudson is a fine navigator. You will have an excellent teacher on that voyage."

The professor then gave me a copy of his latest paper, *Tables for the Improvement of Navigation* and a faded copy of Mercator's Arctic map. "Take these with you, Master Woodhouse. You might find them useful someday. And, perhaps, you will be able to bring Mercator's map up to date for me? I would appreciate that very much."

I started home for Gravesend in a state of euphoria. Nothing could dampen my spirits, not even the torrential rain that persisted over the Thames all the way in the Long Ferry. Sheltering under my cloak as much as possible, I watched the raindrops pock-marking the river beside me, imagining I was already on board a ship bound for the Arctic. My youthful enthusiasm could not be contained. As I stepped ashore at Gravesend, my excitement was such that I was careless. Forgetting that the dark of night can be an evil cloak worn by criminals, my mind was on Captain Hudson and the forthcoming Arctic expedition. I failed to notice someone following me through the narrow streets.

CHAPTER 6

My first indication of approaching danger came in the form of running footsteps echoing off the cobblestones. I flattened my back against a wall as I drew my sword and prepared to defend myself. The footpads came at me from two directions at once. Working as a team, their intention was obvious: to rob me of any valuables and to cause me harm if I resisted.

"Nah then, young gennelman," one of them said, his voice a sinister drawl. "Put up your sword and ye'll come to no 'arm."

My reply was a slash at his dim figure with my sword. That momentary distraction allowed the other thief to stab at me with a long knife. I felt it cut into my left arm and yelled in pain.

"Nah we've got 'im. Take 'is sword."

The wound hurt, but not enough to incapacitate me. I slashed again and heard a scream of pain from one of the felons as he went down. With him out of action, I assumed a guard position and invited the other to try his luck again. He did not wish to do so. Hurling a string of unpleasant epithets in my direction, he ran away. At home a few minutes later, one of the maids cleaned and bound my arm before I went in to see Papa. He noticed the dressing, and the blood on my clothes immediately.

"What happened, Thomas?"

I explained about the attempted robbery. Papa pursed his lips in disgust, muttering something unpleasant about the criminal element of the city and the dangers decent folk had to face. His concern for my welfare showed as he pointed to my arm and asked, "Are you hurt bad, Thomas?"

"No, Papa. The cut is superficial. It is a flesh wound, nothing more. Elsie has cleaned and dressed it for me."

"Well, then, that's good news." He indicated the drinks cabinet, "Pour yourself a measure. I think you need it – and pour me one at the same time, if you will."

I handed him a snifter and took a seat opposite his beside the coal fire. He put his head on one side, looked at me with his quizzical parent's expression and asked, "Well, Thomas?"

I told him of my discussion with Captain Hudson and that I had accepted a position as an able seaman on his forthcoming Arctic voyage. Papa, of course – as predicted, did not take the news too well. He had so hoped to see me placed with the reputable East India Company.

"What do you know of this Captain Hudson?" he asked me. "Do you understand he is considered by many to be a traitor? He worked for the Dutch as an explorer for many years. He might be a scoundrel."

"Yes, Papa, I know he worked for the Dutch, but only for one year, I believe. Sir Dudley explained it all to me. But recently Captain Hudson has had an audience with the king, and he has taken a commission from Sir Thomas Smythe, Sir Dudley Digges and Sir John Wolstenholme. If they believe in his honesty; his capability, he must be respectable. And, let's not forget, Papa, you are always happy to trade with those same Dutch merchants, are you not?"

"Hmm." Papa scowled at the intrusion of my unexpected rudeness. "Trading with them is not the same as working for them," he muttered. Then, "I suppose Digges and the others know what they are doing. Where did you say this Captain Hudson is going?"

I leaned forward, my excitement taking over. "We are going north, Papa. North and west to find a navigable passage through the Arctic ice to Cathay. If we can prove this route exists across the top of the New World, Papa, it will cut the shipping time between England and the Orient by months, maybe a year or more. Therefore, it will greatly reduce transportation costs to the merchants. Think how advantageous that would be for a business such as yours."

Father stared at the faded world map on his wall for long moments, as if seeking inspiration from it. I walked over and traced the route we hoped to take with my finger. Papa watched me without comment. He nodded to himself a few times; then shook his head, as if ridding himself of a flying pest. As I sat down again, he scratched at his grey, pointed beard and said, "Frobisher couldn't find that damned sea route. Neither could George Weymouth. The brilliant John Davis failed too. They all tried hard and they were all fine seamen with strong ships under them. What makes you think this Captain Hudson will be successful?"

I knew I had him hooked on the idea by then. When Papa started asking me questions, he was giving me his cautious approval for my immediate future. I explained why I thought Frobisher had failed.

"Frobisher missed his opportunity each time he went to the Arctic. He ventured into that long bay that he believed to be a straight. But it is not a straight. It is a dead-end. I'm sure of it. The real straight is a few leagues to the south. Weymouth got it right, I believe. He fought through the Furious Overfall and managed to work his ship about one hundred leagues to the west, against a strong current and drifting ice, before conditions forced him to turn back."

Papa smiled as he listened to my youthful arrogance. Having dispensed with Frobisher and Weymouth, I then told him what I knew of Captain Hudson's three earlier expeditions.

"Captain Hudson worked for the Muscovy Company on two of his expeditions, and for the Dutch on a third." I raised my hand to stall my father's anticipated interjection. "I know that latter sounds treasonous to many, as you have suggested, but he was pardoned by King James and has received approval for this new venture."

"Hmph. What did Hudson do for the Muscovy people, and for the Dutch, to make him so interesting?"

I leaned forward again, my enthusiasm obvious; my wound forgotten. "Under contract to the Muscovy Company, he discovered new whaling grounds near the North Pole. He sailed a ship, named *Hopewell*, further east across the north shore of Russia in the Arctic than any man before him. Captain Hudson only turned back when ice made onward travel impossible. It was a magnificent achievement of seamanship and navigation."

"Yes, yes. I understand that, but if he didn't get across the top of the world to Cathay, what was the economic value of the voyage, if anything?"

"It is true, he did not discover any new lands, but he was able to improve the accuracy of navigation charts for that part of the world, and he reported on the abundance of walrus herds in the Arctic. The oil from their blubber and the ivory from their tusks, both have high economic value."

"And for the Dutch? What did he achieve for them to account for his treasonous voyage?"

"Captain Hudson went back to the Arctic again in 1609, this time for the Dutch, on a second attempt to breach the north east passage. Again he was stalled by ice, however, instead of returning to Amsterdam, as he should have done, he took his ship, *Halve Moen*, across the Atlantic to the New World. There he explored the coast as far south as the Virginia Colony before turning north again. He discovered a great river flowing out of the interior and he traded with the savages far up stream. That voyage was a success, to an extent, although not in the way his Dutch masters had expected."

"I seem to recall Captain Hudson found himself in trouble with both the Dutch and with his Majesty after that voyage. What makes you think he can succeed next time?"

"I believe Captain Hudson will succeed, Papa, because he is tenacious. He truly believes in the value of his expeditions and always does everything in his power to win through."

Papa held up his empty brandy glass, his eyes on mine. "I think we can have one more before we retire for the night," he said.

I took the hint and poured two more drinks. We sat there on either side of the fire in silence for a while. I swirled the brandy in my glass, wondering what he was thinking. At last he spoke, his voice low and, unusual for him, it trembled.

"We'll miss you, of course, your mother and I, not to mention the other children. How long do you expect to be gone?"

"Possibly a year, maybe two. It depends on how long it takes us to find the passage and navigate through the ice.

That will be the most difficult part of the voyage. So far the ice has thwarted all previous attempts to find the passage."

"One year. Two years. That's a long time to be away, Thomas. A very long time. When you come home you will be different, I'm sure of that. Will you then try to settle down and be my business partner?"

"Yes, sir. That is my intention, but who knows what the future will bring?"

With that less than satisfactory answer from me we embarked on another long discussion about our future business relationship. We talked for a long time, each determined to have his say. Each determined to gain the upper hand. The fire died and the room cooled. The level in the brandy decanter went down and still we talked. The rest of the house was quiet. Even the servants had gone to bed – although the butler would probably remain awake and alert until we retired. In the end, much later, we called a truce. My father accepted that his eldest son would sail to the Arctic with Captain Hudson and live his dream – through good times and bad. The future would have to look after itself. For my part, my already considerable respect for my father grew beyond all measure that evening. When we bade each other goodnight, we were still father and son; we were still close friends.

Mama invited me to join her for a glass of wine and conversation the following afternoon. We sat in the drawing room talking about the life I had lived so far; her aspirations for my future and her wishes to see me settle down once my Arctic adventures were behind me.

"Take this with you, Thomas, and write in it every day for me." She handed me a thick leather-bound book of blank pages. I thanked her with a kiss on the cheek. I knew there had to be more on her mind and waited for the real reason for our *tête à tête.* It wasn't long in coming. Reminding me that I would be 21 the next year, she then brought up the subject of marriage and mentioned, quite in passing she insisted, the names of three suitable young women of marriageable age from good families. She even hinted that I might consider becoming betrothed to one of them before leaving for the Arctic. I knew all three ladies, having met them socially on a few occasions; I liked them all. Mama's first choice – she made no secret of the fact – was a tall, slim beauty with red hair and blue eyes named Miss Jane Montrose. The very same beauty who had allowed me to kiss her at the New Year's Eve ball a few weeks earlier. Mama had of course noticed my interest in her namesake, either that evening or possibly at church a few times. Plus, no doubt, Emily had had her say on the subject. Now, Mama was using her maternal wiles to match me with Jane or, if that failed, with one of the others. I declined as politely as possible, pointing out that such a course of action would hardly be fair to any young lady.

"I like Miss Montrose very much, Mama. Very much indeed. Even so, I cannot consider a betrothal at this time. There is so much I want to do. I have even discussed my exploration plans with Miss Montrose. Once I have made my mark as an explorer, Mama, we can talk about this again."

Mama accepted my logic with reluctance. She had something more to discuss. "Emily tells me you have a tattoo, Thomas. May I see it?"

"That little witch! No, Mama, I would prefer you didn't. It is in a rather embarrassing place."

That was not true but the only way I could think of to avoid the disclosure of my raven.

"Embarrassing for whom?" she asked with a broad smile. "I am your mother. You forget that there is no part of you that I have not seen."

I could feel the blood rushing to my face. "I would prefer to keep the tattoo hidden, if you don't mind, Mama."

She accepted that and returned to the subject of marriage as I was about to leave her. "Come home soon, Thomas," she said. "These lovely young ladies will not wait for ever. I can assure you of that. And, you know that Jane Montrose would be a splendid match for you. She comes from an excellent family. She is intelligent; well educated. She is sophisticated. She has a considerable dowry and..."

"And she's beautiful," I completed the catalogue with a wry smile.

At the end of March, only two weeks before I was due to sail with Captain Hudson on *Discovery,* I stood on the Gravesend waterfront with my father and many other citizens and waved my hat in the air as the mighty *Trades Increase* sailed by. She was a grand sight escorted by a new pinnace, the whimsically named *Peppercorne*, which would keep station with her all the way around the southern cape of Africa to the markets of Arabia and then on to the Spice Islands of Asia. Did I feel a trace of envy for the men on the elegant merchant ship passing by? Yes, I did to an extent, but that was mollified by the excitement of knowing that soon, I too would be outward bound for the, to me, equally exotic lands of the Arctic and, if all went well, eventually to those same Spice Islands.

There were many among my acquaintances who wondered how I could give up my comfortable life and again go to sea as a common sailor.

"If you must go off to sea, why don't you have your father buy you a commission in His Majesty's navy?" asked some.

The answer was simple. I wanted to become an explorer. I wanted to sail with Captain Henry Hudson. I wanted to learn from an expert. In all of those short responses, I was naïve. I really had no idea what I was letting myself in for. Ahead of me, my future was waiting to create havoc with my life. Captain Henry Hudson would prove to have an Achilles heel that would echo through my world and far beyond. That unhappy disclosure was still many months away. For the moment, I was excited that Captain Hudson had accepted me as a member of his crew.

A few nights before my departure I called on Jane Montrose. We sat close together, as close as convention allowed, in her mother's drawing room, with only a maid in discreet attendance as a chaperone in a corner of the room. I found it difficult to keep the excitement out of my voice as I explained that my orders had come through.

"I am to join Captain Hudson on board *Discovery* in two days," I told her. "We depart soon after for the Arctic. I expect to be gone for at least a year, maybe longer."

Jane reached out and touched my hand. "And what then, Thomas?" she asked. "What will you do when you return to Gravesend? Will you join your father in his business?"

"My father believes this expedition will change me. In what way, or to what extent, he couldn't say. I imagine I will be different when I return, too; certainly a little older. Beyond that, who knows? Whatever happens. I shall still be me."

"Yes, Thomas. You will still be you, I hope," Jane replied.

When I stood to leave, Jane addressed her maid, "Stay there, Sally. I shall see Mr. Woodhouse to the door."

I wrapped my cloak around me, took my hat in one hand and looked at Jane. She smiled, understanding that I was at a loss, not knowing what to do next. She looked behind her. None of the servants were in sight. Opening her arms, she pulled me to her and kissed me full on the lips. We held each other tight for a second or two and then pulled apart.

"May I call on you when I return, Jane?" I asked.

"Are you asking me to wait for you, Thomas?" she stood back, waiting for my answer.

"No, Jane. I have no right to do that. I have no idea what is in store for me during the next year or two."

Jane nodded, a hint of tears glistening in her eyes. "That is true, Thomas. You have no right to ask me to wait. If, indeed, I decide to wait for your return, that will be my decision and mine alone."

There were no more words to say. I felt we had an unspoken agreement, but neither of us was prepared to give it voice. "I will send you a message by the fastest ship when we reach Cathay," I said, doing my best to sound positive.

"Yes, Thomas. If you reach Cathay, do write and tell me about your journey." Jane held my hand for a moment more and then added, "May God keep you safe and bring you home in good health." She didn't add, "...To me." No, she didn't add those two words, but I heard them anyway.

My last day in Gravesend, before I travelled to London to take my place on board *Discovery,* was a busy one and, in many ways, a sad one. I took lunch with friends in the *Eagle and Child* to fortify myself for the evening, which I had no doubt would be difficult.

That night Cook prepared a dinner fit for King James himself, highlighted by two roasted pheasants stuffed with bacon and chestnuts that had been sautéed in port wine. The six of us: Mama and Papa, Emily, James, Mary and myself, talked as if the evening had no special significance for any of us, although much of the gaiety seemed forced.

Soon after dinner came the difficult part. I had to make my farewells to my family and to the servants, all of whom lined up to say a few words before we all retired for the night. There would be no time in the morning for I had to be away long before dawn to catch the early Long Ferry to Greenwich. Emily and Mary, both of whom had promised to behave like proper ladies, clung to me in tears and kissed me. Emily whispered in my ear, "Sorry about the tattoo, Thomas."

James stood to one side, shy, not wanting to appear less of a man by any undue show of affection. "Goodbye, old chap," he said, his young voice gruff with emotion, sounding just like Papa. He shook my hand and turned away so I would not see the pain on his face.

Mama held me close as mothers must do and said softly, "Promise me you'll come home, my darling. Promise me."

I promised, the arrogance of my youth convinced that I would come home a hero of the Arctic. Mama had a few more quiet words for me about Jane Montrose before she said goodbye with a smile on her face and her eyes moist.

"I am so proud of you, my son," she said for all to hear.

Our butler, Jackson, who had been with my parents since before I was born, said goodbye to me, a choke in his normally strong voice and with tears in his eyes. "You look after yourself, young master Thomas," he paused and then added, "and you come home safe."

I surprised him by shaking his hand, something I had never done before. "Thank you, Jackson. I'll be home next year some time with many tales to tell."

Papa watched from the door to his study, his face expressionless. I knew it was a mask he used to show indifference when his feelings were quite the opposite.

"Have a snifter with me, Thomas," he said. "Just one before you go."

The rest of the family and all the servants went to their respective beds. I followed Papa into his study. He closed the door behind us, poured two healthy Cognacs and cleared his throat as he handed me one.

"Your mother meant what she said, Thomas. She is proud of you, son. We are all damned proud of you. Wherever this voyage takes you, whatever you do, remember you are a Woodhouse and a gentleman. Remember to say your prayers each night, and may God look after you every day until you enter this house again."

He downed his drink, hugged me briefly, kissed me on the cheek and blurted out, "Goodnight, my Thomas," as he hurried from his study. Looking back, I think he might have had some kind of premonition of disaster, hence his emotional departure.

I sat there alone for the best part of an hour, sipping my Cognac, thinking of the long voyage ahead. Wondering what the future held for me. I was excited and apprehensive at the same time. It never occurred to me that I would never again set foot in the house that had been my home for all of my twenty years.

Book Two
An Arctic Expedition

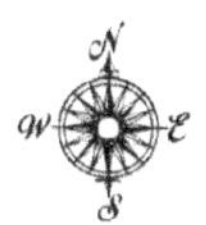

CHAPTER 7

ST. KATHERINE'S POOL, LONDON, APRIL 17, 1610

"All hands on deck," the captain's strong voice rang out from the poopdeck.

We assembled at the mainmast: some excited about the coming voyage, others more blasé. Excited or not, all eyes were on Captain Hudson.

"Men," he called, "today we embark on a voyage of exploration. It will be long. It will be dangerous. The work will be arduous and often unpleasant. I expect you to attend to your assigned duties with proper diligence. I expect you to prove that you are the equal, if not the better, of any English seamen. We will all work when we have to, for as many hours each day as we must. We will all rest when we can. Completing the voyage safely is the most important consideration. Do all of that and I will ask no more of you. Take a good look around you at your homeland as we sail down the Thames because you'll not see England again for a year or more. When we succeed, and I do intend to succeed, I promise you it will be rewarding for all hands. I assure you all, it is my intention that we will come home to this port safely and in triumph."

The captain's confidence made me feel very special at that moment. He stopped talking; looked at us over his Bible, his eyes flicking from one man to the next until he had noted us all.

"Caps off," a voice as yet unknown called. Each man removed whatever head covering he had and held it in both hands in front of him. The captain nodded his approval, glanced down at his Bible and began to read. I immediately recognized the text as part of Psalm 107. As Captain Hudson read the words, I recited them under my breath from memory.

They that go down to the sea in ships, that do business in great waters;
These see the wonders of the Lord, and his wonders in the deep.
For he commandeth, and raiseth the stormy wind, which lifteth up the waves thereof.
They mount up to the heaven, they go down again to the depths: their soul is melted because of trouble.
They reel to and fro, and stagger like a drunken man, and are at their wit's end.
Then they cry unto the Lord in their trouble, and he bringeth them out of their distresses.
He maketh the storm a calm, so that the waves thereof are still.
Then they are glad because they be quiet; so he bringeth them unto their desired haven.

Captain Hudson closed his Bible and looked at us, his crew. When he spoke again his voice was strong. "I promise you, with God's help, we will reach our desired haven and we shall return safely once again to this city." He nodded once or twice as if satisfied with what he saw, and then finished with a gentle, "Amen." Every man of the twenty-two of us assembled on *Discovery*'s decks echoed that final sentiment. The prayer for our future over, the ship returned to normal routine. The orders began in loud, authoritative voices.

"All hands, prepare for sea. Let go fore. Let go aft. Bring her round, Mr. Colebourne, if you please."

On *Discovery* all members of the crew manned their stations, on deck and aloft, as the ship responded to the breeze, slowly gaining way under a small foresail. I took my place in the rigging and waved to the few watchers on shore. I was one week past my 20th birthday and off on a magnificent adventure. I was so very excited. Guided by the quartermaster at the whipstaff, *Discovery* eased her sixty-five feet of hull out of St. Katherine's Pool and into the river. A trio of gentlemen, all of whom had visited with Captain Hudson that morning in his cabin on board *Discovery*, stood on the wharf watching our departure. They each raised their hat in salute as we made our turn.

"God speed, Captain Hudson," one called.

I knew that the youngest of the men was our own Prince Henry, son of King James. Another was one of the expedition's financial backers, and my patron, Sir Dudley Digges. The third, so someone said, was the captain's friend, a man named Richard Hakluyt, the eminent historian, clergyman and gentleman of letters that John Hudson had told me about when we first met.

The Thames was full, with the tide just starting to ebb. A light breeze blew from the west. The skies were overcast and sombre. Captain Hudson called for the main courses to be set. The mate – Mr. William Colebourne – relayed the order and we climbed out onto the yards to work for the first time this voyage. As the sails filled with wind, *Discovery* dipped her bowsprit in farewell to the City of London. Our great expedition, to find a sea route through the Arctic to the riches of far Cathay, had begun.

We didn't go far. We had no sooner lost sight of St. Katherine's when the westerly wind failed. As we drifted downstream with the current, a mid-April fog billowed in from the North Sea, clouding everything in its clammy embrace.

"All Hands. Prepare to come about. Let go the anchor." There was nothing else for it. We had to furl our sails and stop where we were. We could not risk navigating the many bends in the busy river while running blind.

"Where are we?" asked a voice from the foredeck, muted by the fog.

"Dunno. Can't see. Somewhere off Blackwall, I should think," came the answer.

"Should be able to see the masts from all them ships bein' built, if we are, I reckon," a voice called.

"I'll take a look from the masthead," I offered and scrambled up the ratlines to the topmast. From there, my head above the fog, I could see a forest of masts and spars close by to mark the shipyards.

"Yes. We are abeam of Blackwall," I said when I returned to the deck. "I can see the topmasts of a dozen or more ships. This fog is only about thirty feet thick but it is getting worse, I think."

Only a league or so from our starting point and the Arctic expedition had stalled, waiting for the thick fog to disperse. We waited at anchor for the best part of five days. The fog remained, wrapped around us like a damp, grey blanket. Five valuable days lost from the all too short Arctic navigation season. Being at anchor did not mean we could be lazy. Mr. Colebourne kept us all busy for those long hours behind London's spring veil. There were last minute stores for ship's maintenance to be packed away. We had to stow the final delivery of food provisions wherever there was space. Able seamen checked and re-checked the rigging, and secured the spare sails where we could reach them at any time. When all other work was exhausted, we scrubbed the decks. I sent a message ashore for delivery to my family and another to Jane Montrose, telling them of the delay. The captain sent some notes of his own ashore also.

Although many in the crew looked upon me as no more than a boy, Captain Hudson knew I had already spent over one year at Oxford University reading mathematics, and that I was a sailor. My fellow crew members soon learned that my able seaman rating had been earned the hard way. The Arctic voyage in *Discovery* was not my first time at sea. Because of my passion, and thanks to my father, the few months I had spent on *Ravenswing* sailing to Antwerp and to Portugal had turned me into a competent sailor. That experience would now stand me in good stead.

In my possession, stowed away in my sea chest, I had the two valuable papers on navigation and the Arctic map given to me by Professor Henry Briggs. Now, as an able seaman on Captain Hudson's ship, I hoped to improve my navigational skills. I could study the movements of the sun, moon and stars, and learn how to use them as guides on sea and on land. I had learned much about the exotic voyages of Drake, Frobisher and Hawkins, in addition to John Davis – the Arctic master. I was confident of my future. And, I tell you, without wishing to appear boastful,

I hoped someday to emulate – perhaps even eclipse – their voyages of exploration. How naïve I was at that age.

Discovery was ideal for our expedition. She was a bluff-browed, three-masted barque displacing some 50 tons, stoutly built of English oak over elm ribs. She carried a full complement of six sails and replacements for each, plus spare canvas to fashion more if needed. We had loaded a shallop in pieces below decks. The carpenter would assemble that ready for use when we reached Arctic waters. We also carried a smaller boat on the main deck, used for rowing crew ashore, among other duties. *Discovery*, so aptly named, had proved her reliability on an earlier expedition to the Arctic under the command of Sir George Weymouth. A tough ship, she had recently been refitted for our voyage. She carried a complement of 23 men on this expedition, including the captain.

When the fog at last dispersed, we slipped downstream on the outgoing tide. Passing Gravesend, my hometown, on April 22, I could see the redoubtable blockhouses on each side of the river and thought of the boom lying dormant on the riverbed, almost exactly under our keel. I watched the town drift past from up on the mast for as long as I could, wondering when I should see my home again. I fancied that I could see my father and mother on the shore with my brother and sisters. I wondered if the lovely Jane Montrose was there as well to wave a handkerchief in my honour. Little did I know then that most of them I would never see again in this life, and for two – it would be more than half a lifetime before we again came face to face.

As we flowed with the current north round the great bend east of Gravesend, we picked up some extra wind. The river changed to the east again, spreading out and pushing the land away on both sides as it made its way to the North

Sea. Instead of sailing east and north, the captain kept us close to the south shore as we crossed the mouth of the River Medway and approached the Isle of Sheppey. I was too excited at being under way to wonder why. Abreast of Sheerness, Captain Hudson ordered us to come about, furl the sails and stand to anchor. That did get my attention. What now? I asked myself. The weather was good. The wind was fair. Why were we stopping again so early in the voyage? I had been high in the rigging, up at the royal yard when we passed Gravesend and was still working there when we dropped anchor. I could see no reason for our sudden stop.

Captain Hudson hailed a pink tacking up stream and ordered Mr. Colebourne to board her and return to London with a letter for his sponsors. Although the mate was very much distressed at being sent away from *Discovery*, the captain would accept no argument. Knowing better than to voice our opinions, or to ask questions, we worried at the meaning behind this unusual action so soon in the voyage. Soon after, a small boat put out from Sheerness and pulled alongside. We took on two more men: visitors, we thought. One of the visitors was extremely well dressed, though we never learned his name. Perhaps he was one of the expedition's many financial sponsors. He was not on board long enough for us to find out. The other seemed vaguely familiar to me.

With Colebourne gone, the captain promoted Mr. Robert Juet to mate. The oldest man on board and said to be almost as experienced as Henry Hudson, Juet was on his third Arctic voyage with the captain. Rumour had it that he was a hard man with a mercurial temper, and quick to use his fists. Others who had sailed with both the captain and Juet before said the two men did not like each other. If so, it was not a good mix for a long voyage, I thought, but it had nothing to do with me. John Hudson admitted he was not happy about Juet being on board again. I decided Mr. Juet would be one to watch and to avoid, if at all possible.

Getting out of the Thames estuary and making way for the north meant sailing across a blustery wind out of the north-east for many hours. The captain set a course a little south of east until we reached the open sea. Out of sight of land, with plenty of sea room, *Discovery* came round onto a course to take her to the north and west. The wind changed direction with us, veering round the compass to blow from the south-south-west; a fair wind at last for *Discovery*.

The elder of the two visitors on board spent most of his brief time on the ship at the captain's side. He left *Discovery* when we called at Harwich in the mouth of the River Stour on April 28. We never learned his purpose. The other, not so much a visitor it proved, was named Henry Greene. He was a friend of the captain's and was said to come from a good Kentish family. Rumour had it that for some weeks he had been living at the captain's house in London. It occurred to me that he was the young man waiting by the stairs the day I had my interview with the captain. Greene sailed with us for the Arctic when we left Harwich on the first day of May, though he was on board without benefit of pay, we soon learned.

Greene was a cocky, arrogant young man; well-dressed and quite handsome in a sullen sort of way. I didn't like him at all. He was shy of real work, so not much use above decks, or below. He played the violin tolerably well, but he was openly against religion and sneered at those of us who prayed. He was a clever card player, though not, I suspect, an honest one. A couple of weeks into the voyage we learned he was a strong pugilist when he picked a fight with a deckhand and quickly defeated him. That skill, however, he used mostly to bully the weaker men and the less accomplished in the crew. He made one attempt to push me around. It was his last. I clenched my fists, adopted a pugilistic stance and acquitted myself at least as well as he did in the next few minutes. Henry Greene never bothered me again.

John Hudson, the captain's son, was only 17 but he was already one of the most experienced sailors on *Discovery*. This voyage was to be his fourth Arctic voyage with his father since he first went to sea at the age of 14. We had met in London some weeks before and now, working together day after day, we soon became friends. Nicholas Simms, the cabin boy, was a couple of years younger than John. He was on his first voyage and almost as excited as I was. Then there was Abacuck Prickett. He was a strange man of about the captain's age: strange, though kind in an offhand sort of way. He had large, staring blue eyes and a prominent chin. His most memorable feature was his nose. I had never seen one so big or so veined in red and blue. It dominated his face. Rumour on board said he was in the employ of Sir Dudley Digges, one of the expedition's three main sponsors. He was not a sailor; that was soon obvious to all of us. Prickett was a scribe – placed on board *Discovery* to observe and to report on the expedition directly to Sir Dudley when we should return to England. I heard from the cook that Prickett was an un-frocked priest, but no one else ever spoke of it.

Philip Staffe was the ship's carpenter. He had sailed with Captain Hudson to the Arctic on an earlier voyage. Staffe was a strong, thoughtful man who avoided arguments whenever possible. He impressed me as a man with principles. Two seamen, Arnold Ludlowe and Michael Perse, had also sailed with the captain before – and with Juet. They cautioned me to steer clear of the new mate if at all possible, but would say no more. How many more warnings would I receive about Juet? I wondered.

The rest of us were newcomers to the captain. Edward Wilson was the ship's doctor though only a year or two older than I. Francis Clements was bo'sun. He was older than my father and had been at sea most of his life. This would be his first Arctic voyage. John King was an excellent quartermaster, but often bad-tempered. Bennet Matthews was the cook and a kindly man. His culinary ability was limited but he did keep us well fed until the provisions started to run out. Michael Butt, Adrian Moore, Syracke Fanning, Andrew Motter, William Wilson and John Thomas were ordinary seamen. John Williams was an ordinary seaman too – he was also the gunner. Sylvanus Bond was the cooper. Part of his job was to maintain the barrels of fresh water, beer and food on board, also to make new barrels if and when necessary. Robert Bylot was an able seaman like me though with a few years' experience. Captain Hudson promoted him to second mate when he made Juet up to first mate after the departure of Mr. Colebourne.

We lived in close quarters, though each with an assigned berth. I slept just outside the cook's area in a narrow bunk – sometimes in a hammock slung from deck beams. John Hudson, Syracke Fanning and the surgeon were in the same confined space. The other crewmen slept tucked into corners wherever there was enough room, either in a hammock or in a bunk. Only the captain and the first mate had their own cabins and the second of those was no larger than a small cupboard.

Our voyage up the North Sea was helped by a brisk southerly wind. On May 2nd we passed the great chalk cliffs of Flamborough Head in Yorkshire. Three days later we rounded the north end of the Orkney Islands and set course for the west. I asked Philip Staffe why we had not taken the shorter route between the Scottish mainland and the south side of the Orkneys. The gap between the two land formations had been easy to see in the clear weather. Staffe's answer was more than I expected.

"That's the Pentland Firth. That narrow strait can be dangerous," he said. "Wicked currents fight the tides in there. It's a graveyard for ships."

As the Orkney Islands slid away astern, I heard the captain comment to Mr. Juet that, according to his observations, the north coast of Scotland – and the Orkney Islands, were not as far north as had been believed until then. That was interesting news to me as a fledgling navigator. I made a note of the fact in my journal and vowed to ask the captain for the details when Mr. Juet was elsewhere.

So far all was well on board. The crew worked their allotted tasks with a will, often singing popular shanties. Most I have now forgotten, but I do remember a couple of lines from one of my favourites:

Hale and ho rum below
Stir well the good ship and let the winds blow

For the most part, we were happy and enjoying life at sea. Captain Hudson seemed happy too. He smiled most of the time when he stood on the poopdeck, staring to the north and west. He was a fine man and, as far as I could see, he had the respect of all the crew. One afternoon when I was off watch, somewhere between Orkney and the Faroe

Islands, Captain Hudson stopped me on deck for a conversation.

"You are an educated young man, Woodhouse. What do you know of the explorations of the Frenchman, Jacques Cartier?"

"Well, sir. I know Cartier made a series of voyages to the New World in the last century – about thirty-five years before Frobisher. He was looking for a sea route to Cathay, just as we are. And I know he discovered a wide river heading far inland, a long way north of the river you discovered last year."

"Indeed, Woodhouse. Indeed. Do you understand where that wide river lies in respect to our planned voyage?"

"Yes, sir. I think so. Cartier's river, he called it the Rivière du Canada, is far to the south of the Arctic. I have seen it on a map. It appears to flow into the ocean from the west-south-west. Cartier sailed up it between 50° of latitude and 45°. The route you have planned for us through the Arctic will be north of 63°. That's a mean difference of at least 300 leagues."

"Well done, Woodhouse. Well done." So saying, the captain walked away leaving me to wonder at the reason behind his questions. Perhaps, I thought, Captain Hudson believed that the Rivière du Canada eventually curves to the north-west. Perhaps we would meet that river in the Arctic. Perhaps it might prove to be part of the passage we sought.

My knowledge of Jacques Cartier's three voyages was limited, but I did know that he had sailed far up the Rivière du Canada on his last expedition. He was only stopped by dangerous rapids spanning the width of the river, up stream from a place he called Hochelaga. I couldn't help but wonder whether the route we sought was actually Cartier's river, or whether we would find it far to the north, in the Arctic – where we were bound.

We passed to the south of the Faroe Islands on the 8th of May. When I was sure Mr. Juet was below, I borrowed the captain's backstaff and took a sight, calculating we were at 62° 20'. Captain Hudson later corrected my work to 62° 24'. He had no reason for a visit to the Faroes, so we continued on course for Iceland. This was to be our first stop since leaving England. I wondered what we should find there. The name suggested a cold and barren land. It suggested an Arctic environment. I was excited at the prospect of setting foot on that exotic alien island.

CHAPTER 8

By the time we reached the Atlantic Ocean we had all adjusted to shipboard routine. The wind filled our sails; the ship moved forward. The waves lifted us, rolled under us, broke over us and rippled alongside. Movement was the constant we could all count on. Wherever we were on *Discovery*, at any time of day or night, we clung to the old maxim of the sea – one hand for yourself and one for the ship. Some days it rained. Some days the sun shone through to warm our tired bodies. We stood our watches, by day and by night, in fair weather and in storms. Although we sailed mostly west, each day, we knew, took us a little closer to the time when we would make a course change in a northerly direction to find the Arctic. Nick Simms, the youngest on board and a first-time sailor, suffered much for the first week or two from sea sickness. Of course, he received little or no sympathy from the seasoned sailors. They had seen it all before.

After three weeks on board, we hove-to in a thick fog off the south east coast of Iceland on May 11th. We couldn't see the land but could hear the surf pounding the shoreline. There was some ice drifting in the area and we assumed there would be more to the west. *Discovery* went to anchor until the fog cleared.

I had had little opportunity of trying my navigation skills thus far, apart from taking the brief sight off the Faroes. Captain Hudson and Mr. Juet looked after those tasks and the latter would accept no interference or help from me. Once, somewhere between Orkney and the Faroes, when I asked the mate if I could assist in determining our position, he pushed me away with rough hands.

"Get back to work, you lazy bastard," he yelled. Juet would have punched me in the face if I hadn't ducked under his fist and scampered back to the main deck. Had we been on land, and armed with swords, I would have challenged him. At sea, and his subordinate, I had to take his insults as well as I could. After that unfortunate confrontation, I made my own backstaff, with the help of the carpenter, and did my own calculations when the weather and my duties allowed.

Being at anchor and having to maintain a watch on the ship at all hours, we whiled away the time fishing for cod, ling and halibut until the fog lifted the following day. Sailing west as the ice retreated before us, with the coast visible to starboard, we passed a land where angry mountains spewed liquid fire and hot ash into the sky. Prickett told me he had heard about these volcanoes. Pointing to one of the highest and most active, he said, "That must be Mount Hecla. When that blows hot, bad weather will follow. You mark my words, young 'un."

The weather closed in again as we followed the coastline. Fields of drift ice surrounded the ship, carrying us beyond the land to the west and then north. Off Westmonie, the north-west coast of Iceland, an icy gale blew in and carried us north. I wondered if this was the storm Prickett had foretold by seeing Hecla exploding. We sailed well beyond the land, until we were stopped by thick ice stretching as far as the eye could see from west to east. Arnold Ludlowe looked at the wall of white and shivered.

"That be the polar ice cap," he said. "The edge of the North Pole."

There was no alternative but to retreat to open water and return to Iceland. Following the indented coastline south a few leagues, we stopped in a small bay on the west coast. The captain said he thought it was Dyre Fjord and allowed us to go ashore. Some, myself included, took muskets with us. Although not one of us could claim to be an expert shot, between us we brought down over one hundred ducks, geese and other large birds. Many more escaped our attentions. Once plucked, gutted and salted, they would become tasty additions to our provisions. I first tasted fresh water from a stream on Iceland and found it clear, cold and refreshing. Iceland's pristine inland waters were a far cry from the stinking pollution of the Thames and other rivers of my homeland.

When the weather relented we stood out to sea again, reaching for the north. The wind refused to play its part, holding us back while a cold rain squall washed our decks. The head wind continued, visibility worsened. At last the captain turned south again, looking for the fjord we had recently enjoyed. The inclement weather obscured the entrance so we missed it and took shelter in another small gulf a few leagues further south. There, again, the captain allowed us time ashore to hunt for more geese and ducks. It was there on that lovely green and white island that Henry Greene showed the truly unpleasant side of his dark character.

Greene and the doctor, Edward Wilson, got into a pointless fist fight over ownership of a goose one of them had shot. It didn't matter who shot it – the goose was headed for the ship's galley anyway for all to share. Greene, using his pugilistic skills, beat the doctor viciously. He would have kicked him in the face but two of the men held him off. Wilson was by then bloodied about the head and lying on the ground in agony.

After the fight, seeing steam rising from a small pond, we stripped off our garments and washed ourselves, and our clothes, in the heated pool. We needed the cleansing. By this time we were all suffering from lice, about our bodies and in our clothes. The heat, we hoped, would rid us of the pests. I had always hated being dirty. On *Discovery* I was getting used to the lack of hygiene but never accepted it.

"This water is so hot it would scald a fowl," said Abacuck Prickett, wincing as he stepped naked into the steaming pond.

We enjoyed our brief stay and we enjoyed the cleansing opportunity. One sailor, with an acute sense of humour, labelled the inlet Lousie Bay. As the first tendrils of fog began to waft over the sea and creep across the land, the gunner fired a cannon shot to recall us to *Discovery.*

Back on board, Robert Bylot attended to the doctor's injuries. He had contusions on his face and bruised ribs. We heard Prickett report the beating to Captain Hudson. He was right to do so. Mr. Wilson, as our doctor, was an officer and Greene no more than an ordinary seaman. The captain should have severely punished Greene, if not put him ashore. Instead, the captain would have none of it. He commented, "Leave it be, Prickett. The doctor has a tongue on him that would harm any man."

Wilson was incensed at the captain's attitude. "I demand to be put ashore. I'll not sail with that wicked monster," he said, pointing at Greene. The men, myself included, argued with him, finally persuading him that we needed him on board with us. We also reminded him that he had a duty to look after our physical welfare. Upon that, he agreed to stay but insisted, "Keep that man away from me or I'll see him in hell." He pointed again at Greene, who glared back at him and mouthed an obscenity.

Mr. Juet, who had obviously been into the rum cask, then chose to stir the embers into flame. His thoughts should have been kept to himself, instead he expressed them loud enough for those of us close by to hear. "I swear there'll be blood shed aboard this ship before the voyage is over."

In a louder voice, he cautioned the crew to keep swords and muskets close to hand. Turning towards Captain Hudson, he threatened to turn the ship and take all aboard home to England. This was mutinous talk; the captain should have stopped it immediately. Instead, showing much indecision, Captain Hudson at first remonstrated with Juet.

"Enough of that talk, Mr. Juet. I have a mind to put you ashore at Lousie Bay and leave you to fend for yourself. I'll hear no more of such scurrilous words." Then, apparently thinking better of it, he said, "We'll talk more on this, Mr. Juet; you mark my words. Now, back to your duties."

Juet continued to mumble against the captain while he ordered us to prepare for departure. By this time the mood on board was tense. The fuse had been lit. Unless Captain Hudson did something to stamp it out, we knew the explosion had to follow in due course.

On June 1st we set sail, this time for the west. After a few hours the lookout shouted that land was dead ahead. As we sailed closer, taking a few hours to get there, it became obvious that the lookout had mistaken a thick fog bank for land. *Discovery* turned south-west until we sighted the towering white mountains of Greenland on June 4th. I had hoped we might have an opportunity of going ashore. It was not to be. There was too much drift ice along the shore for a boat to attempt a landing.

For the next four anxious days we dodged icebergs and large fields of ice, with Greenland off our starboard quarter. The combination of snow-covered mountains, huge bergs and rafting ice was a magnificent sight, though frightening to us in our insignificant little ship. I was near the end of my watch and using my backstaff to find our position one noon when the captain's voice interrupted me.

"What are you doing, young Woodhouse?" he asked.

I stammered a bit but managed to answer that I was practicing my navigation. The captain nodded and tugged at his beard. I noticed for the first time that he had long, slender fingers. They reminded me somewhat of my mother's.

"So, you really do believe you are a navigator as well as a scholar, do you? What do you know of latitude?"

I swallowed hard and marshalled my thoughts. "Latitude is calculated from the Equator, and has been since before the time of Ptolemy. It cannot be measured in any other way."

"And how would you calculate the latitude on which we find ourselves this day?" asked Captain Hudson.

"I believe most experienced sailors can determine the latitude of their location by the angle of the sun, the length of the day, or, at night, by the stars, sir. I can do the same."

"Yes, Woodhouse. All that is true. Are you an experienced enough sailor, I wonder? Can you determine our latitude?"

"Yes, sir. I can. My backstaff will give me the angle of the sun and from that I can find our latitude. I have already done so, in fact, sir. We are at sixty degrees north."

"Show me your calculations."

I did as he ordered and then, to my surprise, Captain Hudson took my backstaff from me and made a sight of his own. A few minutes later he looked at me with a smile and said, "Well done, Woodhouse. Well done. That's very close. Now, you'd best get back to work before Mr. Juet loses his patience."

With that he walked away. But it was not the end of my experiments at navigation. On two later occasions he invited me to join him when he checked our positions with his backstaff and with an astrolabe. On the second of those I asked him to explain the facts of the incorrect chart positions for north Scotland and the Orkneys. He did so, even showing me the correct positions on his chart. It was then that he gave me the correct latitude of the Faroes. On one such occasion the captain discussed the problems of ascertaining a ship's actual position on a line of latitude.

"What has Ptolemy taught you about measuring distances at sea along a line of latitude from his prime meridian?" asked the captain.

"Well, nothing, sir. There is no known way to measure distance from east to west, or vice versa. Ptolemy was a skilled mathematician and astronomer, yet he could not determine a longitudinal position with any degree of accuracy. Neither can we. Can we, sir?"

"No, we cannot. The question is, why not?"

"I believe the answer has something to do with time, sir. No matter where we are, we cannot know the exact time at any hour with any precision. To measure longitude, we would need to know the exact time in more than one location at the same time. Our timepieces give us no more than a rough idea of the time and then only where we are."

Mr. Juet was not pleased about my navigation sessions with the captain and gave me extra work for, as he put it, "Thinking myself more than I was." I didn't care what Juet thought. I was happy to be using my mathematical skills and delighted that the captain had seen fit to let me work with him at last.

Passing the southern tip of Greenland, where the winds were the fiercest we had encountered to that day, we continued to change course regularly, sometimes even coming about to avoid heavy drift ice. We saw a few whales spouting in the distance, too far away to give chase – even if we had had the inclination. Then three humpback whales came close to the ship; one having the temerity to swim under our hull. They studied us as we studied them. After a few minutes watching us they sounded together and disappeared into the depths.

Fog, drift ice and icebergs accompanied us. We sailed slowly north and west into Davis Strait, leaving the icy mountains of Greenland far off to starboard and then astern. Our course was then west and half a point north. The ice scattered over the sea caused concern for all on board. Some of the bergs stood higher than our topmast head. I know that because I climbed up as high as possible and was still below the level of some ice. Close up the ice proved to contain many colours and tones, varying from pure white to shades of green bright enough to rival the finest jade. The larger bergs were in a constant state of change. As I watched from my highest viewpoint, trickles of shiny particles cascaded down their flanks creating avalanches of ice. Occasionally huge pieces would calve away with thunderous cracks, plummeting into the sea, sending spray higher than our masthead and creating chaos all around. Large floes drifted with the bergs, wallowing around the ship, each one a danger to our survival. Among the ice, wherever there was a lead, or patch of open water, we saw many triangular black fins and the spray from spouts on the back of the creatures' heads. Some came so close, I fancied I could reach out and touch them.

"They be grampuses," one of the old Arctic hands told me. "Vicious killers, they be. I've seen them gangin' up on whales ten times their size. They hang on to their mouths and drown them. Sometimes, if they see a mother and a calf, they separate them and drown the calf before tearing it apart."

Fascinating though the gruesome tale was, it was not the sort of story I wanted to hear. I vowed to be extra careful when in the rigging. A fall into that sea, with so many grampuses, could result in a death far worse than drowning.

John Hudson saw me exercising with my quarterstaff on the main deck one afternoon as we crossed Davis Strait. He watched for a while and then asked me if he could join in. I nodded my agreement, even though he had no weapon that I could see. John was resourceful, he took a pikestaff, removed the sharp metal end and placed himself in front of me.

"Step back a bit further, John, and watch what I do. Then try it yourself," I said.

We worked together for an hour or more, gradually getting to the point where we were giving and taking blows. I was vaguely away of other men watching and, as sailors will, they chose sides and were betting on the results of the contest. As the more experienced fighter, I won, though John proved to be a tough opponent. At the end of the impromptu bout we shook hands and agreed we would have a return match when time allowed. The audience drifted away, some complaining because they had forfeited part of their grog ration, others happy to be among the winners.

On June 25 the lookout at the mast head called, "Land ho!" He pointed to the west.

CHAPTER 9

"Land ho!" Normally, those words represented a welcoming call for almost any sailor after a hard voyage. Here, though, in sub-Arctic waters, it was more a shout of danger in sight. A couple of older hands who had been to Davis Strait before identified the shape as Resolution Island.

"That high land behind. That be the land Frobisher called Meta Incognita, I reckon," said one.

As we closed with Resolution Captain Hudson set a course to take us round the north end of the island. The wind gusted hard from the north-west, forcing *Discovery* to the south instead, into a strong current filled with drift ice. We were carried past the island and then hard to the west, all the while threatened by the most broken ice we had seen until that day. The land to starboard was rugged, a catastrophe of rocks and ice, with nowhere to put ashore. Out of control, *Discovery* was swept south, a fragile shell amidst a sea of white danger. All hands stood at the rails with long poles to fend off the floes as they drifted past. The work was hard but we reached open water without incident and steered westwards into the strait John Davis had named the Furious Overfall: the strait that had defeated both Sir Martin Frobisher and Sir George Weymouth.

I had read much about Frobisher, as indeed I had about all the Arctic explorers. Frobisher made three voyages to this barren region, also in search of a North-West Passage. His voyages between 1576 and 1578 were unsuccessful in that he did not find the North-West Passage, yet he added a vast amount to our knowledge of navigation in ice and of the lands through which we must pass. Frobisher penetrated the Furious Overfall only for a few leagues before being forced to turn back by ice. Sir George Weymouth had taken this very ship 100 leagues into the strait in 1602 before being forced to turn back by the lateness of the season, by ice and because of a difficult crew, many suffering from illness. For *Discovery* the Furious Overfall was nothing new. For her officers and crew, however, it was uncharted and unknown territory.

The riptide and erratic currents took us west then, with a change in the wind, to the south. Icebergs rolled over in front of us and beside us with deafening booms. The sudden large waves created by the capsizing bergs crashed into *Discovery*, adding to the confusion, rolling her from beam to beam and from stem to stern. Our three stout masts whipped back and forth, and from side to side, threatening to snap under the strain. The rigging thrummed and twanged in agony. Vast fields of floating ice and drifting, broken bergs littered the turbulent sea. The rocky shores on the north side of the strait disappeared in the spray and shore-bound fog. I had never been in such a dangerous place and wondered how *Discovery* could possibly survive such violence. The wind began to blow hard from the west. We sailed across it, south, sometimes south-east, and south-west whenever we could, dodging ice for many days as we traversed the unknown sea. In the midst of the worst ice concentration the captain had us make the ship fast to a great floe of ice until conditions became more stable. Some of the men showed signs of fear at the extreme danger all around us. That fear manifested itself in anger and in not a few tears. I reflected that, perhaps, Weymouth's crew on *Discovery* had reacted to the perils of ice in the same way. On July 5th we sighted land near 59° N and a new potential peril.

"Look there," a voice called from the foredeck. Its owner pointed to port where a mountain of ice towering over smaller bergs drifted with the current. "Look, I tell you. Look," he shouted again.

We looked towards the ice. Two large white bears stood tall on hind legs on one of the smaller bergs. They were, it was obvious, watching us. Without warning they leapt into the sea together. At first they appeared to be aiming for us. As one, we reached for pikes to repel them if they tried to get aboard. Instead, after a few minutes hard paddling in our direction, they climbed out onto a floe of ice, shook themselves and ambled away. The bears are beautiful beasts with rippling coats of yellowish-white fur, large paws, long necks and, as I found out a few years later, jaws strong enough to crush the largest bones.

The land was barren and inhospitable, with no anchorage along the rocks and ice of the foreshore. *Discovery* turned to the north and west, and back again to the south, fighting for distance against the wintry hell. The ice made terrible sounds as the wind and currents swept the floes and bergs into each other. They crashed together with booms like heavy thunder overhead. They rafted up on top of each other, scattering smaller pieces of ice far and wide. We watched in horror as one immense island of ice cracked and turned over with a mighty roar, creating huge freezing waves to wash over us. The captain did everything he could to keep the violence from overwhelming our ship. We did our part too, obeying shouted orders faster than we had ever done. None of us wanted to see *Discovery* crushed by the enormous power of that icy mayhem. The ship dodged left and right, each turn taking a long time as we heaved on the braces to swing the yards in response to the orders. I have to admit, I was scared. Very scared. So were the rest of the crew, if their faces told the truth. The captain was no exception. After the rolling sea almost swept us up onto the rocks in front of a high island while trying to navigate away from the ice, I heard Captain Hudson talking by the port rail with Abacuck Prickett. The master sounded much concerned saying, "I fear we may never get out of this ice, Prickett. I fear we shall all perish in this dreadful wilderness of white."

This lack of confidence from a captain was something I had never heard before and I doubt that any other of our crew had ever heard similar. We expected strength from our leader, not an attack of nerves. If the other men noticed the captain's fears, they kept it to themselves, as did I. Even so, I found myself watching the captain's mood swings with more curiosity each hour. Henry Hudson's next actions filled me with dread. The ice lay all around us, moving restlessly. For the moment the ship was in the lee of the land and so out of danger. Leaving Prickett, the captain went to his cabin and retrieved his navigation card. Prickett leaned against the rail, his eyes narrowed, brow creased and rubbed his beard thoughtfully.

"Mr. Juet," Captain Hudson called when he returned to the deck. "Have the men muster at the mainmast. All of them. Immediately."

"Aye, aye, sir." Turning, Juet cupped his hands to his mouth and yelled, "All hands on deck. All hands on deck. Now!"

Once we were all there, standing in small groups, most wondering what was so important, the captain held up his navigation card for all to see.

"Listen to me now, men," he said, his voice a little shaky. "I have taken this good ship many leagues further west in the Arctic than any English sea captain has ever gone before." That wasn't true but I had no intention of reminding him of Weymouth's voyage. Captain Hudson looked around at us assembled on the deck. "We have come this far in our quest," he said. "We have no idea what lies ahead but we do know of the perils behind us. I leave it to you now to decide whether you would go on or would you wear ship and go home."

Turn around and go home? I could hardly believe my ears. Was the captain really offering us a choice? Us, a crew of misfits, most of whom were illiterate? Was he really prepared to give up his dream, ignore the expedition sponsors' instructions, and return to England with nothing to show for our efforts? I had started this voyage with great admiration and respect for Captain Hudson, but this was a strange turn of events indeed and one that worried me greatly. There began much talk back and forth among the crew. Some wanted to go home, others determined to go on, all wishing to be free of the ice as soon as possible. The captain and Mr. Juet, the latter wearing his perpetual scowl, remained silent, listening to the debate swaying back and forth on deck. Henry Greene, supposedly the captain's friend, stood to one side of the crew, watching and listening.

Adrian Motter, normally a quiet man, spoke up loud and clear for all to understand. He addressed his remarks to

Captain Hudson. "If you offered me one hundred pounds, sir, I would give ninety of them to go back to England right now."

Some men smiled, nodding their heads in agreement. A few gave soft cheers. Philip Staffe, the carpenter, was of a different mind. He stepped forward and said, "If I had one hundred pounds I would not give ten upon such condition, but would think it to be as good money as ever I had." We understood that to mean he was willing to go forward.

The argument moved from one voice to another. Some outspoken enough to demand a return to England. Others, more loyal to the captain, said to go on with the expedition. The mood of some of the men was as close to mutiny that day as it could be without actually stepping over the line. I kept silent until I felt the captain's eyes on me.

"What about you, Woodhouse? You are an educated young man. Would you have me turn the ship, or would you go on to seek the North-West passage?"

"Onward, Captain. I would go onward. North and west, sir," I said in as strong a voice as I could muster, all the while pointing in the direction I felt we should be exploring.

I watched Henry Greene. He had taken no part in the discussion. He just stood there listening, watching and, I'm sure, remembering who said what. What was going through his deceitful mind? I wondered. The ice ended the unprecedented debate.

"Wind's changed, sir," Philip Staffe called. "The ice is closing in fast."

The captain, startled, looked around him. "All hands," he shouted, "back to work. Mr. Juet, get a crew to fend off that ice. You men," he pointed in my general direction, "shake out those sails; sharply now or I'll have your hides."

Along with three others I raced into the rigging to attend to the sails. For the next few hours we toiled without rest to get *Discovery* clear of the dangers. The offer to return home was forgotten, for the moment. We worked our ship north and west and when fronted by ice or cliffs, we worked her south and west. There we came in sight of a high land with sloping green pastures, but much covered in snow. It must have impressed the captain because he named it Desire Provoketh. We could hear the roar of surf on the shore and see great spouts of water where the ever restless sea crashed against the land. I must say, that piece of land did not instill any desire to attempt a landing for me. The captain watched the land for some time, his eyes roaming from the waves breaking against the rocks to the high cliffs above. He looked lonely and very much alone. Turning away from the desperate scene with a deep sigh, he ordered the quartermaster to change course for the north-west again. On the main deck we hauled the yards round to help the sails catch the wind.

The ice lay all around us, no matter which way we turned. Some huge bergs were aground. It was hard to believe, but they were, and in over one hundred fathoms of water. Early that evening, we tied up for a while for protection to an enormous field of thick ice. With *Discovery* safe for the moment, we were allowed to leave the ship for a while. Eager to stretch our legs, we ran races on the ice while the carpenter checked the ship's hull from the outside. We made slides on the ice and we played a form of cricket and other silly games on the ice. I was at bat when someone, a Welsh crew member, called, "Look you, there's a big white bear."

On a nearby chunk of ice, no more than two or three ship lengths away, a bear stared at us. Two of the men grabbed their pikes, launched one of the ship's boats and rowed hard towards it. The bear, seeming to understand their intent was less than friendly, made itself scarce. The men returned empty handed, but laughing anyway. They had no idea how close to unstoppable danger they had been.

When we set sail again, there was no longer any question of which way to go. Captain Hudson had made his offer, perhaps to avoid the threat of a mutiny. That offer had not been forgotten; not by any of us. Since then we had been too busy avoiding ice most of the time to discuss it among ourselves. I was sure the subject would arise again when the men had had time to think more about it. As *Discovery* continued to point her bowsprit to the west, it was obvious that we were going on, west and north, to search for a passage through the icy hell until we reached the warmer waters of far Cathay. Those who would have turned the ship for England had lost their opportunity, for the moment. We would have to battle the ice, the fog and the strong currents for every moment of the hundreds of leagues ahead of us in the strait.

At a place the captain named Isles of God's Mercy, Abacuck Prickett and Philip Staffe were ordered to select a handful of men and go ashore to climb a height of land to see what lay before us to the west, north-west and south-west. Prickett looked at me and raised his eyebrows.

"Yes," I agreed, "I'll go with you. Wait for me while I get a musket, powder and shot."

"Well, hurry it up, Thomas."

With the weapon in my hand, I scrambled over the side into the boat before Captain Hudson or Juet could find a reason for me to stay.

Walking on land for the first time since Iceland was good for my legs. Unfortunately, the barren, wet rocky ground was home to hordes of vicious, flying biting insects. They descended on our hands and faces in dense clouds, leaving us covered in welts and spots of our own blood. The bites itched unmercifully and, we later discovered, the annoyance lasted for days. We could do nothing to alleviate the torment of those wicked pests. All we could do was try not to scratch the welts.

I tried to talk with Prickett about the captain's strange offer as we walked ahead of the other men, but he had nothing to say on that score, except, "The captain knows what he is about, I reckon. He'll see us through this."

Prickett's conciliatory words conflicted with the expression on his face. I could see that he didn't believe what he'd said any more than I did. We walked on in silence, each with his own worried thoughts. Preoccupied as we were, we surprised a covey of partridges. We were almost on them before we saw them and before they sensed our presence. As they took off in alarm, I fired the musket at them but only managed to bring one down – and an old one at that. I was embarrassed enough to shrug my shoulders at my poor marksmanship. My shipmates were too busy fending off the flying insects to offer more than a half-hearted jeer at my incompetence. On board later, the cook's reaction was a little kinder. "Better than nothing, I suppose."

We took a supply of driftwood aboard for firewood and reported to the captain the welcome news that the way ahead, beyond the other side of this land, was free of ice as far as the eyes could see. First though, there was a sea of white to navigate safely before we could reach open water. Once back on the ship and ready to get under way again, the cold breeze kept the insects away from us. We were thankful for that small mercy because it took us almost eight hours of hard work to clear the ice gathered against the shore. Out on the open sea again, with room to manoeuvre, the wind turned fair for a while and swept us to the west.

The land to port was much protected by inhospitable islands and jagged islets of rock and ice. For a while the natural hazards stood to the south and west, causing Captain Hudson to sail north to clear the danger. A storm blew in and took us within sight of the high, craggy cliffs of the north shore of the strait. Once more we pointed our bowsprit to the south and west, hoping to regain proximity to the southern shore. The storm continued, taking us well to the west until we again fell in with the south land. As we passed, noting the geographical features as they changed, the captain named each promontory and bay. Soon we sighted a high hill, prominent enough for the captain to name it Mount Charles. After passing an island, and with an almost clear sea ahead, a lookout in the bow called the alarm when he saw an unusual disturbance upon the sea. "Shoaling, sir. I think," he bellowed.

Cautious of running onto a rock shelf, the captain ordered Mr. Juet to have the lead cast. There was no bottom. The rippling and apparent distress of the sea's surface could only have been from a conflict between currents.

We sailed west for a few days, keeping no more than a league off the coast, until we sighted a high island. The captain named it Cape Digges for his primary sponsor and a nearby height of land on the main for Sir Thomas Wolstenholme. With no immediate danger from ice, the captain sent Prickett and a small crew, including myself, ashore to explore the land near Wolstenholme. Not knowing what manner of beast or persons we might encounter, we went armed with muskets and pikes as usual.

The weather closed in on us soon after we landed. A violent storm of freezing rain, thunder and lightning swept over the land. There was no shelter so we forged on to complete our observations as soon as possible in order to return to the ship and get dry. In the distance we saw a herd of more than a dozen deer, but too far away for a musket shot. Following orders, we crossed the land to a high, rugged prominence, too steep to ascend without ropes. I estimated the hill to be about 1,000 feet above the sea. A series of waterfalls cascaded off the heights, keeping the land at the foot of the hill lush and green. The green, we soon discovered was sorrel and scurvy grass. Ignoring the clouds of flying insects, we gathered as much of the grasses as we could carry. The cook would make good use of it over the next few days.

The fertile land on which we stood was home to an abundance of fowl. Before we scared them away with our muskets, for they were too distant for a guaranteed kill, we crept closer past a pile of rocks that gave the appearance of having been stacked by human hands.

"Look at this," Prickett said as he lifted the uppermost stone. "It's hollow inside, like a tomb."

Between us we removed a couple more slabs of rock to reveal a great surprise, the interior was a storehouse of fowl hanging by their necks. We forgot all about the flock of distant live fowl. Those hollow, rocky cairns served as a form of outdoor larder. They could only have been made by human hands. We looked around us in all directions. There were no signs of habitation or other obvious clues to the ownership of the birds. Most important, there were no people, friendly or otherwise in sight.

"We need to report this to the captain," I said. "He will surely want to locate the owners of this cache of food."

Robert Bylot sent Prickett and Greene back to our landing place to bring the boat around. The rain stopped while the rest of us descended a pleasant valley, with Bylot in the lead, to the shore where we waited. As our boat came in sight round a headland, we heard two shots from the cannon, calling us to the return to the ship. It was then that we saw the fog creeping in from the north.

"Make haste there, Prickett. And you Greene. Pull for all you're worth. Fog's a coming in," Bylot shouted through cupped hands.

On board we described what we had seen to the captain and asked that we should anchor at this desirable place for a few days to stock up with birds and fresh water. Ignoring the advantages, the captain would have none of it.

"No. There is no time to waste. The season is late and we must continue with all speed," he growled. We sailed on, leaving the abundance of ducks and geese behind.

The land now curved away to the south and west for a few leagues until we lost sight of it altogether as it changed direction and fell away to the south and east. There was little ice yet the winds were cold and snow yet stood on the land we had recently passed. We changed course again to meet the land, coming in to a deceptively rocky and shallow bay where we went to anchor. We were held there for a day to ride out a storm.

I had some misgivings at this point about our direction. I believed the passage we sought had to be somewhat further to the north and west. Everything I had learned about the possibility of a north-west passage suggested it had to be north and west of our position – that seemed obvious to my mind; yet we were sailing south and, often, more to the east, following the shape of the land. There had been no opportunity for me to check our latitude with my backstaff, so I hesitated to broach this subject with the captain. I felt he had enough on his mind. He did not need to hear the concerns of one such as I. When we set sail again, we continued south and a little to the east. The skies cleared and I took the opportunity of taking a sun sight. The results showed we were now at 58° and continuing south. It didn't make sense to me. We were going the wrong way. I had no opportunity of checking my work as the backstaff was suddenly snatched from my hands. Mr. Juet stood there his face wearing its customary angry scowl.

"What the hell do you think you're doing, Woodhouse?" he yelled. "You are not the ship's navigator." Having said that, he snapped my backstaff across his knee and tossed the pieces overboard. I almost lost my reason. Doing my best to control my temper, I stood there glaring at him, my fists clenched at my sides.

"Just try it, Woodhouse," he sneered, his face close enough to mine that I could smell his foul breath. "Just try it and I'll clap you in irons for striking an officer."

Shaking with fury, I turned my back on him and climbed into the rigging. Ignoring his shouted orders to get back on deck, I made my way to the masthead. There, far out of his reach, I screamed my anger and frustration to the winds until my throat hurt. I stayed there, aloft and alone for hours. Up there, with a vast sea spread out to starboard, it occurred to me that, perhaps, Captain Hudson believed we were now on the ocean and that over there, beyond the west horizon, we would find Cathay. The only way to be sure would be to sail due west until we sighted land again. But we were not sailing west. We were sailing south. By the time I returned to the deck, cold and miserable, Juet had forgotten all about me.

Our course remained steady to the south until we reached latitude 53°. I know that because Robert Bylot told me where we were and why we were there. He had learned it from the captain.

"Captain Hudson thinks this bay might lead us to a big river to take us west."

"Well, why don't we cross this sea to the west and find out what's there?" I asked.

Bylot shook his head. "Not my decision."

This latitude was almost as far south as my home in England. Again I wondered at the captain's choices. There was no evidence to suggest a big river to the south, unless he was thinking in terms of Cartier's Rivière du Canada, but that should be hundreds of leagues away. I asked myself again, why were we not looking across the sea to the west? Or to the north-west? That was where we were supposed to be going. On the 10th of September, 1610, with none of us having any clear idea of where we were or where we were going, the captain put the expedition in jeopardy again.

Chapter 10

September 10, 1610

The Master has had enough of Mr. Juet's ill words and actions. After our dinner this evening he called all the men together on deck to address the situation. It was, in effect, a court and the man on trial was Mr. Juet, the first mate – an officer, if you can believe it. I wrote in my journal:

"There were proved so many and great abuses, and mutinous matters against the master, and action by Juet, that there was danger to have suffered them longer; and it was fit time to punish and cut off further occasions of the like mutinies."

The first to speak against Juet was the cook, Bennet Matthews. He reminded all that Juet had warned of bloodshed to come when we were at Iceland. Matthews also spoke of Juet's threat to turn the ship for home as we were leaving Iceland's Lousie Bay.

"Ah, that was but a joke, Matthews. Could you not see that?" Juet countered. If the faces all around were honest in their expressions, no one believed him.

Philip Staffe spoke up, as did Arnold Ludlowe. They both swore on the Holy Bible that Juet had told them to keep their muskets charged with shot and swords ready, because those weapons would be needed before the voyage was over. Staffe then talked of the near mutiny off Desire Provoketh and of how Juet had deliberately stirred the emotions of many of the crew with his slanderous comments about their captain.

Staffe reminded us, "When we were stuck in the ice, Juet spoke words that suggested mutiny and slander. Those words easily had an effect on the timorous among the crew. Had not our Master prevented it, those dangerous words could have overthrown the voyage and endangered all our lives. Only yesterday, I heard Juet mocking Captain Hudson's belief that we might reach the Spice Islands by Candlemass."

Juet stood there in silence, his face an ugly mask of loathing. He said nothing, because he had no defence. He could see that, despite his machinations, most – but not all – of the crew were against him and on the side of Captain Hudson, our Master.

On any other ship and under any other captain, Juet would have suffered the full weight of the law of the sea. Many captains would certainly have hung him from a yardarm immediately. The more lenient would have cast irons on his ankles and wrists and confined him to the chain locker in the forepeak for the duration of the voyage. Captain Hudson did neither. Instead, showing a distinct lack of authority, he let Juet off lightly.

"Mr. Juet, you are demoted to able seaman. Mr. Bylot will take your place as mate," the captain ordered. "And you, Francis Clement, for continually siding with Juet, you are demoted from bo'sun to ordinary seaman. William Wilson, you are now bo'sun."

There were murmurings among the crew but no one voiced a complaint, not even the men demoted. The captain had more to say, "Adrian Motter, you are now made up to bos'un's mate."

These changes would affect us all, none more so than Captain Hudson who was in grave danger of losing control of his crew and, therefore, his ship.

Juet stood there before the men, his face contorted with rage. Much of his evil mood was directed towards Robert Bylot. His obvious hatred became even more intense when the captain announced that Bylot would henceforth receive Juet's pay. There was no mention of continued pay to Juet, not even as an able seaman. The Master closed the proceedings with a few conciliatory words to Juet and to Clement – in effect – a promise for the future.

"If you behave yourselves honestly from this day forward, I would consider that good behaviour and would consider forgetting the slanders and other injuries you have cast upon me."

We were aghast. Such talk was unheard of from a ship's captain. His word was law. No one could speak against him for fear of dire punishment. Why was he letting Juet and Clement off so lightly? Was he afraid of them or, perhaps, afraid of their standing with the crew? These were not the words of a strong leader. They were not the words or deeds of a man for whom I had once had so much respect. I thought about Captain Hudson's words and the meaning behind them for a long time afterwards. Was he truly as weak as he now appeared to be, I wondered? Was he always to vacillate between right and wrong? Could he not see the damage his lack of leadership was doing to the morale on our ship? Could he not see that his grand expedition was falling apart?

Now the captain's actions became more and more erratic. After the trial, we sailed north. Then we sailed south. We sailed north again and once more to the south, until we came to anchor in a shallow bay. The wind held us there, much too close to the land on a lee shore, for a full eight days. When at last it began to relent, but still blowing with a force, Captain Hudson ordered the anchor weighed. That action was a disaster waiting to happen and the captain should have recognized it. The wind was too strong; the seas still too high. As the anchor cleared the water a large sea hit us hard. All of us on the capstan were hurled from it; some sustaining injuries to arms and legs. The anchor would have plunged to the seabed, taking its rode with it had not the carpenter severed the cable with a mighty blow from his axe. The anchor went to the depths alone, never to be retrieved. We managed to save most of the valuable cable.

We sailed south and we sailed south-west on a clear sea. The depths varied from deep to shallow and to deep again. And then we came to a strange phenomenon – a sea of two colours, one black and one almost white. The lead showed 16 fathoms beneath our keel as we sailed west along the demarcation line between the two extremes. After 4 or 5 leagues, with night fast approaching, we took in all but our main and foresails. The wind blew steady enough to keep us moving. The leadsman in the bow called out the depths as darkness fell.

"Six fathoms, by the lead, sir. Five fathoms by the lead, sir," he announced.

Although the sea was becoming shallower by the minute, due to the dark we could not see land ahead but none of doubted its existence or proximity. I waited for the order that had to come, and soon.

"Wear ship. Wear ship," Henry Hudson's voice bellowed across the decks.

All hands had been waiting at their stations for the order. We went into action immediately. As we turned the yards and the quartermaster turned the rudder, *Discovery* began to heel over as she crossed the wind. Slowly, with the rigging straining and rubbing and the masts creaking and groaning, she came around and soon found deep water again. The captain changed course again, this time once more to the south; then the south-west until we entered a small bay where we anchored just off the north shore for the night.

Wrapped in my blanket, swinging to the rhythm of the ship in a hammock while off watch, I often dreamed of home. I dreamed of my parents and of my brother and my darling sisters. I dreamed of Jane Montrose and the unspoken promise of more kisses in the future. At times, I dreamed of Brenda, the serving wench from Oxford. I was lonely and, suddenly, I was homesick. The Arctic voyage that I had wanted so badly months before was far from what I had expected. There was no adventure here. There was no sense of discovery. I felt trapped amid the vague wanderings of a man who increasingly showed a tendency to madness.

Captain Hudson sent a boat ashore to explore the land at daylight. The water shoaled quickly so that the small boat could no longer float. The men on board took to the water and walked ashore through the shallows. There, on a thin layer of snow among the rocks, they found the footprints of a man and others of a duck, or a goose. There was much dead wood scattered along the shore, a good supply of which our men collected and brought back to the ship.

The water was clear in this bay. Clear enough to see far into the deep. I climbed to the masthead and looked around me. A submerged ledge of rock showed to the north of the ship and another to the south. The rocks were covered at high tide but a definite hazard at any time. I could also see rocks, above and below the surface along the course we had taken to enter the bay. It seemed to me that in the darkness we had only found our way in by luck and the leadsman's skill.

At midnight we retrieved our anchor and set sail again, on the reverse course to that we had used to fetch the bay. The carpenter, risking a torrent of abuse from the captain or the mate, spoke up.

"Sir," he called, looking up at the poopdeck. His voice was anxious. "There be rocks dead ahead. I've seen them. We'll be on them afore we knows it."

Captain Hudson replied, "Nay, Mr. Staffe, calm yourself. We are past the rocks. Have no fear."

Minutes later we sailed onto a rock with a crash that jarred all on board and most of the ship's timbers too. Philip Staffe picked himself up from the deck and glared at the captain but wisely kept his mouth shut. We were stuck there, canted over to port, for the next twelve hours until a sea lifted us off. By then the carpenter had determined that none of the timbers had been sprung. The damage to the ship was slight; not enough to cause alarm. Our faith in the captain, however, had suffered another blow. Afloat and watertight, by the grace of God and the shipwrights' skills, we stood to the east once again until we saw three hills lying north to south. We steered for the most southerly and passed it to enter a pleasant bay without obvious rocks and came again to anchor. By this time, in late October, the nights were long and they were cold. Snow covered the nearby land. We all knew we would have to stay here, or somewhere close by, for the winter. It was not a happy prospect.

Captain Hudson sent Philip Staffe and Abacuck Prickett off in a ship's boat to explore the coast to the south. After the last three months wandering in what Prickett referred to as "a labyrinth without end," we were sore in need of some comfort. The two returned a few hours later with news of a good anchorage to the south. On the 1st of November, 1610, we came into this place at 52° North latitude, found it acceptable and all hands gathered to haul the ship aground in a safe place. The shore was rocky, some smooth and many sharp. The land was flat, with no appreciable prominences. The forest, which stretched almost to the water's edge in places, stood on soft, spongy ground, like a peat bog. Immediately to the south of our position was a river flowing fast into the sea from the east. This then was to be our home for the winter months. Philip Staffe suggested to the Master that he and other men should go ashore and build a house out of spare wooden planks, stowed on board in London for just that purpose. The Master would not hear of it.

"*Discovery* will be comfortable enough for us all through the winter," he said.

Ten days after we secured the ship, the temperature dropped below freezing and the ice closed us in.

When we departed London, we understood the victuallers were supposed to have provisioned the ship for eight months. We all knew that, whatever amounts the victuallers had supplied, a certain amount of the food would have gone directly to the Master's home. All captains, as far as I knew, did the same. Therefore, we had no way of knowing exactly how much food had actually been stowed away in *Discovery*'s hold. Whatever that amount was, it would not add up to provisions enough for eight months. To add to our unspecified stock, we had caught fish and we had kept a store of ducks and geese. By this time, in early November, we had been at sea for six and a half months. Food was running low but not yet a concern. We expected to supplement the provisions left with more fowl, with fish if they could be found beneath the ice, and with beasts from the forests. Captain Hudson offered a reward to any man who killed a duck, goose, fish or wild beast that winter. He did not specify what the reward would be.

I am not ashamed to admit, I wanted to go home. If the winter should prove to last as long as English winters, we were looking at four months before spring warmed the land. Unlike the comforts and joys of home, that meant another four months cooped up on the ship with limited activity and an unhappy crew serving a captain who had lost the respect his position demanded. It was not good to think of the cold, bleak days ahead. John Williams, the gunner, couldn't wait for spring. He died in the middle of November from unknown causes. His death created more tension aboard ship and more dissension.

It is the custom of the sea that when a man dies his belongings are displayed at the main mast and there they are auctioned to the crew; the highest bidder taking the item. John Williams owned a fine cloak of heavy grey wool. Henry Greene persuaded Captain Hudson to let him have the cloak for a trifle. There were those who objected to this favouritism and spoke out against it. The captain, however, insisted that Greene should have the cloak and that was the end of it, or so we thought.

To give us more living space than the cramped quarters on the ship, Captain Hudson then decided we should have additional accommodation, as suggested by the carpenter earlier. "Mr. Staffe," he called. "I want you to go ashore. Take your tools, lengths of wood and as many men as you need and build us a house."

Staffe looked at him as if he were mad. "No, sir," he replied, "Beggin' yer pardon, sir, but I can't do that. I offered to help build a house when we first came to this place. Now it's too late. The snow and frost will make the work almost impossible. Besides," he added with sum truculence, "I am a ship's carpenter, not a house builder."

Captain Hudson was so angry he struck him hard in the face, called him foul names and threatened to hang him. Staffe, to his credit, stood his ground.

"Punish me all you want, Captain," he said, "but I am not a house carpenter. However, I do know that this frost would complicate the work beyond measure. We would never be able to put down any kind of foundation."

Captain Hudson, furious though he was at being disobeyed, allowed Staffe to leave the deck without further punishment. I had expected the captain to put Staffe in chains for his words. I thought the idea of a house, or some such accommodation on shore, would be a good idea so we could spread out. I felt we should have started work on the house as soon as the ship had been secured for the winter – as Staffe had originally suggested – but, how difficult could it be to build a temporary house? I wondered. Four walls, a roof and a few bunks, that's all. With the ground harder than granite, a foundation was unnecessary. By the time the land thawed in the spring, we would be off sailing again with no further need of a house.

"Captain," I volunteered. "With your approval, and if I could borrow the carpenter's tools, I could build this house, with some help from two or three others."

The captain glared at me, without speaking. I shrugged and said to John Hudson and Nick Simms, "You would help me, would you not?" They both nodded their agreement.

"Well, then, Mr. Woodhouse. It seems you have a job to do," the captain said. "I want that house built and ready for occupancy in three days. Three days, do you hear me?"

"Aye, aye, sir. I hear you," I answered. "C'mon, lads, let's get started."

We built the house, if one could call it that, in the allotted three days. At least, it had four straight walls and a roof that didn't sag. Not that it mattered much. The shack was rarely used anyway. Most of the men preferred the cramped quarters aboard ship, for the warmth and the familiarity.

The day after his confrontation with the captain, Staffe decided to go hunting on shore. There was a general order on board that no man could go ashore alone, only in pairs. Each pair must take one musket and one pike with them, for protection and to kill beasts for food. Staffe invited Greene to go with him and they prepared to depart. Captain Hudson threw another tantrum at this news. Perhaps feeling that Greene was now conspiring with Staffe against him, he ordered the late gunner's cloak be given to Robert Bylot, instead of Greene.

This pettiness provoked an argument on the main deck that I doubt had a parallel in the annals of life at sea. I had gone back on board to collect some loose planks and heard it all. Henry Greene and Captain Henry Hudson stood face to face, a common seaman and the ship's master, shouting at each other for all to hear. Greene demanded the return of the cloak for which, he said, he would pay out of wages due to him. The captain refused, yelling words of abuse and saying, "None of your friends would so much as trust you with twenty shillings. Therefore, why should I trust you? As for wages, you have none and none shall you have if you continue to displease me. Now, get out of my sight."

Greene swore at the captain as he left the deck. Much concerned and embarrassed by this unseemly turn of events, the rest of us looked away, most finding work wherever they could, determined not to catch the captain's attention. I went ashore to my construction work for safety. The threat of mutiny had been hanging over *Discovery* for a few months. With this latest assault on the master's God-given superiority, we took another step closer to outright rebellion.

Discovery was as safe as she could be – half on land and half in the water. Ice had formed around the hull to lock her in place. Plus, we had lines out in many directions to anchor her to shore using convenient rocks and trees. Regular falls of snow had built up a barrier against her hull and a thick carpet on deck, all of which, we found to our pleasure, helped to insulate the vessel from the extreme low temperatures. We insulated the shack on shore the same way, spending hours packing snow against the walls and on the roof. Despite that assistance, we suffered agonies from frozen feet and fingers. I have never known such wicked cold.

We took down the sails and dried them over the log fire in the shack. When the heat had steamed all the frost and moisture out of them, we folded each one with care and stowed them away on the ship between decks to keep them dry. When the ice eventually melted on the bay and spring returned to warm the air, the sails would be ready and in good condition for quick use. We also took down the top masts and their associated rigging. The topmasts were secured on deck. The rigging went below with the sails. The captain assigned a roster of men to keep the ice off the cables and anchor rodes tethering *Discovery* to the land. They also had to keep the hawses clear of ice and snow. Those tasks had to be done each day throughout the months we sheltered on the edge of the shore. Shrouded as she was in winter's cold blanket, from a distance the ship began to look more and more like a ghostly sculpture from nature's infinite repertoire of exotic designs.

CHAPTER 11

Occasionally during those long winter months John Hudson and I would take our hammocks and bedrolls to the shack on shore and sleep there, as much for the cleaner air as for the peace and solitude. I found the constant farting, belching, snoring, hawking and spitting on the ship to be ever more repugnant. In the shack, even with a wood fire burning day and night, it was colder than on the ship, but the additional living space and the privacy was worth the suffering. On those occasions, armed as ordered, we would be up at first light and trudging through the deep snow of the forest in search of game, or people. On one of these expeditions we climbed a prominent hill on a rounded peninsula. From there we could see long distances, but saw no sign of human life.

One night on board ship as we rested in our berths trying to keep warm while a blizzard blew outside, John Hudson came to me and said, "Happy New Year, Thomas."

Happy New Year? Christmas had passed a week before and no one had noticed or, if they had, had not shared the knowledge with us.

"Is it? Then Happy New Year to you too, John," I answered. A chorus of sleepy voices passed around the greetings. Soon Robert Bylot appeared with mugs of hot rum for all hands. "Happy New Year, men," he sang out.

Later, warmed by the rum, I lay there thinking of the previous New Year's Eve and the elegant ball I had attended. How far removed I was from that now. My mind strayed to Miss Jane Montrose and the kiss that could have become more. I wondered what she was doing that winter's night in the far away land called home. I wondered if she ever thought of me. Such thoughts, especially of Jane, were pleasant but unsettling in the extreme. I did my best to shut her from my mind. I was left with the snoring of the other lonely men around me.

We were fortunate over those first winter months that Mother Nature did not desert us. Snowy white partridges, with plump healthy bodies arrived in their thousands. Between us, the members of the crew shot over twelve hundred for the cook's use. We were always cold, but never over those few desperate months of isolation did we go hungry. Looking back to that winter, I often wondered how it was that no savages came to visit us. We were never sparing of our shots. Almost every day one could hear them echoing through the forest. There was always smoke in the air from our cooking fires – on the ship and on shore; we talked in loud voices, yet not once did we meet another human being. Likewise, we never saw any signs that suggested human presence. Not once did we see smoke from fires other than our own, unlike in the autumn when we had regularly seen smoke. It was as though we were the only people left of earth.

On board, when we weren't working, we entertained ourselves as best we could. Some men played cards or dice. Some slept. Some picked arguments. I read my books and exercised whenever I could in the small space available. Captain Hudson kept very much to himself.

For three weeks in January we were confined to the ship while a blizzard raged all around. Hour after hour, day and night, the wind screamed and buffeted *Discovery*. The snow became deeper on deck. Each day men were sent up to clear the worst, even at the height of the storm. We all suffered through those terrifying days with little else to do but to confront our own demons – in addition to the devils attacking our ship. We could not hunt. We dared not leave the ship for to do so would be suicide. We would have been lost within seconds. We melted snow and ice from the deck for water. Our stock of fire logs dwindled. Our food supply dropped day by day. By the time the storm had blown itself to oblivion, our fuel was almost exhausted. The captain sent four men out with axes to replenish our stock in case of another bad blow. They had to struggle through thigh-deep snow for hours to find dead trees suitable for burning, chop them into manageable lengths and carry them back to the ship.

As the long winter exhausted itself and spring began to melt the snow, the partridges flew north, all together and all at once. A few swans, geese and ducks came down to rest from their migratory flights, but they were rare. We hoped the bigger game birds would stay, maybe to use the surrounding land for a breeding site but it was not to be. After a short while, they continued their journeys to the north. As the winter retreated so they went with it. Our diet now deteriorated. Some men set traps to catch small mammals, with little success. Others broke holes in the ice and tried fishing – again with limited success. We went out on forays to gather anything remotely edible, even such bitter vegetable matter as mosses and lichen, and the loathsome frogs – of which there were an abundance. I experimented with the trees, searching for anything that might offer sustenance. There were no nuts or berries yet but I did find an interesting bud, which was rich with a substance reminiscent of turpentine. I wondered if it had any medicinal properties. Hopeful of a positive outcome, I collected some and took them back to the ship. Our surgeon, Edward Wilson, made a concoction from the buds and fed it to the men suffering from the ague or scurvy. Sometime after they drank it they began to feel better. Abacuck Prickett pronounced it a miracle cure, saying, "I received great and present ease of my pains."

I went out to collect more in the hope that it would help all of us recover our strength after the tiring winter months. It was a bitter drink but palatable enough for all that with boiled water and a little sugar – even better laced with a portion of rum.

As the ice began to break up around *Discovery* we returned to normal watch-keeping duties. Bylot measured each tide, marking its height on the rocks and on our hull. We all knew we would require a high tide and, at its peak, a lot of muscle power from all crew to get the ship afloat again. Using the small rowing boat, we ran out a kedge anchor well to the west of the ship. When the time came, with the tide peaking at six feet above the low, everyone worked together in teams at the capstan to reel in the cable and so to move the ship back off the rock ledge. Even two lame men did as much as they could. When men tired, Captain Hudson lent his weight to the task alongside his son. Slowly, her keel making an awful sound as it scraped over the rock, like an animal in agony, we manoeuvred *Discovery* into deep water and made her secure.

"Man the pumps," Bylot cried out. "Carpenter, check all seams. Make sure she's water tight."

We were lucky. The shipwrights at Woolwich had done their work well those first few weeks of the previous year. *Discovery* was strong. Staffe found little repair work to be done, except for some caulking required in the bilge. The work, however, was not over. The topmasts had to be re-rigged and the sails bent onto the yards. It was late in the evening and very dark before we finished. The captain was so pleased with our efforts that day that he ordered an extra ration of hot rum for all hands.

We had waited for the ice to break up for so long; now we found ourselves in danger again from drifting floes as the wind turned them and ground them against the ship's sides. All hands turned to, using poles and pikes to fend off the dangers. A ruptured hull from marauding ice could yet sink the ship if we relaxed our vigilance for a moment. Soon we were buffeted from both sides at once. *Discovery* shuddered and tossed her bowsprit like a horse in distress. The wind blew from the north-west. The current flowed to the north. The ice rocked and danced, this way and that, as the conflicting forces fought for dominance. Caught in the middle, *Discovery* was at the mercy of all three. We worked so hard during those long hours to keep our ship safe. We fended off the ice until we thought our muscles could do no more, and then we continued until the next watch relieved us or we dropped. All the while, we prayed for a change in the wind.

CHAPTER 12

"The ice in the bay has begun to break up and drift away with the northbound current. Our long winter incarceration is coming to an end. Soon, we all hope, when the wind returns, we will be able to sail away from this icy hell and continue our search for a passage to the Spice Islands. That is, after all, why we came here to this Arctic environment. I have been somewhat lax over the past few months in taking note of dates. Often I don't even know what day it is. I must do better."

I shared thoughts such as those with my journal regularly, and I wrote occasionally of the happenings on board but the days merged. Surprising then that, as the ice began to move and the weather improved, my thoughts turned to spring - and the comforting scent of spring flowers. That warm memory reminded me that I must have passed my 21st birthday sometime within the past few weeks and not even noticed. Somehow it did not seem important.

A savage came to visit us soon after we relaunched *Discovery*. The first sign of human life we had seen since the previous summer in the Furious Overfall, apart from the footprints in the snow. He paddled in a canoe along the shore from the south, working his way through the ice with great dexterity to *Discovery*'s anchorage. Off our port quarter, he made signs that he wished to come aboard. Captain Hudson agreed and invited the man to the poopdeck. The savage walked right past me as he crossed the deck, so close I could have touched him. He wore breeches of a tan coloured material, which might have been the cured skin of an animal. His shirt was the same colour and material, as were the slippers on his feet. He was tall, maybe a little taller than most of our crew, including me, and I was among the tallest. The native's black hair was tied back into a queue hanging down his back. He wore two long feathers, one black and one white, in the hair on the side of his head. His skin was the colour of a fine brandy. By any reckoning, he was a handsome man. To my surprise, he greeted the captain in heavily accented French. "Bonjour, Monsieur."

I knew Captain Hudson did not speak French. His languages were limited to English and some Dutch. I stepped forward.

"Excuse me, Captain," I said. "I believe I can understand this man. He is speaking a form of French."

"Go ahead, Woodhouse. See what you can do," the captain ordered.

I greeted the savage and then asked where he had learned to speak French. His reply was halting and I soon found his knowledge of the language was limited to no more than a few words or sentences.

"From a Frenchman, a fur trader," he answered, and then lapsed into an incomprehensible tongue. That initial greeting seemed to be close to the extent of his linguistic ability.

In French, I asked him his name, placing my hand on his chest. He answered, "Chogan." I repeated the gesture with my hand on my own chest. "Thomas," I said. He smiled, touched my chest and repeated, "Thomas." I pointed to Captain Hudson. "Captain," I said. Chogan smiled and nodded his understanding. That was as far as we could take that conversation. Captain Hudson was eager to trade and to find out where the man's village was situated.

"Ask him where he lives, Woodhouse."

I posed the question. Chogan looked around the horizon. He nodded to the north, south, east and west. "La bas," he said. "Partout." Over there. Everywhere.

Exasperated by what he took to be deliberate evasion, Captain Hudson appeared to be losing his temper. Prickett forestalled a potentially difficult situation with a suggestion.

"Captain, sir. Perhaps if you give him a few gifts he will return with information, or trade goods."

Captain Hudson glared at Prickett for his impudence. Even so, he gave the man a knife, some shiny buttons and a looking glass. The native smiled his thanks and signalled his intention to return after he had slept. He was soon kneeling in his canoe, paddling with sure strokes through the gaps in the ice for the land to the south.

"Men," Captain Hudson addressed us all, "when this savage comes back, and I believe he will, I expect him to bring goods for trade. I want every man aboard to surrender his knife and his hatchet so we have more to trade from our side."

This was not a popular order. The men were sailors. All sailors carried a knife. It was part of their clothing, an extension of their hands. They used knives for protection from others and for the security a sharp blade could afford if needed to cut away tangled rigging. Only two men obeyed the captain. I was not one of them. I watched to see what would happen. Abacuck Prickett handed over his knife and so did John King. They were the only ones to do so. To my surprise, the captain did not repeat his order. Neither did he reprimand those of us who had not stepped forward to present our knives. He looked disappointed, and perturbed, but he said nothing. He just turned his back on the men and went to his cabin. It was another strange turn of events.

The native returned the next morning. He came along the land, pulling a sled over the snow all by himself. When he climbed aboard, he brought with him two beaver pelts and two heavy deer skins draped over his powerful shoulders. He placed the knife he had received the day before on one beaver pelt and the looking glass and buttons on the other. Captain Hudson nodded and took the two beaver pelts. The native placed the knife, looking glass and buttons in a bag hanging from his shoulder. The captain then showed a hatchet and motioned that he wanted both deer skins for it. The native refused, offering only one of the skins. Captain Hudson stood his ground and, after a few minutes of arm waving and unintelligible words, the native agreed, though he was obviously unhappy with the deal. Then, touching himself on the chest, he made signs that there were more people like him to the north, the south, east and west. He tapped his chest once more.

"Chogan," he said. We understood him to be reminding us of his name. Captain Hudson tapped his own chest and said, "Captain."

Chogan looked at us sailors on the main deck. His eyes swept over the crew until he saw me. He came down the steps and touched my shoulder. "Thomas," he said, drawing out the syllables.

Looking back at the captain, the native gave signs that he would return with other traders in a few days. I watched until he had pulled his now empty sled out of sight. I scanned that part of the horizon for a long time, looking for smoke from village fires. There was nothing. The native named Chogan was gone. I could not know then that he would soon become an important factor in my life.

Much of the ice had left the bay by this time. With open water all around, the captain sent seven sailors out in a small boat to set fishing nets. That day they hauled in over 500 fish at one attempt. Most were trout or grayling. They were of no great size, but all became valuable additions to our dwindling food supplies. The same men, William Wilson, Henry Greene, Michael Perse, Arnold Ludlowe, Andrew Motter, Bennet Matthews and John Thomas went out on subsequent days but never again brought in anywhere near as many fish. It seemed to me that they had chanced upon a couple of large shoals of fish passing the ship on the first day. That bounty had now moved on and little remained. Soon our bellies again began to shrink from hunger.

While the men fished, carpenter Philip Staffe had assembled the shallop, a larger vessel than the rowing boat. I heard Henry Greene and William Wilson plotting to take that new boat, supposedly to fish for everyone, but instead to flee the ship and fend for themselves. Captain Hudson, who could not have known of the plan, forestalled them when he announced he would be taking the shallop on a short journey to try to find a native village. He took two men with him, plus food for a week or so, and headed south. The rest of us received orders to collect wood for fuel, fresh water and big stones for ballast. Greene was much angered by the captain's decision but could do nothing about it.

"My time will come," he seethed as the trio sailed away. "You mark my words."

When the shallop returned many days later, there were no canoes following them. No natives gathered on the shoreline. There was just the captain and his two companions. They had seen and smelled the smoke from fires, but had not been successful in locating them. They had not encountered any natives at all although they knew people were there. To stop the captain and his men from reaching their location, the savages had set fire to the forest causing an immediate retreat to the sea. The expedition had been a waste of time and precious food.

On his return to the ship, our disappointed captain again showed signs of concern for the welfare of the expedition, and for the stomachs of his crew. Unfortunately, he again issued orders that made no sense and went against the accepted practice of life aboard ship. He had all the ship's bread collected and shared equally among the men. Each of us received about one pound. Some could not think of tomorrow, or the next day. They devoured the bread within minutes to please their tortured bellies. I held on to my bread, determined to ration it so it would last a few days.

Captain Hudson then did something that shocked me even more, despite all that I had learned about the weakness of his character. He gave every man a letter, which was, he said, to be shown on return to England, to acknowledge that the captain had shared out the bread of his own volition, not because of any threats from the crew. He was, in effect, absolving us of any mutinous thoughts or deeds. I walked away, the letter in my hand, shaking my head in wonder at the unseemliness of the Master's actions.

The fish boat went out again on Friday morning and didn't return until late on Sunday. I had begun to think that

Greene and his companions might have abandoned us. They returned but with only fourscore small fish: not enough to feed a crew of hungry sailors for long.

It soon became apparent that Chogan would not be returning to the ship with more furs to trade. That evening we sailed out of our wintering place and came to anchor in deeper water some distance away. At daylight we sailed north until we reached the mouth of the bay where we had been trapped for months. There, in sight of the great sea to the north, we again went to anchor. That evening the captain divided the remaining seven rounds of cheese, some of which had grown exceedingly mouldy. Assembling the men, he shared out all the cheese, in equal parts good and bad, among the officers and crew. Some had already eaten all their bread and now proceeded to devour the cheese without thought of the immediate future.

I was sorely perplexed by this extraordinary behaviour from Captain Hudson. Nothing he did made sense any more. He had no control over his crew, except by virtue of these recent bribes – and I use the term with deliberation for I could not find any other word for his actions.

Henry Greene gave his share of bread and cheese to a friend for safekeeping and insisted he dole out only small portions to him each day. I felt this required an act of loyalty from Greene's friend far above and far beyond the strength of character shown by most of the crew so far, including that man. I kept my cheese hidden away with the remains of my bread. At this juncture, I didn't trust anybody.

The wind turned in our favour. The weather improved. With our sails full, we made way for the north. Concerned though I was at Captain Hudson's strange attitude, being under way again, I felt that the situation would resolve itself to everyone's advantage. The rest of the crew went about their duties as if nothing was amiss and yet, there were furtive glances passed between many. Some looked worried. Some showed the residue of anger. Only one or two acted with indifference. Most important, all were sailors and sailors know how to work, and they are happiest when their ship is at sea and sailing well. On the night of June 18th, we came up to a thick barrier of ice. Up in the rigging, while furling the sails, I could see that the ice field stretched far to the north, to the east and to the west.

The wind veered during the night to blow a westerly, hard enough to hold *Discovery* tight against the ice. We were stuck there, in sight of land to the east for a full week. I was not unhappy with our present lack of progress. I was suffering from the ague and a few days of rest could only be beneficial. Now, just when we thought we were finished with the troubles on board, the captain again made a remarkable decision.

"Simms," he called to the cabin boy. "I want you to search every man's possessions for any hoarded bread or cheese and bring it to me."

The men were exceedingly upset at this latest development and started to grumble among themselves. I began to regret my decision to store my portions and ration it to myself once each day. I regretted it even more when Nick's search yielded thirty cakes of bread and some cheese, including mine, which he took to the captain.

The crew were furious. I was no exception. The grumbles grew louder. We only had about two weeks of food supplies left in the ship. None of us could afford to lose the rations of bread that the captain had himself doled out to us earlier. Those among us who had saved our bread and cheese and eaten it sparingly, were to be punished for our foresight while the greedy ones would benefit. The situation was ripe for trouble and it was not too long in coming.

CHAPTER 13

JUNE 21, 1611

There's mutiny in the air. I can sense it and I can smell it. There have been warnings of it before, once at Iceland and again on that strange day in the icy strait, but not this strong. I heard Greene and William Wilson talking to Abacuck. If I heard right, they planned to put the weak and injured men adrift in the shallop and I'm sure Greene said that Captain Hudson would have to go with them. The weak and injured, I assumed, included me as the ague was still upon me. Despite his lack of leadership, the captain was still in charge of *Discovery* and he still claimed my loyalty. To make sure I had heard correctly, I watched and I listened whenever Greene or Wilson spoke to any of the men. I heard Prickett arguing with Greene after dark.

"Do you not understand?" exclaimed Prickett. "What you are proposing is mutiny, and that is a hanging offence. You'll be dancing from the gallows as soon as you get home."

"Hold your tongue, Prickett," Greene raised his voice. "I would rather be hanged at home than starved abroad. We have food for less than fourteen days. We have to do something."

Their voices faded as they walked away from my hearing. Mutiny! It was the most vile crime perpetrated at sea. The law was clear on the punishment. Mutineers would be hunted down, no matter where they tried to hide. They would be hunted down, captured, returned to their homeland in irons and there they would face the ultimate penalty. The threat of hanging, it seemed, was not sufficient deterrent to the likes of Greene and Wilson. This was evil news that the captain needed to hear at once. The hour was late; the captain's door closed. I was about to knock when Juet appeared.

"The captain's abed. Don't disturb him, Woodhouse," he said.

I went back to the deck. Wilson and Greene were talking with Prickett by the starboard rail. Greene was angry. Every time Prickett tried to say something, he cut him off. I noticed Prickett had his Bible in one hand. Greene saw it too.

"Give me that Bible, Prickett," he hissed, "I have need of it."

Prickett handed it over and begged, "Give me three days, Greene. Just three days to talk with the captain. Maybe we can sort this out."

"There is no time for that. I will not give you three days. I will not give you twelve hours even. The time for talk is over," Greene held the Bible aloft.

"Take note of this, Prickett. I swear I will do no man harm. All that I do is for the good of the ship. If necessary, I will have every member of the crew swear the same."

Wilson took the Bible from Greene and swore a similar oath. I remained out of sight, waiting for my chance to warn the captain. Prickett continued to argue against the mutiny but Greene, swearing he would slit the throat of anyone who acted against the plan, left him talking to Wilson and went below. Greene returned a few minutes later followed by five other members of the crew. They were: Juet, Bennet, Motter, Perse and John Thomas. Greene now held Prickett's Bible aloft so all could see, even in the dark.

"You men will now swear an oath, as I and Wilson have sworn. Raise your right hand and repeat after me..." And so Greene took one step closer to outright mutiny. The oath he spoke to lead the others is ingrained in my memory.

"I shall swear truth to God, my prince and my country that I shall do nothing but to the glory of God and the good of the action in hand, and cause harm to no man."

When they all left the deck, I stayed for some time, musing on the oath and its meaning, knowing I would be doing the right thing by reporting these events to the captain – if I could get to him without being seen. I couldn't approach John Hudson about it. He slept too close to other crew who might be involved.

I was about to go below when Greene and Prickett returned to the deck, soon followed by Wilson. They stood close together by the mainmast, barely visible. I crouched on the foredeck, making myself as small and invisible as possible. Prickett asked a question which I did not hear well enough to comprehend. Greene answered, his voice harsh.

"Don't you see what the captain has done? He has replaced Juet, who can read and write, with Bylot who can do neither. Only the Master, and now Bylot, have access to the ship's logs. But Bylot can't read or write, or navigate, as far as we know. That means the captain can chart any course he wants and, Bylot told me, the captain has ordered him to collect any and all writing materials and journals from the crew. None of us who can write will be allowed to keep any record of our voyage from now on. The captain has no plans to take us home, men. If he has his way, we will all die in this wilderness."

They talked some more, but with lowered voices. Unable to hear and too scared to move, I stayed where I was until they dispersed. For a while afterwards I walked the deck, thinking over Greene's words. They made sense and yet, our sole reason for being here was to find a navigable passage to Cathay. We had come so far. We had survived so much hardship. Giving up now because the captain's behaviour was not to our liking was to admit defeat. I thought about that strong, repugnant word for some time. Defeat. My dream was to be an explorer, not a sailor who gave up when conditions became difficult. I recalled my Papa's last conversation with me. Yes, indeed, I was a Woodhouse and a gentleman. I would make my family proud of me. Defeat? No. It could never be. Such an attitude was not for Thomas Woodhouse, son of Barnaby and Jane Woodhouse.

The sound of Greene's violin playing a gentle melody interrupted my thoughts. That gave me the opportunity I needed. The music would cover the sound of my knock on the captain's door. There was no one in sight. I went down the companionway and was about to knock when I realized the music was coming from inside the captain's cabin. Then I heard voices. Greene and the captain were inside, talking amicably. What now? I asked myself. What is Greene doing? Perhaps he had come to his senses. I hoped so. Greene was with the captain, there was nothing I could do to warn our Master that night. In the morning I would decide what had to be done. My procrastination sealed the captain's fate, and my own.

On the morning of June 22, 1611, just about daybreak, the dangerous rebellion began. For the mutineers, there would be no turning back. For me it was the beginning of the worst day of my life so far.

John Hudson must have heard whisperings of trouble for he was found hiding below decks, in the gun room – which was not where he slept. When he was discovered there by Juet he held a pike in his hands, ready to do battle. Despite his obvious courage, John was no match for the older sailor who soon disarmed him and marched him to the open deck. There his father stood, his hands tied behind him. Father and son looked at each other without a word. All who cared to notice could see the despair in those two pairs of eyes.

Desperate for escape from his captors, the captain called out to the carpenter, "Help me, Mr. Staffe for I am bound."

There was no answer because Staffe was below decks, held there at the point of a sword. Then Arnold Ludlowe and Michael Butt spoke up, shouting at Greene and his mutinous men to desist. "No good will come of this, Greene. No good at all," said Ludlowe.

Greene ignored him and ordered the shallop hauled alongside where it was held by one of the mutineers. As William Wilson roughly manhandled the first of the sick and lame over the side and down into the shallop, Philip Staffe was brought to the deck, his hands bound behind him. Greene released him and offered him the freedom to stay on board *Discovery*. I supposed that was because of his skills as a carpenter. Staffe replied with a question.

"Are you, Henry Greene, and all you other men, prepared to hang when you reach England? For surely you will."

He glared at Greene, daring him to answer. Greene took his time and then said, "You have a choice. You stay or you leave. Which is it to be?"

Staffe spoke loudly for all to hear. "I will not stay. I serve the captain. I will not be branded a mutineer, unless you make me stay by force of arms."

Greene shrugged his shoulders, waved his sword in dismissal and said, "Then go, Philip Staffe. We do not need you. I will not keep you here."

Staffe then demanded the right to take his chest of tools with him. Greene agreed without argument. With that acceptance, I felt we had some hope. Those tools could be used to build us shelter on shore, or a bigger boat.

"What about you, Woodhouse? Where do your loyalties stand?" Greene asked me, an unpleasant expression on his face. I did not hesitate. No matter what the risk in being cast adrift, I would not disgrace my family and my good name by becoming a mutineer.

"I stand with Captain Hudson, Mr. Greene. I go where he goes and I do my duty."

"Then begone, Woodhouse." Greene pushed me to the rail.

"I would take my sword with me. It was a gift from my father."

"Your sword stays here," Greene sneered. "We have need of it. Now, over the side with you."

"At least allow me to collect my journal and some clothes."

"No. You take nothing. Get into the shallop."

Unarmed, apart from the knife at my belt, and faced by a ring of mutineers brandishing swords, pikes and muskets, I had no choice but to step over the rail and into the smaller boat.

John Hudson lowered himself into the shallop soon after, reaching up with his strong arms to help his father onto a seat. As we found places to sit, I looked around me. The shallop contained nine men: Captain Hudson, John Hudson, John King, Michael Butt, Syracke Fanning, Arnold Ludlowe, Adrian Moore, Philip Staffe and myself, Thomas Woodhouse. Above us, lining the port rail in silence, we could see the mutineers clustered around their new leader – Henry Greene. What folly it was, I thought, for Captain Hudson to have brought that evil man along on the voyage. I noticed that Abacuck Prickett stood apart from his shipmates on *Discovery*. His face was troubled. Nicholas Simms was there too. He had tears running down his young cheeks. There was no sign of Robert Bylot.

In addition to Staffe's tool chest, we took with us a musket, powder and shot, some pikestaffs, plus an iron pot containing food. The loss of my journal weighed on my mind, along with the loss of my beloved sword.

In the beginning, as she sought a way out of the ice, *Discovery* towed the shallop behind her. When the mother ship reached close to open water, the little boat was set free to the accompaniment of jeers from among the mutineers. Once clear of the ice, Greene's depleted crew loosed the topsails and *Discovery* soon made way for the north and east. We followed as fast as we could under our small sail, but soon lost sight of her. With a fair wind, we sailed north in *Discovery*'s wake, with little hope of catching her. A few hours later, while some of the men slept, John Hudson pointed to the north-east.

"There she is again," he cried. "There is *Discovery*. I can see her topsails."

We came up to her quite quickly, as she was by then hove to. We were hoping the mutineers might have had a change of heart and be willing to negotiate. We hoped to return on board and take our rightful places in the crew again. It was not to be. Someone on deck saw us and called the alarm. They crowded on sail and *Discovery* again pulled away from the much slower shallop. Soon we could see no more than a hint of her topsails. Then she was gone from sight. We never saw the ship again. We were alone.

CHAPTER 14

With no possibility of catching up to *Discovery*, which had long since disappeared over the northern horizon, Captain Hudson turned the shallop to the south. There was little wind that day but enough to keep the shallop moving under its single sail. Built to accommodate no more than ten men on short excursions from the mother ship, the little boat now held nine men and some of their possessions. This, however, was no short excursion. Whichever direction we took; wherever we went, the voyage to safety would be dangerous and far from comfortable.

"We have two choices. We can go north and attempt to get through the ice to Davis Strait. If we succeed, maybe there will be whalers there to take us to safety. Or we can go south to place ourselves at the mercy of any savages we meet. Tell me what you wish to do."

This was too much for me. The captain was supposed to be the authority – the one with the experience and knowledge. This was not the time to let the crew make a choice. I looked around at the men. No one had moved. No one spoke up. Most looked at their hands in silence. I raised myself up from a sitting position so I was half standing, holding on to Staffe's shoulder with one hand.

"Captain," I said. "We are but sailors. We will abide by your decision, whatever that may be."

I heard a murmuring of assent from the men around me. The captain looked at me and then at his small crew.

"Thank you, Thomas," he said at length. "We'll go back to the place where we spent last winter." His voice sounded harsh with anger and, perhaps, with sadness. "There we shall try and contact the savages. With their help we can make our way overland to safety. Jacques Cartier's river must be south of there, perhaps only a few leagues, possibly as far as two hundred or more, and all through unknown territory."

"How far is the wintering place, Captain?" asked Ludlowe. "How long will it take us to get there?"

"I estimate one hundred leagues so, if this wind prevails, no more than three or four days."

I thought that was a little optimistic but, still feeling some of the effects of the ague, I kept my own counsel. I had already reminded Captain Hudson that he was still in charge. It was enough. Although I felt he trusted my judgement to an extent, I was no more than an able seaman. While he lived, he must make the decisions. I could only hope he wouldn't fail those of us who had supported him.

I sat down again and tucked my body in between Philip Staffe and Syracke Fanning. We all kept as low as possible to maintain warmth in our bodies. I was scared, so were the others. We all did our best not to show our fears. Young John Hudson sat at his father's side. His face showed no emotion except for a twitch in his eyes. Captain Hudson stared ahead: a captain still, but now in command of a very small ship.

We sailed south under grey skies and on a rolling sea. Captain Hudson took the helm, the rest of us huddled down and tried to sleep. After a while I sensed movement and opened my eyes. John Hudson was sitting up straight, staring into the distance. He raised his head higher and looked beyond the bow, his eyes focused on the horizon.

"There's an island dead ahead," he said. "Maybe we can find food and shelter there."

I stood, holding on to Philip Staffe's shoulder again for support. Just visible under the clouds were two islands, side by side. We should be able to land on one of them. We came upon them a few hours later. The larger island had a forbidding prospect with waves breaking on the west side. The smaller, overshadowed by its neighbour and sheltered from the worst of the wind and waves, showed a foreground of smooth rocks and sand bars. It looked much more promising for our needs. We landed in the late afternoon on a shore littered with driftwood. Never was I happier to set foot on *terra firma.* Without asking permission, Philip Staffe took charge as soon as he stepped ashore.

"Tom, help John King gather wood for a fire. We also need four, maybe six long straight lengths to trim as corner supports for the sail – that will give us some shelter."

Captain Hudson sat on the bow of the shallop, as if guarding the men still crouched inside. His face was blank. John Hudson said something to him, but there was no response. As I stepped ashore, John left his father and said he would help us collect wood. We scoured the shoreline and returned with an armful of small branches each. With that dry fuel, Philip Staffe was able to light a fire in minutes. I hacked one end of a straight piece of wood, about two-thirds my height and as thick as my wrist, into a point and rammed it deep into the sandy soil. John King and John

Hudson helped me with the other lengths. Once we had a perimeter of posts standing erect reasonably close to the fire, we took the sail and spread it over the uprights, tying the ends down to prevent the wind taking it from us. It wasn't the best shelter, but it would do while we assessed our situation. Captain Hudson settled our two injured shipmates under the awning and suggested in a tired voice that we should hunt for food.

The short Arctic summer night was yet a few hours away. John King and Philip Staffe went off to explore the island and hunt for game. They took with them a sword and a musket with some powder and ball. During their absence we collected a load of grasses and pots of fresh water. Once boiled, the grasses, though bitter to the taste, became acceptable as a thin and nutritious soup. If our hunters returned empty handed, we would at least have some additional sustenance to supplement the meale taken from the ship. John and Philip came back to the camp that evening with more wild vegetables and a rabbit Philip had shot.

For those of us suffering from the beginnings of scurvy, the grasses and other vegetable matter proved beneficial in the extreme. The rabbit didn't go far when shared between nine hungry men but we each had enough of a taste of cooked meat to revive our spirits. The carcass, including the head, we stewed in a pot with the vegetables and saved for later when we would be hungry again. Philip cleaned the entrails and threw them in too. He looked at the bloody pelt draped over a rock and said, "We'll save that for later. If we get hungry enough, we can cook it."

Feeling stronger after my meal and having slept for a few hours, I volunteered to go hunting with John Hudson. John shot another rabbit while I brought down a partridge with a heavy stick. It was a lucky throw that would have missed had not the partridge stayed close to the ground. While we were gone other men foraged along the seashore for additional food, returning with small crabs, mussels and limpets.

We stayed two and a half days on the island to regain our strength. We left our camp early in the morning, rigging the sail where it belonged and leaving the corner posts of our shelter standing and the fire yet smoking. The wind was fair, the seas calm. Captain Hudson, who had hardly spoken for over two days, steered for the south. We were all hopeful of an easy voyage for the final few leagues to the mainland. The weather had other ideas.

As the afternoon wore on black clouds began to form on the starboard horizon. The wind veered to westerly and the seas began to develop a sinister roll. The shallop rolled with it. There was no land in sight; no safe haven for us. We would have to take our chances and try to ride out the coming storm.

"Reef that sail, Mr. Woodhouse," the captain called. "Look lively now. We are in for a strong blow."

Out on a stormy sea is no place for a small, open sailing boat. The first heavy gust of wind almost turned us over. Without waiting for orders, Staffe and King dropped the sail and bundled it around us for warmth. As we turned to run before the wind, the first big wave broke to starboard and shed its foaming crest into the shallop. We were instantly soaked. A parade of waves marched down on us out of the west. Each one held the power of life or death over us. We rode them for some time, Captain Hudson using the tiller with considerable skill to keep us stable.

A larger wave than most hit us hard and slewed us round. The next wave completed the assault. Captain

Hudson had no opportunity to correct our drift. We broached and over we went. I sensed I heard the mast snap as we rolled and then I was under water. The sea was icy cold. I managed to surface beside the upturned shallop, gasping for breath, with the captain and John Hudson beside me. Philip Staffe joined us, as did John King, both spluttering and spitting out salt water. Between us, with much effort and by judicious use of the oncoming waves, we were able to right the shallop and help each other aboard. The broken mast with sail attached floated alongside. We hauled mast and sail on board while searching the waves for our shipmates. There was no sign of the missing four. We knew they had to have drowned.

Huddled together, we were five wet and frozen sailors, with only the soaking wet sail for protection. We were at the mercy of the wind and the waves. What little food we had kept from our brief stop on the island was gone. Our drinking water was gone. Our meagre possessions were scattered on the sea bed. The carpenter's tools were there too, along with the few weapons we had had between us. We knew then that our survival was unlikely in the extreme.

John King was in a bad way. He had a long gash on the side of his head with the bone showing through. His face grew paler by the moment as the blood washed out of him. He soon fell unconscious and died at the height of the storm without a word of goodbye. We set his body over the side and into the deep without ceremony, although I did offer a silent prayer and make the sign of the cross over my chest. Only four of us left. Who would be next? I wondered and silently prayed for deliverance. Shivering with cold and a deep-rooted fear, I fell into a sort of sleep. When I awoke the shallop was still afloat. The storm continued to toss the small boat from end to end and from side to side. Philip

Staffe's head was on my shoulder. I tried to push him upright but his head would not obey.

"He's dead, Thomas," said the captain. "He's gone to his reward. I fear we'll be joining him soon enough."

The storm swept over the bay throughout that night. We had no idea where we were or where the wind was taking the shallop. The wind goaded the waves into a fury. The waves attacked us with a force we could not resist. Sometime not long before dawn, I estimated, the captain sat up and stared around him. He cupped his hands to his left ear and listened. I heard it too: the most frightening sound to a mariner's ears.

"Breakers, dead ahead," the captain and I yelled at the same instant. As one we reached for the tiller and tried to turn the shallop into the wind. We were too late. A wave picked us up and hurled us onto the rocks. The shallop disintegrated with the impact. I landed hard, half drowned and winded. Somehow, more by desperation than any rational thought, I clawed my way out of the sea's clutches. I was alive, just, on an alien shore. I lay there in the cold, bruised and battered but sheltered from the wind and waves by a cluster of boulders, and fought to get my strength back. As if from a distance, I heard my name.

"Tom. Tom. Where are you?" John Hudson's voice carried on the wind. It was faint. It gave me hope. Oh, how it gave me hope.

"Over here, John. Over here," I shouted as loud as I could. Staggering to my feet I went looking for my friend and the captain.

I found them huddled together on the rocks near the boat's wreckage, with waves breaking over them. John had a broken leg. Captain Hudson was in a bad way. He had been thrown out of the shallop when we hit the shore and landed chest down on a sharp rock. The impact had crushed his ribs and torn his chest wide open. He died in his son's arms soon after. This, for me, was the saddest day of the voyage. We had lost six of our fellow castaways in the storm. Now we had lost our Master. I thought of the words spoken by Socrates to his judges after they had condemned him to death: "The hour of parting has come...We go our separate ways, I to die and you to live. Which is better, only the Gods know." Only the Gods know indeed. Bowing my head, I said a prayer for the safety of Henry Hudson's soul; then, with John's help, I pushed the captain's body into the sea and away from shore, leaving it to the currents to choose his final resting place in the bay.

The storm passed but the effects stayed with us. Only two of us were left. One was injured and the other weakened by recent illness; both slowly starving to death. We had no food. The only drinkable water was what we found in depressions in the rocks. What little there was tasted brackish from salt spray.

"Well now, John," I said, trying to sound cheerful, "we must look to your leg. We can fashion a splint from the wreck."

"Why?" he asked, his head in his hands. "We are done for, Tom. This is the end for us."

"Come now, lad," I replied. "We are not dead yet. We can make a raft from the remains of the shallop. I remember the current here from late last year. That current should carry us south, to the river mouth, somewhere near *Discovery*'s wintering place. If we are lucky, the shack we built should still be there."

I fashioned a rude splint for John's leg and found a piece of thin driftwood for him to use as a crutch. Between us, working when we had the strength, it took three days to gather enough wood to build a raft, some from the shallop and some driftwood. We tied the bundles together as tight as we could in our weakened condition with strips of canvas torn from the sail. The storm had abated by this time and the sea was calmer. We were able to drag our raft into the water and hold it close to the rocks. I helped John aboard and settled him down on his back. After covering him with what was left of the sail, I said a prayer for our salvation from the sea; then pushed away from the shore.

"You just stay there and rest, lad. I'll paddle for a while," I told John.

Without a backward glance, I paddled our new craft out to sea, using a length of broken planking. The current took hold of the raft and carried her south, as I had hoped. For two more days and nights we drifted. Neither of us spoke. Occasionally I raised my head, hoping to see us in sight of the place where we had wintered. Hoping to see the high hill that I had climbed months before. I must have fallen asleep because a rhythmic banging on the raft brought me to my senses. The wind and current had pushed us ashore where we wallowed between two rocks.

"Come on, John, lad. Come on. We've made it," I said as I tried to stand. I looked down. John had not moved. His eyes were closed. His head rolled from side to side with the movement of the raft. Afraid of what I would find, I put my hand on his heart. There was no beat. I tried the pulse in his neck. Not a murmur. John Hudson had died and I hadn't even noticed. It took me a few moments before I could accept the stark truth. I was truly alone in an unknown wilderness. Worse, I was ill clad, with no food and no sure means of catching any – apart from my knife and my bare hands. At that moment, I felt my chances of survival were so very slim. I sat with John's body for a while.

His corpse was my last link with home and I was reluctant to break the contact. I was more scared than I had ever been.

CHAPTER 15

The thick, dark clouds that had brought such dismal weather for many days began to break up. The wind dropped to a whisper. The sun came out, forcing its light through the layers of clouds and spread its warmth on the land. I took John's knife from his belt and tucked it into mine, on the opposite side from my own knife. As an afterthought, knowing he had no further use of clothing, I removed John's shirt and his leather belt. The shirt I kept for future use. It was in better condition than mine. The belt I wrapped around my waist above my own belt. After a brief prayer, I pushed the raft with John's body on it back out into the current. Maybe, I thought, maybe somewhere he and his father would be reunited.

Very much alone, I lay there on the smooth rocks out of reach of the waves for a long time, resting and drying my clothes. At first, I broke down and sobbed. I hesitate to admit it, but the dramas of the past days had eroded my physical and mental strengths. I was so alone and so scared. Feeling better late in the day, I went in search of food. I found some berries, not yet ripe. I knew to eat them would probably cause me more suffering, though I also knew I didn't have much choice. A thin croak spurred me on. Within a few minutes I had collected and killed about a dozen frogs. Using a piece of wood, I mashed them into a thick paste, pounded some unripe berries in with the resultant mess and ate it raw. I cared not about the bitter taste, of which there was little. It was food. That was the important thing. The crude meal helped to restore my spirits and some of my energy.

I was more frightened and lonely those first few days alone than I could ever have imagined. The only way to keep from going out of my mind was to find work – to find food and shelter; to keep busy. In the tidal pools among the rocks I found a handful of crabs and a few tiny fish. Also, there were many mussels. I broke open the crabs and mussels and consumed the flesh raw. The little fish I swallowed alive and whole.

While I sat there on the rocks, only a few paces from the forest, a twittering caught my attention. I stayed still, thinking it was a bird. Thinking I might be able to kill it with a stick. Instead, a strange creature, the like of which I had never seen, peered at me from the fork of a tree. It was an animal, like a small fox, but with dark rings around its eyes and its long, bushy tail was portioned into horizontal stripes of brown and white. I threw a large stone at the creature, hoping to stun or kill it. I missed and hit the tree instead. The dark-ringed eyes and striped tail disappeared. That failure prompted me to carve a spear from a straight length of wood. Using some of the remains of our sail, I bound John's knife to the end. Now I had a useful hunting weapon, if I could learn to use it effectively.

At Oxford University, in the fields beside the Cherwell River, I had experimented with some fellow students to see who could light a fire by rubbing sticks together. That boyish contest wasted the best part of an afternoon when we should have been studying for exams. However, I did manage to create some smoke and then a small flame. Now, more than two years later, I decided to try again. If I could build a fire, I could keep warm when the sun went down. I could cook any food I caught. Maybe, I could signal for help with the smoke. It was worth a try. First, I had to find dry wood, dry leaves and dry twigs. With warmth and food inside me, I could go in search of the shack we had built on the shore somewhere not far away.

My first attempt at making fire was a disaster. I had found a convenient rock with a shallow groove in it. I rubbed the end of a stick in it until my arms tired but could not generate any heat. Tired and despondent, I buried myself in a thicket and slept fitfully through the evening and night. By morning, my stomach rumbling with hunger, I determined to try the fire again.

With daylight brightening the sparse forest and the sun showing its inviting face, the biting insects came out in force from the damp, spongy ground. Soon annoying red bites covered all my exposed skin – my face, neck, hands and arms. Doing my best to ignore the itching, I worked hard to light a fire and succeeded after a desperate struggle using dry moss and a handful of wood shavings. Once the fire was burning brightly, I added twigs and small branches. As these took flame, I added larger pieces of wood. The fire heated up and glowed red throughout. I piled damp leaves on top to create thick smoke in the hope that someone might see my primitive signal. I found the smoke had another, more salutary effect – it kept the biting insects at bay.

A squirrel chattered at me from a low branch on a nearby tree. I sat still with a stick of wood in one hand, hoping it would come closer. After a few minutes the little creature's natural curiosity caused it to come within range. I had no thoughts of niceties. The squirrel represented food. Even a small meal would be beneficial to me at that stage. I distracted the rodent by tapping the fingers of my left hand on the rock. As it approached to inspect the movements I clubbed it with the stick, killing it instantly.

In England all the squirrels I had seen were either grey or grey tinged with red. This one was covered with black fur. I pondered on this unusual colouring as I stripped the pelt from the body and head. Fifteen minutes later, after holding the small carcass on a stick over the hottest part of the fire, I had my first hot meal in a long time, which I devoured in less than a minute. I kept the pelt and tail, scraping the inside clean with my knife then leaving it on the rocks to dry for a while.

Much as I detested the flying insects, I knew I couldn't sit by my fire all day in the smoke to avoid them. I estimated there was enough fuel on the fire to keep it burning without attention for an hour or more. That gave me time to forage for additional food and fuel along the shore. I returned with a small bounty wrapped up in poor John's shirt. I had found a few crabs, some shrimp, snails and a small fish. I had nothing in which to cook my collection, although a sea food stew would have been appetising. In the absence of a cooking pot, I held the crabs over the fire impaled on a stick. The shrimp, snails and fish, I mashed into a paste on a rock and ate the gritty mess raw.

My situation was bleak. I knew that, yet I also knew it wasn't without hope. There were savages living somewhere reasonably close. All I had to do was find them. Maybe even find the one called Chogan. He had been friendly. There was no reason to believe others of his kind would want to do me harm. Even so, I knew I would have to approach any savages with extreme caution.

I had another important concern. I could not guarantee to be able to start a fire whenever I wanted. In order to travel I needed a method of carrying a permanent fire with me, in some small measure. A cup of some kind, such as a stone hollowed out by wind or wave action would be ideal. Finding one was the problem. I wrapped John's shirt around my head and neck for protection against the torment of flying insects and searched the seashore for hours. There were no rocks that suited my purpose, instead I found a thick piece of driftwood, seasoned by immersion in saltwater, that offered possibilities. I took it back to my fire and worked on it with my knife.

The wood was hard and difficult to carve. That made it almost ideal for my purpose. I worked on it for well over an hour until I had removed enough of the centre to make a crude bowl. This I held over the fire long enough to burn off any roughness and to further harden the wood. The final touch was to bore three holes near the rim of the bowl. I achieved that by heating my knife in the hottest embers of my fire and using the glowing tip as a drill. Finding something to use as twine became my next quest. I found the answer in John's belt. Laying it on a flat rock, I cut three long, thin strips of leather without otherwise damaging the belt. Those three leather strips would act as durable strings from which to hang my portable fire pit. I could then carry hot coals with me wherever I went. With care, I need never be without fire again.

When the black squirrel fur had cured, which took only a short while held over the fire, I wrapped it around my right wrist, in part for decoration, also to add strength to that arm. Without really being aware of it, I was becoming a self-sufficient wilderness man.

Before moving south in search of *Discovery*'s winter shack, I laid out my meagre belongings and tools on the ground. I had two sailor's knives, a spear cut from a sapling, two belts and a means of carrying fire. In addition, I had a spare shirt plus the breeches and shirt that I already wore and a length of sail canvas. My feet were bare as I had lost my shoes in the storm that capsized us, and that was a problem. The soles were not tough enough for me to walk far without injury. I would have to exercise caution and watch every step. The journey would be slow.

In preparation for departure, I wrapped John's shirt around my head as a form of hat – protection against the insects. I buckled his belt above mine around my waist, with the two knives tucked in where I could reach them in seconds. The remnant of sail I draped around my shoulders. I carried my spear in my right hand and my fire bowl in the left. It was time to go.

I had not kept track of the days, so had no true idea of the date. The mutiny had taken place on June 22nd, just after the summer solstice – the longest day of the year. How appropriate that seemed – the longest day indeed. I estimated that had been no more than two weeks before. Therefore, the date had to be somewhere in early July. That meant the long days and short nights were slowly changing. Each day would be a few minutes shorter; each night that much longer. I calculated that there would be, at best, about three more months of reasonable weather. I had to get far to the south before another winter froze the land near the bay. The clear weather allowed greater visibility. In the distance, to the south, I could see a height of land that resembled the hill I had climbed with John Hudson near our wintering place. Whether it was or not, it was something to aim for.

For two hard days I followed the seashore south, reaching the high hill and passing it, until I came to the river almost opposite our wintering place. Crossing from one side to the other would prove to be another challenge. The river was too deep to wade across. Although I could swim, keeping my fire dry would be impossible without some kind of help. On the shore, where the river's slow current and the tide had clashed, there was much driftwood. Tree trunks, stripped of their branches, mingled with lengths of wood from smaller, long dead trees. Collecting as many of the smaller pieces as possible, I wove them into a fragile raft about four feet square. The day was calm, the river sluggish and no more than twenty long paces wide. Stripping naked and placing my precious fire bowl in the middle of the raft on top of my clothes, I pushed it out into the river and followed. Steering the raft with two hands to keep it on an even keel, I paddled with my feet. The water was cold. I splashed with my feet as hard as I dared until the raft touched the opposite shore.

There, a few minutes' walk from the shore, almost hidden among the trees, was the shack we had built at the beginning of the last winter. My feet were cut and bleeding. I was hungry and I was tired. To offset that, I now had a roof over my head and four walls to protect me. I also had my fire. There was no time to rest. I collected dead wood and built a substantial blaze to dry my clothes and to warm my body. The smoke curled up and fled through the hole we had left in the roof for that purpose. The warmth from the fire, my long walk and recent swim had worn me out. Although my stomach cried out for food, a state of lassitude swept over me. I curled up on the floor beside my fire and fell into a deep sleep. I awoke some time later to find a foot on my chest and the point of a wooden spear at my throat.

Book Three
Life with the People of the Muskeg

CHAPTER 16

I had gone to sleep certain that I was alone in the wilderness. Waking up to find a spear poised to rip into my throat and a foot pressing down on my chest, I froze, willing my muscles to be still. The silhouette of a savage stood over me. He lifted his foot and stabbed the point of his spear into the earthen floor by my head. Before I could react, or defend myself, he rolled me over and pinned my arms behind me. I felt him binding my wrists together with some kind of thong. He pulled me to me feet and turned me to face him. I recognized him immediately. He was the same savage who had visited us on *Discovery* at the end of winter. We had not treated him very fairly at that time. I did not expect any different for myself. I called him by name, hopeful that he would remember me; trying to sound friendly.

"Chogan," I said. "Je suis Thomas." He looked startled for a second, though he did not comment. Instead, he placed a noose of rawhide around my neck and tied the loose end to his own wrist. I was obviously his prisoner. Collecting his spear, and without saying a word, he tugged at my bonds and set off along the edge of the forest, within reach of the sea. What was to become of me? I wondered.

Could these savages be cannibals? Had I survived a mutiny and a shipwreck, only to be captured, killed and – perhaps – eaten?

We walked at a leisurely pace over the rough ground for maybe an hour or more. Clouds of biting insects buzzed around our heads, attacking our exposed skin and sucking our blood. Chogan ignored them, as if they did not exist. With my hands bound behind me, I had no defense against their vicious predations and suffered grievously. Not once did Chogan turn to look at me or acknowledge my presence. No words passed between us. He walked, I followed on the end of a leash. I had plenty of time to study his back. He was about my height, maybe a fraction taller, a little broader in the shoulders and somewhat heavier. He wore his long black hair in two braids down his back and decorated with feathers. Also on his back, he carried a bow and a quiver full of arrows.

When we stopped for the first time he tied me to a tree. Satisfied that I could not escape, he vanished into the forest and was gone for half a day, as near as I could tell from the sun. I was beginning to worry that he had abandoned me and left me to die when he returned with a dead animal slung over his shoulder.

Chogan started a fire with a stick of wood, a rock and some dry moss. It took him seconds. Leaving me tied to the tree, he gutted the animal, a small deer, throwing the entrails into the fire and muttering a few words over the smoke. Next, he skinned the carcass with deft flicks of his knife; chopped off the limbs and threw them into the hot coals. Freeing me from my bonds, he made signs that I should watch the meat as it cooked. Chogan then went to the sea and washed the blood off his hands. When he came back he crouched by the fire, pulled out a thin leg and began to strip the cooked meat off it with his knife. He looked at me, indicated the meat and spoke for the first time – and in French.

"Asseyez." Sit. He commanded and then, "Mangez." Eat.

The meat was delicious, tasting of venison. I was so hungry. I cracked the remaining bone and sucked out the warm marrow. After eating his fill, Chogan suspended the carcass horizontally over the fire, with its head still attached. It cooked slowly over the next few hours. I leaned back against a tree and slept for a while.

My feet were in bad shape after the long walk over rough terrain with no shoes. Chogan looked at the bloody cuts and abrasions and grunted. Cutting two equal size pieces of deer hide, he soon made me a pair of soft shoes, with the short fur inside.

"Pakekineskisina," he said as he gave them to me to try on. They were soft and comfortable. Grateful for the gift, I smiled back and said, "Merci, Chogan."

Once the deer had cooked to his satisfaction, he wrapped the meat in the rest of the skin and tied it up in the fork of a tree. Tying my hands again, and fastening me to the base of the same tree, with enough scope to allow me to lay down, he made signs that we should sleep.

At daybreak he released me. We sat on opposite sides of the now dead fire and each ate a piece of cold meat washed down with clear water from a nearby spring. We set off for the south soon after: Chogan in the lead carrying the deer carcass; me at the end of my leash. My feet felt so much better in the deerskin shoes. Late in the day we came to a wide, fast-flowing river. There was no way that I could see for us to cross. Chogan proved me wrong. A few minutes up stream, hidden in a thicket of thorny bushes, he dragged out a canoe.

Paddling a lightweight canoe was a new experience for me. Chogan placed the deer meat in the centre. Motioning me to sit towards the bow, he took his place at the stern.

"Thomas," he called. I was so surprised to hear my name, I almost fell out of the canoe. Chogan had nothing more to say. He just wanted my attention, and he had got it. Waving a paddle, he pointed to a second paddle tucked in beside me. I picked it up and held it poised over the port side of the canoe. Chogan grunted his approval. Working together as well as we could, for I had no experience with a canoe, we paddled up stream against the current, slowly angling towards the opposite shore. When we came close, Chogan gave me a sign to stop paddling. He took us in to a perfect landing, almost exactly opposite our starting point.

A significant change came over our strange partnership as we pulled the canoe out of the water together and hid it in some bushes. Chogan pointed south and, without my leash and with my hands loose for the first time since he captured me, I was free, although not free to leave alone. This time though, I had a burden. The deer meat he strapped to my back weighed me down. I understood that Chogan had offered me a position of trust. If I disappointed him in any way, he would replace my bonds, or he would probably kill me. For my part I was happy to go with him, just so long as we continued on a southerly course. I would have followed him all the way to the Rivière du Canada, if that had been his destination. Unfortunately, we didn't have anywhere near that far to go. After about two hours we came to the banks of another river, much wider than the last one. Chogan nodded at the distant opposite side.

"Waskagahanish," he said. I had no idea what he meant. Was it a statement? If so, what was he telling me? Was it an order? It didn't sound like one and I couldn't imagine what it would signify, even if it was. I looked at him and put my head on one side.

"Qu'est ce que c'est, Waskagahanish?" I asked, stumbling over the long, unfamiliar word.

"Ihtâwin," he answered. I did not understand that word either, never having heard his native tongue before. My facial expression must have told of my ignorance.

"Waskagahanish, Chogan ihtâwin," he explained. I was really none the wiser, except to understand that possibly Chogan's home was somewhere over there.

The river bank where we stood was bare. I looked up and down stream. There were no canoes pulled up on this side of the river. Chogan collected pieces of wood and built a small fire. When it was burning well, he added some wet spongy sod creating a thick pillar of smoke. Then he waited, squatting on his haunches; watching the river. Soon he grunted and stood up. I followed his gaze. A canoe with two people in it angled up stream from the opposite side to cross the current and then drifted down towards our position.

Chogan hailed them, a smile spreading over his face. They called back, their voices light and musical, like laughter. They were women and they were beautiful. Close up it became apparent that they were mother and daughter, their features so much alike. Seeing me with Chogan was obviously a huge surprise. As they ran the canoe ashore they chattered to each other and to Chogan, their voices high. I had no doubt that I was the reason for their excitement. Chogan smiled a lot, nodding happily. He touched me on the shoulder and said my name.

"Thomas," the two women repeated. They pronounced it more like Dommass.

The elder of the two asked Chogan a question. He nodded, still smiling. She turned to me, touched her chest

– pointed to Chogan and said, "Wikimak." I repeated the name and smiled at her. The younger woman, no more than a girl really, touched herself and said, "Alsoomse." I repeated it. "Alsoomse," I said, drawing out the vowels. Alsoomse clapped her hands and laughed with delight. She had been watching me carefully, almost too close for comfort. She reached out and touched my long blond hair, a frown on her face. She stared into my eyes, moving from side to side to see them in different lights. She touched one of her own eyes, which were the darkest brown, and touched one of mine. She uttered a few words of surprise. I assumed she had said, "His eyes are blue."

The introductions over, and Alsoomse's detailed examination of my hair and eyes complete, Chogan piled our burdens in the middle of the canoe. Wikimak, who I assumed to be his wife, took her place in the bow. Only later did I learn that Wikimak meant wife. Alsoomse knelt behind her mother. Chogan placed me behind the cargo before pushing us out into the current. He jumped aboard in the stern and yelled an order. The two women took up their paddles and settled in to a rhythm matched by Chogan. I reached for a spare paddle, looking back at Chogan to see if he wanted my help. He nodded, indicating I should paddle on the starboard side with him while the women paddled on the port side. In this fashion we soon crossed the wide river.

Chogan loaded the fur and skins on his back and the bundle of meat on mine. Walking single file, with the two women chattering behind us, we wound our way over the bog and through a copse of small trees to an open area in sight of a rough stockade of driftwood. The open area was a cultivated field, with ankle-deep wet ground and neat rows of small green shoots. We followed a narrow path through the field and pushed through a gate of thin branches. A group of children came running to meet us. Seeing me, they stopped and crowded together in confusion. Then one shouted, "Emistikôšiw. Emistikôšiw." The others joined in until their cries echoed throughout the village.

I asked Chogan in French what the children had said. He pointed to my face and replied, "Homme blanc." White man.

I learned later that I was in the settlement of Waskagahanish in the land known as Eeyou Istchee. My captor, Chogan, was chief of the local Omushkegowak tribe, or group of families. Omushkegowak referred to the people of the muskeg, or marshlands. I believe I was the first white man most of these people had ever encountered. They were as interested in me as I was in them.

I had survived a mutiny and a shipwreck. Now I had become a slave to a band of savages living in the wilderness. Chogan was my owner. He made that clear. He and his wife ruled my life for the first few months, as did their eldest daughter, Alsoomse. Wikimak was fair though demanding. She had a sharp tongue and a keen eye for her daughter's interests. Anytime Alsoomse came near me during those first weeks in captivity, Wikimak was close by.

The village to which I had been taken lay close to the shore at the southern end of the small bay, although it was not visible from the water. It was a short distance inland from a wide, fast-flowing river called Nemaska. Protected by a stockade made from driftwood standing taller than a man, some of the dwellings were built of saplings covered with thin bark from silver coloured trees. Many others were covered in animal skins. Some of the dwellings, called wigwams, were rounded in shape, others more conical were known as teepees.

Chogan and his family lived in a large conical home. In a mixture of sign language and broken French, Chogan told me it was now my home too. It was my home, but I was a captive – a slave in effect, and would have to work for the family. I slept where they slept. I ate the same food as the rest of the family and they treated well. My clothes were in sad shape. I wore a ragged shirt and torn breeches, with John Hudson's shirt tied round my shoulders by the sleeves, all that I had left of my English clothing. Alsoomse and her mother looked me up and down, said a few words to each other and started work. In short order they made me a shirt, breeches and another pair of thin slippers from soft animal skin, similar to those worn by Chogan and the other men.

My hair was very long and matted. Alsoomse exercised her fascination with my golden tresses by ordering me to wash it in the river. Afterwards she brushed the tangles out with a comb made from animal bones. Then she tied the long hair back at the nape of my neck with a leather thong. Ironic though it might appear, I began to feel somewhat civilized again. I was a young man. I began to look at Alsoomse with more than a passing interest. Even though we lived in close quarters, when any of us dressed or undressed, we did so in the most discreet way possible. I never saw Alsoomse, or Wikimak, in anything other than full dress.

I soon learned that Chogan means blackbird. He had a dark birthmark on his left shoulder that resembled a bird in flight. Chogan and Wikimak had three children, Alsoomse – named for her independent nature, another younger daughter named Kanti and a son. I guessed Alsoomse was two or three years younger than I. The boy, affectionately known as squirrel, was about ten or eleven.

He was already a hunter having killed his first animal – a squirrel, Chogan told me, his pride in his young son evident.

In a surprise move, Chogan returned my knife to me, but kept John's tucked in his belt. The considerate gesture pleased me. I said a thank you but that meant nothing to Chogan. I tried to acknowledge the gift with my smile instead and said, "Merci." He understood the smile and the French word.

When Chogan and the other hunters left the stockade, I had to stay behind. My job was to haul water from the river, collect dry wood for the cooking fires and otherwise help the women whenever and wherever they needed me. I learned that the large cultivated patch outside the stockade was wild rice, one of the staples of the Omushkegowak diet. I had heard of rice but never tasted it. When I eventually did, I found I preferred it to potatoes. While I worked with the women, I thought of ways to escape. The day after Chogan left, with no clear plan in mind, I secreted some food in my shirt and walked away from Waskagahanish. No one noticed. Chogan and his hunters had gone to the east. I turned south, following a river and breaking into a run as soon as I was out of sight. The only weapon I had with which to defend myself, if I should need to, was my knife. I used it to cut and trim a sapling long enough to use as a quarterstaff or a spear. Without thinking of the consequences, I threw the wood shavings into the river. As I ran south, the river took my tell-tale shavings north past Waskagahanish, for all to see.

My freedom lasted a little more than two days. Chogan and another hunter caught up with me as the sun lengthened the shadows on the third day. I did not put up a fight. There was no point. Without my sword, I knew I could not hope to win against two men and escape without injury. Chogan spoke harshly to me, took my knife away, tied my hands behind me and pushed me ahead of him. When we arrived back at Waskagahanish there was much merriment. Everyone seemed to think my failed attempt at escape was a huge joke: everyone that is except Alsoomse. She made it clear that she was offended and refused to speak to me for many hours.

Living and working with the family, in close proximity to Alsoomse much of the time soon became extremely disturbing for me. Alsoomse was the most exotic creature I had ever seen; even more beautiful than Jane Montrose. She had long black hair, dark brown eyes; a sensuous mouth with perfect lips. Her nose was slender; her chin strong. She had skin the colour of light bronze. Dare I say that her breasts were full and proud; her hips finely curved? She spoke softly, her voice rising and falling in a gentle cadence. She moved with such sensuous grace. I found it difficult to keep my eyes off her. Every time I saw her I felt the same pulsating tension in my loins. I seemed to have a perpetual erection when I was in her presence, a fact that embarrassed me in the extreme but did not seem to concern her. She couldn't help but notice my plight, I'm sure. Confidant lady that she was, Alsoomse just smiled and went about her work. Wikimak watched me like a hawk, determined that I should not get too close to her daughter. The only cure for me, at those moments, was to immerse myself in the deep, cold waters of the river until my blood cooled.

I learned that the Omushkego name for the southernmost part of the great bay was Winipekw. The land on which they lived was Eeyou Istchee, which means "the people's land" and their village was Waskagahanish, which means “little house.” The fast flowing river coursing in from the east is the Nemaska. There was another river a short distance away, which flowed into Winipekw from the south. The Omushkego called it Natuweu Nipi.

Chogan made it clear that I could never escape and would be foolish to try it again. Despite his warning, I resolved to make another attempt as soon as I could. Winter could not be far away and I needed to travel as far south as possible before it blanketed the land with snow and ice. First, I needed weapons. Chogan had taken John’s knife from me when he found me asleep in *Discovery*’s winter shack. He also again had my knife and wore both of them in his own belt.

Most Omushkego men are skilled hunters with bow and arrow, as well as with the spear. Recalling my archery days at Oxford, I made myself a bow and a set of arrows with chipped stone points. I couldn’t help but notice the apparent scorn on the men’s faces when they saw me practicing using a post in the stockade wall as a target. A few days before, while shooting alone outside the stockade, I had found that by increasing the tension of the gut string, I could project an arrow across a distance I estimated to be at least one hundred yards. Now, within the stockade I was working to perfect my aim.

One of the younger men approached with his own bow and a selection of arrows. Standing beside me he loosed an arrow that pierced a knot in one of the posts. He indicated that I should try to hit the same spot. My first arrow hit the correct post but was too low. I knocked another arrow and raised the bow higher. This time, when the arrow streaked across the intervening earth, it smacked into the post beside his arrow. He laughed with delight and loosed another arrow. That too landed beside the others. We spent the rest of that afternoon competing, with more young men joining us as the word of the impromptu archery contest spread. At the end I felt I had acquitted myself well and, to my pleasure, had made a few friends. The archery contest had been a useful distraction. Later, in the night, the loneliness of my position came back.

My thoughts continually turned to England. Despite my attraction to Alsoomse, my desire to escape and find some way to get home became stronger by the day. I knew the river nearby flowed from the east. The other, a few leagues down the coast from Waskagahanish, flowed from the south. It was the same river I was planning to follow on my first wasted escape attempt. That river could lead me from one river to the next and an eventual route to the sea. I remembered Captain Hudson talking about the Frenchman, Jacques Cartier, who sailed up a long wide river which, according to Captain Hudson and maps I had seen, had its mouth in the vicinity of latitude 49 degrees. Cartier claimed to have sailed inland against the current in a south-westerly direction to the latitude of 45 degrees. If that river was a passageway between east and west, it could flow somewhere close to those latitudes for much of its length. Our wintering place with *Discovery* was at about 50°. Therefore, the mean difference between Waskagahanish and Cartier's river had to be approximately 4 degrees. One degree of latitude equals 20 leagues. That equated to a possible 80 leagues from Waskagahanish to the big river, as the crow flies. If only I had some way to determine longitude, my escape journey would have been somewhat less daunting. As it was, without a clock or even an hourglass, and without knowing accurate time anywhere, I could not place myself on a line of longitude. My journey could be twice the distance I had calculated, or even more.

I was confident that, given the strength and food for sustenance, I could find my way to civilization by navigating using the sun by day and the stars by night. That, however, would rely on clear skies at all times.

I soon began to understand that my original assessment of these people as savages was far from correct. They had a well-ordered form of civilization, which, although quite different from European values, especially those held in England, was nonetheless efficient. Despite that, at first I suspected they were God-less people, at least as we understand religion.

As I learned the Omushkego language from Chogan and his family, so Alsoomse became a student of English. She brought me items of clothing and demanded to know the name in my language. We walked together in the forest, or by the river, and we named all the things we saw. Alsoomse gave me the Omushkego name. Whenever I could, I told her the English equivalent. Our conversations made no sense to anyone else yet, somehow, we began to understand each other more and more.

Alsoomse asked me one day how I came to be on their land when Chogan found me. I told her about my long voyage in *Discovery*, even sketching a ship under sail for her in the earth. She could not imagine a canoe big enough to carry so many men, or understand the concept of a sail, which she thought represented clouds. Remembering my childhood games beside the Thames River, I carved a small boat from a block of wood. When it was shaped to my satisfaction, I added a stick for a mast and a piece of thin cloth for a square sail.

"Come with me to the river," I said. "I want to show you something."

The wind was blowing up stream, ideal for my demonstration. I set the boat on the water in an eddy where there was little movement from the water.

"Watch," I instructed Alsoomse. "Watch what happens when it finds the wind."

No sooner said than done. The wind caught the sail, turned the boat so its carved bow faced into the current and began to push it up stream, one boat length at a time. I was thrilled to see a small bow wave appear where it should be.

"Now, do you see, Alsoomse? The wind is pushing the boat up river against the current. I came to Winipekw in a huge canoe with many big sails like this one." I spread my arms out wide for emphasis.

Alsoomse picked up my little boat and examined it, turning it from side to side and end to end. She put it back in the river and gave it a little push. The miniature boat picked up speed, was pushed into the current and soon lost to sight.

"Will you build a big canoe, Thomas?" she spread her arms wide. "Will you build a big canoe with clouds on top and go away from us to your own people?"

"I don't know how to build a big canoe and even if I did, I could not sail it alone."

"Then I will help you and I will go with you." It was a statement of intent; not a question.

"Perhaps. One day," I answered. "Come, it's time for your English lessons."

In addition to educating Alsoomse, I was also teaching the village children. I spent an hour or so each day, when possible, sitting with them, my back against a tree, and telling them stories of my homeland and of my life at sea. They did not understand most of my words, even so, they appeared to enjoy my performance. Given enough time, I hoped, one day, to teach them to speak English and French. After one such session, Alsoomse came to me.

"You, not Thomas," she announced. "You now Otácimow – the storyteller." And so from that moment on I left Thomas behind and became Otácimow. I felt as though this change of name reflected another positive stage in my assimilation into the Omushkigowak way of life.

I have learned to my distinct pleasure that the Omushkegowak do believe in a deity rather like ours. They call him Kitchimanito, the Great Spirit. He lives in the sky and when people die, they go to join him in the spirit world. It's not Christianity and yet, in its simplest form, it is so similar. Discussing the Great Spirit with Alsoomse one day, I told her of our churches, even sketching an outline of the abbey at Dorchester on the ground. Alsoomse did not understand the concept of a church, or a priest. It made no sense to her.

"The Great Spirit is everywhere. He sees everything. Why do you need to hide behind walls, or under a roof? He can see you and hear you out in the forest, or on the river."

Unable to explain, I could only agree with her; asking myself why my family had ever gone to church when God was everywhere, just like the Great Spirit. The subject came up again one evening when the heavens erupted into green, purple and white lights, like a parade of colourful, shimmering ghosts. I confess, I was afraid – thinking the display might be a portent for the imminent end of the world. Alsoomse had no such fears. She stood with me beside Winipekw watching the sky with a beatific smile on her face.

"What is it?" I asked. "What is happening? What does this mean?"

She could sense my fear and held my hand in both of hers. "Don't be afraid, Otácimow," she said. "Those are the spirits of our ancestors come to see us again and to make sure we are happy."

As I watched, I felt sure there must be a more rational explanation for the eerie phenomenon but could not think of one. Alsoomse's version was the best I could get. It would have to suffice. I tried another question.

"If those are spirits, does the Great Spirit look like that? Does he look like colours in the sky?" I wondered aloud.

"I don't know," answered Alsoomse, with a frown. "No one knows. No one has ever seen the Great Spirit."

We watched the heavenly parade of rippling lights until they softened and faded from view, leaving the sky dark until the stars could again sparkle through. The extraordinary show of lights had unsettled me, probing at my mind; turning it into a confusion of conflicting ideas. With no higher intellectual authority - such as Professor Rushworth - to help settle my thoughts, I needed my mind to return to reality: to return to more earthly questions. I needed to concentrate on the subject of escape, to be precise.

My captors had lightweight canoes, like the one that brought me across the river with Chogan. I was surprised when Chogan told me that the women of Waskagahanish build canoes as well as the men. I could not imagine any of the women I knew in England even attempting such a task. There were four large canoes at the riverside belonging to the people of Waskagahanish, and a few smaller ones – they seem to be communal property. I had studied their construction carefully. The framework was made from saplings – I don't know from what tree. It appeared to be somewhat similar to willow but with a reddish colour. The frames were bound together with cord, which, Chogan told me, came from the intestines of forest animals, such as bears, caribou, or beaver. The canoe builders sealed the knots in the cords with dried resin or sap from selected trees. The skin of the canoes intrigued me most of all. It was thin, yet strong, rather like a parchment. I suspected this was the bark from a form of birch tree. I asked Chogan where the skin came from.

"From trees," he answered, and pointed up river. "Up there, above the first big waterfall, there is a beautiful grove of these trees. We peel the bark in strips from the living tree."

Gradually a new escape plan was forming in my mind. If I could build a lightweight canoe and get some provisions, I could paddle up the river, travelling so much faster than on land. I vowed to ask Alsoomse to help me with the canoe, without telling her of my ultimate plan.

Sitting beside our smoky fire with Chogan, talking about the art of canoe building, he showed me a large piece of delicate birch-bark with beautiful patterns, like butterfly wings, somehow stencilled on it. I had never seen a form of art like it. Yet, at once, I could see its potential for decoration, or for trade.

"Is this for your new canoe?" I asked. "How does the pattern get on the bark?"

Chogan answered, "Mazinibaganjigan." Seeing I did not follow the complicated word, he looked around him. "Alsoomse," he called. When she appeared, he spoke rapidly to her, much too fast for me to follow the guttural sounds. Alsoomse took the decorated bark in one hand, folded it carefully without creasing it and held it to her mouth, showing her teeth. Then, she made a motion of biting the bark. I understood at once. The patterns had been placed on the bark by an artist's teeth, but what had been used for a dye, or ink? I left that question for another time when I understood more of the language. I made a mental vow to go and see this stand of birch trees for myself. Another idea was already forming in my mind. In addition to building my own canoe, I could use the thinnest bark as paper – for writing paper, if I could find something to use as ink.

The next time Chogan went up river to collect birch-bark, I went with him. We paddled a large canoe as far as possible against the fast current and then took to the land. Above a thundering waterfall, just as Chogan had said, stood a beautiful grove of white birch trees. Chogan taught me how to cut and peel the thin bark without tearing it. After a few false starts I found it quite easy to do, although a slow process requiring a steady hand. We returned to the village with enough bark for two canoes and more left over for my writing needs.

There were many dogs at Waskagahanish. Every family seemed to have at least one or two. Most were scruffy, bad-tempered mutts. Few were considered pets. They all shared a single purpose – to assist in hunting. The dogs were fed on scraps of leftover food, plus whatever they could hunt on the nearby land. Alsoomse had her own dog. She called him Samoset, "He who walks a long way." He was an exception, being a hunting dog and a much loved pet at the same time. I called him Sammy and he responded to either name. Sammy was of unknown breed, a mixture of many, I suspect, with a lot of wolf in him. Alsoomse groomed his thick coat regularly, a process he enjoyed very much. She said he followed her everywhere, until I arrived. Perhaps sensing a similar need in Alsoomse's strange new friend, Sammy soon attached himself to me and was rarely far from my heels after that.

Chogan took me hunting with him towards the end of summer. Sammy went with us. Chogan had seen my prowess with bow and arrow, and my skill with a spear. Now he wanted to see if I could put these accomplishments to a real test. Much as I wanted to find a way to escape, I was excited at this new opportunity. I even wondered if I might be able to flee while Chogan's attention was elsewhere. That, of course, was unlikely to happen. We paddled one of the canoes up the river that flowed from the east. Close to the waterfall we had climbed on our expedition to cut birch-bark, we stopped, hauled the canoe ashore and made a rudimentary camp. We would hunt inland from there. Chogan was hoping for deer, but any large game animal would be acceptable.

I had seen white bears from *Discovery*'s decks. From that safe viewpoint, I really did not have any idea how powerful bears could be. I had never seen a live black bear, although there was a pelt from one stretched on a rack in the village. Even the size of that coat had not prepared me for a face to face encounter with a living beast. Sammy warned us of the proximity of danger. He extended the ruff on his back and neck and a low growl rumbled in his chest. Chogan saw the bear first and cautioned me to be still. At my signal, Sammy crouched low, the growling soft yet menacing. The bear was cross wind from us; not an ideal situation. The bear stood about fifty paces away and showed no sign that it knew of our presence. It continued foraging for berries and stuffing them into its mouth to help sustain it through the coming long hibernation.

Chogan whispered to me to stay put. He began a slow walk sideways to get downwind of the beast. I knocked an arrow and stood still. The bear either sensed our presence or heard the slight sound and immediately charged. Sammy launched himself forward. Chogan shouted as loud as he could and waved his arms. The bear changed direction, racing straight for him. Sammy changed direction to intercept the bear. Although Chogan had shouted to protect me, his actions put him in immediate danger but gave me a clear shot. The bear was a big target, broadside to me and halfway across the gap to Chogan when I loosed my arrow. Sammy was already snapping at the big creature's heels. I had aimed for the bear's large body, hoping to hit it anywhere and disable it. Instead my arrow pierced the beast under its right front armpit and must have gone straight to its heart. The dead bear tumbled head over heels and came to rest on its back at Chogan's feet with Sammy snarling and snapping his teeth close by.

"Hiyhiy," Chogan chanted. "Thank you." He clapped me on the shoulder and said, "Now you are a hunter like the Omushkegowak."

At that moment I could not imagine any higher praise. We stood grinning at each for a few moments until our hearts slowed to normal and we could breathe again. Chogan then showed me how to skin the bear without damaging the pelt. He started from the snout and finished with the feet. With his skills, the process was fast and efficient. I knew it would take me a lot of practice before I could perform the task half as well. After washing as much of the blood off as possible in the river, we folded the pelt and loaded it into the canoe. We cooked some of the meat, which was delicious although quite strong in flavour, and threw a few bloody scraps to Sammy to reward his bravery. The rest we piled into the canoe and set off downstream for Waskagahanish. Our hunt was over for now. We had enough meat to feed many families for a few days and I had the material for a winter coat. On our arrival Chogan was most effusive with his praise of my bravery and my hunting skills. He told everyone who would listen and, as he was the chief, that meant all in the village. I had become a respected hunter with one lucky shot.

Autumn arrived bringing with it a splendour I could never have imagined. The many varieties of trees put on their finest presentations of the year. As if to celebrate the change of seasons, they painted their leaves in tones far beyond my experience. The trees delighted in their own extravagance. They showered the land in red, in yellow, in gold and green, in dark shades and in light. Walking through this wonderland, with Sammy snuffling through the bushes sampling the fresh smells of autumn, I had no doubt that only a supreme being could have made such a beautiful country. I sat at the base of an old spruce and said a prayer of thanks to my God for sharing his extraordinary artistic talents with me.

The winter at Waskagahanish was quite different from the previous winter aboard the frozen ship *Discovery* and occasionally in the shack on shore. At the end of autumn, before the first snow fell, I discovered why we had not encountered any native people during *Discovery*'s winter sojourn in the ice and why we never saw smoke from cooking fires over those long months. One morning Alsoomse said to me, “Today we leave for the winter hunting grounds.”

CHAPTER 17

Everyone was leaving. Waskagahanish would lie empty and quiet until the spring. All the families were busy packing their homes and belongings. All that would be left to tell of our summer presence was the stockade. The strongest hunters went ahead, following the river upstream. The other men, women and children followed, foraging for food on the way. Some of us travelled by canoe; the rest by land. All would meet far to the east in the deep forests of the high lands beyond the waterfalls.

Alsoomse and I travelled together in a canoe she and her mother had built on the river bank near Waskagahanish. Sammy divided his time between the land and the river. Much of the time he ran along the river bank with the other dogs, hunting small creatures as he went. When he tired he would bark at us to let him ride in the canoe. For all the dogs, the annual migration was an exciting event. Indeed, it was an exciting event for all of us, perhaps especially for me as our destination was unknown. I hoped it would take me nearer my eventual goal.

We travelled for five days. To my disappointment, I noted we were moving east, ever east, not south where I wanted to go. We passed the waterfall where I had killed the black bear a few weeks before. We camped beside the grove of birch trees. We passed two more falls, carrying the canoes on our shoulders to reach the river above. Everything we owned had to be carried in this way. Each waterfall required many trips on land to get everything to the top. At the end of the fifth day we arrived on the shores of a small lake where there was the semblance of a tired old wooden stockade.

"Nemiskau," announced Alsoomse. That, I soon learned, was their name for the lake and their winter hunting grounds.

A village of tepees and rounded wigwams soon built up inside the enclosure. I was put to work with the women, strengthening the stockade while the hunters set off into the forest. A trio of older men took one of the canoes and a fishing net out onto the lake. As I worked, I came to accept that escape from this place at this time of the year would not be possible. I would have to bide my time until we returned to Waskagahanish in the spring.

Life at the winter camp was not at all unpleasant. The biting insects of summer had all gone. We dressed in animal furs to keep warm. We always had log fires burning in the teepees and wigwams. I wore a suit of black bear fur over my deerskin shirt and breeches: the same bear I had killed at the end of summer. Alsoomse had a similar wardrobe. Chogan was most impressive in a suit made from a great white bear he had killed a year or two before. When he went out into the snow to hunt, he could merge into the whiteness until none but the sharpest eyes could see him. On our feet we wore knee-high boots with fur inside and out. Worn over thin socks of soft animal skin, they were surprisingly warm. I soon found that walking in deep snow without help was tiring. The Omushkegowak had solved that problem by tying special racks to the soles of their feet. They called them Asam.

The snow shoes, for that is the only way I can describe them in English, were shaped like giant tear drops, usually two or three times longer than a man's foot. They were constructed by the same skilled men and women who build the lightweight canoes, and with similar materials. The snowshoes were strong and they were light, with wood frames containing a tight network of string – dried intestines of animals. They were efficient. Most snowshoes had the forward edge curved up to avoid digging into the snow and the trailing edge tapering off to a long rigid tail. They really were remarkable contraptions. Wikimak and Alsoomse showed me how to make a pair to fit my big feet. Once I mastered their use, I found walking on snow easy to do and was surprised at how fast I could move.

As the winter advanced, we set our traplines for snow hares. Larger than the variety of hares found in England, their coats turn white in winter for camouflage. We also tried for other small mammals, plus the much larger caribou – a form of deer. We hunted a large wild cat that left tracks around our camp, but without success. And we came faced to face with one of the most dangerous creatures I had ever encountered, the formidable wolverine – Chogan called it a kayvik. We never saw the great white bears in winter. Chogan told me they hunted seals far out on the ice of Kitchikumi. The black and the brown bears were all asleep in dens dug into the ground beneath the snow. He said they would sleep all winter and only come out when spring warmed the land.

The wolverine looks like a bad-tempered bear, though much smaller. We surprised one in the afternoon a few leagues from the camp. The wolverine was feasting on a deer that had succumbed to the winter snows. We approached from downwind, without being aware of its presence at first until one of the older hunters held up a hand for silence and for us to halt. He sniffed the air, whispered to Chogan and pointed directly ahead. Following hand signals, we fanned out in a line and moved forward. The wolverine must have sensed the presence of danger for it stood up on the carcass of its prey and glared at us – no more than one hundred paces away. I noticed its paws were large, out of all proportion to its body and head. In overall size, it wasn't much bigger than a large dog.

The hunters raced left and right on snowshoes to cut off its escape. I stayed with Chogan where the beast could see us. It sprayed a smelly musk on the deer carcass, snarled at us in anger and turned away. A dog or almost any other four-legged creature would have sunk up to its belly in the deep snow. The wolverine did not sink. It ran across the top of the snow (I assumed it was able to do that due to its over-large paws) and took refuge in the fork of a tree. Chogan cautioned me not to get close. He made signs that the beast could leap from the tree and attack.

The first arrow to hit the wolverine caught it high up on its padded shoulder. It screamed in fury and launched itself from the tree towards one of our men. A volley of arrows whined across the snow towards the animal as it charged. Most of them missed. We were lucky no one was hurt. The wolverine took three more arrows in its body before it slumped into the snow, spreading bright red blood over the pristine white. The hunter who had fired the first successful arrow claimed the kill, as was his right, although he shared the overall honour with three other men. They all stood around the body thanking the wolverine for giving its life for us. I don't think my arrow went anywhere near the wolverine. I was too nervous and excited to aim properly.

Hunting was always like that. There were moments of extreme concentration tinged with fear, offset by sometimes hours, or days of tracking and often frustration and hunger. Each season was different. Hunting in summer was a little easier than in winter. Hunting moose in the autumn was more comfortable than hunting geese in spring when the snows were melting and the ground became soft and spongy. Apart from trapping in the snows, we cut holes in the ice of Lake Nemiskau and fished for a variety of large species, such as the formidable fighting pike and the tasty trout.

My friendship with Alsoomse blossomed over the winter. When I was not working with the women or hunting with the other men, I spent much time with her maintaining a line of traps that spread out two or three leagues from the camp. We laughed a lot together. Jane Montrose spent more and more time tucked away in the recesses of my memory. Alsoomse particularly showed amusement at my frequent mistakes when setting traps in the early days. I suppose it was inevitable that our friendship would grow into a romance. We were young and we were healthy. We worked together. We smiled at each other a lot. We allowed our hands to touch whenever possible. Sometimes when we were alone, following our traps through the forest, she would trip me over and we would wrestle for a few minutes in the snow. Always she would be the first one to break away and get to her feet. The happy smile never left her face.

The nights were most uncomfortable and frustrating. As one of Chogan's family, I slept with he and his wife, their younger daughter, their son and Alsoomse, all scattered around the floor of the tepee. Sammy usually crept in and curled up beside Alsoomse while I lay awake in the dark desperate to hold her in my arms. She had made it clear that nothing of an intimate nature could happen between us without her father's consent. As I was his slave, he was unlikely to agree to such a union. Knowing, therefore, that Alsoomse could never be mine made the frustrations even worse. I began to spend more and more time away from the winter camp hunting with the other young men. Often we would be gone for a week or two at a time. On our return, Alsoomse always greeted me with her broad smile and sparkling dark brown eyes. She would reach out and touch my hand, or my shoulder, but no more. The ache in my heart and in my loins reminded me to plan for my escape as soon as the weather improved and we were back at Waskagahanish.

In the spring, as the winter snows melted and the land turned green again, we returned to the old stockade near Winipekw and prepared for warmer weather and a new season of living, planting rice and vegetables and hunting.

CHAPTER 18

About a week after we returned to Waskagahanish, while I was repairing a canoe with Alsoomse and her mother outside Chogan's tepee, I became aware that someone was watching me. A warrior leaned against a post in the stockade wall his eyes fixed on us. He was well muscled, maybe a year or two older than I. He was handsome enough but the scowl on his face gave him a sinister appearance. I had noticed him watching us a few days before.

"Who is that?" I asked Alsoomse, nodding in his direction. "He wasn't with us at the winter camp."

"His name is Eagle Heart. He is a skilled hunter. He has been away hunting all winter near Waswanipi, far away. He is kahkentam, jealous of you, because he wants me for his woman." She shuddered a little, yet Alsoomse's statement made it sound as though their eventual union was a foregone conclusion. I bristled at the thought. I was an outsider, a white man, a slave. None of that changed the way I felt about Alsoomse. I was hopelessly in love with her. I think I had been since I first saw her on my arrival at Waskagahanish as her father's captive. Noting the expression of loathing on my face as I glared back at the man named Eagle Heart, Alsoomse said softly, "Be careful of that one, Otácimow. He is a strong fighter and, akwatišiw – he is cruel."

Cruel or not, instinct told me I would have to fight him, sooner or later, if I wanted any possibility of making Alsoomse my own. Having long since fully recovered from my lonely survival ordeal of the previous year, regained my strength, put on some much needed weight and toned my muscles over the winter, I was at my strongest. I decided to choose my time carefully, if I could. My future adversary had a different plan.

Eagle Heart sauntered over to where we sat. He grabbed Alsoomse by the arm and pulled her to her feet, kicking over the framework of the canoe we were working on. Alsoomse struggled and yelled at him to let her go. He laughed and dragged her away. The challenge was unmistakeable. The decision of timing had been taken from me. I could sit back and do nothing or... I'm afraid my impetuous nature took over. Sooner or later became now. I rose to my feet, reaching for my wooden spear.

"Eagle Heart," I called. "Let her go."

Eagle Heart pushed Alsoomse roughly aside so that she fell to the ground on her face. With a cry of triumph, he reached for his spear, which he had left stuck upright in the earth close by. His face creased into a satisfied smile. He was ready for battle.

Stick fighting, or pole fighting, using a quarterstaff was a popular sport among my friends in Gravesend and, indeed, while at university. I had become rather proficient at the game, though I had not practised for a long time: not since on *Discovery* with John Hudson, in fact. For this contest, which could mean a fight to the death, I would have to recover all my earlier skills at once. My wooden spear would have to serve a dual purpose – spear and quarterstaff. I twirled it in both hands, spinning the weapon on its own axis. The balance was okay. It felt good in my hands, but I was nervous. I changed my stance and assumed the low guard – my left hand on the butt of the staff and my right hand halfway up the shaft. My right hand and right foot pointed forward, facing towards Eagle Heart. Insofar as it was possible, I was ready.

My opponent faced me, balancing on the balls of his feet. He held his spear in one hand above his right shoulder like a javelin. His intent was clear, to impale me with his first thrust. I stood still and waited. Eagle Heart screamed something at me. It sounded unpleasant. I stayed silent and stayed still. He moved two steps forward, making stabbing motions with the spear. It occurred to me at that moment that he too was nervous. Something in his eyes told me he was about to attack. With a mighty throw, he launched the missile at me. The spear crossed the intervening space between us in a second or so. Had I stayed still, the point would have split my heart in two.

Instead, I moved half a pace to the right, turned a little to the left and deflected the spear with a flick of my wrist and a touch of my staff. The spear grazed my shoulder as it flew past, tearing my shirt but not drawing blood, before ripping through the birch-bark fabric near the top of Chogan's tepee beyond. Round one to me, I thought.

Eagle Heart grunted in annoyance. He signalled to one of his friends who threw him another spear. This time Eagle Heart held the spear with both hands, like holding a pikestaff, and took a few paces towards me. I stood my ground. He shook the spear at me as he advanced, growling deep in his throat like an angry bear.

I was aware of the attention of most of the villagers, including Chogan. He stood to one side, his arms folded across his chest and a thoughtful expression on his face. Alsoomse stood beside him, her face an expressionless mask behind the streaks of dirt from her fall. Wikimak stood with a group of women. Apart from an occasional shouted comment from one of Eagle Heart's supporters, the villagers remained silent; watching and, I assumed, wondering how long I would last against one of their best warriors.

"Keep coming. Keep coming," I breathed softly to myself. Eagle Heart continued his approach, dancing in his anticipation. He was a graceful yet ominous sight as he growled at me, stabbing at the air with the point of his spear. I noticed he had changed his approach. Now he was moving sideways, to his left, as well as forwards. I turned a fraction, maintaining my stance. With a scream that came from far inside, he attacked. As he ran forward he changed his grip on the spear, copying the way I held mine. He was fast, closing the gap between us in one breath.

He raised his spear to bring it crashing down on my head. I parried the blow so it glanced off my temple and then my jaw. Even so, the spear opened a cut above my eye, split my lip and caused me to bite my tongue. Stepping aside, I turned him with a strong clout of my own; then tripped him by thrusting my staff between his legs as he blundered past. Eagle Heart rolled in the dust, cursing and spitting. Round two to me, I thought.

I should have hit him hard right there and then while he was down and finished the fight. Instead, my ingrained sense of fair play took over. I faced him and waited as he slowly got to his feet. Now I had to defeat not only his strength but also his anger. I could only hope that rage would make him careless.

As Eagle Heart rushed me, I reversed my staff, making as if to hit his legs again. He jumped high in the air, his legs apart. Seeing my opening, I changed my grip, and brought the butt end of the staff up between his legs as he came down from his jump. Powerless to avoid the blow, he took it hard in his crotch and doubled over, gasping in pain. Showing no mercy now, I swung my staff in a circle, catching him on the side of his head. He collapsed in a heap, out like a candle in a hurricane wind. I am not one for coarse language, yet the fight had brought out the worst in me.

"Fuck you, Eagle Heart," I shouted as I spat blood and saliva into the dust.

As I walked away, I ripped off my blooded shirt and threw it on the ground. Spitting blood from my split lip and tongue, I turned to look at Chogan and Alsoomse, blood streaming down one side of my face and dripping onto my shoulder. For the first time the people of Waskagahanish saw me with a bare chest. There was a collective gasp of surprise. Alsoomse stood with her mouth open. I glanced at Wikimak. She was looking at Alsoomse, an expression of concern on her face. Chogan unfolded his arms and walked towards me, a severe look in his eyes. He reached out and touched the prominent tattoo on my right shoulder.

"Kakako," he said, his voice filled with awe.

"Yes," I replied. "It is a raven."

He removed his buckskin shirt to bare his own chest. The vivid birthmark resembling a blackbird in flight showed clearly on his left shoulder. Chogan stood beside me, his left side against my right. He held up his hands to quell the murmurings from his people.

"This emistikôšiw (he used their name for a white man, or European), Otácimow, who came to us from far away across Kitchikumi, the great sea, is a powerful warrior, as you have seen today. He is a good hunter and has already killed Masko, the black bear. He is also our storyteller."

Chogan pointed to my tattoo and then to his own birthmark. "Otácimow has been marked by the Great Spirit, as I, your chief, have been marked," he thundered. "I tell you now, he is as my son. He is a free man."

Chogan spoke a few rapid words to Wikimak, who furrowed her brow before nodding her agreement. He motioned Alsoomse forward. Placing her left hand in mine, he said to me in a loud, clear voice so all could hear, "Otácimow, you are now a man of the Omushkegowak. If you want my daughter, Alsoomse, and if she wants you, then you have earned the right."

In a quieter voice he said, "You should have killed Eagle Heart when you had the chance, Otácimow. Now you will have to fight him again someday, and next time he will kill you, if you do not act first."

I glanced sideways to where Eagle Heart had fallen. He had gone. All that was left was a pool of vomit and some blood. I had no doubt he would return some day.

CHAPTER 19

My only experiences of the congress between a man and a woman had been the urgent couplings of my youth at Oxford with Brenda, the serving girl. Rough and ready though most of our encounters had been, in alleys and in hay lofts, Brenda had taken the time to teach me where and when to touch her. She had coached me when to be gentle and when to be forceful. The lessons learned from that lusty girl would now stand me in good stead with Alsoomse.

Among the Omushkegowak there was no such thing as a formal marriage ceremony, not as I understood it from an English point of view. Chogan asked me if I would take care of his daughter. He asked if I would hunt for her and feed her well. He asked if I would give her strong babies. I answered in the affirmative to all his requests and that was that. I was a married man with a beautiful native wife.

Alsoomse's mother had taught her the mysteries of the union between man and woman. That first night together, after she had bathed my lip and the cut on my forehead, we went to a small tepee of our own. There, in peace and privacy we removed all our clothes and united our bodies and our lives in the most pleasant way possible. All thoughts of escaping were gone. I still missed my English home and family. They were always there in my mind yet, at last, I was content.

Wikimak accepted me with a certain amount of reluctance. I'm sure I would not have been her first choice of husband for Alsoomse. However, Chogan had spoken and Chogan's word was law. There was not much Wikimak could do about the union. For the first few weeks she watched from a distance as Alsoomse and I began to share our lives. Her concern, I assumed, was perhaps typical of a mother-in-law.

I had been experimenting for some time with fluids taken from insects and from young trees, trying to create a form of ink. I had sheets of birch-bark ready for use and eagle's feathers sharpened for quills. So far I had not been able to write legibly. My first attempts at making primitive ink faded almost as soon as it touched the thin bark. I asked Alsoomse for help. She took me into the forest where we spent hours collecting a certain type of beetle. Once we had enough, she crushed them to produce a thin stream of dark, almost black liquid. It worked perfectly on the bark paper and the ink retained its density once it dried. At last I could write.

I made myself a new backstaff. It was far from perfect in appearance but should, I hoped, assist me in determining my position. One morning I took Chogan's canoe and paddled alone down to the mouth of the river, where it opens into the bay. There, when the sun was at its zenith, I took a series of readings. To my great surprise, I ascertained that Waskagahanish is on almost the same latitude as my hometown of Gravesend. As near as I could judge, they are both on latitude 51° N. Why then, I wondered, why is the winter weather so much worse here at Waskagahanish than in southern England? If the two areas are on the same latitude, they are the same distance north of the equator. Why is it so much colder here in winter than in Gravesend? I experimented over a few weeks, taking sun sights whenever I could. Each time my calculations led me to the same conclusion. Waskagahanish and Gravesend were on the same degree of latitude.

One morning, soon after I had reached my conclusions, I tried to explain the concept to Alsoomse. Pointing to the east, where the sun was just beginning to spread its warmth over the forests and rivers, I said, "My home is over there. Beyond the sunrise."

"Then we must go to your village and meet your people," she announced and started gathering our bedroll and cooking pot.

"No. No, Alsoomse. It is not so easy. My village is on the far side of a great sea. It would take many moons in the biggest canoe ever built to cross."

Alsoomse looked at me in surprise, and then shook her head. "Otácimow," she said, turning me to face the north-west, "Kitchikumi, the great sea, is there beyond Winipekw. It is there, not – there." She pointed first to the north-west, and then to the east.

"Alsoomse, my love. There is another sea. A sea even greater than Kitchikumi. It is wahnaw, far away." I pointed to the east again. "It is over there, where the sun comes up. I think it is many moons beyond Eeyou Istchee."

Seeing the puzzled expression on her face, I took a stick and sketched what I believed to be a reasonable representation of the New World in the earth at our feet. That crude map reminded me of how far I was from the land of my birth and my English family. It reminded me how different I had become from the sophisticated young gentleman who had sailed away from England. I could almost hear Papa saying, "When you come home, you will be different."

That night, under a cloudless sky, we stood together and watched the stars. I pointed out Polaris, the North Star, well known to all mariners. Alsoomse told me the Omushkego name was Kewatino Achak. Tracing the seven stars we know as the Big Dipper, Alsoomse said, "Ochekatak." Looking at the familiar constellations, as I often did, a brief sense of longing for my homeland and my family passed over me. The stars we were looking at were the same constellations I had studied in my youth. They were the same stars that brightened the night sky over my far away home. I imagined I could journey to the stars and from their lofty viewpoint see into my family's house in Gravesend. Would they approve of Alsoomse, I wondered, knowing the answer was almost certainly no, they would not, because they would consider her a savage and, therefore, far beneath me.

Out hunting alone one day, with only Sammy for company, I shot an arrow at a ring-tailed creature in the fork of a tree. As the arrow sped towards its target a young raven playing with a stick flew across its path. The arrow clipped the bird's wing and brought it tumbling down. Deflected from its purpose, the arrow missed its intended victim and disappeared into the forest.

The raven flapped about on the ground, trying to get its damaged wing to work properly. Sammy pranced around the injured bird barking with excitement. When I picked it up, the raven pecked me at first and voided its bowels over my hand. It settled down as I stroked its wing feathers, seeming to understand I was a saviour, trying to help it.

We took the raven home with us where I put a splint on its wing in the hope that it might set properly. It never did.

Alsoomse didn't understand why I had not killed the bird outright.

"Because it's a raven, a kakako," I told her. "It is my symbol."

From that day on the young raven, now named Kacky, was with me most of my waking hours. When she wasn't riding on my shoulder nuzzling my ear, she rode on Sammy's back, hanging on to the ruff of his neck. One morning she found her way to the apex of our tepee and perched there, her eyes constantly on the lookout for anything edible. When a large dragonfly flew past, also questing for food, Kacky launched herself from her lofty perch – forgetting she could not fly. She spiralled out of control and crashed at Sammy's feet, missing the dragonfly by a wide margin. Sammy grinned at her and received an irritable peck on the nose. Kacky was not amused. With a loud squawk she jumped onto Sammy's back, complaining at full voice. Alsoomse and I laughed so much we almost cried.

We ate a lot of fish, which Sammy and Kacky both enjoyed as much as we did. We took them from the rivers and from the bay. We fished with nets strung out in the river from the bank to an anchor of stone marked with a block of wood for a float. It is an efficient way of catching fish yet lacks the simple pleasure of sitting on a riverbank with a rod and line attached to a baited hook. Alsoomse had never seen a fish hook of the kind we used in England and I could not find the words to describe the tool to her in her own language. Instead I resorted to drawing a hook in the dirt and then showing her with my fingers how small it needed to be. A few days later she gave me a tiny hook, complete with barb and eyelet, carved from a piece of bone and polished to a shine. I only used it for fishing once, successfully I should add. After that, especially pleased with the carving, I hung it around my neck as an ornament. I don't think I had ever been happier than in those first few months with Alsoomse. My former life in England was far away and slipping further from my mind each day. As a free man, I could have walked away whenever I wished. I didn't. I was happy with Alsoomse and my native family. I no longer considered any form of escape.

Chapter 20

I had not seen Eagle Heart since I beat him with my staff in the early spring. His absence lulled me into a false sense of security. I was surprised, therefore, when he and his two friends returned to Waskagahanish at the summer solstice. They carried with them a substantial load of moose meat, some pieces on their backs and the rest on two trellis frames dragging behind them. Most of our people, Chogan included, greeted the returning hunters with the warmth they deserved for supplying the village with such a bounty. I stayed away, unsure of how to act. Eagle Heart reminded me that the animosity between us had not faded. He looked in my direction, cleared his throat and spat phlegm towards me. His two friends laughed. I nodded, knowing that the time was close when we would fight again.

For the next few days, I carried my spear and my knife with me wherever I went, even within the confines of the village. I warned Alsoomse that Eagle Heart was back and to be careful. She had concerns of her own.

"Do not trust him, or his friends. They will challenge you when you least expect it and they will work together to bring you down, just like the wolves."

During Eagle Heart's absence from the village I had practised daily with my staff, a new spear and my knives. I could hit even the smallest target from a long distance with knife or spear. And, thanks to energetic exercising, I was nimble on my feet and with my hands. I was carrying fresh water from the river to our tepee with Alsoome when one of Eagle Heart's bullies tripped me, spilling all the water. I picked myself up and said, "I have no fight with you, Black Crow, yet you spill our water." I held the skin bucket out to him. "Now go and fill this for us in apology."

Black Crow knocked the bucket from my hand and grunted an insult. I knew Eagle Heart could not be far away and would be watching my reactions. Black Crow had a squat face like a toad. He was a powerful young man with huge shoulders and a barrel chest. He moved with a lumbering walk that belied his natural speed. I knew he would be a dangerous adversary if I let him frighten me. Without warning, I drove my clenched fist into Black Crow's stomach. As he doubled over I brought my knee up to break his nose and down he went. Picking up the bucket, I said to Alsoomse, "I'll refill this; then it's time to go home."

We walked without haste to our tepee carrying the heavy bucket of water between us. There I collected my knife and my spear.

"Stay here, please," I told my wife.

"My place is by your side," she answered and followed me out into the afternoon sun.

Eagle Heart stood in the open, a knife in his left hand and his spear in the right. His two friends stood a little behind, one to each side. I noticed with considerable satisfaction that blood was still running from Black Crow's broken nose.

A few minutes before the open area in the middle of the village had been empty, now, as if at a pre-arranged signal, there were men, women and children thronged around the open space, including Chogan and the elders.

"Go to your father, over there," I ordered Alsoomse. "I can handle this alone."

She held on to my arm. "No. He will kill you," she said, her voice trembling.

"No, he won't. Today, if anyone dies, it will be Eagle Heart." I was not nearly as confident as I sounded. Raising my voice, I called, "What do you want with me, Eagle Heart?"

He smiled, his lips curling from humour into a sneer. "You have attacked and injured my friend, Black Crow," he said. "Now you must fight me."

"I have no wish to quarrel with you, Eagle Heart," I called. "It is not necessary for us to fight again."

Eagle Heart sneered at me and spat, "Ushaakuteheu!"

Coward. That was arguably the most unpleasant word in his language, and one of the worst insults to a man in mine. I sighed with sorrow. Eagle Heart and his friends had backed me into a corner, so to speak. There was no way out of it without more bloodshed in a final contest. Taking off my shirt, so the raven could feel the air, I prepared for battle.

Alsoomse stood near her father and other elders, close but not touching Chogan for support. She stood alone. Yet she stood tall and proud, with her hands by her side. I smiled at her. She smiled back. Her bravery, which had never been in question, made me so proud to be her husband at that moment. I hoped I would not disappoint her in the coming duel. I took a deep breath, my eyes on my opponent. Making the sign of the cross over my head and chest with my right hand, I prepared for the fight of my life.

Eagle Heart moved slowly to his right, like a cat on the prowl. He held his spear high above his shoulder, its point aimed at my heart. His knife was ready in the other hand to stab the life out of me. Behind him and off to each side, his henchmen waited. I noticed one carried a spear and a knife, with a heavy wooden club at his feet. The other held a drum and stick. The battle would not necessarily be one on one.

I walked, one short step at a time, also to my right, my staff now spinning between two hands, a blur of motion. My eyes focused on Eagle Heart's dark, hooded eyes. The drum started to beat. My opponent began to dance. He appeared to ignore my presence as he whirled and twirled, his feet stamping the earth to dust. His movements were hypnotic. To control my nerves, I put my staff through all the moves I expected to have to make to win this contest. I fell into a pattern. Without intention, I was exercising to the insistent beat of the same drum that drove Eagle Heart. For those few rhythmic moments, the two of us, bitter enemies, were, briefly, in unison. I knew, instinctively, when the beat stopped, Eagle Heart would strike and for one of us, death would follow.

The rest of our village, and although I couldn't see them, I am sure they were all there, stood around the perimeter in silence. Even the children seemed to sense something momentous was about to happen. They stood in front of their parents, imitating their silence, maintaining the sombre emotion of the challenge.

Without warning, the drum beat changed. It speeded up to double time and Eagle Heart's gyrations followed. His dance became an exotic blur. I balanced on the balls of my feet, my staff ready to defend the imminent attack. The beat stopped. Sudden silence dominated Waskagahanish.

Eagle Heart's spear was halfway to my heart before the drum's final echo bounced off the stockade wall. I was slow to react: much too slow. I fended off the missile, turning it with my staff so it missed my chest. Instead, Eagle Heart's spear hit me in the fleshy part of my left shoulder and knocked me off my feet.

There was no pain, at first. The spear had torn my flesh, leaving a long open wound. I rolled with the blow, still holding my staff, and found my feet. Eagle Heart was halfway across the clearing, running at me with his knife in one hand and a club in the other. I knew I had to keep him at bay with my staff. If he got inside my guard, I would be finished in no time. Fighting in the sporting style of an English gentleman was out of the question. I had to take charge and win this battle by fair means or foul, and I had to do it as fast as possible.

Unable to use my left arm with any skill, I battered at Eagle Heart with my staff, using one hand only. He concentrated on swinging his club at my already injured left arm and shoulder. For a few moments we hammered at each other. Eagle Heart remained on the offensive. I had to defend against each blow. As I turned to protect my left, he changed his stance, swinging his club horizontally and knocking my staff from my hand. I just had time to draw my knife from my belt before he was on me.

As Eagle Heart closed with me a second time, he threw his club away, the blade of his knife alone searching for my throat. In desperation, I knocked his arm aside and pulled him to me in a chest-to-chest embrace. As I did so, I thrust my knife up between his ribs and deep into his heart. My adversary died with no more sound than a gentle sigh.

Leaving my knife in him, for I would never want to use it again, I lowered Eagle Heart's body to the ground. I was covered in blood, his and mine. It mingled with the sweat from my exertions and ran in crimson streams to soak into the waist of my breeches. In death, my enemy and I had become brothers in blood. Facing his henchmen, I flexed my arm and shoulder, trying to get some life back into it as the pain began. I took a deep breath and spoke to them, and to them alone in a loud voice.

"Do you wish to fight me as well? If so, you must do it now, together or one at a time, because after this day this bloody feud will be finished. Make your choice now."

I was angry. I was sad. I had had enough. My determination and my emotions were obvious to all watchers. "Well, Black Crow," I called. "What is it to be, death now or peace for ever more?"

Black Crow looked at Chogan who stood there expressionless. He turned to the assembled villagers. There was no encouragement there. He said something to his friend who nodded. Laying their weapons on the ground, they stepped back. The battle was over but I hadn't finished with them.

"Listen to the words of Otácimow," I called in their language so all could understand. "Here lies the body of Eagle Heart. He was a great hunter. He was a mighty warrior. He was a brave man. He was your friend. Take him now, honour him and wash him in preparation for his journey to meet the Great Spirit."

Having said my piece, I retired to my tepee. Alsoomse followed me in. Without a word, except a low keening, she cleaned and dressed my wounds. When at last she spoke, her voice was soft and low.

"It is over now, Otácimow. It is over." She brushed my lips with hers and held me close. No matter what she said, it wasn't over. Not for me, and I knew it never would be. I had killed a man. Nothing could ever change that. I felt the tears streaming down my face as, exhausted, I fell asleep wrapped in my lover's arms.

I awoke some hours later. Alsoomse was beside me, sleeping in peace. I lay there, thinking of Eagle Heart, the man I had murdered. Making the sign of the cross, I prayed for his soul and for my own. Even now, from the vantage point of many years, I shudder to think of that awful day. I am not a violent man. I never have been. I am a good Christian. I could have subdued Eagle Heart without taking his life. I should have subdued him. I would never be able to forgive myself for that final vicious thrust with my knife: the thrust that ended a young man's life. It was a memory that I would never be able to erase.

While I slept in Alsoomse's loving embrace, Eagle Heart's two friends took him from the village and buried him in the forest. In accordance with custom, they laid him in his grave wrapped in his bearskin cloak, with his club, his knives and his spear beside him. They never did return to Waskagahanish. It was as if they had died with their leader.

CHAPTER 21

Although the land on the western and southern shores of Winipekw are marshland and mostly bare of trees, except for small shrubs, the eastern shore is somewhat dryer and is well endowed with forests of trees, from many different species. In summer the mosquitoes and the vicious blackflies were far more numerous and active over the western marshes. For that reason, we lived and hunted on the eastern land although there were still many areas of soft marsh and many insects. We kept the pests at bay with liberal applications of bear grease on our exposed skin.

We were out foraging one day in late summer, walking along the marshy land close to the shores of Winipekw where the ducks and geese landed to feed among the flocks of smaller wading birds. We had been gone from the village for a few days, camping out on the land with Sammy. Alsoomse was explaining the difference between the various plants – which ones were edible and which ones poisonous. Neither of us was paying much attention to the surrounding terrain. Alsoomse was deep in thought and I was watching the birds when I fell into a mud and water-filled hole in the muskeg. I went down feet first and was sinking quickly, to my knees, waist and soon to my shoulders.

"Alsoomse," I yelled. "Take my staff and pull hard. I'm sinking."

Alsoomse pulled with all her might. I moved with my feet as much as I could while holding the other end of the staff. When I was close enough to touch, Alsoomse lay face down on the marsh and reached out her hands to mine. Sammy barked his concern and his encouragement, reaching forward to take the sleeve of my shirt in his teeth. Slowly, inch by inch, they helped me to safety. We lay there on the damp muskeg side by side, both gasping for air while Sammy showed his affection with his tongue. We stayed there for a long time. Then Alsoomse rolled over and kissed me.

"You are not supposed to frighten a future mother," she said.

My brain took a few minutes to process her words. I sat up and stared at her, asking a question with my eyes.

"Yes, Otácimow," she laughed. "You will have a son when the next winter snows have melted."

I stood up; pulled Alsoomse to her feet and held her to me. We were both soaking wet but laughing with happiness. Next spring, a son, she said. The news was almost too much for me to take in.

"How do you know this baby will be a boy?" I had to ask, being completely innocent of such events as birth. Perhaps mothers-to-be received a special sign. "How do you know?"

"I feel it here, deep inside. You, too, will know soon, when he starts to kick in the night."

We went home to our tepee arm in arm, a couple of very happy young people. Our happiness was short-lived. Waskagahanish was in mourning. Chogan sat outside his tepee with his face in his hands. I could hear Wikimak sobbing inside. The villagers were silent, except for a child's cry and women expressing their grief.

"What has happened?" Alsoomse asked. "Why is everyone so sad?"

Chogan made no sound although his pain was evident. We learned the story from a young hunter. Chogan and Wikimak's son, Alsoomse's younger brother, Squirrel, had been hunting above the rapids with a friend. On their way home, racing down the rapids, the canoe had turned over. Squirrel had drowned. This was the worst calamity that had befallen the village since I had been there. Chogan, his wife and daughters, and the rest of us, mourned Squirrel for many weeks. Chogan rarely came out of his tepee during that sad time.

The autumn turned to winter. At the Nemiskau hunting grounds Chogan slowly recovered his former strength of mind and character, though he never smiled or laughed. We hunted together many times, while at home Alsoomse grew bigger by the week. The baby would soon be with us.

My relationship with Chogan had gone through many changes. We had progressed from captor and slave to a family bond. He was my father-in-law. He was my mentor. He had become my friend.

I was hunting with Chogan, soon after we returned to Waskagahanish as the snows melted. We had left Sammy at home with Alsoomse, who was getting near her time. We should have taken the dog with us. His instincts and his nose were far more attuned to the air than ours. We followed caribou tracks along the seashore where the breeze off the sea kept the clouds of biting insects at bay. The caribou we tracked was either injured or old, Chogan told me. He guessed it was lame. Killing it would be a mercy for the caribou and a substantial store of food for the village.

We expected it to be tiring and when it did, we planned to be there to finish it off. After two days we lost the tracks on a long ledge of flat stones beside the water. Chogan cast around for some minutes trying to pick up a sign. He moved away about twenty paces from me, off to my right and a little ahead where there were still patches of snow. I was looking down, trying to pick up the tracks when Chogan said.

"Otácimow, caribou came this way. A white bear is following it. We will wait here."

I ran to his side, jumping over a snow hummock that suddenly moved. Startled, I rolled sideways, hit the ground and came face to face with a little white head fronted by a black nose and wistful eyes. Without thinking, I grabbed the bear cub and stood up to see Death in white with blood around its mouth coming to its hind feet behind Chogan. The baby's mother had scented us and turned back. She rose up behind my friend, towering over him.

"Chogan," I screamed, "Nanuk. Right behind you."

Chogan didn't look over his shoulder as I would probably have done. He turned his complete body to meet the danger. Holding his spear ready to defend us, he challenged the bear to attack him. The struggling bear cub whimpered. I held it high above my head and shouted abuse at the giant facing Chogan. The bear stopped. She stood there, her huge paws waving at shoulder height. Her nose sniffed at the air. Her eyes fixed on her cub. A deep growl rumbled from her open mouth. Chogan took a step back.

"I'm going left," I told him, moving at the same time, still holding the struggling cub; still shouting. Desperate to distract the deadly bear so Chogan could either go for its heart or get away.

"I'm going to throw the cub at the bear," I yelled, my voice harsh with fear. "You get ready."

Chogan nodded his understanding but his eyes never strayed from the bear. I kept moving, slowly, always holding the cub high where it could be seen. The bear watched me sidestepping away from Chogan. When I was far enough that he should have been out of the bear's peripheral vision, I hurled the cub with both hands at its mother, hitting her in the chest with the screaming bundle. For a second or two the bear fumbled with her baby. That was all the time it took for Chogan to roll forward in smooth somersault. He came up on one knee with the butt of his spear on the ground, the point at about 50 degrees and already reaching for the bear's heart. Chogan gave a mighty upward thrust. His aim was true and the bear toppled forward, the cub still cradled in her arms. When we rolled the dead bear over we found the cub had been killed in the fall: crushed between the weight of its mother and the hard ground. Even in death the bear held her baby close. It was, I reflected, a sad tableau.

We found the dead caribou not far away. The bear had caught it and broken its neck. The caribou also had an old injury on one of its forelegs. The great white bear's powerful jaws had bitten almost all the way through one of the hind legs. As we were skinning the bear later, Chogan stopped. Leaning back on his haunches, he looked at me with a shake of his head.

"Otácimow," he said, "we were very lucky today. What you did was brave but stupid. I don't think that would ever work again." He grinned at me. The first time I had seen his smile since Squirrel's death. "I wouldn't try it. But I'm happy you did."

I laughed, more a reflex of nerves than humour. "I expected you to run, not stay and fight. That bear could have killed you."

Chogan ran the blade of his knife down one of the bear's legs and peeled back the pelt. "Never run from a bear, especially a white bear," he said. "You either have to fight or die. No man can run faster than Nanuk."

I made a mental vow to avoid bears whenever possible. Soon my son would be born. He would need a father to guide him in the ways of the hunt. One blow from a bear could deprive him of all that.

We now had an abundance of fresh meat, far more than we could carry between us. We also had the heavy pelt of a white bear, a much smaller pelt from the cub and the valuable skin of a full-grown caribou. Between us we assembled a rude sledge. It wasn't pretty but it carried our burdens, it ran smoothly and, harnessed in tandem, we could pull it over the grass and snow patches without undue effort

.

Chapter 22

Our son was born with a shout that was more laughter than a cry of indignation. He took his first real breath and he smiled. When the midwife and Wikimak finally allowed me to hold him he was asleep, sated by his first feed of mother's milk. Wikimak watched me with my son, ready to step forward and catch him if I should drop the baby. When she saw how I held him and, I expect, the look of love in my eyes, she relaxed and rewarded me with a beaming grandmotherly smile. He slept. He fed. He burped; he slept some more. When he was awake, he smiled or chuckled. He was a happy boy. We soon found out that he also had a temper, especially when hungry or soiled. His bad moods though never lasted long.

"What is our son's name?" I asked Alsoomse, knowing she would have already chosen something appropriate,

"His name is Ahanu. It means one who laughs a lot," she answered.

"Ahanu," I said, letting him curl his tiny fingers around my thumb. Then I added, "Ahanu Thomas Barnaby Woodhouse." I thought it a fine name for a half-English, half Omushkego boy born in the forests of a New World.

From that day on, until he could manage on his own two feet, Ahanu went everywhere with us, held securely in a soft skin bag on Alsoomse's back. All that could be seen was his little face and a pair of bright brown eyes that seemed to notice everything. Ahanu grew quickly. As he took his first cautious steps when he was nine months old, he hung on to the fur on Sammy's back with one chubby fist. Sammy, by then in the middle years of his life, adored his little friend. Kacky, now an old bird with a bad temper, was not so fond of the child. She did her best to avoid Ahanu's attentions by clawing her way up the tepee and screaming abuse from the top.

That did not deter Ahanu in the least. He took hold of the tepee's skin covering and shook it as hard as his little muscles would allow, all the while calling Kacky to come and play. Kacky would have none of it. Until Ahanu lost interest, she would stay far out of reach, only coming down when I snapped my fingers at her, and then only to perch on my shoulder – still out of the little boy's reach. Despite their difference of opinions about Ahanu, somehow, in the wisdom of their advancing years, the two animals seemed to understand the importance of the new life that had come to Waskagahanish. They seemed to understand, also, that their time was slowly coming to an end.

Kacky left us first when Ahanu was two years old. We heard Sammy whining outside the tepee and found him full length on the ground, his once raucous and rowdy pal lying still between his paws. Ahanu helped me bury Kacky in the forest. When we returned to Alsoomse, Ahanu announced, "Mama, Kacky gone to meet Great Spirit."

CHAPTER 23

Living in the forest for so long and hunting fur-bearing animals, my thoughts strayed back to the day that Chogan had visited us on *Discovery*. I thought of the small number of furs he had to trade on that occasion and Captain Hudson's interest in them. Holding a cured beaver pelt in my hands, I wondered what it's value might be in England, or elsewhere in Europe. I looked around my tepee at the pile of furs we used for floor covering, for blankets, for clothing and for decoration. We had black bears and brown bears. We had deer, wild cat, beaver, raccoon, mink, muskrat and more. Their meat had sustained us through the annual seasons. We had never taken more than we needed. What, I wondered, would we do with all the meat if we hunted more for trade than for our existence? My musings left me with much to think about for the future.

When Ahanu was seven we took him with us on an extended hunting expedition. By then he was already showing signs of the man he would become. His black hair was long, tied back at the nape of his neck. His keen eyes noticed everything. He had a long, slim body and longer legs. Although still only a child, he carried his weapons with confidence and he was fearless. Ahanu had known none of the privileges of my childhood, yet he was a happy boy with a marked intelligence.

After three weeks following and servicing our long trapline far inland, we were on our way home to Waskagahanish, Alsoomse and I each with a load of furs strapped to our backs. Ahanu trotted along beside us with his bow and arrows at hand to protect us if necessary. Alsoomse stopped suddenly; held up her hand for silence. I listened, but could not hear anything unusual. Standing straight beside us, Sammy raised the hair on his back, a sure sign of trouble. He began to bark. Alsoomse quieted him with a hand over his face.

"What is it?" I whispered, drawing my knife from my belt. "What can you hear? Is it a bear?"

"No," she answered. "It's not that. She sniffed the air. "Iskotewakan," she said, her voice betraying a certain amount of fear. I sniffed the air. Yes, I could smell fire too. Two nights before we had sheltered under a homemade lean-to from a violent storm, with thunder rumbling and crashing through the clouds and lightning stabbing jagged bolts of fire at the forest. One of those strikes must have hit a dry tree and ignited it. Under the hot, brittle conditions of mid summer, the fire could easily have spread along the ground, feeding on the undergrowth and had now grown into a raging menace.

"Pimipahta. Pimipahta. Run. Run, Otácimow. We must get to the river if we can."

With unerring skill, Alsoomse darted through the forest, jumping over fallen logs, squeezing through bushes and racing over soft open ground with Ahanu at her side. Burdened as I was with a heavier load of pelts, I was slower but my longer legs made up for the difference in agility. Sammy ran with Alsoomse and Ahanu. Squirrels, raccoons, rabbits, foxes, skunks, wolves and an old black bear ran from the danger. In their panic, they ignored us and we, including Sammy, ignored them. Some ran one way, some another, all desperate to get beyond reach of the flames. We ran until a wall of smoke and flame blocked our route.

"This way," shouted Alsoomse, changing direction; now running parallel to the fire and into the light breeze. "We must get beyond it or find a way through. The river is just over there." She pointed towards the flames. At a place where the fire thinned out enough, Alsoomse took Ahanu by the hand and changed direction, charging through the wall of flames. Without hesitation, I followed her. My eyebrows, hands and the fringes on my shirt got singed in the terrifying heat. I closed my eyes against the smoke and ran on. With a splash, I blundered into the river, landing beside my wife and son. We were lucky to have landed in a shallow eddy where the strong current could not reach us. Taking off our heavy packs and jamming them into the low bank, we crouched as close to the water's surface as possible, leaving just enough room to breathe. We had all suffered burns, though none too serious. The fire burned most fiercely among the trees about twenty paces inland. Smaller bushes along the riverbank smouldered but none had caught fire, so far.

"Where is Samoset?" cried Alsoomse. "He didn't follow us?"

"No, he didn't. He will find his own way to safety. He'll be close to the river somewhere downstream."

A black bear and her cub floated past, keeping far enough off shore to stay clear of the fire, but not so far that the cub would not be able to swim to land when it began to tire. I'm sure they saw us but were too busy avoiding the flames to care about our presence. In the distance, almost drowned out by the roaring and crackling of the forest fire, I heard a plaintive bark. Sammy was still alive and letting us know his location. I shouted his name as loud as I could. Ahanu joined in with his much smaller voice. After that the ominous sounds of the fire dominated everything. I estimated an hour went by; then another. As the fire closest to us decreased in ferocity, we heard heavy breathing coming towards us. A few minutes later Sammy came into view. Paddling against the current and keeping close to the shore, he was working as hard as he could to make headway. I reached out and caught him by the scruff of his neck as he reached the eddy where we waited. Ahanu clutched his pal to him with both arms around the dog's neck.

"Sammy. My Sammy," he crooned into the dog's wet fur.

A change in the wind took the remnants of the fire away from us. I lifted Ahanu and then Sammy onto the riverbank and climbed out after them. Alsoomse handed me our heavy packs before I pulled her up to join us. Sammy was so excited we were all together again. He shook water all over us. He danced with joy, spinning in circles in his happiness. Thanks to the fact that we were all soaked, and so were the furs we carried, we were able to walk roughly parallel to the now dwindling fire along the riverbank without getting scorched. Our clothes steamed; so did the furs. We didn't care. We were alive.

Over the next few years we watched our son growing into a young man. Alsoomse taught him to set efficient traps. I taught him to hunt using stealth and skill. His grandfather passed on to him the legends and history of the Omushkegowak. His grandmother consoled him when he lost his first love. Between us, we schooled him in languages and I made him study a crude map I had drawn of the world on birch-bark. At night I told him stories from the history of England.

Sammy grew old. He spent most of his time either sleeping in the sun or staggering around behind Ahanu on his old legs. Only the enthusiastic wagging of his tail reminding us of the hunter he had once been. Sammy died quietly in his sleep one afternoon. Ahanu found him and came to tell me.

"Papa," he said, as I sat sharing a pipe with Chogan, "Sammy has gone to see the Great Spirit."

Once again Ahanu and I went into the forest where we put our old friend to rest beside his pal, Kacky.

Chapter 24

At seventeen Ahanu was a big, strong lad, his skin coloured gold by his mixed race parentage. His hair had the same ebony sheen as Alsoomse's; his eyes reflected the darkest leaves from autumn's artistry. His laughter, which had reverberated around Waskagahanish since he was born, was as clear and fresh as it had always been. Everyone considered Ahanu a man. He had proved himself worthy of the name. Because of his hunting skills and his looks, the young women of our tribe admired him very much.

Ahanu had made his first kill at the tender age of ten when he put an arrow through a raccoon from fifty paces away. He became a warrior at fourteen in a brief skirmish with some Iroquois bandits. During the fight against the intruders, he took another man's life to save mine.

We were cutting birch-bark with two others of our people, far up the river that flows from the east, in the grove above the first waterfall, when the seven strangers attacked. Due to the noise from the nearby cataract, they were able to come into the large stand of birch trees where we worked without a sound. Ahanu was the first to sense their hostile presence.

"Pîtosiyiniw," he warned me in a whisper. Enemy.

I looked around, my knife at the ready. A movement among the trees betrayed the first of the intruders. An unknown man stood there with an arrow pointed straight at me. My friend, Omikikon, hefted his spear, threw it hard and took the man down. An arrow ricocheted off a tree trunk by my left shoulder. Six remaining warriors glided into the clearing, each armed for war. Each prepared to fight us and, if necessary, to die.

Ahanu called to them in our language, asking who they were and why they wanted to fight. One of them shouted back, saying they were Iroquois from far to the south come to hunt and we were in their way.

"This is not your land," replied Ahanu, his voice strong and loud. "This is the land of Eeyou Istchee and we are Omushkego. It is our land; our hunting grounds."

The Iroquois ignored him and attacked. The three of us stood with our backs to each other in a defensive triangle. The enemy circled us, holding their spears, axes and knives at the ready.

"Two each," said Ahanu, with more than a hint of bravado. "We can take them down."

All three of us waited. "We are too close together. Move apart," Ahanu ordered, taking two steps forward. We obeyed him to give the enemy less bulky targets. A warrior flew across the clearing to me, too fast for me to react as I should have. Before I could defend myself he had me by the throat with one hand and was about to plunge a knife into my guts with the other. Ahanu reached sideways, grabbed my assailant by the long hair, pulled his head back and slit his throat.

The fight went out of the others as their leader fell. Omikikon took down a second warrior with a well-aimed throw from his axe. The three remaining Iroquois made threatening gestures but came no closer. One, in a last stand at defiance, knocked an arrow and shot it at Ahanu. It missing him by the thickness of my son's skin. That was the last move the warrior made. Ahanu speared him through the chest.

We talked about the attack with our elders when we reached home a day later. Our words would go into the immense store of Omushkegowak legends and be passed on from the elders when the winds blew cold around the cooking fires in winter. I made my own record, preferring the incident to be in writing. Chogan said he had never heard of Iroquois this far north. One of the other elders disagreed. He said, "They came once before, when I was a boy. They killed some of our people and stole two of our women. My father had to track them for many days before he and his warriors caught them on the edge of Eeyou Istchee."

"Was your father able to rescue the women?" I asked, even though I knew the story. The old man looked sad. "No," he said. "The Iroquois killed them, right in front of my father's eyes. One of them was my mother."

That final confrontation, as I knew from the stories passed down, had resulted in a bloody battle that had lasted for days until the Omushkegowak avenged the loss. Few of the Omushkegowak I had known showed aggressive tendencies. Most were happy to live their lives in peace, hunting, trapping, growing vegetables, raising children and following the seasons. Peaceful they were: afraid to defend their people they were not. I hoped the Iroquois would have the sense to stay in their own lands to the south.

Thinking back to the day I had shown Alsoomse how a sail worked, I built a model canoe as long as my arm, added a lee board that could be raised and lowered, installed a slim mast and dressed it with a square sail. I played with it on the edge of the river, watched by Ahanu and Alsoomse. When I felt I had the balance right and could trust the canoe on the river, I tethered it to my hand with a long cord and set the sail. The canoe responded to the wind and stayed upright.

"What are you doing, Papa?" asked Ahanu.

Alsoomse stood beside our son, her arms folded across her chest, a slight smile on her face. The recognition dawned suddenly. She looked at me and laughed. I knew at once she remembered the story of *Discovery* and had guessed my intentions.

"So, Otácimow, at last you will build the big canoe with clouds on top," she said, her eyes sparkling with delight.

"Yes. This is a model. I wanted to see if it would work as well as I hoped. I think I can convert one of the big canoes to this system. I'll try anyway."

Over the next week, with Chogan's blessing, I took one of the four-place canoes and went to work. I added reinforcements to the hull amidships and to the sides in the same area, plus an extra length of wood inside as a keelson. A tall sapling became my mast. I had decided to use a lateen sail but there was no cloth available. Animal skins were too heavy. Alsoomse suggested using birch-bark, with the pieces stitched together into a patchwork arrangement. It worked tolerably well although I could see that raising and lowering the sail would eventually result in the thin bark cracking. Alsoomse solved that problem too. She spread a thin seam of resin along the potential problem areas and left it to dry in the sun.

"Where are we going in this canoe?" Alsoomse asked after I had tested it on the river for an afternoon.

"I want to explore the west coast of Winipekw to see what is there," I answered. "I was there once before on *Discovery* but did not go ashore. This canoe will take me along the coast in safety."

"You will take Ahanu with you?" It was a question and a statement at the same time.

"Yes, if he wishes. Don't you want to go with us?"

"Oh, no. Too many flies and mosquitoes over there," Alsoomse shook her head. This was to be a journey for men only.

"Ahanu. Will you go with me?" I asked.

"Of course, Papa. I'll get my weapons." Ahanu loped back to the village. His excitement at the coming adventure evident in his long strides. Alsoomse tucked her arm through mine and we walked close together, following our son.

"You will look after him," she said, looking up at my eyes.

"Yes, my love, and Ahanu will look after me."

"Good, then I have no need to worry about either of you," Alsoomse reached up and kissed me, still holding tight to my arm. "How long will you be away?"

"I honestly do not know. The distance is long, the weather unpredictable. Perhaps until the next full moon, maybe a little longer," was the best answer I could give.

My son had become a wonderful hunting companion. We still went out with Chogan at times and on occasion with Alsoomse, but our times alone – just father and son – were special. Loading the big canoe with our weapons, bedrolls, basic supplies, my backstaff and extra birch-bark for writing – and with Alsoomse's approval – Ahanu and I set off to go exploring.

Chapter 25

The first day we paddled for many hours into a slight breeze from the west. With the wind from that direction, there was nothing the sail could do to help us. The sea was calm, with little or no wave action. We forced the canoe west across the bay for an estimated three leagues before following the indentations in the coast – north, west, and south – covering many leagues until we began to tire. At a signal from me, Ahanu acknowledged with a wave of his paddle and we took to the land for a rest and a meal. The days passed in a blur of sea on one side; the muskeg and forest on the other. We sailed when we could, happy to rest our arms and shoulders.

Late on the third day we met an old Omushkego hunter from a village on an island in the mouth of a wide river. At his invitation we stopped there for a day and two nights. While I talked with the elders, having to explain my relationship to Ahanu and to the Omushkegowak, my son spent most of his time in the company of a young lady of his own age. One of the elders, who had been listening to my story with great interest, suddenly asked me if I was the white man who had killed Eagle Heart many years before. I admitted that was so, hoping I would not have to say any more. The elder listened. He nodded. He pointed to me with his pipe and said, "I knew that boy, Eagle Heart. He was bad in here." He tapped his chest and nodded a few more times. I breathed a soft sigh of relief. No danger from that source.

On the second morning the wind was fair, blowing almost uniformly from the south. It was time to leave. Most of the village came to the water's edge to watch as our canoe found the wind and sailed north. Ahanu watched the crowd on shore for a long time, his eyes on just one person. I said nothing, knowing he would talk with me about the girl when he was ready. The wind was kind to us that day, carrying us far – I estimated ten leagues that day.

And so our days passed. We hunted on shore, taking a variety of pelts and meat from small mammals. I sketched a chart of the coast on the birch-bark. We passed between the mainland and a large, low-lying island.

"We'll stop there and look around on our way back, if the weather is kind," I told Ahanu.

"I would like to stop at the Omushkego village as well," he replied. "Perhaps for a few days, if you don't mind." He looked back over his shoulder and gave me a wide grin as he spoke. That was the only time he hinted at his interest in a girl as we travelled north.

Walking along the shoreline one afternoon tracking caribou, we moved inland with them. Ahanu was in the lead when he stopped and called, "Look at this, Papa."

At his feet, laid out on a few rocks, was the skeleton of a dog. My first thought was that it was a wolf, until Ahanu pointed to its neck. The skeleton was wearing a thick leather collar studded with short metal spikes. I noticed the skeleton had a broken shoulder and assumed it had fallen foul of a bear. Ahanu took off the collar and handed it to me. The leather was worn, but in good condition. Where it was stitched to accommodate the buckle, a faint outline showed. I was sure it was a maker's stamp but too faint to read.

"How on earth did this get here?" I wondered aloud.

"What is this for?" asked Ahanu, for he had never seen a dog collar.

"White men use them to keep their dogs in check. To hold them back, on a leash," I answered. My mind was in turmoil. This skeleton was that of a dog; a domestic dog. It did not look too weathered by the elements so could not have been there very long. The collar worried me. It had been made in England. I was sure of it. Yet, how did it come to be here?

Ahanu took the collar from me and wrapped it twice around his wrist before buckling it. He held his arm up for me to see. "I will keep it," he said.

We heard wolves howling that night and for the next few nights though none came near us during the day, at first. We had made a habit of camping on the shore above high water mark, wherever we could find dry land. Finding a large, dry, open place, we hauled the canoe out and went hunting. Hours later we came back empty handed, apart from a plump goose that Ahanu had taken with a well-aimed arrow.

"There is a wolf following us," he said. "I haven't seen it yet, but I know it is there. If we go back some distance, we'll find its tracks."

"One wolf will not harm us," I answered. "It's probably curious, that's all."

That night we slept on either side of a fire of driftwood as was our custom. I awoke just before the sun and looked over the remaining hot coals to Ahanu. He was still asleep.

A few paces away, lying full length with its head between its front paws and looking straight at me, was a large dog. Not a wolf, although that had been my first impression. I raised myself into a sitting position. The dog raised its head and wagged its tail slowly.

"Ahanu," I whispered. "Ahanu, we have company."

Ahanu sat up and followed my gaze. The dog whined, wagged its tail. It stayed there, watching us. Ahanu stretched out a hand and allowed the dog to smell him, then lick his palm. The dog shuffled forward on its belly towards him. Wrinkling its nose, the dog reached over to the collar on Ahanu's wrist and began to sniff it, then lick it. We stayed still. The dog licked the collar, inhaling its scent and blowing out its nostrils, then it whined and pawed at the collar. Ahanu held it up out of reach. The dog watched. When Ahanu lowered his arm again, the dog stretched over his lap and resumed licking the collar.

"She and the skeleton knew each other, I think," said Ahanu.

"Yes, I think so too. But where did two dogs like this come from? She reminds me of dogs I saw in England. I think she is a cross-breed between a mastiff and a bloodhound. They were hunting dogs and both quite fearless."

"We have not heard of any white people in this area," said Ahanu. "Perhaps the dogs came from far away – to the south?"

I shook my head, having no answers. We assumed the dog had probably lived with a wolf pack for some time during the recent past and only left when she picked up our scent. When we packed the canoe that morning the dog watched. As soon as we pushed out onto the water and climbed in, the dog followed, swimming strongly after us.

We paddled back to shore; the dog again followed. After shaking water all over us, she jumped into the canoe and curled up near Ahanu.

"I think you have a dog now, Ahanu. What will you call her?" I asked.

"Masko," he replied. "She looks like a small bear. I will give her this collar." He took the collar from his wrist and buckled it around Masko's neck. And so Masko became the third member of our exploration party.

Where the waters of Winipekw meet Kitchikumi the land fell away to the west. The broad expanse of Kitchikumi – the great bay where we had wandered so haphazardly in *Discovery* – lay before us. It was calm, almost inviting, with only a few clusters of ice far off shore. I resisted the temptation to sail due north. I knew from painful experience how quickly storms could turn these waters into a death trap for a small boat.

"This is as far as we go, Ahanu," I announced as we stood on a low cape looking down on the vast sea. "It's time to start for home."

"Yes," he answered, "and with an important stop on the way." His smile was all the explanation I needed. He was in a hurry to get back to a certain young lady living in a village on an island at the mouth of a wide river.

I took one last look at Kitchikumi, my mind in the long distant past. Then, with a light slap on the back to my son, I strode down to the water where we had beached the big canoe. A few minutes later we were paddling hard for the south, hoping for a following wind to fill our sail. We paddled for three long days before we were rewarded with a breeze out of the north-west.

A few days later, sheltering on land under the upturned canoe from a downpour of rain that obliterated everything from sight more than a few paces away, I considered our position. The wind that had carried the thick, dark rain clouds to us had arrived almost without warning. If we took a chance on crossing the wide straight to the big island we had seen on the way north, we could be trapped there for many days – weeks, perhaps. The risk did not seem worth the possible reward. The island could be barren, devoid of wildlife or anything else of interest. Ahanu was sleeping with Masko's head wrapped in his arms. When they awoke, I suggested a change of plan.

"The weather is changing, Ahanu. I think we should make all haste to get back to the Omushkego village and rest for a day or two, then continue for home. Do you agree?"

"I'm ready, Papa. As soon as this rain stops, I'm ready to go." His eyes sparkled in the semi-darkness of our shelter.

The rain held us there under the canoe for two and a half days. When it cleared, the clouds remained. The wind was down but there was an ominous swell on the waters of Winipekw. I watched the sea while Ahanu packed the canoe.

"We must keep close to shore for safety," I told him. "All we need is a foot of water. We'll have to keep crossing the incoming waves, but they are small here and should not cause too much of a problem. Let's try it."

We stowed the sail and the leeboard, keeping them ready for use if the weather changed in our favour. A thick fog crept in from the sea late that morning sending us once again to the land to wait. Ahanu explored the waterfront with Masko while I waited with the canoe. The fog felt cold, clammy and deadened all sound. Ahanu and Masko came back, arriving so suddenly I heard no sound.

"There are many tracks of Nanuk to the south, not far," he warned. "They appear to be from an old female; large but not heavy. It might be very hungry and will be dangerous. Masko will tell us if she comes close."

When the fog dispersed as the sun burned through the layers, we set off again, keeping close to the land as before. We saw the white bear as she stood up on her hind legs to view us more clearly. Masko went into a frenzy of barking. Nothing we could do would stop her. The bear dropped to all fours and ambled to the water's edge. Her matted coat rippled, showing her ribs and her poor physical condition with each forward step.

"She's coming after us," shouted Ahanu.

We turned the canoe out to sea and paddled hard to keep the bear at a distance. She kept on coming. We crashed through the waves, covering ourselves with spray. I took a quick look over my shoulder, the white bear was halfway from the shore to us. We could not afford to fight her from the canoe. One blow from her massive paws would shatter our fragile hull. Out of the corner of my eye I saw ripples on the sea. A cat's paw of wind.

"Go left, Ahanu. Left, now."

We paddled with all our combined strength until we felt the breeze in our faces. While I continued to paddle, Ahanu raised the sail and we began to pick up speed, outdistancing the bear. When she was no more than a white speck far behind us, we relaxed and let the wind work for us without our help. Masko had stopped barking but never took her eyes of the distant bear.

"That was close," I shook my head to clear the salty spray from my eyes. "The sky looks okay for the moment. We'll stay out here for as long as the wind holds and get as far south of that demon as we can."

Many hours later, as the sky took on the greyish tones of twilight – harbinger of the dark that would not come back for many weeks yet – we paddled ashore for a rest and a hot meal. The white bear was far to the north, although we were both aware she could travel long distances while we slept. I calculated that she was too old and too starved to have enough energy for such an extended journey. With Masko as our warning system, we should be able to sleep in peace.

Our arrival at the Omushkego village some days later was greeted with much excitement and shouting. We had a load of fresh meat from a caribou we had killed late the day before, which we handed over to the women to cook for all to share. While I sat and recounted our adventures to the elders, Ahanu went off on his own pleasures. Masko explored the village alone; picked a fight with two of the local dogs and acquitted herself well, coming back to me with blood on her muzzle, patches of fur missing from the scruff of her neck and a satisfied look on her face.

That night there was much feasting and merriment. We all ate too much. We talked too much. We laughed a lot. In the early hours of the morning, I stretched out in my bedroll beside the canoe with a puzzled Masko beside me. Of Ahanu there was no sign. In mid-morning Ahanu came to me leading a shy, very pretty girl by the hand.

"Papa, I would like you to meet Wapun," he introduced her formally. "She wants to travel with us," he added.

"Does, she? Well, hello, Wapun. I am pleased to meet you."

Masko assessed Ahanu's new friend in her own way, her nose inspecting Wapun at close quarters. My son squared his shoulders and looked me in the eyes. "Wapun is coming with us, Papa," he stated, his voice strong and determined.

"What about her parents? What do they say about this idea? Have you talked with them?"

"No, Papa. Wapun is an orphan. She has no family here. If you ask the elders, I think they will let her go with us." Ahanu had it all worked out.

We left the village after two days. I took the stern position as was my custom. Ahanu sat in the bow. Wapun sat behind him, leaning back against our pile of furs. Masko, with some reluctance, had to sit closer to me than to her master. Wapun spoke little during the long journey home to Waskagahanish. She did her share of the work on shore; collecting firewood, preparing meals and talking quietly with Ahanu. With me she was polite but reserved. She had never seen a white man and didn't know what to expect from me. I did my best to act as I always did – I was Ahanu's father and an elder, no more; no less.

When we stepped ashore at Waskagahanish a crowd awaited us. We had been seen from afar and the word had spread throughout the village. Chogan stood in the foreground, Alsoomse by his side. Ahanu was first ashore. He greeted his mother with a kiss on the cheek and a brief hug. Turning to Chogan, he placed his closed fist over his heart and held it there, his face beaming. Chogan repeated the gesture. Masko jumped out of the canoe and loped towards the village. I stepped out and embraced my wife. Wapun stayed in the canoe until Ahanu reached out his hand to her.

"Come with me," he said and she followed.

"Mama, this is Wapun," he introduced her to Alsoomse. "She is my woman."

Alsoomse looked at me, her eyebrows raised and a question on her face. I shrugged my shoulders and showed the palms of my hands in a gesture meaning, "Don't look at me like that. I had nothing to do with this."

Wapun watched Alsoomse, keeping herself close to Ahanu's side. I noticed she did not try to hide as some might have done. She watched and she waited. Alsoomse gave me a look that I knew meant a serious discussion when we were alone. She reached out her hand to Wapun and said, "Hello, Wapun. I am Ahanu's mother. My name is Alsoomse. You are welcome to stay with us. Come with me."

Ahanu looked at me. His smile said it all. In the distance we could hear the snarling and yapping of a dog fight. Masko was making herself known to the other dogs with her usual flair.

"Well, Ahanu. There is still work to be done. Let's get this canoe unloaded," I tried to sound stern but failed. He laughed and said, "I'll do it, Papa. You go and talk with Grandpa. I know he's waiting to hear about our adventures."

Sitting outside Chogan's tepee sharing a pipe, I recounted our voyage in the Omushkego manner, taking my time and leaving nothing out. Masko came to sit with me, bloodied but unbowed. We were home and the village was richer by one person. I was happy and I hoped Alsoomse would be too. I would find out later. When I joined Alsoomse in bed in the early hours of the morning she was still awake.

"Do you approve of this union between our son and this girl?" she asked.

"It's not for me to approve or disapprove. Our son has made his own decision. That's all there is to it," I answered.

We lay there, side by side in silence for a while. Then Alsoomse rolled over on top of me. She traced the outline of my eyes, nose and mouth with her fingertips. She kissed me and said, “I missed you, Otácimow. I missed you very much.”

Without moving off me, she slid one hand down between my legs and guided me into her. And then we were one. I was home.

Wapun soon made herself a favourite member of our family. She was a natural peacemaker who somehow echoed my mother’s happy attitude to life. One year after she stepped from our canoe on the shore by Waskagahanish Wapun delivered a daughter. Ahanu was a proud father. He asked me if they could name the baby Jane for the English grandmother he had never known. Of course, I knew my mother would have approved. Jane was the image of her father, even to the dark tone of his eyes. As we soon learned, she also had inherited Alsoomse’s independent streak and Wapun’s gift for making people smile.

CHAPTER 26

We first noticed a change in Alsoomse when Ahanu was 21 by my account. I had kept a record of the years in my birch-bark journal. I was reasonably confident of their accuracy. Alsoomse began to lose weight. She became pale and thin and little remained of her once impressive energy. I feared she was wasting away. Her illness had started three moons before, with a cold and a cough. The cold dried up but the cough persisted and gradually became worse. Often the violence of her coughing caused blood to fleck her lips. She complained of pains in her chest. Some days the cough was so bad she could hardly swallow food or water.

The shaman came to see her and cast a few spells while chanting a prayer of some sort. He danced around Alsoomse, scattered a few dusty ingredients over her and achieved nothing. I added my own prayers daily and nightly, hoping for an improvement. Wapun nursed her mother-in-law with great care for they had become firm friends. Each day she would bring in Jane for Alsoomse to hold for a while. Ahanu visited us each day and sat with his mother for many hours. When Ahanu and his family left, Chogan and Wikimak came in regularly, asking why

Alsoomse was not recovering. I could not answer them. I had no skills as a doctor. I knew so little of medicine.

Wikimak brought in a hot drink made from sweetgrass. In appearance, texture and smell, it was much like the Holy grass grown in England. Wikimak believed it had medicinal properties. I could only hope she was right. I was so desperate for Alsoomse to recover I would have tried anything to make her well again. Remembering the tree buds of a turpentine-like substance that had proved beneficial to some of *Discovery*'s crew during our first winter, I collected a handful and crushed them to a liquid pulp. Mixed with warm water the pulp gave off a pungent smell. Alsoomse said the concoction tasted awful. It did nothing for her. The sweetgrass drink did help her relax for a while and helped control her cough. Nothing, however, seemed to alleviate the pain in her chest. I believed something unpleasant must be growing inside her but could do nothing to help. The days and nights became a blur. I refused to go anywhere. I could not leave my lover's side. In the early hours of one morning Alsoomse called my name.

"Otácimow."

I was already there with her, holding her in my arms as I did every day and every night. I brushed her damp hair from her eyes and spoke soothing words to her.

"Otácimow, my beloved husband," she whispered, "I must leave you." She coughed up some blood. which I wiped away with my fingers.

"No, Alsoomse. Please, don't go. Keep fighting. I love you and need you here, so does Ahanu." I almost choked on the words.

"The Great Spirit has called to me and I must go. We will see each other again among the stars."

After those few words, Alsoomse gave a gentle sigh, laid her head on my shoulder and passed on to the spirit world. The Omushkego belief of life after death is not so different from that taught in the scriptures by priests in England. Long after her spirit had taken its gentle flight to the heavens, I held Alsoomse in my arms and prayed to my God that he would take care of her soul. I prayed to the Great Spirit too, mindful of her strong beliefs. We stayed that way, locked together, until the dawn broke. In the darkness of those lonely hours, I wept until my eyes had no more tears to shed; then I went to tell our son.

Alsoomse was the daughter of a chief. Her funeral would reflect her status. Chogan and Wikimak stood with Ahanu, Wapun and Jane in the middle of the main clearing at Waskagahanish. I stood off to one side. We waited. In my tepee the women were preparing Alsoomse for her final journey. They came out carrying her body on a stretcher of fresh saplings and plaited grass. The love of my life lay there with her face uncovered but her eyes closed; her hands clasped on her middle. Women had braided her shiny black hair into a single long queue dressed with an eagle's feather. It rested across her breast. Ahanu and I placed some wild flowers in her hands. Somewhere a drum began a mournful, monotonous beat.

I walked ahead of the women carrying my wife. Ahanu walked by my side. Chogan and Wikimak followed with Wapun and Jane and the rest of Chogan's family. We led them into the peaceful forest, to a glade where Alsoomse loved to walk and where she would rest until eternity.

Book Four
A Return to Disappointment

CHAPTER 27

"Since my beloved Alsoomse passed away in the early summer one year ago, I have been thinking more and more of England. The seasons have come and gone without the attendant pleasures and problems we shared. Summer disappeared in a daze, my mind too filled with thoughts of my loved one to notice much more than the inevitable passing of the days."

I wrote those words in my wilderness journal to remind me that I had almost given in to my despair at losing Alsoomse. The first autumn without her passed without my noticing the colours. Winter, always a busy time at the hunting grounds, helped me slowly adjust to being alone. I hunted with Ahanu during the days. We both enjoyed being together but Ahanu had a wife and young daughter to look after. He spent less and less time with me. At night, I lay in the thick furs of my bed, with others of the family asleep around me, and I thought of Alsoomse. Late in the night, when all others were dreaming, I wept silent tears for the love I would never see or hold again.

Perhaps the loneliness brought on the desire to return to England. Perhaps the loneliness reminded me that I would like to learn what happened to *Discovery* and the mutinous crew who cast us away in a small boat so many years ago. Did they return to England safely? Were they all hanged as mutineers? Suddenly, I want to know. My son was a strong young man of 22. He didn't need me anymore. He was a respected member of our small community with his own family. Without Alsoomse, I didn't feel able to stay any longer at Waskagahanish, much as I had enjoyed my life in those beautiful forests.

Chogan had told me many times of a huge river far to the south. He said he learned of it from the Iroquois and from a French fur trader when he was hunting in the interior as a young man. He said the fur trader believed the river flowed into a sea even greater than Winipekw. I think it is possible that this river is the one Jacques Cartier discovered: the one he called Rivière du Canada. The one I thought of escaping to soon after my capture by the Omushkegowak over half my life ago. Now that I am a free man and an elder of the tribe, there are no restrictions on me. Also, as a man in mourning, I can come and go as I wish and stay away for months if I choose to. I have decided to go and find Cartier's river. Perhaps this huge river will lead me to that great sea. Perhaps that great sea is the Atlantic Ocean. Perhaps, somewhere there, I might find a ship sailing for England, or some other nearby nation, maybe to France or to the Dutch port of Antwerp. There is no certainty, only conjecture. Despite that, I feel strongly enough to make the attempt. My earlier thoughts about trading in furs came back to me and I vowed to research that possibility in England.

I discussed my plans with Chogan and the other elders for many hours. Chogan did not want me to leave. He reminded me that as he had no blood son now since

Squirrel's death, I would be chief when the time came for him to join the Great Spirit in the sky. I knew it could be so, but my mind was made up. I had to go to England, somehow. I had to find the answers to the questions that now disturbed my lonely mind.

Based on my current latitude and on the mean latitude between the mouth of the Rivière du Canada and his furthest point upstream as stated by Jacques Cartier, and taking into consideration the estimated number of leagues we travelled west in *Discovery*, I calculated the distance in a straight line to be roughly 160 leagues. Travelling by river when possible and overland when necessary, I expected to have to cover perhaps half that distance again. Therefore, my journey could be up to 240 leagues over unknown terrain, although Chogan knew parts of the route and could explain them to me. Experience had shown me that I could cover an average of five leagues each day – both on land and on the rivers. If I could maintain that speed, I could possibly reach the big river in about 48 days.

Against me would be the possibility of hostile tribes, the certainty of dangerous rapids and waterfalls, the need to stop and hunt for food along the way, and to keep myself fit. If I should fall and break a leg or an ankle, without help, of which there would be none, I would die in the wilderness. I believed the journey would be worth the risks

After an emotional farewell to my friends and family, especially Chogan, Wikimak, Wapun and my little granddaughter, I left Waskagahanish by canoe, heading up the Natuweu Nipi to above the second set of rapids where the river becomes a long, thin lake – like a finger. Ahanu and one of his friends travelled beside me in another canoe, helping me up the rapids. They left me at the head of the finger lake where we camped together for three nights.

While his friend packed their canoe on the last day, Ahanu put his hands on my shoulders and looked me in the eyes.

"You will come back, Papa?" he asked.

"Yes, my son. I shall return one day, if I can."

Ahanu hugged me and then, without another word, he helped push the canoes into deeper water. He and his friend both saluted me with their paddles as they turned for home. The last I saw of them was two strong, bare backs with rippling muscles, paddling hard for the first rapids. Alone again, and feeling rather lost, I loaded my canoe and set off in the opposite direction. The marshlands continued on each side of the river for many days. The mosquitoes and other biting insects attacked me on land so I spent as many hours each day as possible on the lakes and rivers.

Although it was time consuming, I never attempted to ascend or descend a rapid without having first studied its full length by walking the banks. Also, I never travelled up or down a rapid until I had carried my pack to a safe place. By the time I started my journey, after over 25 years of experience, I could handle a canoe under most conditions. That didn't mean I could afford to take chances. My pack contained furs for trade or sale, my few personal belongings – including my backstaff and my precious birch-bark journal – and some food. I also had my weapons – bow and arrows, my spear, a bone knife I had carved after the fight with Eagle Heart in my youth, and John Hudson's knife, which Chogan had given me the day I left. I could not afford to lose any of them.

As I travelled, I lived on freshwater fish taken in a net, the meat of small mammals I caught in traps or shot with my bow and arrow, plus an assortment of berries, nuts and edible roots. I did not try for big game as those creatures provided more meat than I could carry or eat. The years with the Omushkegowak had taught me never to take more than I needed.

The rivers seemed endless. Whenever I could, at least once each day if possible, I took a sun sight to determine my rough latitude – to see how far south I had travelled. The rapids continued against me, therefore I was still climbing slowly inland. Soon, I knew not where or when, the land would lead me downhill to the big river. Most of the lakes were really nothing more than wide parts of the rivers, until I came to a lake that spread from east to west. The wind was strong that day and blowing from the north, kicking up waves that could swamp my light canoe. I had to stay close to the north shore and choose between paddling east or west. I chose east and dodged from cove to cove to keep out of the wind until a river presented itself.

This new stream was no more than two or three leagues in length; then it widened out into a small lake. That was followed by another short stretch of river and yet another, larger lake. I could see the lake was dotted with what looked like many small islands. I chose one with a fine copse of trees to rest on for a day or two. The choice of camp was excellent, the timing all wrong. My journey could have ended there.

On my second day, as I began a meal of pike baked over hot coals, I heard voices. Coming straight towards my camp was a large canoe with six men on board. There was no time to hide my canoe. They had obviously seen the smoke from my fire and were coming to investigate. If they were intent on war, I was in trouble. Hiding was pointless. The island was small. They would find me in minutes. I did the only thing I could think of. I went to the base of a tree overlooking the lake, where I could see and be seen and stood there without my weapons.

As the men came ashore, they called to me in a dialect that sounded similar yet was not quite of the Omushkego that I knew. I found I could understand most words although not all. I answered and told them I was a friend, inviting them to share my fish. They were quite concerned to meet me. They had never met a white man before. Despite my clothing, and my facility with their language, my hair, my eyes and my skin told of a different ancestry from theirs. It took me a while, explaining who I was and where I had come from, before they began to relax. They were a hunting party from a village to the south east they called Waswanipi. I mentally translated that to something akin to 'Light over water' and wondered at its provenance.

Adding more fish to my pot, I listened as the visitors told me they were on their way home from somewhere to the north-east with a load of moose meat. When I told them where I was bound, they invited me to travel with them.

"Our village is Waswanipi. It is in the same direction," said one of the younger men.

Although none of them had been to the big river, they all knew of it. Their versions of the possible distance to cover, however, varied from the ludicrous to the extreme. Happy to have company for a while, we left together at first light next morning. One of the visitors joined me in my canoe to help me keep station with the larger canoe and its five paddlers. Waswanipi was only a few leagues away. The river was calm, with no rapids. My companion paddler kept me busy all the way asking questions about me, and about my travels.

"How did you come to live near Winipekw?" he asked. My answer was long. The time passed quickly. Soon we saw thin spirals of smoke from cooking fires, followed by the barking of dogs and shouts of children. We came ashore at the village edge and walked in so I could meet the chief and pay my respects. Every one I met treated me as an honoured guest, everyone, that is, except one man.

At Waswanipi my memory threw me back to my first year at Waskagahanish when I saw a familiar ugly face. It looked like a bad-tempered toad. He watched me from the shadows of a wigwam entrance. He had broad shoulders, a little rounded with age, and a barrel chest. He was about my height. The most significant feature I noticed was his broken nose. I had broken that nose in a brief tussle after he tripped me to spill my container of water. His name was Black Crow.

CHAPTER 28

Seeing Black Crow, I knew I would have to be careful. Did he harbour a grudge against me for the long ago fight with Eagle Heart? Would he want revenge for his broken nose? I made up my mind to leave Waswanipi immediately to avoid further trouble. Black Crow took the initiative from me. He strode across the space between us until we were only three or four paces apart. He planted his feet wide and blocked my path. He had a knife in his belt and a club in one hand. The knife was the one with which I had killed Eagle Heart.

"Otácimow," he hissed.

Sensing a conflict, my new friends backed away. One called out, "What is this, Black Crow? Do you mean harm to our visitor?"

Black Crow snarled his reply, leaving me and everyone else in no doubt as to his intentions. "He killed my friend, Eagle Heart, and he broke my nose. Now it is his turn to die, this white man."

I was unarmed, apart from a knife at my belt. My spear and my bow and arrows were all in my canoe. I had not thought to carry them into Waswanipi. I had come in peace, not to wage war. Black Crow made it obvious that peace would not be possible between us. He raised his club in a threatening gesture. I looked around me. One of the young men of Waswanipi carried a spear. It looked strong enough to double as a quarterstaff. I snapped my fingers at him and pointed to the spear. He nodded and threw it to me so I caught it midway down its length. At least one of the watchers believed in fair play.

Once again, as I had done in front of Eagle Heart, I twirled the staff in both hands. Its balance was almost perfect. I smiled a brief thanks to its owner and faced Black Crow.

"If you wish to fight, then you must strike the first blow," I said.

He didn't hesitate. He swung his club at my head hard enough to smash my skull. I leaned away and poked him in the ribs with the pointed end of the spear. He roared with rage and swung again. His anger made him careless. I was able to step out of his reach and again my borrowed spear hit him in the chest, that time with just enough force to draw blood. By the time he was aware he had been cut, I had moved beyond his reach again. Black Crow dropped his club, drew his knife and rushed me. The spear became a blur of motion as I defended against his attack, pounding on his upper arms and his body. As he fell back, screaming curses at me, I followed. A cold rage was building behind my eyes. The fight had to end immediately or I would kill him. I feinted low, as if to trip him. Black Crow jumped sideways as I reversed the spear, swung it in a wide circle and hit him hard at the temple. He went down in a heap. Turning to the watchers and the men who had brought me to the village I said, "I'm sorry. I did not want this to happen. I will leave you now."

I handed the spear back to its owner with a nod of thanks and went to my canoe. One of the young men pointed east and said, "Oujè Bougamou, the next friendly village, is about four or five day's travel away by river."

I thanked him and paddled away without a backward glance. My thoughts were on Eagle Heart; the man I had killed to defend Alsoomse. I had no wish to kill another man; not even one such as Black Crow. I hoped by letting him live I had not put my immediate future in jeopardy. My arms and my paddle reflected my sense of urgency. They worked in unison, stroke after stroke, eating up the leagues as we raced the river upstream. I had been told to take the left fork at the first intersection and a much narrower left fork at the second a few days later. From there my instructions were to leave the river at an obvious portage site and then strike north to Oujè Bougamou. That route would leave a trail and be easy to follow, if Black Crow had a mind to do so. I ignored the directions and continued past the portage.

A day passed. The river opened out into a series of small lakes. I paddled across each one, slowing down a little to enjoy the lush scenery, always heading south-east. Leaving the last lake, I crossed a strip of land to find a narrow stream. The sound of fast-running water put me on alert. Pulling my canoe onto the bank and piling my belongings beside it, I walked a few hundred paces to find the rapids. The first thing I noticed was that the white water was running away from me. That meant I had crossed the divide and was on my way downhill. The second was that only a fool would attempt that rocky drop in a canoe, and I was no fool. Elated at my progress, I ran back to my canoe and paddled it as close to the lip of the cascade as I dared. Again I hauled it out of the water.

Within an hour I had carried my worldly possessions and my canoe to the eddies at the bottom of the rapids, reloaded and was on my way again. There would be many more rapids and falls ahead, that was a given. I paddled smooth water for a few hours, enjoying the susurrus of ripples against my hull. I manhandled everything I owned past a succession of rapids. I paddled again. Each night I slept in the open with the sound of the river lulling me to sleep. On one evening, soon after dark, a soft green light shimmered across the sky. It appeared to be reaching for me. It stayed there over my head for only a few minutes but I knew, without question, Alsoomse was watching over my journey.

The days and nights passed. Always the current carried me downstream. The Rivière du Canada had to be getting closer. I began to feel that nothing could stop me.

CHAPTER 29

My confidence was misplaced. A moment's inattention in a fast current wrecked my canoe. I had pulled the craft up onto a grassy bank and tied it to a tree. I then carried my pack along a narrow game trail on the north east side of the river. At the foot of the rapids, close to a large eddy, I left my pack hanging from the fork of a prominent tree and walked back. The rapids were not serious enough for me to portage the canoe. I could see at least two safe lines to take me down the chute. I chose the most obvious one, pushed myself out into the stream, paddling hard to increase my speed for more control. Just before I plunged over the fall a black bear appeared on a rock to my right, almost close enough to touch. I shied away, glanced off a sharp rock and the canoe was ripped open from end to end.

The current tore the wrecked canoe away from me as I surfaced. Letting the current carry me away from the white water, I struck out across the flow to reach the north-east bank. My arms were strong enough that I was able to get ashore some distance downstream from my pack. However, the effort of swimming while fighting to cross the current had been exhausting. I lay there on the river bank in bright sunshine long enough to recover my breath. Walking back to retrieve my pack later was a pleasure, considering I could have lost my life in the rapids. Shouldering all that I owned, I set off downstream on foot. At the end of the day, having walked for an estimated five hours, the river opened into a wide inlet at the end of which, in the distance, I could see what looked like the open sea. It was a good place to make camp for the night.

In the morning I walked the north-west shore of the inlet until, somewhat to my disappointment, it opened up into a large lake; not the sea I had hoped to find. Undeterred, for my life had suffered many setbacks, I continued my walk for three more days. I had to cross a few rivers, each one its own challenge, until at the end of the lake I came to a river flowing almost due east – the direction I desired. Appealing though the magnificent lakeland scenery was, I had no time to waste on more than a brief acceptance of the beauty. I knew by instinct this river would lead me to my goal.

For the next two and a half weeks, I walked long hours each day, always keeping the river on my right. The river had immense power. I had the impression that running it in a canoe would be a formidable challenge. Often when I looked down at the dangerous rapids I was happy to be walking. After a few days, maybe five or six, the river opened out into an inlet with sheer sides. I made camp there and was able to catch a fine trout in my net soon after I arrived. That evening, sitting by a log fire with my fish dinner cooking over the hot coals, I noticed something that excited me very much. This wider part of the river was tidal. That meant I had to be within reach of the sea at last. My long, arduous journey from Waskagahanish was almost over.

My belief that the sea was close became stronger by the appearance of a dozen or so white whales. Beyond them I could see geysers of mist that could only have come from larger creatures. I was soon able to identify them as a pair of humpback whales, having seen similar at close quarters off the coast of southern Greenland. The waterway was a deep fjord with steep rugged sides of granite for much of its length, almost devoid of vegetation except for a number of tenacious trees clinging to the rock with no soil visible. There was danger on the trail too. I found fresh scat from black bears on a game trail in the edge of the forest. To avoid a confrontation, I climbed to the highest point I could find. That fjord hike was the hardest walking I have ever done. To keep in site of the river far below, I walked the crest day after day, climbing over gigantic boulders, struggling up hill and down.

Some of the land close to the fjord had been cultivated and planted with maize. Walking through the tidy fields, I knew I was nearing the end of my journey. I arrived at a fur trading village, surrounded by a wooden stockade, at the confluence of the river of white whales and a much wider river 63 days after I left Waskagahanish. One look at the massive river flowing past, into which the river of white whales flowed, told me I had probably reached Cartier's Rivière du Canada. The Atlantic Ocean was still far to the east, but now accessible if a ship should come in from that direction. I sat there for a long time just staring at the river I had travelled so far to find.

The first person I spoke to was a Frenchman, although from his colouring he might have been half native. He told me the place was called Tadoussac and it had been a trading centre in furs for decades between the Innu – the local natives – and the French. It seemed that my idea of trading in furs was not a new one.

"There is a mission here," he told me. "You should go and meet the priests. They are in charge of everything, including the sale of furs."

CHAPTER 30

Delighted as I was to discover Europeans, the French, I knew, could be a problem. I hoped England and France were not at war. My fears were groundless. Le Mission de L'Exaltation-de-la-Sainte-Croix-de-Tadoussac proved to be a welcoming haven. Even though the two resident priests were Papists, I was happy to meet the first real Europeans I had seen for over 25 years. The Innu called the small settlement, Totouskak. The French priests called it Tadoussac. I traded my furs to the priests for enough food to sustain me for a few weeks.

Père Henri d' Eschambault was in charge of the mission. He was about ten years my senior and had lived at Tadoussac for 20 years. He was a strange, fiery little man of God, no taller than my shoulder, yet with boundless energy. His dark eyes twinkled like stars throughout the day. He always seemed to have a smile on his thin face. His unruly mop of snowy hair was a plaything for the breezes. Papist though he was, I soon grew to like him very much. By contrast, Henri's assistant, the other priest, was a giant of a man with a face of perpetual misery. We never liked each other and avoided contact whenever possible.

I had not received any information about Europe, on either side of the channel, since I left home in the spring of 1610. Although Henri's knowledge of events across the ocean was at least one year old, it was all news to me. That evening he told me some of what he knew. Most of what he had to relate was of little consequence in my life. He told me of the murder of a French king, the marriage of an English princess to a high-born German, more colonies being established in the New World – though far south of Tadoussac. One story in particular intrigued me. In 1620, or thereabouts, he said, an English ship called *Mayflower* had sailed from Plymouth with over 100 pilgrims on board. They had landed somewhere between the Virginia Colony and the Rivière du Canada, but the priest could not tell me exactly where.

"The Atlantic Ocean has to be that way," I said, pointing to the east. Looking west, I asked, "What is that way? Have you ever travelled up stream?"

Père Henri shook his head. "Quebec is there, that was Samuel de Champlain's base. Further on, I've heard, there might be a place called Hochelaga. But, no, I have not travelled that way. I have enough to do here at Tadoussac."

We were standing outside the mission chapel looking at the great river a few days after I arrived at Tadoussac. I had so many questions crowding in my mind. "How often do trading ships, any ships, come up this river?" I asked him.

"There was a ship here recently from France. It called in here on its way back from Quebec about two weeks before you arrived. There will not be another this autumn, unless it is God's will," he shrugged. Continuing his answer, he added, "I think there will be a ship in the spring, after the ice breaks up."

My disappointment was acute. I had missed a ship bound for France by a mere two weeks. Suddenly I was desperate to keep moving, down that big river to the open sea and far beyond. I begged the good priest to send me word as soon as the sails of another ship came in sight.

"You have only just arrived. Now you are in a hurry to leave us, Thomas. Perhaps you should join me in a prayer for a ship?"

"I've forgotten how to pray, Père Henri. I have not prayed since my wife died. And even if I remembered how to, my prayers would not be your Catholic prayers."

The priest burst out laughing and patted me on the shoulder. "Come with me, Thomas," he said. "We shall pray together. We share the same God. He hears prayers in many languages and from many different people. Perhaps he will even listen to a heretic such as you."

So saying he took me by the elbow and walked me into the chapel where we knelt side by side, each to pray in his own way. *The Lord's Prayer* was the only one I could recall, and even then only the first couple of lines. Beside me Père Henri smiled as my tongue stumbled over the Latin words. He nodded to me and then began to pray out loud.

Pater noster, qui es in cœlis;
sanctificatur nomen tuum:

I joined in after the second line as my memory found the words I had been seeking; the Latin words and phrases my mother had drilled into me so long ago.

Adveniat regnum tuum;
fiat voluntas tua,
sicut in cœlo, et in terra.
Panem nostrum cotidianum da nobis hodie:
Et dimitte nobis debita nostra,
sicut et nos dimittimus debitoribus nostris:
et ne nos inducas in tentationem:
sed libera nos a malo.

I finished with a quiet "Amen" and made the sign of the cross over my chest. Père Henri did the same. We stood and he clasped my right hand between his much smaller hands.

"You see, Thomas, prayer is not so difficult. You have not forgotten. We are different yet we are all the same in the eyes of God. Come in and pray whenever you wish. This door is always unlocked. Now, tell me how you came to visit us."

"Indeed I will, if you will tell me more about the world I have not heard of since I was a young man," I agreed

Hours later, having told me his news, Père Henri, in his turn, listened intently to my story of living with the Omushkegowak for so many years. He was particularly interested in the possibilities of trading for furs with my people at Winipekw. I did not disclose my thoughts on that subject to him, preferring to wait until I had talked with my own people in England. We spent many pleasant evenings like that, sharing tales from our respective lives. The first time the little priest produced a bottle of Cognac from his cellar the image of my father sprang to mind. For a few moments the potent combination of strong drink and my emotions prevented me from speaking. I knew, somehow, that my mother and father were unlikely to be alive. If they were, they would be close to 70 years old. That made me feel very sad. And what of my sisters and my brother? Suddenly, with absolute clarity, I could see my sister, Emily, standing with Jane Montrose outside St. George's Church in Gravesend. I had not thought of Jane for many years, probably not for all the time I was with Alsoomse.

I already knew that no ships would be coming to Tadoussac for many months. It was too late in the open water season. The harsh winter was almost upon us and soon ice would begin to form on the Saguenay and, so Père

Henri told me, ice would also cover much of the vast expanse of the Rivière du Canada. Perhaps, I hoped, God would hear our prayers and send me a ship early in the spring, as soon as the ice had been carried away by the current and tides.

The winter advanced with determined force. A few sprinkles of snow dusted the ground. The daytime temperature dropped to freezing point; the nights became much colder. A blizzard blew in from the west bringing with it a heavy fall of snow. The temperature dropped lower. Ice began to form on the Saguenay and along the shores of the Rivière du Canada. The whales had left before the first snow fell. Without birch-bark or enough animal skins, I could not build a tepee or a wigwam. Instead I spent the first few weeks at Tadoussac building myself a small dwelling – I could hardly call it a house. I felled the necessary trees myself, using a long-handled axe borrowed from Henri. Each one I dragged alone through the snow to Tadoussac. Each one, I positioned myself according to a rough plan laid out in my mind. With only one room, four solid walls of spruce and a pitched roof it wasn't much to look at but, thanks to half-forgotten mathematical skills, the four corners were accurate to form a square and the walls were vertical.

Taking advice from a local fur trader, I caulked between the logs with dried moss and wet mud, and did the same with the thinner logs on the roof. Windows, I decided, would be an unnecessary affectation. I hadn't used a window since I left home in 1610. A window would let in light. It would also create drafts. To keep warm, I could live with the gloom, brightened only by a central fire. Using the same techniques as in a tepee or a wigwam, I left an opening in the roof for the smoke to escape. The earthen floor was cold and hard but my bearskin bedroll was warm and thick enough to alleviate some of that discomfort.

Before the ice covered the fjord (the priests told me the name they have given to the river of white whales is the Saguenay), I set out a net each day and collected enough fish to freeze and store for the immediate future. Next, I had to study the surrounding land for signs of wildlife and set out a trapline away from others already in use by people from Tadoussac. That meant travelling a longer distance than most. I hoped the trap lines would prove worthwhile. The furs I needed for warmth and for trade. The meat was for sustenance.

That winter of 1637 to 1638 was harsh. The winds blew with a ferocity I had never experienced at the winter hunting grounds at Nemiskau. Blizzards often lasted for many days, making travel dangerous, even for short distances. The probability of losing one's way was too extreme. Wicked storms of ice created scenes of exotic beauty while keeping all at Tadoussac housebound. Running out of food became a real threat for all in the village. As the winter wore on, to ward off hunger as long as possible, I often told stories from my life at sea and with the Omushkegowak in exchange for food. At first I entertained locals in their homes and ate supper with them. Later, as my talks became popular and I needed more room, Père Henri allowed me to use the church, providing I remembered to give God the credit for all my bounties and the devil the blame for my misfortunes.

Slowly the winter passed. When the weather permitted, my trap lines brought in some food and a few additional furs to trade for more. I chipped holes in the ice on the Saguenay and caught fish every time. With each one that I pulled out of the water, I thought of Alsoomse and fingered the bone hook she had carved for me when we were young. It had been hanging around my neck ever since. The blizzards blew less frequently. The snows fell less often. The sun beamed its life-giving presence, burning the clouds away and beginning to warm the land and the rivers. Ice began to break up and drift away in large floes. The birds came back to Tadoussac, building nests in trees, bushes and on ledges lining the fjord. The shrill honking of hundreds of geese filled the air. Flowers opened up their hearts and welcomed the sun. Bears came out of hibernation, introducing new-born cubs to the world they must inherit. Beavers set to work strengthening their lodges, and repairing dams broken by flood water from melting snows. Spring was a magical time along the banks of the Rivière du Canada and the Saguenay fjord.

A few weeks after the last of the snows melted from the land, I was on my way back to Tadoussac with a haul of beaver furs and a stack of fresh meat. From the distance I heard the tolling of a bell: the mission bell at Tadoussac. The day was not Sunday, or any other holy day as far as I knew. That meant the bell, which was being rung with extreme energy, signalled something momentous; something that would affect all at the settlement. I hoped it was a ship and increased my strides. Henri greeted me with much excitement as I arrived at the mission an hour later.

“Come, Thomas. Come,” he helped me off with my pack, took my arm and led me to the waterfront, almost running to keep up with my long strides. “Look there,” he said. “Look there. Do you see what’s there?”

She was still a few leagues off but there was no mistaking the filled sails of a large ship working her way up stream. What a beautiful sight. Sailing ships had been so much a part of my early life. Not having seen one since

Discovery sailed away from me in 1611, I stood there in awe. I watched her approach for a long time, taking in every nuance of her sails, the shape of her hull and the way she rode upon the river. I could see from her three masts and her sail plan that she was a barquentine and looked to be quite large. As she came to anchor off the settlement, her ensign became clear. She flew the Tricolour at her stern and was, therefore, as expected, a French ship.

CHAPTER 31

The ship, *La Sirene*, had brought supplies for the mission, common European goods to trade for furs and a few hardy settlers – all men. The latter came ashore in a longboat and were greeted by Tadoussac's two priests. Whether they wanted his religious attentions or not, Père Henri was God's servant and he was determined to keep the newcomers on a good Christian path. Before they had taken half a dozen paces on the soil of the New World he had informed them of the times for Mass and reminded them to respect and revere God in all things. None of them appeared to be listening.

The captain came ashore in the first boat with the settlers. He listened to the good priest's admonishments with a cynical smile on his weather-beaten face. When Henri had finished his personal form of welcome, he turned to the captain and asked, "Did you bring me a keg or two of Cognac, Captain?" And then, as if remembering his manners, he introduced himself. "Père Henri d'Eschambault à votre service."

"Capitaine Yves Durand," the officer replied, holding out his hand in greeting. "Yes, old father. I have Cognac for you, and a keg of rum, plus wine for the Mass. Have any fur traders come in yet?"

"Yes, our storeroom is full of furs and all yours for the choosing. This man," he indicated me, "is a trapper. He has been living with the natives far inland for many years. He is English."

The captain looked at me, his curiosity obvious. "Anglais?" he asked. "Vous êtes Anglais? Parlez-vous Francais?"

"Yes, Captain Durand," I answered in his language, "I speak fluent French. My name is Thomas Woodhouse. I was shipwrecked on the shores of a great bay many leagues to the north-west in 1611. I have lived with the Omushkegowak ever since. Now I am looking for a ship to take me back to England, or to France."

"Indeed. Can you pay?"

"No, sir. I have no silver or gold, only a few furs to trade or sell. But I can work. I was an able seaman on my last ship. Though long ago, I have not forgotten how to climb a mast, to handle rigging, reef a sail, or steer a straight course. I can navigate too. I was once a mathematician."

The captain looked at me for a few minutes. Then he addressed Henri. "I lost two good men overboard in a storm south of Cape Farewell. I shall need to replace them here if possible. Will you vouch for this man? This Anglais?"

"We will say a special Mass for those unfortunate sailors and pray for their souls. This man? Thomas? Oh, yes. I will vouch for him. He is not of our true Catholic faith but he is a good enough Christian for all that. He's a hard worker, and intelligent too."

Of course, there was no schedule set for the ship's departure. She would leave when her holds were full of furs and not before. Henri's kind words had secured me a place on board as an ordinary seaman. When the ship sailed, I would be on board. Until then I returned to my trap lines. For a week I roamed the interior collecting furs and bringing in my traps. I would not be needing them again. The night before we were due to sail, I sat with Henri and shared a large Cognac with him. He gave me a parting gift of some oiled cloth to keep my rolls of birch-bark journal dry and an exquisitely made wooden box in which to carry them.

"I made the box from wood left over when you built your house," he told me.

I left him with my traps, my spears, bow and arrows, my remaining furs and the last of my meat, all of which he could use, sell or trade to help the mission. I was sad to be leaving Tadoussac for the little priest had become a good friend over the winter months. Despite that, I was anxious to be on my way to the Atlantic Ocean again.

The French barquentine, *La Sirene*, sailed downstream from Tadoussac at the end of May. Her destination was St. Malo, a channel port only forty or so leagues south of England. St. Malo, I knew, was Jacques Cartier's place of birth. The Rivière du Canada was wide, so much so that often the south bank was invisible. After a few days we sailed out of the estuary into a huge sea which, I later found from the captain's charts, had two exits to the ocean, one in the south east and the other in the north east. *La Sirene* was bound for the north eastern passage.

Our voyage to the Atlantic Ocean took many days. The wind was fair, yet the distance far greater than I had believed. The land to port passed slowly as the wind took us through a long strait named for Jacques Cartier, between the mainland and a long island the French called Anticosti. The weather remained fair although on many mornings a thick mist drifted across the water until the sun dispersed it.

Passing through a narrow strait, no more than six leagues at its narrowest, the second mate told me the south side was called New Founde Land, an English name given by Sir Humphrey Gilbert, and the north was Labrador. Small icebergs drifted in the area, coming south from the coast of Greenland. Whales crossed our course. They were en route to their feeding grounds in Davis Strait and beyond. We were sailing east for an old French port. We had no time to give chase to the whales and no reason to interfere with them in any way.

I became something of a focal point on the ship. Everyone knew I had lived with the natives deep in the forests for many years. They all wanted to know what my life had been like. I spent many hours when off watch telling small groups of men stories from Waskagahanish and the winter hunting grounds at Nemiskau. Even the captain showed interest, inviting me to dine with him occasionally and asking me many questions about the abundance of fur-bearing animals to be hunted and where they might be found. His interest, I could see, was purely mercenary. I stored that information for possible future use.

Talking with an old sailor one evening while we were on watch, I mentioned the difference in winter climates between Waskagahanish and southern England, or northern France.

"Do you know how this could be?" I asked. "They are on the same latitude, the same distance north of the equator."

The old sailor drew on his pipe and thought for a while. Then he said, "I know nothing of these things. But, I do know that there is a strong current flowing across the ocean from the New World to Europe: to La Manche, the channel between France and England. We are in that current now. I believe this current has warmer water than the rest of the Atlantic. Maybe, there is an answer somewhere there."

The Atlantic had not improved its moods since I last crossed it in *Discovery*. It is a monstrous sea that never stops moving. It rolls without cease, day and night. When the wind taunts it into fury, the rolling swells become peaked waves with spitting white caps. *La Sirene* sliced through and over the swells, making good distances for the first few days. Then the clouds built over us from horizon to horizon. The wind kicked the waves into aggressive action. The waves attacked *la Sirene* with unprecedented force.

We rode out the first storm without damage. The subsequent gale a week or so later caused us considerable grief as it pounded the ship from all angles. By the time it blew itself out we had lost four sails, some rigging; had a damaged royal yard and a cracked mizzen mast. We bent on new sails and worked at the other repairs until the next storm slammed into us a day later. The hours passed in a daze as we struggled keep our ship afloat and to stay alive. We fought to stay on board as wave after wave washed over us and we fought to save our ship. Many of us expected to founder in those dreadful, mountainous seas. But survive we did, for a while.

That last storm forced us far off course. We were by then almost within reach of France. The storm blew us a long way to the south of Ushant and into deep trouble. A malignant wave slammed into *La Sirene*'s stern and sheered off her rudder. Crippled, the ship was at the mercy of unbeatable forces. Another giant wave broke over the decks, snapping the foremast and sweeping it over the side. Held there alongside by strands of rigging, we had to cut away the thick mast at the height of the storm to avoid suffering even more damage. The cracked mizzen mast went next, sliced away from the deck by the wicked wind. The rigging became a tangled mess of torn and frayed lines, and we were leaking like a sieve. The Bay of Biscay, where the storm had taken us, is no place for a crippled ship with another gale in the offing. My first and only experience of a storm on the Bay of Biscay was aboard a ship named *Ravenswing* when I was but a lad of seventeen. That storm on the south side of the bay almost sank a fine ship. Somehow she stayed afloat and took us safely home to England. I feared this time, I would not be so fortunate. This fine French ship, already much damaged by the ferocity of bad weather on the Atlantic, felt doomed.

Under the captain's direction, we jury-rigged another rudder and set a staysail between the mainmast and the stub of the foremast. If the weather played fair, we might have been able to keep the ship afloat long enough to reach a safe haven. The look of the sea and the clouds suggested otherwise. The Bay of Biscay was preparing for another bad blow. It wasn't long in coming. The wind screamed across the sea, driving the waves before it and building them up into angry peaks of furious white. The first wave picked us up and skidded the ship sideways. The next slammed into our port side, bursting through the thick planking and *La Sirene* filled with water as she turned over.

All hands were on deck to deal with the storm so no one was trapped below. That was small consolation. Unable to cling to any part of the ship against the power of the sea, we were washed overboard. I came up for air to find debris scattered all over the trough that held me between the waves. Nearby was a barrel bobbing nervously amongst the flotsam. I swam for it and held on. It was buoyant enough to keep me afloat, providing I could maintain a grip on the two ends, which was far from easy. The barrel wanted to roll, first one way, then the other. Holding on became an exercise in skill dependent on the strength of my fingers. I was one of the few sailors who could swim more than a few strokes, and that was no guarantee of survival in those tempestuous seas. As far as I know, none of my shipmates lived through that catastrophic day.

I fought the erratic gyrations of the barrel until I could hold on no longer. Seeing a large plank of wood on the crest of a wave, I swam over the same wave to find it. Banging against each other in a trough between the waves I found planks of many sizes, all splintered at the ends. With them was the remains of the mizzen mast, wrapped in rigging. Tied tight to the mast, strangled by the ropes, was the body of one of the officers. There was no point in cutting him free. He was already dead. I collected a few long planks and stretched out across them, trying to keep them together and myself afloat at the same time. It was a precarious way to travel but the best I could do. Slowly, ever moving with the waves and guided by the wind, the planks took me to safety. Pounded by the surf, I struggled ashore into a salt marsh that stretched a long way inland. There was no sign of *La Sirene* or any of her crew.

CHAPTER 32

When I had recovered sufficiently, I patrolled the seafront day after day, searching among the debris for a wooden box containing my roll of birch-bark wrapped in a form of oiled cloth. Both the box and the oiled cloth had been a parting gift from Père Henri. The task seemed hopeless but my desire to find my precious records was such that the time felt well spent. I suppose I was delusional after the shipwreck. The possibility of finding my box was remote in the extreme. My mind forced me to continue.

I lived on the edge of the marshes for a few weeks. There, food was never a problem. As a skilled hunter, I was able to snare game birds whenever necessary. I caught small fish in tidal pools with my cupped hands; I dug clams out of the sands and more than a few crabs as they tried to scuttle away to safety. Lush grasses supplemented my diet. During those weeks I must have walked as much as three leagues or more in each direction along the Bay of Biscay coast each day, stopping to examine any piece of wood or other wreckage that could have come from the unfortunate *La Sirene.* Some of the wood I used to build a small shelter above high tide. Some I used to fuel my cooking fire. I had begun to despair of ever finding my precious roll of memories. Thinking of moving on towards the English Channel to find a ship to England, I decided to make one more effort before I left.

As always, I walked close to the water's edge in one direction and returned along the high tide mark, where much of the sea's flotsam came to rest. The sun was high; the air warm. Sand fleas and small flies buzzed around my head, many more hovered over random piles of drying seaweed. Using a long stick I stirred the smelly weed, turning it over and scattering it on the beach. In one such pile I found remnants of clothing. In another a worn leather boot. A noisy gathering of seagulls dominated a section of beach at the southern extremity of my search. Close up I could see and smell a decomposing body. After beating off the gulls and turning the corpse, there was no way I could see of identifying him. I assumed he was one of the crew from my ship. Saltwater and the sea birds had done their destructive work. I left the gulls to their gruesome feast.

Searching the debris marking the limit of high tide I chanced to glance at the sea, which was more than fifty paces away. Something shiny had caught my attention. I watched for a while, trying to recapture the image. The sun glinted off the crests of small waves, each one creating its own momentary mirror effect. My eyes were tired from the strain of daily searching but something out there in the shallows was not natural. The waves broke on the beach creating small, wide foamy rivers that ran back to the sea as soon as their forward motion was exhausted. Behind them, moving in an awkward parody of the fluid dance of the incoming waves, was a block of wood. I ran into the water until it reached my knees, my thighs and then my waist. Heedless of the cold water, I launched myself into a flat dive and struck out hard for the object. A wave kicked it away from me, hiding it from my view. I bobbed up and down in the surf, my eyes constantly seeking something unusual, something that should not be there. A small shape, out of context with the sea, gave me hope. This time I reached it and held on tight. My long search had been rewarded. The block of wood was my own box, made by the skilled hands of a faraway priest from the seasoned wood of a tree I had felled beside the Saguenay River.

Sitting in my driftwood shelter with a blazing fire in front of me, I opened the two small metal clasps and raised the lid. There was a trace of water inside, but not enough to create damage. More important, the oilcloth was intact. Inside, my precious rolls of birch-bark were dry.

The next morning at daybreak, I loaded the box onto my back using lengths of cloth collected along the beach as a sling. It was not comfortable but I cared little for that. I had my memories again. Now it was time to strike out for the north coast and find a ship to take me across the channel to England.

CHAPTER 33

Many days (I had lost count of the number) after leaving the beach beside the Bay of Biscay, I walked into the port of Havre de Grâce. Like most seaports, large and small, it was crowded with ships, with sailors, with taverns and, of course, with whores. I only had need of a ship; a ship to take me across the Channel, or further along the coast – perhaps as far as Antwerp if necessary. I went to each vessel moored alongside the harbour. None were going where I wished to go. I asked at all the taverns if anyone knew of a ship going to England. None were, or if they were, no one would tell me.

Havre de Grâce, despite its gentle name, was a rough place. I had not seen the like since I left London. The town was dirty. Petty crime was rife. Violent crime was habitual. The inhabitants appeared to be mostly sailors, from all across Europe. They were a tough and, for many, a lawless breed. I managed to steer clear of trouble most of the time, although my precious box attracted more attention than it warranted. I had to use my staff, fists and feet daily to keep it from being stolen from me.

I camped in a grove of trees an hour's walk away from the port. There I could sleep in peace on a bed of thin branches and piles of leaves. I could snare rabbits and I could cook them over a small fire without gathering unwanted visitors. I took fresh water from a nearby stream to drink and to wash occasionally. Each day, after I had eaten a few morsels of meat left over from my dinner, I returned to Havre de Grâce. Each day, I went from ship to ship and from tavern to tavern, always looking for a way to cross the channel to England. My quest went on for over three weeks. In late afternoon, tired of asking and tired of looking, I had made up my mind to cross the Seine River and search further along the coast when I heard a rasping voice that could only have begun life in the docklands of London.

"You, sir," I called. "Are you English?"

The object of my attention was startled to hear me. He put his hand on his knife, prepared to defend himself if necessary.

"Nay. Nay. Belay that," I said. "I mean you no harm. I am English too. Where is your ship?"

"What's it to ya?" the sailor asked, his tone belligerent. "What d'ya want?"

"I need passage to England. I am an experienced sailor. Does your captain require any crew?"

"We always need crew, mate. Always. That's the captain over there," he indicated an equally scruffy individual lighting a pipe. "Oy, Captain," he yelled. "This geezer needs a job."

The ship was a small lugger, a two-masted coastal vessel with fore and aft sails. The captain agreed to take me on for the channel crossing, but I would have to work and there was no food unless I could pay for it. Hard work was no more than I expected. The lack of food bothered me not at all.

We landed at Portsmouth after a tedious rolling passage of two days, during which I worked without sleep. I didn't wait for permission to go ashore. As soon as the ship stopped moving, while men secured her lines to a dock, I slung my box on my back and jumped. When my feet touched my native soil for the first time in 28 years I expected to feel some form of emotion, some sense of nostalgia. It wasn't so. My feet were on land, nothing more. The land on which I stood could have been anywhere. I had never been to Portsmouth so there was nothing familiar to my eyes. Even the voices on the wharf sounded strange, their harsh accents so different from the smooth French I had been listening to in recent months. I walked away from the ship without a backward glance. It had been my transport across a body of water. Other than that, it meant nothing to me. I walked through the people thronging the dock area without seeing them. My mind was on the last leg of my long journey. Gravesend was 30 leagues away as the crow flies; slightly more on the route I would have to follow. Putting Portsmouth and the sea behind me, I strode inland.

I walked. I rode on the backs of wagons. I walked. I worked when I could, earning a few coins for chopping wood, running errands, catching rabbits, anything to keep food in my belly as I made my way across southern England through towns and villages to Gravesend. Always, my box of memories was either on my back or close to hand.

Finding my English family took longer than I expected. My father's Gravesend warehouse was still there on the waterfront, but locked. Strangers owned the house I was born in. No one knew of my parents. A neighbour, however, directed me to London where, he said, he thought my sister lived with her husband, Sir Giles Trent. Sir Giles, he told me, was a wealthy ship-owner.

In my youth I had always travelled between Gravesend and London as a passenger on the Long Ferry barge. I had no money for such luxuries this time. The capital city was only seven leagues away to the west. Not so far for a man who had walked from the salt marshes of the Bay of Biscay to Havre de Grâce and from Portsmouth to Gravesend.

Had I not known that my sister's husband was a ship-owner, I would have had no idea where to begin my search. Armed with this knowledge, however, I knew where to ask questions. The walk from Gravesend to Greenwich took me two days. From there I helped row a heavily loaded wherry across to St. Katherine's Pool in exchange for free transport. The Pool was just as I remembered it from the day we sailed out to our destinies in *Discovery.* A forest of masts and spars speared the sky. Coarse voices of stevedores echoed from wharf to wharf. Men loaded ships. More men unloaded other ships. It was a noisy, colourful and vibrant scene. Dirty, too. The smells were just as bad as they had been decades before. Refuse, ordure from horses, dogs and cattle clogged the muddy streets. People pushed and shoved each other as they went about their business. I found the combined effects of noise, unpleasant odours and crowds of ill-mannered people to be overwhelming.

Obtaining the information I required took little time. I asked a gentleman getting out of a coach at the first warehouse if he could direct me to one of Sir Giles Trent's ships. He ignored me and pushed past, a perfumed handkerchief over his nose and face. I asked the coachman the same question.

"Ask at that warehouse there," he pointed to the third in a row of large buildings. I thanked him and set off. The warehouse proved to be owned by Sir Giles. After questioning four or five workers, I finally learned the Trents lived on Philip Lane – about a league or so walk to the north. I had been to Philip Lane once before to meet Sir Dudley Digges in January 1610.

I was far from well-dressed when I arrived at the elegant mansion, appearing more of a dirty tramp than a once promising mathematician. My hair was long and untidy and my beard a mess. I had to make a dreadful fuss before the butler would call for my sister. Emily came to the door, quite flustered by all the commotion. She was older but still had the vibrant look of her early womanhood. She looked me up and down with disdain written all over her face.

"I know not this man. Give him a few small coins and get rid of him," she said to the butler.

"Emily. Emily. It's me, your brother Thomas," I cried. "You cannot turn me away."

"My brother Thomas has been dead these many years," she replied. "How dare you claim his name, you scoundrel?" She turned to go inside.

"Please, Emily. Listen to me. I sailed from London with Captain Hudson on board the ship *Discovery* in April 1610. I am the only survivor of that tragedy."

"Can it be? Is it possible? There is something in your voice that reminds me..." Emily looked as though she might faint any moment.

"I tell you, I am Thomas Woodhouse, your brother," this time I shouted my name. "I am Thomas Woodhouse."

The butler pushed me away from the door, saying, "Be gone, whoever you are."

I dropped to my knees and opened my shirt so the raven was visible. "Emily," I sobbed, "don't you remember my tattoo? Don't you remember how you used to scream and run away when I chased you and your friend Alice with a frog?"

Emily turned, looked at my tattoo and stared hard into my eyes, her mouth open in surprise. "Thomas?" she whispered. "You really are Thomas?"

"Aye," I said, getting to my feet, fastening my shirt and standing tall, "I am Thomas, come back from the dead."

Chapter 34

That evening was bitter sweet. After my first hot bath in many years, a shave, and wearing someone else's clothes, I related a brief version of my story to Emily and her husband, Sir Giles Trent, over dinner. At first I stumbled over the words, my thoughts being marshalled in the Omushkego language before my mind translated them into English. I related the story of the mutiny that changed my life and embarked on my years with the Omushkegowak. When I introduced the subject of Alsoomse and explained our relationship, Emily's face reflected the horror she obviously felt. Her hand flew up to cover her mouth and her face paled. Giles was aghast. His features grew red with anger and disdain.

"You married a savage. Is that what you are saying? A savage?" He looked as if he would explode. "Surely you didn't actually marry her – with a priest?"

"Alsoomse was not a savage. She was the daughter of a chief of the Eeyou Istchee Omushkegowak."

I glared at my brother-in-law as I explained, slowly and clearly with, no doubt, a hint of menace in my voice. "Understand this, Giles Trent, the Omushkegowak are a civilized people, but in a different way from the English concept of civilization. They are most certainly not savages."

Giles continued to frown at me. Emily spoke first, offering an attempted voice of reason. "But surely, Thomas, you cannot expect us to believe that a native from a foreign land is the equal of an English person?"

Seeing his opening, Giles dived in with, "That's right, my dear. How dare you suggest such a thing, Thomas. Your experiences appear to have addled your mind. Savages. Bah!"

I thought about the filth I had seen on the streets, the stink of the dirty brown river coursing through London, the ordure floating in it, and the deplorable state of many of the people I had encountered as I made my way across the city to this elegant house. The Omushkegowak would never have accepted such squalor in their communities. I tried to explain.

"Being born English does not make us superior to other people." My eyes strayed from Emily to Giles and back to Emily again. "The Omushkegowak live in a vastly different style, I agree." I swept my right hand around the room to encompass all the lush fittings and comfortable furnishings in a single gesture. "They certainly would not understand any of this, or your attitude. It's true, none of them can discuss the political situation in England or, indeed in Europe. But they do talk politics, as it relates to the various tribes in the region. They have their hierarchy. They have their leaders. They have their traditions – many of which are centuries older than most traditions in England. They hunt for much of their food. They grow vegetables. Nothing is ever wasted, unlike here. Look around you, outside. It is impossible to walk anywhere without seeing piles of rubbish and other filth."

Giles started to interrupt. I held up a hand, palm facing him. "Wait. Hear me out, Giles, please. There is much you don't understand about the people I have lived with – shared more than half my life with, in fact."

Giles would not listen. "But, Thomas, by your own admission, you were taken as a slave. How can you justify that as civilized behaviour?"

I almost exploded. "That is the most inappropriate statement I have heard since I left England. Are you not aware that Englishmen have been involved in slavery since the time of Drake and Hawkins? Do you consider that civilized behaviour?"

"That's quite different, Thomas," Giles was beginning to bluster. "Those slaves were savages from the jungles of Africa. You are an English gentleman."

"A slave is a slave, no matter what his origins, Giles," I countered. "Slavery is wrong. There's no denying that. And yet, even though a slave, I was always well treated. I eventually earned my freedom and became a respected hunter, member of the tribe and a member of the chief's family. Had I stayed, I would have become chief when my friend Chogan died. Yes, the Omushkegowak looked after me well. They saved my life. And now I am a widower with a son, a daughter-in-law and a granddaughter – and they all have Omushkego blood in them, as well as English for my son and granddaughter."

I looked from Emily to Giles. It was obvious that neither of them understood or agreed with me. I forced a change of subject by asking after Mama and Papa. Emily told me both our parents had died of the plague in 1625. "Papa must have caught it in London and taken it home with him. Mama and Papa died within days of each other. They are buried side by side in the cemetery of St. George's Church in Gravesend."

"I don't imagine any of the Omushkegowak, or other tribes in the New World ever died of the plague, and they are unlikely to – unless they happen to catch the dreadful disease from a white man," I interjected. There was an embarrassed silence for a few minutes; then Emily told me a little of her children, two girls, both married to gentlemen. One lived in London and the other in Canterbury.

"And what news of Mary and our brother, James? You haven't mentioned them," I asked, eager to see them as soon as possible. Emily was silent, her eyes filled with tears as she turned her face away.

"Mary died from consumption soon after you went away to sea," Sir Giles told me. "James grew into a fine young man. But, like you, he rejected the opportunity of working at your father's business. Instead, he followed his older brother and went to sea. He received a commission as an officer in His Majesty's navy." Giles fell silent for a moment, then, "James was lost at sea off Denmark almost twenty years ago. That almost broke your father's heart, having already lost you – his eldest – and little Mary, his youngest child."

Saddened though I was to learn of the tragic deaths in my English family, I had no tears to shed for my parents, or my siblings. They were all so much a part of my distant long lost youth, besides, I had shed all the tears I owned over my Alsoomse's grave. Emily brought me out of my reverie with a question from the distant past. "Do you remember Miss Jane Montrose, Thomas?"

"Yes, of course I do. Mother wanted me to marry her," I answered.

"She waited for you, Thomas," Emily said quietly. "She waited for you as faithful as a lover until word came that you had died in the Arctic. Even then she waited for a long time, hoping the news was false."

"I'm sorry, Emily, indeed I am, but it was a long time ago. My life took a different path through no fault of my own."

"I know, Thomas," Emily reached out and touched my hand. "I know. Jane became a close friend. She is, in fact, my sister-in-law having married Giles's older brother. He died some years ago. Jane lives not far from here. She has a son, a Captain in His Majesty's Navy serving on HMS *Leopard*. I'm sure she would welcome a visit from you."

Leaving me with much to think about, Emily went to bed, exhausted by the day's events. I sat with my brother-in-law, sipping port, while he talked about the happenings in England and Europe since I had sailed away. King James had died in 1625 leaving the throne to his son Charles. More to my interest, as I had no means of financial support, other than a few almost worthless coins, he told me there was an inheritance waiting for me from my father. Emily had kept it in the hope that I might one day return.

"It's not a lot," warned Sir Giles, "but it should pay you around two hundred pounds a year."

Two hundred pounds a year? That was a huge fortune to me. I could now afford lodgings. I could afford decent clothes and I could afford regular meals. Once I was settled, I told Giles, I planned to find out if *Discovery* had ever been heard from in England.

"Indeed, yes," Giles said at once. "I can answer that question for you. *Discovery* returned to England with a small crew. I was with your father in his warehouse when word came that Captain Hudson's *Discovery* had arrived at Gravesend. That was in late August 1611."

"What took you to Gravesend," I asked. "Were you negotiating business with my father?"

"No. Not at first. I had gone to Gravesend to ask him for Emily's hand in marriage."

I smiled at the idea, remembering how much Papa had doted on his two pretty girls.

"That must have been a daunting prospect, Giles. Papa could be quite formidable at times. Obviously he liked you enough to give his approval."

"No, he didn't. He was still playing the role of a father reluctant to lose a daughter when a messenger burst in with the news of the ship's arrival. We hastened directly to the pier, expecting to meet you. My request for Emily's hand was forgotten – at least, it was by him until..."

"Tell me about *Discovery*," I interrupted Giles. "How did she look? Was she shipshape?"

"To be perfectly honest, she was a mess. Even from a distance we could see that she was dirty beyond belief. Close up we could see her rigging was much in need of repair. Her bulwarks were damaged, with parts of them missing. Her sails hung from the yards like rags. She was not a pretty sight and the smell was even worse."

"Did you meet any of the crew – the mutineers?"

"Yes, we met a man named Abacuck Prickett. He was coming ashore when we reached the ship. Your father hailed him, calling, 'You there. Is my son Thomas Woodhouse still aboard?'"

"I knew Prickett well. Like me he was on the ship due to the influence of one of the sponsors. How did he answer my father?"

"We asked his name, which he told us but he was much more reticent about answering any other questions. When asked about you, Prickett stammered a bit and tried to walk away, but I held tight to his arm. Then he told us Tom Woodhouse had died somewhere on a great bay in the Arctic wastes. Your father immediately demanded to see someone in authority. 'Take me to the captain,' he demanded. 'Take me to Captain Hudson. If my son has indeed died, I would hear it from Captain Hudson's own tongue.'

"'That be impossible, sir. Captain Hudson died at the same place. Last spring it were.' Prickett pointed to the poopdeck where a man had just appeared. 'That's Captain Bylot. He's in charge now. He's the one that bought us home.'

"With that Prickett touched his knuckled right hand to his forehead in salute, shrugged my hand from his arm and pushed his way through the crowd that had gathered to see the ship," Giles explained. He stopped for a moment to collect his thoughts, then continued.

"'Captain Bylot,' your father called. 'A word with you, if you please.' Bylot leaned over the ship's rail and studied the two of us. 'Well, what is it?' he answered.

'Allow me to come aboard, sir? I wish to talk with you about my son.'

"While your father talked with Bylot on the poopdeck, I remained on the main deck by the mast and looked around me. I tell you, Thomas, I did not like what I saw. There were dark stains on the planking and on the inside of the bulwarks, plus some splashed on the lower part of the mast. Those dark stains were blood: I'd stake my life on it."

Giles sat for a while, lost in thought, his eyes down, his focus on a memory. I hesitated to interrupt him, although I was almost bursting with more questions. When he looked up at me again, he continued his narrative – his voice soft and reflective.

"It was a long time ago; nearly thirty years. Yet that day is still clear in my mind. What struck me most, Thomas, was the quiet. I have visited many ships recently arrived in port from foreign lands, before and since. Without exception, they are bustling with action. There are men hauling off cargo; sailors, happy to be home, talking and waving to friends and family on shore. There is always an air of excitement. There was none of that lively atmosphere on the *Discovery*'s decks. No crew members, other than Captain Bylot and the aforementioned Abacuck Prickett, were in evidence. The ship was quiet, like – like a grave. Only later did I learn that the few crew members to survive the voyage back to England had fled over the side as soon as the ship tied up to the jetty."

Giles suddenly stood up. "That reminds me. I have something that belongs to you. Two things, in fact."

When he returned he carried my sword in one hand and my journal in the other. He handed them to me. I couldn't speak at first. I turned the sword over and over in my hand, feeling the emotion in my eyes, remembering the day my father had presented it to me when I was a boy.

"Thank you, Giles. Thank you. How did you come by these treasures?" I asked.

"Your father demanded that Bylot hand over any of your belongings. His demeanour left Bylot in no doubt that a refusal would result in more trouble than it was worth. Bylot went to his cabin and returned with those two items. Your chest of clothes, he told us, had been shared out among the crew after you died."

I held my sword and my journal on my lap. I was unable to speak, the emotions raging through me, taking away my ability to think clearly.

"My father gave me this sword when I was a little boy," I said at length. "And my mother gave me the journal just before we sailed for the Arctic. These two items mean the world to me. They are all I have left of my early life. Thank you."

"I know," said Giles. "That's why I kept them, in case you ever came home."

"Tell me, Giles, what sad story did Bylot tell you and my father about my death?"

"He, like Prickett, said you died in a great bay in the Arctic, but Bylot added that you were killed in a battle with savages. They had obviously prepared their story together. Your father wept for a long time before he could find the strength to go home and tell your mother. It was a sad day for all of us."

We sat in silence for a while, each with his own memories of that year of infamy. Giles poured two more glasses of port. Standing with his back to the window, he took a sip of his; then cleared his throat.

"Emily and I married less than a year later. I had an inheritance from my father so I invested in the Woodhouse Trading and Shipping Company and became a partner. I have been running the business as Woodhouse-Trent since your father became ill from the plague in 1625. My daughter, who has a keen head for business, helps me."

"Why then do you live in London," I asked. "Do you not still maintain the warehouse in Gravesend?"

"No. We sold the Gravesend buildings many years ago. The warehouse and the family home were the last to go. We moved here and opened a new, larger warehouse at St. Katherine's Pool."

"Yes, I have been there," I put in. "That's how I found your address, from the foreman in charge."

"I predict that London, more specifically, St. Katherine's Pool and the docklands nearby, will become the primary shipping port for southern England. I believe Gravesend will soon see a decline in the cargo business," Giles added.

When I mentioned going to Gravesend to visit the graves of my family, Sir Giles cautioned me to be careful. The roads, he said, were unsafe due to the many villains preying on travellers. It didn't seem to occur to him that I had walked that road alone only recently.

"Go by river, on the Long Ferry" he said. "It is still in service. You can get a barge from Greenwich which will take you to Gravesend in safety, if not in comfort."

The following day Giles introduced me to his tailor. Within a few hours I was again dressed like a gentleman – for the first time since the spring of 1610. That evening over dinner we talked of my forthcoming visit to Gravesend where I planned to find accommodation. Emily wanted me to live in London but I felt the need to be somewhere more familiar. I did agree that I would take advantage of their hospitality whenever I was in the city. Unable to convince me to stay permanently, she asked me to delay my departure for a few days so we could tell each other more about the missing years – even about my other family in the New World. It never occurred to me that my sister had an ulterior motive.

Chapter 35

As part of my quest to find anyone and everyone linked to the *Discovery* expedition, I went to the house where Captain Hudson had interviewed me in early 1610. The Hudson family's old home at St. Katherine's was still there but under new ownership. Mistress Hudson and her family had not been seen for many years. The new owner believed she had gone out to India with her youngest son a year or so after *Discovery* returned without Henry and John.

I went back to Philip Lane to find my sister entertaining a guest for the afternoon. I suppose I should have expected something of the kind but, still finding my way about the modern world of England, and preoccupied by my search for answers to the mutiny, I missed the obvious.

"Ah, Thomas," Emily beamed at me as I entered the room, "may I introduce Lady Trent, my sister-in-law?"

I was conscious of the fact that my once golden hair had long since turned to grey, though it was clean and tied back in a neat queue with a black silk ribbon. The skin of my face was dark from exposure to all weathers and creased by the remorseless assault of time. My hands were rough and scarred, the way seamen's and wilderness peoples' hands always are. By contrast, the former Jane Montrose was just as I remembered her. Slim, lovely figure, red hair, clear blue eyes: the face of a young woman, though with a few faint lines at the corners of her eyes. The years had not diminished her beauty. She smiled at me; put out a hand, over which I bowed and touched with my lips.

"Lady Trent," I murmured.

"Hello, Thomas Woodhouse," she said in the soft, yet confident voice I remembered most clearly from a few seconds after we had kissed so many years before. "Welcome back from the dead. Emily has been telling me thrilling stories of your adventures since we last met."

"Please, Thomas, sit down," Emily patted the seat beside her. "Will you take wine with us?"

I must confess, I was at a loss as to what to do or say. So many years had passed since I had employed the social graces of my youth. I sat, as Emily ordered. I accepted a crystal glass of red wine and sipped. Finding my voice at last, I addressed Emily's guest.

"It's a surprise and a pleasure to see you again, uh... Lady Trent," I said, hesitating before saying her name and trying not to appear too uncomfortable. Jane and Emily laughed, each with a hand over her mouth.

"Thomas, please, my name is still Jane and, don't forget, we are now related by marriage."

She sounded wistful though her smile appeared almost mocking. I sat through an hour of pleasantries, perched on the edge of my seat. My discomfort must have been obvious to both Jane and Emily but neither commented. When at last I felt I could leave with some of my dignity intact, Lady Trent offered me her hand again.

"Shall we see you again soon, Thomas? Or are you running off on another adventure?"

"I hope I shall be here to greet you again, Lady Trent," I answered, still holding her hand. "I must go to Gravesend for a while. Later, I have people to see in London regarding the events of my Arctic voyage."

"Of course you will see Thomas again, Jane," Emily stepped in. "He has promised to stay with us whenever he is in London."

I let go of Jane's hand. "Yes, yes, I expect to be a regular visitor for a while."

"Wonderful," said Emily, clapping her hands together. "I know. We shall have a dinner party to welcome you home properly."

I cringed at the thought but knew that I could not possibly avoid it. Even as a child, once Emily made her mind up about something, there was no stopping her. Even Papa had always to accept her plans.

"Thank you, Emily," I said, mustering a smile. I bowed once to Jane – Lady Trent – and made my escape. Emily's plan was obvious. She would do everything in her considerable powers to put Thomas Woodhouse and Lady Jane Trent close to each other as often as possible. I had no doubt that she and Giles had a large group of affluent friends, as did Jane. London society would soon be introduced to a man who had married a savage, of all things. I shuddered at the thought of being on display at a dinner but knew that nothing short of my death would save me from the occasion.

I visited the graves of my parents and my sister, Mary, in Gravesend as soon as I could. St. George's Church looked exactly as it had in my youth. I sat for a while in what used to be the family pew, even imagining I could see Miss Montrose across the aisle. The peace and quiet suited me yet I found it impossible to pray. A young priest came by, his slippered feet shuffling on the cold smooth granite stones of the floor. I introduced myself and for a few minutes we talked about his predecessor, the priest I had known before I went to the Arctic.

Later, in front of my family's headstones, with my hat in one hand, I knelt and made the sign of the cross, blinked away tears, but no words came. I couldn't even say goodbye. Their names were carved in bold letters on the vertical blocks of marble, even so, I could not imagine the bodies of my mother, father and little Mary, deep under the earth in their lonely wooden coffins. As I made my way to the cemetery gate I came across another stone marked with the name *Pocahontas.* She, the inscription said, was a native princess from the Powhatan people of the Virginia Colony. Pocahontas had died on a ship anchored off Gravesend in 1617 while on her way home. She died at my home town while I lived among other, similar natives far north of Virginia. I pondered on Pocahontas's story for a long time. It seemed to parallel mine in a strange sort of way.

About this time, I was able to find suitable lodgings in Gravesend, a valet to look after my clothes and a cook to prepare my meals. With a roof over my head and comfortable accommodation, I could then continue my purpose: to find out, if at all possible, what had happened to the mutineers and to *Discovery.* That meant a return to London for a few days.

I found most of the answers buried in the archives at Trinity House in Deptford, on the south bank of the Thames near Greenwich. Toughened by the years though I was, the results of my searches filled me with sorrow even, for a few minutes, bringing tears to my eyes. The records though, told a far different story from that related to my father by Robert Bylot on the day *Discovery* returned to Gravesend.

After we were cast adrift, *Discovery* sailed north with Henry Greene as captain. Greene, a scoundrel if ever there was one and leader of the mutiny, was killed by natives in the northern sector of the great bay. He was no loss to me. Michael Perse, John Thomas and Andrew Motter were all killed in the same battle. The bodies of all four of them were sent over the side without ceremony; their bones to stir restlessly under the ice on the sea bed of the great bay. With Greene's death, Robert Bylot took command of the ship.

Robert Juet, another scoundrel, died of starvation on the return voyage just to the west of Ireland. His body was also tossed overboard. The ship and remaining mutineers made landfall on the south-west coast of Ireland at Bere Haven. The men were starving. The ship was in a terrible state. No one in Bere Haven would help *Discovery*'s crew until the master of a barque from the Cornish port of Fowey gave them money in return for an anchor and cable. At last they were able to buy food and continue their voyage to England. *Discovery* called in at Plymouth to await a fair wind on the Channel. With the wind at her back, she then sailed east along the south coast of her homeland, past the Downs and so north and west into the Thames estuary. As Sir Giles had told me, *Discovery* returned to Gravesend in August, 1611.

The seven survivors, five of whom had fled as soon as the ship docked, were rounded up and imprisoned in London. Eventually, each was forced to give his account of the voyage and the subsequent mutiny to the officials of Trinity House. At first the mutineers were ordered to be held in custody until such time as Captain Hudson could be rescued, or proof was learned of his death. In the latter event all would be held in prison for the remainder of their lives. It wasn't to be so. The seven depositions, when taken together, apparently showed reasonable cause for the mutiny. All seven survivors were set free. Not one of the mutineers was sent to the gallows for the crime of mutiny, or murder. Not one. How could that be? I asked myself, time and time again.

In the files of Trinity House, I found a copy of the decision that freed the seven sailors. It was dated October 24, 1611:

"By examination of the seven of the company of that ship that endeavoured to make the north-west discovery, it appears that the Master and the rest of those men which are lost were put out of the ship by consent of all such as are come home and in good health. The plot was begun by Henry Greene and Wm. Wilson, but that Juet, whom they considered to be their pilot, was privy to the plot.

Abacuck Prickett clears Robert Bylot, who came home Master, of being acquainted with the plot at the beginning. Prickett said Bylot was only chosen to take charge of the ship after the Master had been put away in the shallop. They all charged Master Hudson with having wasted or stolen the victuals. All conclude that, to save some from starving, they were content to put so many away."

One of the charges against the Master was that he had hoarded food himself and shared it only with his favourites among the officers and crew. That was preposterous. I knew the seven men had collaborated to confuse the truth. I knew it deep in my soul, but could do nothing about it after the lapse of close to 28 years. Besides, my research showed that Robert Bylot was exonerated of any wrongdoing and sent once again to the sea that I thought of as Hudson Bay in 1612. Bylot became a respected man. To my surprise, and to my consternation, I learned he had gone back to the great bay as captain of our old ship, *Discovery,* as part of a two-ship expedition under the command of Sir Thomas Button. Even more surprising, Abacuck Prickett went with Bylot. I have no idea of the places they explored. I do know they could not have been searching for Captain Henry Hudson and the rest of us castaways. Once they found their way through the Furious Overfall, they must have stayed in the northern regions of the great bay. They certainly did not sail into Winipekw, the smaller extremity in the far south, close to where we had been cast adrift by the mutineers.

The unpleasant truth astounded me. Although those two English expedition ships were there in that great bay only one year after we were so cruelly treated, and two of the survivors of the mutiny were on board, they did not have the heart to sail south to search for us. I lived, hunted and fished in that area with my Omushkego family every spring, summer and autumn, for twenty-seven years. Had a big sailing ship come within sight at any time, I would have known about it. No one came looking for us.

In London I heard that Bylot, now long dead, had become famous as an Arctic explorer, having made at least two other voyages to the northern regions – and even had an island named for him. That was the final insult to the late Captain Hudson, as far as I was concerned. Although he had proved to be a flawed man, I believe Henry Hudson was without equal in the annals of Arctic exploration. The other survivors of the mutiny, Prickett included eventually, all disappeared into the English countryside or towns, never to be seen again in London.

The expedition's three main sponsors, Sir Dudley Digges, Sir John Wolstenholme and Sir Thomas Smythe were all dead. Smythe had passed on in 1625. Digges and Wolstenholme both died shortly before I returned to England. Professor Richard Hakluyt had died long before in

1616. There was no one left to be interested in my account of the mutiny or of Captain Hudson's death. A callow young clerk at Trinity House claimed he had never even heard of Henry Hudson. On a more trivial note, there was no one left from whom I could claim the pay owed to me from the time we left England, until the mutiny at least.

Trinity House records showed that the High Court of the Admiralty had also taken an interest in the case on two occasions, five years apart. Nothing conclusive was decided and the surviving crew members were again not charged with mutiny. I left Trinity House with a heavy heart, thinking much of Captain Hudson, and of my shipmates on that long ago voyage.

Although Bylot and Prickett had not sailed south into Winipekw to look for the castaways in 1612, I did find out that another English ship had sailed into the area in 1631. Under the command of Captain Thomas James, a Welshman who sailed out of Bristol, the one-ship expedition spent the winter of 1631 to '32 on a large island almost opposite *Discovery*'s wintering place of over 20 years before. They reported finding evidence of possible white men on a nearby smaller island, just east of their island. That evidence consisted of an obvious fire pit and two thick sharpened wooden stakes. We, the castaways from *Discovery*, had left those sharpened stakes there, with others, as part of the supports for a primitive shelter. I thought it rather strange that Captain James would not have looked at those stakes and thought of the possible relationship with Captain Hudson's castaways. If he did, he did not mention the possible connection in his journal.

I was much saddened to know that some of my fellow countrymen had passed a winter on a piece of land James named Charlton Island for Prince Charles. I knew the island as Kaamischii. It was no more than about 15 leagues to the north-west of Waskagahanish. As none of the Omushkegowak had seen them, their anchorage must have been on the west side of the island, out of sight of the east coast of the bay. Most of us, of course, were far inland throughout the winter at the hunting grounds beyond the waterfalls. Reading Captain James's powerful story from beginning to end, I wondered had I chanced to meet them, would I have gone home to England with them? Would I have taken Alsoomse and Ahanu with me? They were questions without answers.

In his journal, Captain James mentioned having two dogs on board. A dog and a bitch, they ate too much food and stole rations from the men, so he put them ashore south of a cape he named Henrietta Maria after his ship. The male dog wore a collar. There, by the merest chance, for I had not expected to read Captain James's journal, I had the answer to the mystery of the dog skeleton wearing a collar and its mate, now an old hunting pal named Masko. They could only have come from James's ship.

An interesting comment arose in Captain James's story. When he accepted he would not be able to get out of the bay to the north with winter's ice so close, he expressed a desire to sail to the most southerly recesses of the bay (in a rush of ego, he named it James Bay for himself) and from there find his way to Cartier's Rivière du Canada. Captain James wrote. "I resolved...to go down into the bottom of Hudson's Bay; and see if I could discover a way into the River of Canada."

Captain Hudson had hoped to do the same after being cast out from *Discovery*. Armed with an abundance of local knowledge, I had done exactly that many years later.

Because he could not find a navigable waterway in the south, the rivers being too shallow for a big ship, he sailed a short distance north to set up winter quarters on Charlton Island. Captain James's reference to the great bay north of his James Bay as Hudson's Bay pleased me. If the name finds its way onto maps and charts of the area, and I hope it does, it would be a fitting tribute to a fine explorer. Captain James also referred to the icy strait leading to the ocean as Hudson Strait.

Although six men died that winter from accidents and illness, Captain James and his surviving crew were able to free their ship, *Henrietta Maria*, from the ice in the spring of 1632 and set sail for Bristol. After a desperate struggle to avoid the heavy drifting ice and icebergs in Hudson Bay and in Hudson Strait, they reached their home port on October 22nd, 1632. With the end of that voyage, it seemed, the case of Captain Henry Hudson was closed.

While in London, I enquired as to the fate of my boyhood hero – Sir Walter Raleigh – sentenced to death by King James in late 1603. I remembered the king had later commuted his sentence to life imprisonment. One of the clerks at Trinity House told me Raleigh had been released in 1616 to lead an expedition to find a place the Spaniards called El Dorado. He was unsuccessful, which angered the king. Raleigh, I was told, made more trouble for himself by attacking Spanish ships, despite an order against such actions from his sovereign. As a result, at the end of that adventure King James reinstated his original sentence. Raleigh was beheaded at the Tower in October 1618. That was a sad day for England, in my opinion.

I also learned at Trinity House that the enormous East Indiaman *Trades Increase,* on which I had once been offered a midshipman's position by Sir Dudley Digges, had foundered in the Spice Islands on her maiden voyage with appalling loss of life. How strange are the fates that govern our lives?

Chapter 36

Emily announced her dinner party to welcome home her long lost brother for the following Saturday. Giles, who seemed to understand how I felt, warned me not to forget.

"Emily will never forgive you if you disappear again, especially before Saturday. Now, how about a snifter? I have some excellent Cognac in my study." So saying, he led me to his private haven and the comfort of a well-padded leather armchair.

"Put your feet up, Thomas. You are safe from Emily in here," he said with a laugh. With more seriousness, he added, "You do realize that Emily is bound and determined to marry you off to my sister-in-law, don't you?"

"Yes. I remember all too well how her mind worked as a child. It seems not so much has changed. How many people are you expecting to attend on Saturday?"

Giles swirled the Cognac in his glass, deep in thought. "Well, Emily's soirées tend to be rather extravagant. I have never been able to reign her in. When she gets the bit between her teeth, so to speak, well... you can imagine what she's like."

"Yes, I can. But how many guests will there be?"

"Emily has promised me that this will be an intimate occasion, so no more than about thirty – I should hope." Giles didn't sound convinced by his own words.

On the dreaded evening, Emily made it clear to all that her sister-in-law, Lady Trent, was there as my companion. Delightful company though Jane was, I did not approve of being partnered in that way. Giles cautioned me to, "Grin and bear it, old chap."

A steady flow of affluence arrived dressed in their finest to greet Emily and Giles, Jane and the guest of honour – Thomas Woodhouse, lately risen from the dead. My sister knew everyone who was anyone in London. Thirty of the crème de la crème came to gaze upon my weathered face. I shook hands with every man at least once and kissed a bevy of silk-gloved hands. Jane, I must admit, was a tower of strength. Sensing my acute discomfort, she steered me through many pointless conversations and inane questions. Never once did she leave my side. For the most part she stood close with one hand resting lightly on my forearm. One future dowager asked, "But what did you do in the forest all day long, Mister Woodhouse?"

"I hunted, ma'am. We always needed fresh meat."

"You hunted? All the time? Was there not a butcher, grocer or some such tradesman – whatever they are called – one could count on?"

"No, ma'am. There are no such amenities in the forests where I lived. We looked after ourselves."

"Surely, you don't mean... you couldn't, surely?"

"Mean what, ma'am? I'm afraid I don't follow you." I kept a straight face and attempted to sound interested. Jane pinched my arm and stifled a giggle with her other hand.

"Well, I mean... Did you actually shoot the wild animals, with a musket? Wasn't that terribly dangerous?"

"Yes, and no, ma'am. Yes, most often I shot them, but no, not with a musket. I did not possess a firearm. I used a bow and arrow, or a spear, like the rest of my tribe." Getting into my stride, I added, "As for danger, well, sometimes, when the beasts came close enough, I wrestled them to the ground and dispatched them with my knife. Especially the bears. They were dangerous but they seemed to enjoy wrestling. After that I skinned and butchered them." I could feel Jane shaking with suppressed mirth beside me.

"How very interesting," murmured the future dowager, her face the image of a sour lemon. "Yes, very interesting indeed."

Being the centre of attention in London society after half a lifetime spent living in a forest was unnerving. Without Jane by my side I doubt that I could have navigated through the guests with so little effort. Most of the people I spoke with had never been out of England. They had no idea what life was like in any other country. They certainly could not understand how I had lived. That did not stop them from asking questions that bordered on the infantile from some, and outright impertinence from others. I don't recall who was worse, the women or the men.

One young lady, revealing her deeper interests by blushing as Jane introduced her to me, wanted to know where the doctor came from who attended to Alsoomse at Ahanu's birth. I explained that there were no doctors in the forest. I told her that some of the women assisted my wife. The young lady shuddered in horror and turned pale enough for me to be concerned that she might faint. She held on to my arm to steady herself.

"Don't you think that was a rather indelicate question?" Jane leaned over and asked her.

"Actually, there was nothing unusual or difficult about the birth. A couple of hours later my wife was out working on a canoe with me," I offered, hoping that would free me from the conversation. It did and very quickly.

Some of the men, particularly one of the younger ones, were curious to the point of rudeness. One, positioning himself so as to avoid Jane hearing, leaned over and asked me in what he assumed was a low voice, "I hear you were married to a savage, old boy. What was that like? Must have been wild in bed, what? Haw. Haw. Haw."

He laughed like a donkey braying. Jane stiffened and gave a gentle tug on my arm. I refused to budge. Beckoning the donkey to come closer, I whispered in his ear, "My savage wife would have cut your testicles off and stuffed them down your throat. And so will I if you say another word to me." Leaning back to see his face light up in scarlet anger, I smiled at him and turned away, with Jane on my arm.

"What was that all about, Thomas? Was he being rude?" she asked, not having heard the exchange, only seen the facial expressions.

"Oh, he thought he was being funny. I simply reminded him to act like a gentleman. It's nothing to worry about."

I could have gone home with Jane that night, I'm sure of it. The desire was certainly there on my part, and the look on her face, plus the pressure of her fingers on my hand suggested her feelings, but the possible consequences for both of us held me back. I helped her into her coach and told the footman to make sure she reached home safely. The hour was late, all the other guests had gone home, only Emily and Giles would have known, plus a few servants, yet I sent Jane away and retired to my own bed. Sleep was a long time in coming that night. My mind played with images of Jane in various stages of undress. My mind played with images of Alsoomse and our life in the forest. My mind mixed and mingled Jane and Alsoomse. My mind and my body were at odds.

Over breakfast in the morning, Emily announced that she and Giles had been invited to a small gathering that afternoon. I was invited too and Jane would be there. I began to feel that the social vultures were circling to feast on my emotions. I begged off, explaining that I needed to hasten back to Gravesend on urgent business. To avoid appearing rude, or inconsiderate, I sent word to Jane that I would call on her when next I visited London.

At home again in Gravesend, and relieved to be away from the gossip and inquisitive minds of London society, I set myself to the task of transcribing my birch-bark notes onto real paper and adding more detail. When my eyes began to tire, I walked along the waterfront to the Blockhouse and sat by the wall if the weather allowed, sometimes reading my journal, at other times I just held it tight in my hand, closed my eyes and thought of the long distant past. As I wrote, more and more memories came flooding back – many prompted by the words I had written as a young man. Memories of the Arctic voyage in *Discovery*. Memories of the mutiny and of the mutineers. Those memories were followed by reminders of my early days of slavery with the Omushkegowak, and the warm memories of my subsequent life as a respected storyteller and hunter. Most precious of all were my thoughts of the passionate years with Alsoomse.

Occasionally I travelled to London for a few days, where Emily soon organized me into escorting Jane to a mind-numbing variety of social gatherings each time. One evening I fulfilled a boyhood dream by taking Jane with me to the Globe Theatre to see a performance of *Hamlet.* Shakespeare had died in 1616 but his plays continued to be performed in his theatre. We both enjoyed the drama very much. On the last occasion we were together, as we sat in Jane's drawing room late at night, I tried to explain to her that my life had been so different from the sedate society life she lived that I could not see any future for us. I told her I would be going away again and might never return. Jane was unhappy but her breeding and character shone through. She smiled at me as we were about to part, placed her arms around my neck, kissed me full on the lips and said, "If you do come back to London, Thomas, you will come and see me, won't you?"

I assured her that I would. As I reached the door, Jane said my name softly. I turned to look at her. She was slowly undoing the strings of her pink silk bodice, an enigmatic smile on her face.

"Will you not stay with me this one night, Thomas? Will you not love me just once before you leave?" Jane asked.

We loved each other with a passion born of loneliness and desperation: a passion that had been building in each of us for too long. Much later, after sleeping with Jane in my arms, I awoke as the first nightingales began their morning song. Jane greeted me with a kiss, her beautiful body naked against mine. She moved lower and studied my tattoo.

"The tattoo suits you, Thomas," she said and kissed it. I kissed her lips once more and started to get out of bed. We both knew that something, somewhere far away, called to me.

"I know it is time for you to leave, Thomas. You may go, if you must," she said.

As I dressed, Jane lay there in the bed watching me, her red hair spread out on the white silk pillow, a sheet over her lower body; her breasts uncovered. She smiled though a tear ran down the side of her face.

"Goodbye, Thomas, my darling," she said, her voice gentle, wistful. "Look after yourself and come back to me, if you can."

I leaned over, pulled the sheet up to her chin, kissed her once and nodded my head. "If God wills," I said.

That night after dinner, I told Emily and Giles of my decision. Emily was disappointed enough to be extremely angry with me. She stormed off to her room in tears. Giles was more understanding, though even he had to state a case for his sister-in-law.

"I think you are making a big mistake, old chap. I really do. Jane is a wonderful woman. She would make you a good wife."

Alsoomse had been a good wife. No, far more than that. She had been a wonderful wife. She had been the perfect wife for me. No one could take her place. Not even the lovely Jane Trent. I kept those thoughts to myself, knowing that no one else would understand.

"Oh, Giles. I know only too well that you and Emily would like me to stay and take Jane as my wife, and I understand why. Jane is a lovely lady and would make a fine partner. There would be many other advantages to me, too, not the least of which would be to share in the lives of my English family," I paused, trying to make my words as kind as possible. "But it cannot be. I doubt that I could make Jane happy for very long. I am nothing like the young man she once knew."

"Forgive me for the interruption a moment, Thomas," Giles broke in. "When we see you and Jane together, we see a couple made for each other. Other people see it too. Emily believes that Jane has waited for you all her life, despite having been married to my brother. Does that not warrant more thought on the subject?"

"I have feelings for Jane. I cannot deny that. It is not enough though. I know myself too well, Giles. I would soon grow restless here in the claustrophobic confines of London or Gravesend and want to leave. Every time I saw a ship, I would want to be on it with the wind in my face. Every time I looked to the west, I would think of the forests around Waskagahanish. My heart is already far away."

Giles leaned forward. "You find London claustrophobic. How so? I have never heard of such a thing. London is growing fast. There is nothing claustrophobic about it."

"I'm sorry, Giles, if my use of the word offends you. I am used to living on the edge of a forest beside a river with a vast unpopulated land around me," I explained. "London is claustrophobic to me, as is Gravesend. There are too many houses; too many buildings in general; too many people crowded together. And far too many people poking their noses into their neighbours' affairs. No, it is not for me. I have no desire to be a part of such a society."

We both fell silent, each with his own thoughts. I decided to tell him about the potential for profit in the fur trade. Perhaps then he might have a better understanding of the world I missed.

"I've noticed many gentlemen wearing hats which, I believe, must be made from beaver fur. I saw the same in France. Are there so many beavers left in the countryside of England and Europe?" I asked.

"No. In fact, I have heard that the creatures are becoming more and more difficult to find. They might even be extinct in this country. The same is true of the other furs worn by ladies – most of them come from Russia, I believe. Why do you ask?"

"The forests, rivers and lakes where I live contain an abundance of fur-bearing animals," I replied and starting counting them off. "There are beavers beyond number. There are three different bears, each with a different coloured coat – brown, black and a yellowish white. There are wildcats, wolves, mink, muskrat and so many more. And then there are the deer. Their hides make excellent leather. There is a vast bounty there, Giles, just waiting to be harvested. The French have already made their own advances into lands to the south of my region."

"What are you suggesting, Thomas?" Giles asked, his curiosity aroused.

"Nothing, for the moment. I need to go home. Once there, I will explore the possibilities and, if I can, send word, or an envoy, to recommend the appropriate steps. Before I leave, I would ask you to draw up papers to have most of my inheritance reinvested in Woodhouse-Trent in my son's name. Perhaps, somehow, it will one day benefit he and his family."

I left for Gravesend two days later. From there I sent word of my requirements to the ports of London and Bristol; to Southampton and to Falmouth. I talked to all the captains I met on the waterfront in Gravesend. To all of them I had the same message: I am looking for passage across the North Atlantic. I am prepared to pay and to pay handsomely.

Unfortunately, there were no ships sailing from southern England to the French territory on the Rivière du Canada. I walked to my old haunt – the wall of the Blockhouse beside the Thames – and sat there considering all the possibilities. Seeing a Dutch ensign on a merchant ship anchored in the river, the obvious answer came to me. I would have to make my way to Antwerp, or perhaps to a French channel port first. As the first drops of rain started to speckle the river, I returned along the waterfront to my customary ale house, talking aloud to myself all the way: thinking of the forests around my home. Thinking of the beavers and the bears. Making plans.

EPILOGUE

On a rainy day in May, 1640, a ship sailed downstream from St. Katherine's Pool on the evening tide. She was a three-masted barque, somewhat larger than *Discovery* had been. She called in at Gravesend the following morning to take on some freight from a waterfront warehouse and to board one passenger. She was bound for Antwerp with a heavy mixed cargo of wool and iron. On that day, as the Thames's powerful late morning tide was in flood, the usual customers crowded the *Eagle and Child.* By early afternoon one small table remained unoccupied.

"Where is Master Woodhouse? He's late today." called the landlord. A serving girl moved past, mugs of foaming ale clasped in her hands, and shouted above the din of voices, "Dunno. I ain't seen 'im yet."

Master Woodhouse did not take a seat at his usual table that day. In fact, he never again set foot in the *Eagle and Child,* and was never again seen walking along the Gravesend waterfront or reading by the Blockhouse wall. There is no record of this Thomas Woodhouse anywhere in England after May 1640. It is not known whether he was the lone passenger to board that sailing ship departing Gravesend, or even if he ever found a ship to take him home. No one in England knew whether he returned to his people with more stories to tell, or whether he again went out into the woods to trap furs for clothing or for trade. Only he and his son, Ahanu, held the answers to those questions.

The former Jane Montrose waited in London for him, once again for a long time, but Thomas Woodhouse simply disappeared. Jane, the widowed Lady Trent, settled gracefully into old age. She never remarried.

When the earliest French and later British fur traders arrived in the forests on the southern shore of James Bay, they traded with the chief of an Omushkegowak village called Waskagahanish, on the south bank of a fast-flowing river. The chief was tall, with long black hair showing a few streaks of grey. He had dark brown eyes and a lighter skin than the rest of his people. He spoke a variety of native dialects, plus passable Latin, some Dutch, fluent French and English, the latter with an upper class accent coloured with the subtle tones of the boreal forest. The fur traders soon learned that he was a hard bargainer with a surprising knowledge of the needs in Europe for his product and the prices paid there. He introduced himself as Ahanu Thomas Barnaby Woodhouse.

Many of those same fur traders of the mid 1600s heard rumours of a very old white man living with the Omushkego at Waskagahanish, but no one ever saw him. None of the Omushkegowak spoke of him. No one could or would substantiate the tales. If that old white man was indeed the former mathematician, Thomas Woodhouse, also known as Otácimow – the storyteller, he remained elusive to the end.

ACKNOWLEDGEMENTS & AUTHOR'S NOTES

Although this book is a work of fiction parts of the story are based on actual events, particularly the voyage and subsequent 1611 mutiny by Captain Henry Hudson's crew in the sub-Arctic bay that now bears his name. There was a young mathematician on board Hudson's ship *Discovery*. He was employed as an ordinary seaman and was cast adrift from the ship with Captain Hudson and others by the mutineers. His name was either Thomas Wydowse, Thomas Wydhouse, Thomas Wodehouse or Thomas Woodhouse. I have chosen the latter. Nothing is known of his background or his family. As the real Thomas was a mathematician and could read and write, he was obviously educated; therefore, I chose to give him a family of consequence and a privileged upbringing.

I must stress that Henry Hudson and his fellow castaways were never seen again. My reconstruction of the events immediately following the mutiny in Hudson Bay is the product of my over-active imagination. All characters in this book are either my own creation or are historical figures used fictitiously. Any resemblance to persons living or dead is purely coincidental.

A version of the route that Thomas, also known as Otácimow, followed from Waskagahanish to Tadoussac became an important fur trade route in the mid to late 17th century. The French Catholic mission at Tadoussac is the oldest such establishment in Canada. It was built in 1615 and continues to exist today.

My thanks and appreciation to my group of dedicated First Readers. Steve, Karen, Penny and Bill read the manuscript, pointed out grammatical and punctuation errors, noted a couple of gaps in the plot and questioned elements of my story as they did so. The completed book has been improved thanks to their diligence. Any errors that remain are mine. A special thanks to my long-time friend and occasional co-writer Steve Crowhurst. Steve was one of my First Readers. He also created the maps and designed the excellent cover for this book. And, thanks to Cricket Freeman, literary agent extraordinaire.

The following books were of great assistance to me in the writing of this novel:

Samuel Purchas, *Henry Hudson, The Navigator.* London, 1625.

G.S.P. Freeman-Grenville, *The Wordsworth Book of the Kings & Queens of England.* Wordsworth Reference, 1997.

Dava Sobell, *Longitude.* Walker, New York, 1995.

H.V. Morton, *In Search of London.* Methuen, London, 1951.

GLOSSARY NAUTICAL TERMS

Able Seaman (AB): A sailor who is qualified to handle sails, reef them and steer a ship.

Ague: An illness with symptoms such as shivering and sweating, rather like influenza.

Astrolabe: An early device used in navigation to measure the altitude of the sun or moon.

Backstaff: An early device used in navigation to measure the altitude of the sun or moon. More efficient than the earlier astrolabe.

Barque (also bark): A sailing ship with three or more masts, with all but the stern-most square-rigged. The stern-most, usually a mizzen, being fore-and-aft-rigged.

Barquentine (also barkentine): A sailing ship with three or more masts; with a square-rigged foremast and all other masts rigged with fore-and-aft sails.

Belay 1. To make fast a line around a cleat or belaying pin.

Belay 2. An order to stop a current activity, or to countermand an order prior to its execution.

Bend: To attach sails, as in, to bend on sails.

Bo'sun (also boatswain): A non-commissioned rank responsible for the sails, ropes, rigging and small boats on a ship. The bo'sun also gives orders to seamen by notes on a pipe.

Bowsprit: A wooden spar extending from the bow of a ship to which forestays are attached.

Bulwarks: The extension of a ship's sides above the level of outer decks.

Cable: A thick, strong rope used for mooring a ship.

Capstan: A vertical cylinder or drum with extended spokes used to raise or lower an anchor. In the 17th century the capstan was powered by sailors.

Captain: The Master of a ship.

Caulking: Fibrous material pushed between planks to create a seal and make a vessel watertight.

Course: The route a ship takes to reach a destination.

Courses: Square sails on a traditional sailing ship.

First Mate: A senior officer. One step below the captain on a sailing ship.

Flotsam: Debris thrown up from the sea.

Frames: Transverse ribs attached to a ship's keel to form and strengthen a hull.

Hawse: A hole in the bow of a ship through which anchor cables are run.

Kedge: A method of moving a ship by means of an anchor and line set in a required direction.

Keel: A longitudinal member on which the frames and the hull of ships and boats are built.

Keelson: A length of wood running parallel to the keel of a wooden boat but above the transverse ribs. The keelson fastens the ribs to the keel and strengthens the overall structure.

Lateen: A triangular sail carried on a long yard and rigged at a 45° angle to a mast.

Latitude: Parallel lines running east-west around the world parallel to the equator.

League: A measurement of distance. Usually 1 league = 3 nautical miles at sea, or the distance a man could walk in 1 hour on land.

Lee board: A vertical plank of wood, with the same function as a centreboard, but attached to the leeward side of a sailboat.

Long Ferry: A passenger barge transportation system on the Thames River between Gravesend and Greenwich, started in the early 15th century.

Longitude: Meridians or vertical lines running between the North and South Poles.

Lugger: A small sailboat with two masts, originally with gaff sails.

Master: see Captain

Midshipman: An officer cadet. The lowest rank of the officer class.

Mizzen: The mast aft of the main mast on a sailing ship. Also a sail.

Mutiny: A rebellion against the authority of the captain of a ship.

Navigation card: The forerunner of today's navigation chart. A map for use at sea.

Navigator: The person responsible for ascertaining a ship's position and course at sea.

Pikestaff (also shortened to pike): A wooden shaft topped by a metal spike.

Pinnace: A small boat powered by oars or sail used as a tender by larger vessels.

Poopdeck: A deck forming the roof of a cabin on the aft part of a sailing ship.

Quarter: The sides of a ship aft of the centreline.

Quartermaster: A petty officer with the responsibility for steering a ship.

Ratlines: Thin horizontal lines slung between the shrouds of a sailing ship to form a ladder.

Reef: To reef a sail. To reduce the sail area exposed to the wind.

Ribs: See frames.

Rigging: The masts, yards, sails and cordage on a sailing ship.

Rode: A line connecting an anchor to a ship.

Royal yard: The highest yard, or horizontal arm attached to a mast on a sailing ship.

Scuppers: Openings in the bulwarks of a ship to allow drainage of water.

Scurvy: A disease caused by vitamin C deficiency.

Shallop: A light sailing boat used as a tender by sailing ships.

Shoal: A submerged ridge, rock or bank.

Staysail: A fore and aft rigged sail.

Stevedore: A dock laborer who loads and unloads ships.

Topmast: The uppermost section of a mast on a sailing ship.

Weigh: as in weigh the anchor. To haul up the anchor from the sea bed and bring it aboard.

Wherry: A rowing boat for carrying passengers and small cargoes, particularly on the Thames River.

Whipstaff: A vertical lever connected to a tiller, commonly in use for steering sailing ships before the invention of the ship's wheel in c.1703.

Yard: The horizontal spars connected to masts on square-rigged sailing ships. Square sails hung from the yards.

Yardarm: The extreme end of a yard (see above).

Glossary
Omushkegowak Words

Ahanu: One who laughs a lot.

Akwátišiw: Cruel.

Alsoomse: Independent.

Asam: Snowshoe.

Chogan: Blackbird.

Eeyou Istchee: Where the Omushkegowak lived. Literally, "The people's land." Now a part of Ontario and Quebec, Canada.

Emistikôšiw: A white man or European.

Ihtâwin: A village or settlement.

Innu, also known as Montaignais: One of the First Nations of Canada

Iroquois: One of the First Nations of Canada

Iskotewakan: Forest fire.

Kaamischii: Charlton Island in James Bay

Kakako: Raven.

Kahkentam: Jealous.

Kanti: One who sings.

Kayvik: Wolverine.

Kewatino Achak: Polaris, the North Star.

Kitchikumi: A great sea. To the Omuskegowak, Kitchikumi was Hudson Bay.

Kitchimanito: The Great Spirit.

Masko: A black bear.

Mazinibaganjigan: An art form using dental impressions perfected by eastern artisans of the First Nations of Canada.

Nanuk: A polar bear, or a white bear

Nemiskau: A lake and a small First Nations community in Quebec, Canada.

Natuweu Nipi: In English – the Nottaway River, Quebec

Ochekatak: The Big Dipper, known in the UK as The Plough. An asterism containing 7 stars.

Omushkego: A member of the Omushkegowak.

Omushkegowak: People of the muskeg. Now known as the Swampy Cree, First Nation of Canada.

Otácimow: A storyteller.

Oujè Bougamou: Close to the site of today's Chibougamau, Quebec.

Pahkoemeyikaw: A Roman Catholic priest.

Pakekineskisina: Moccasins.

Pichaw: Far away.

Pîtosiyiniw: Enemy.

Samoset: One who walks a long way.

Tepee: A conical dwelling.

Ushaakuteheu: Coward.

Wahnaw: A long way away.

Wanikochas: Squirrel.

Wapun: Dawn, a girl's name.

Waskagahanish (now Waskaganish, Quebec): Literally, "Little house."

Waswanipi (now a Cree settlement in Quebec): Literally "Light over water."

Wigwam: A rounded dwelling.

Wikimak: Wife.

Winipekw: James Bay, Ontario and Quebec, Canada.

About the Author

ANTHONY DALTON is the award-winning author of 14 non-fiction books, most about adventure, exploration or the sea, and one earlier novel. A former expedition leader, he is a Fellow of the Royal Geographical Society and a Fellow of the Royal Canadian Geographical Society. He is also a former national president of the Canadian Authors Association. Anthony lives on Mayne Island, British Columbia, with his wife, Penny, and yellow Labrador, Rufus. He can be visited at his website: www.anthonydalton.net